The Thief of Chaos

. . . his lover the Harlot, plus the Witch, and her Apprentice

Book 1 of *The Deck of Chaos*

The paths of chaos lead only to damnation.

The Thief of Chaos

. . . his lover the Harlot, plus the Witch, and her Apprentice

A Fantasy of Seduction, Betrayal, and Dark Magic

Book 1 of *The Deck of Chaos*

The paths of chaos lead only to damnation.

by

J. L. Doty

Cover Designed by J. L. Doty

Published by JLD Press

Visit the author's website:
http://www.jldoty.com

ISBN: 978–1–953757–13–5 (eBook)
ISBN: 978–1–953757–14–2 (paperback)
ISBN: 978–1–953757–15–9 (hardcover)

Version 2022.11.16

KEpuz!po!KJNEFTLUPQ:
Formatted using eTools for Writers 3.8.8, Nov 16 2022, 13:33:46
Copyright © 2013-2016 by J. L. Doty

Printed in the United States of America

10 9 8 7 6 5 4 3 2 1

1

Disinherited

"MASTER JAXON."

Standing at the window in his room and staring at the street below, Jax hadn't really been paying attention to the handsome young couple strolling by beneath him. His father's illness had ruled his life for more than a week now, and at sixteen years of age, he feared losing the kindly old man.

"Master Jaxon."

Jax looked again at the young man and woman below, an attractive couple by any standards. The man wore a top hat, tail coat, and shiny black riding boots that ended a little below his knees. The woman wore a light summer dress in pale lavender with an empire waist, and short, puffy sleeves at the shoulders. A stylish bonnet atop her head protected her face from the sun, with a shawl covering her bare neck and shoulders. She laughed at something the man said, and the two of them seemed quite happy. Unlike Jax, they needn't concern themselves that old Bartholomew Escher lay on his deathbed.

"Master Jaxon, your father wishes to see you."

Those words penetrated Jax's thoughts, and he spun to face Betsom. The old retainer stood just within the open doorway of Jax's room, and he looked sad and uncertain. The wispy hairs atop his balding head were in disarray, as if he'd tried to plaster them down with his hand.

Jax crossed the short distance between them, standing eye to eye with the old fellow. "He's conscious, is he?"

"Yes," Betsom said. "For a little while now."

"And lucid?"

"Yes, this time he is, and he's asked for you."

For the past week Jax's father had remained in bed unconscious, his breathing a slow, gurgling wheeze. When he had stirred he hadn't recognized any of them, and often cried out at imaginary beings in the room, his eyes focused on something none of them saw.

Jax followed Betsom down the hall to his father's chambers. As they approached the door it opened and his older half-sister Julia slipped out of the room. Eight years his senior, with blond hair carefully pinned up in a stylish quaff, and attractive hazel eyes, Jax understood that many men found her to be quite attractive. A handsome woman, any man might say.

She paused with the door open, and since he already stood taller than her, she had to look up to meet his eyes. Her mouth curved downward in a look of distaste. "Oh, it's you." She stepped around him and walked down the hall without another word. Thankfully her malice had never manifested in any way other than an unkind word or two.

The door remained partially open. Felix, Julia's older brother by a year, and Jax's half-brother, stepped out of their father's room. Short of stature and wide of girth, where men might consider Julia attractive, Felix would need to boast a good income to attract most women. He had never shown Jax the same open animosity as Julia, but separated by several years and different mothers, they had not been close.

Felix started and hesitated as if Jax's presence in the hallway surprised him. "He wants to see you . . . you."

Felix hid his feelings well, but Jax heard the accusation in his words. Only once had Felix ever voiced any discontent with Jax. Some years ago, when they were both younger, he had said, "Father loves you, and he loved your mother." Implied in those words had been, *And he never loved me, nor did he ever love my mother.* Felix might not have been cruel like Julia, but neither had he been kind.

Felix smiled, more a formal pleasantry than any greeting of warmth. Then he stepped around Jax and followed Julia down the hall.

With Betsom hovering over him, Jax opened the door to his father's bedchamber, though the old retainer did not follow him into the room. His nose told him the chamber pot needed to be emptied, and the air smelled of stale sweat and sickness. Dim light from the only window in the room cast everything in shadow. His father lay on his back in the large canopied bed, propped up on pillows, his wavy, gray hair still full for a man his age. The skin of his face glistened with a sickly sheen, and in many places seemed almost transparent.

To Jax's disappointment, his father's eyes remained closed, and he hoped he hadn't missed his last opportunity to speak with him. But as he tiptoed across the room, the old man must have heard him. His eyes fluttered open and Jax froze. His father extended an arm weakly and clutched at the air between them.

"Jaxon, my boy."

His voice came out so weak that, had Jax been moving, or doing anything to make even the slightest sound, he might not have heard him.

Jax crossed the room quickly, took the old man's hand and clutched it to his breast. His father's fingers were cold and lifeless.

"Jaxon, my boy, you came to see me."

"Of course I did, father. As soon as I heard you were conscious."

The old man seemed to have some trouble using the muscles of his tongue and mouth, and he slurred some of his words. "Julia didn't want me to call you. She must love me very much to want to keep me all to herself, eh?"

"Yes, father, I'm sure she does."

His father blinked his eyes slowly and peered at Jax, as if trying to pierce the haze of a thick fog. "You look good, my boy."

He reached up toward Jax's head, but didn't have the strength to raise his hand that high. Jax bent forward and lowered his head almost to the old man's chest. His father ran a hand through Jax's dark hair, and in times past would have ruffled it, mussing it badly. But he simply rested his hand there for a moment. Jax retrieved the old man's hand before it fell away from his head, and clutched it again to his chest.

His father smiled. "You're going to be tall when you finish growing, taller than me, Julia, or Felix, and you're going to have broad shoulders. You must have gotten your stature from your mother. You got your dark hair and brown eyes from her as well. I wish you could have known her."

"I do too, father."

It had taken Jax the better part of his short life to understand his father's relationship with the two women he had married. As a nobleman, even a minor one, his father's first marriage had been carefully arranged, and according to Julia and Felix there had been no love. After his father's first wife died of some disease, since he had fulfilled the legal requirement to produce an heir, he had been free to wed whom he pleased. He had married Jax's mother for love. She had died in childbirth, but the old man had never blamed Jax for that. Many men might have.

"You were all the parent I ever needed, father."

The old man smiled. "You're kind."

He closed his eyes, and after more than a minute of silence, Jax wasn't sure if he had slipped into unconsciousness again, or simply found sleep.

Jax retrieved a chair from across the room and sat down by his father's bed to wait.

As the time passed Jax grew drowsy and began to nod off. Then the old man cried out, "Jaxon! Jaxon!"

Jax started. "I'm here, father. I'm here."

The old man appeared to have found a moment of clear and lucid thinking. "You shouldn't worry, you know. I've spoken to Julia and Felix, and they've promised to see to it you're taken care of. Our finances are meager, but they'll do for the three of you, if you're frugal."

Jax shook his head. "I wasn't worrying about that."

"No, but they were . . . and are."

His father returned to sleep; at least Jax hoped it was sleep, and not unconsciousness. Jax sat there and listened to the old man's struggled breathing for half an hour, then stood and turned to quietly leave. But on the floor near the bed he noticed the full chamber pot. Someone needed to empty it, so he picked it up and carried it out of the room.

••••

As Jax walked away from his father's bedroom, he heard Julia and Felix arguing in the upstairs parlor.

Julia shrieked, "Well how much do we have?"

Felix answered, pleading like a fearful servant. "I don't know. I sent a message to the bankers, and they responded with a message that they can't discuss it with me."

Jax stopped outside the parlor doors, but didn't want to face Julia when she was in that kind of mood, so he simply stood in the hallway and listened.

"Why can't they discuss it with you? You're his heir."

Felix's pleading stretched into a whimper. "Some sort of legal requirement. They can't discuss a man's holdings and finances with anyone but the man himself, or a legally authorized representative."

"Not even his children, and his heir?"

"No. Not even us. Once he's dead, they'll review his will, a magistrate will declare me his heir, and I'll inherit. Then it'll all be my holdings and finances, and they can discuss with me what I've inherited."

Julia's voice had grown even more shrill. "You don't think he was foolish enough to leave anything to Jaxon, do you?"

"I asked, and the bankers said that would be very rare. The Witch Palace and the High Noble Houses don't like to see estates diluted by multiple inheritances. To leave anything more than a pittance to him would take special dispensation from the Witch herself, or one of the High Houses. I think we're okay there."

"Thank God!"

Jax heard a chair creak, which probably meant Julia had calmed down enough to take a seat.

Felix had calmed down as well. "Father made me promise to take care of him."

Julia didn't say anything in response to that.

••••

The next morning, when Jax returned to his father's bedchamber to comfort the old man, Julia had locked the door and would not allow him entry. He tried again that evening, with no success, and several times the next day. On the third day he awoke to a commotion in the wee hours of the morning. He lit a lamp and donned a robe over his night shirt, noting that like so many things in the house it had seen better days. He paused to examine the robe carefully, knowing in his heart that he was only trying to delay the inevitable.

He steeled himself, opened the door to his room and walked out into the hallway. Old Betsom and plump little Mrs. Dorton, the house cook, stood outside the door to his father's bedroom, both wringing their hands. As Jax approached them, Betsom looked his way and said, "I'm sorry, Master Jaxon."

Mrs. Dorton had tears in her eyes. "Poor young man. Poor young man."

Jax knocked on the door to his father's bedroom. He waited for several seconds, then the door creaked open a crack. Julia stood within blocking the way, as if she must defend the bed chamber against an attack by barbarian hordes from the south. "What do you want?"

Jax didn't want to have this conversation here with two servants looking on. "What do you think I want?"

She spit words into his face. "I don't know. You tell me."

"To see my father."

She shook her head and spoke through gritted teeth. "You can't. The physician is with him."

"He's dead, isn't he?"

Her anger had never been so palpable before. "Why do you think the physician is here?"

Jax shook his head sadly and sighed. "What do you fear of me, Julia? That somehow I'll communicate with a dead man, and convince him to give me all the money you so covet?"

She closed the door in his face, and the latch clacked as she locked it.

Jax returned to his bedroom, pulled off the robe, climbed back into bed, but couldn't sleep.

In the early hours of the morning they carried the body away. Jax intercepted the undertakers at the front door of the house and had just a few seconds to hold his father's lifeless hand. Interestingly enough, neither Julia nor Felix were present to see their father taken away. Jax found them arguing in the downstairs parlor about the wording for a message to be sent to the bankers. He left them there and wandered out to the stables.

When Jax had been a small boy, they'd had a carriage and a team of two draft horses. After Jax had grown a little older, his father had purchased a riding horse for him, and provided lessons so he learned to ride, as every gentleman should. Felix had told him that their father had offered to buy him a horse and riding lessons as well, but Jax's half-brother had cared nothing for riding and turned the offer down. The stables were now empty, the two stable hands dismissed, the carriage and horses sold long ago.

Jax returned to the house, where he heard Felix and Julia arguing. He pulled on a faded tail coat and top hat, then went for a walk. He meandered into the District of High Noble Houses and, as always, marveled at the size of the estates there. Perhaps he envied them their wealth, but he didn't feel that way in his heart. He did envy their happiness.

He walked back to his father's house, then up to his room, and over to the window. In the street below he saw that same young couple, handsome, elegant, and so happy. The late afternoon sun glistened off the fellow's shiny black boots, and that day the young woman wore a peach colored dress, with a matching bonnet.

"I've packed a small valise for you, Master Jaxon."

Old Betsom's voice brought Jax back to the uncertainty surrounding his father's death. He turned away from the window and, as before, Betsom stood just within the open doorway of his room.

It took Jax a moment to recall the old man's words. "Valise?" he asked. "I don't understand."

Julia appeared in the hallway behind Betsom. She stepped past him into the room, elbowing the old fellow aside, her face pinched with anger. She treated everyone with that same unpleasant manner, and perhaps that was why no man had ever sought her hand in marriage.

"You're leaving," she said in a flat, hard voice. Felix walked into the room and stopped behind her. He appeared ill at ease, his eyes downcast.

"Leaving?" Jax asked. "Why? Where am I going?"

"I don't really know," she said. "Nor do I care. You're just leaving, and you'll have to figure that out for yourself."

Felix grimaced and stepped out from behind Julia. "I'm sorry. We've had to make some difficult decisions. Father didn't manage our finances terribly well."

Julia sliced her hand through the air. "Father was a drunk, and an idiot."

It was common knowledge that their father had always had a drink at hand, regardless of the time of day, or night.

Felix turned on her. "Don't speak ill of the dead."

Julia shook her head, and Jax watched her anger boil forth. "House Escher is ruined. We have to sell our home and discharge most of the servants because of him, so I'll not prattle on with kind words for a fool who's gone."

She turned back to Jax, marched two steps toward him, and for a moment he thought she might strike him. But she halted one pace away and pointed a trembling finger at him. "You're leaving. Just take the valise and leave, and be thankful we've given you that much."

"But why?" Jax asked. "You promised father you'd take care of me."

She spit words at him as if he'd wronged her in some way. "After we sell the house, Felix and I will barely have enough to maintain a reasonable lifestyle. We're not about to waste any of it on a young boy to whom we're only half related. So leave, and don't ever show your face here again."

Behind her, Felix said, "We didn't know the state of father's finances until after he died. I'm sorry."

Julia turned toward Felix and vented her anger on him. "Save your pity for us, because we're going to need it." She marched to the door, forcing old Betsom to step aside as she stormed past him. She paused in the doorway, turned about and looked back at Jax. "We've made up our minds, and there's nothing you can do about it." She turned and walked away.

Felix shook his head and lowered his eyes. "I'm sorry. I wish we could do something to help you, but we have to think of . . . ourselves. And you're young. You'll do okay." Without meeting Jax's eyes, he turned and followed Julia out of the room.

Betsom too wouldn't meet Jax's eyes as he said, "Please come with me, Master Jaxon."

Jax started forward, but Betsom quickly glanced over his shoulder, then to Jax he hissed, "Put on your tail coat and top hat. They can't begrudge you that, though we won't be foolish enough to ask them."

Jax pulled on the coat and hat. Then the old retainer led him down to the ground floor where he retrieved a worn and faded, dark-brown, canvas valise. Betsom escorted him out to the street. He handed Jax the valise and said, "There's some clothing, a cloak, and a few silver guineas in this. It's all your older brother could spare, and more than Miss Julia would, if she knew. And though your brother and sister don't know this, I've included a dagger and a small flintlock pistol. If need be, you can conceal them beneath the cloak. I do hope you don't need them, and I wish I could help more, but I'll soon be without employment myself."

Betsom left him on the street clutching the valise against his chest. A horse-drawn carriage approached, its wheels rattling on the cobblestones of the street. To avoid being run down Jax had to step back as it rolled past raising a cloud of dust. The coachman waved a fist at him and shouted something, but Jax couldn't hear his words above the clatter of the coach's wheels and the clop of the horses' hooves, though the man made his meaning clear with his raised fist.

Jax turned and walked down the street with no destination in mind. He wondered where he would go, what he would do, how he would survive.

2

Slumming

AS ONE OF the poorest of the noble families, Jax had grown up on his father's small estate on the edge of the District of Noble Houses. Destitute and now homeless, he wandered aimlessly on the streets of Val d'Ossa for a few hours, though he took care to remain in the district. As night approached, he made his way to a small city park and sat down on a stone bench. He placed the valise next to him on the bench and opened it to examine its contents. In it he found a spare set of undergarments, plus an extra shirt and trousers. There were two silver guineas and some copper coins. He would have to make those last as long as possible, use them only for food.

The dagger had a sharp, pointed blade about six inches long with a simple sheath. In addition to riding, proper gentlemen of Jax's day were also trained in swordsmanship. His father had paid for lessons, and Jax had trained with a light rapier or small-sword, sometimes with a parrying dagger in his left hand called a main gauche. The lessons had given him some familiarity with a blade, but they had been aimed more at teaching him a gentlemanly sport, not a martial art intended to keep him alive. If it came to that, he suspected his skills with the dagger would be sorely lacking.

The flintlock was small, with a barrel only about four inches long. It probably wouldn't kill most men outright, but everyone knew the wound from even a small weapon could fester. Death, or the loss of a limb, would be the likely result, so the small pistol might work to drive someone off. He didn't have any way of refreshing the charge, so after a day or two the odds of it firing would decline rapidly.

The cloak had faded even more than his topcoat. Apparently, Julia had chosen to give him the worst of what they had. But it was thick, and would keep him warm. With winter approaching, the nights would grow chill.

He pulled on the cloak, stuffed his top hat and everything else into the valise, and wrapped the cloak tightly about him. He stretched out on the bench to sleep, using the valise as a lumpy pillow. It was not a comfortable place to lie, and he didn't sleep well.

At dawn he awoke to some sort of stick jabbing him in the ribs. He opened his eyes and looked up to find two city constables standing over him, one old and grizzled, the other young and pink-faced. The younger one had been nudging him with his cudgel.

"Up with you, young sir," the older one said. "Can't be sleeping in the park."

As Jax climbed to his feet, the younger one asked, "What are you doing here?" Both fellows dropped their H's, so *here* came out more like *'ere*.

The older one nudged the younger one in the ribs. "Probably out last night spending his father's money on some whore and too much drink, and couldn't make his way home."

The fellow's comment scandalized Jax, for he didn't whore, and would never get drunk and sleep on a park bench. "No," he said. "That's not it at all."

The older one clearly didn't believe him. The younger one asked, "Then why were you sleeping here?"

"My father died," Jax said, "and my older brother can't afford to care for me."

The younger constable asked, "Threw you out, eh?"

"Yes."

The older one asked, "Disinherited, eh?"

"Yes."

The young one looked Jax up and down carefully, as if he didn't believe him. "Then where do you live now?"

Jax shook his head. "I don't know? It just happened yesterday."

At that, the older constable frowned thoughtfully. "Then you no longer live in this district, do you?"

Jax said, "I guess not."

The older guard considered that carefully, thought for a long moment, then declared, "Well, that means you ain't no longer the son of a nobleman, so I guess that means you'll be sleeping on nothing but park benches from now on."

The younger one curled his upper lip in distaste. "Probably have to sleep in alleys, too."

"Yah," the older fellow said, rubbing his chin thoughtfully. "I suppose he should go to a district where people sleep in alleys."

They escorted Jax out of the District of Noble Houses.

When Jax had walked among the estates of the High Noble Houses, he'd been embarrassed at the limited size and rundown nature of his father's small estate. And as they left the District of Noble Houses, the dwellings they passed grew smaller and smaller. In the heart of the slums where the two constables stopped, people lived in ramshackle structures cobbled together from boards and sheets of tin, and whatever they found that might do.

The old constable left him with one admonishment. "You're no longer a nobleman, lad." He wagged a finger at Jax's nose. "So don't let me be seeing your face among your betters again."

They left him standing there.

That was Jax's first lesson. Had he lied when the constables had first confronted him in the park, and agreed with the old fellow that he had been out whoring and gotten too drunk, they would have assumed he'd walk back to his father's house. They would have left him there and allowed him to go his own way. He could have found another park or alley and spent at least one more night in the District of Noble Houses. There were no parks in the slums, and the alleys near his father's estate were far superior to those in his new home.

••••

During the second day of his life as a destitute commoner, Jax wandered the slums with the valise slung over his shoulder and the strap gripped tightly to his chest. He had heard stories all his life about the denizens of that district and how they preyed upon the unwary. Gentlemen of means were known to frequent some of the establishments Jax walked past, for whoring or other unsavory pleasures. But they entered the slums only in groups, never alone, frequently with a manservant or two to protect them should the need arise. Jax looked over his shoulder constantly, fearful he might become the target of some dangerous cutthroat or ruffian, and it occurred to him he should stop acting like a victim.

As the day wore on, he developed one clear impression: If he wanted to stay alive, he would have to think carefully about everything he did. If they sensed he was an ignorant newcomer, he could easily become a target.

For him, cutpurses and thieves were an intellectual concept. They must exist, but he'd never encountered one before, so he wasn't sure how to protect himself from them. As dusk approached, he made his way toward the edge of the slums, where he would hopefully face less danger. He spied out an empty alley, wandered down it and found the privacy he needed. He quickly retrieved the purse containing the two silver guineas and a few copper coins, tied it to the waist of his pants, then shoved it down inside his breeches where it hung in his crotch.

In early autumn the nights were still reasonably warm, though they had begun to cool a little and the heavy cloak would come in handy. He hadn't eaten since leaving his father's house, and walking through the streets had exhausted him. He found a relatively clean spot in the alley, clutched the pistol in his right hand, the dagger in his left, then shoved both his hands inside his cloak and pulled it tightly about him.

He kicked the valise against the back of a stone building that lined the alley. Then he lay down on the ground on his side with the valise between him and the building. Anyone who might try to steal it would have to wake him first. Exhaustion helped him quickly fall asleep.

••••

"Twenty coppers?" the boy said, his voice rising with anger.

Maelleen quickly glanced around the common room of her father's pub, but that early in the morning there were only two patrons, and neither had taken notice. "Keep your voice down."

He held his voice to a whisper as he hissed. "Twenty coppers? I can have Kimmey for ten."

"Kimmey's old," Maelleen said. "I'm young, and you'd be me first ever." She gave him an inviting smile.

The boy glanced at the cleavage Maelleen had exposed at the top of her blouse. At fifteen her breasts were still growing, and if she was going to make any real money at whoring, she hoped they'd grow to be full and ample.

The boy reluctantly tore his eyes away from her chest. "Okay, twenty it is. But I—" His eyes widened and focused on something behind Maelleen.

She started to glance over her shoulder, but a hand clutched the back of her neck in a painful, iron-fisted grip. She couldn't turn to see who had assaulted her, but she heard her mother shout, "Out with you, you little slack."

The boy clutched his cap in both hands and stood frozen with fear.

"I said out with you. Now get out before I hang your balls above me hearth."

The boy turned and ran.

Like Maelleen, Bethy stood a bit taller than most women but was not large of girth. Still, Maelleen could not have broken free of her mother's grip. "Ow," she shouted. "You're hurting me."

Bethy gave her a shove, releasing her. Maelleen stumbled forward and turned to face the woman. Her mother's eyes had turned diamond hard, her mouth puckered in a straight line of anger.

At that moment Maelleen's father stepped out of the kitchen, wiping his hands on a towel. "What's all the ruckus?"

Nearby, the two patrons hunched their shoulders, lowered their heads, and focused on their mugs of ale.

Bethy turned to face her husband. "She was trying to whore herself to that boy."

Marcus looked about the room. "What boy?"

Maelleen's hoped-for first customer had long since disappeared.

Bethy gave Maelleen a look that made her cringe. "The boy ain't no nevermind. She was whoring, or at least trying to."

Maelleen couldn't contain her frustration. "But you was a whore, ma."

Bethy took one step and closed the distance between them, standing eye-to-eye with Maelleen. "I whored to put food on the table, and I quit when I married your da. We got a roof over our heads and good food for the table. We don't need you whoring."

"But," Maelleen said, her voice sliding into a whine, which added to her frustration. "But I want more'n food and a roof over me head. I want nice things, ma." She didn't add that she had enjoyed herself with a boy from down the street, groping at each other in the alley behind her father's pub, though that had been for free, and for fun. So why not enjoy herself, and at the same time make a little extra money?

Marcus's eyes saddened and he shrugged. "I don't like it neither. But she's old enough to whore if she wants to whore, so's we can't stop her."

Bethy curled her fingers into fists and planted them on her hips. "I can stop her, and you will too."

She didn't wait for either of them to say anything in reply, but marched across the common room, then through the door into the kitchen. She slammed the door with a loud crack.

••••

"Aye, think he's dead?"

Jax awoke to the sound of a young voice behind him.

"Dunno. Dunno. Let's roll him over and check."

There were at least two of them, both boys by the sound of their voices.

"Let's just bash his head and take what's there."

Jax rolled over to face them, pulling his hands out of his cloak to display the dagger in one, and aim the small pistol with the other. Two boys danced back and stepped away from him, their eyes widening as they did so. One appeared to be about Jax's age and the other considerably younger. They wore clothing discolored by smudges of dirt.

Jax sat up, keeping the pistol aimed at the older boy. "I wouldn't take it kindly if you bashed my head."

The older boy said, "We wasn't talking 'bout you."

Jax climbed to his feet and stood taller than both young boys. He looked up and down the alley. "I don't see anyone else whom you might've been talking about."

The older boy shook his head, glanced right and left, then spun on his heel and sprinted away. The younger boy remained frozen where he stood, his mouth open in a round O.

Jax lunged toward him, taking only a single step, and shouting, "Off with you."

The boy spun about, charged out of the alley, turned up the street, and disappeared from view.

Jax put the flintlock in a pocket of the cloak, but kept the dagger handy. He retrieved the small purse from where he had hidden it in the crotch of his pants, selected a few copper coins, then returned it to its hiding place. He held the dagger in his left hand, and kept it hidden from view in a fold of the cloak. He shouldered the valise, and wandered out onto the street.

The sun hadn't yet risen above the rooftops surrounding him, and the shadows of the buildings carried a decided chill in the early morning. Jax found a street vendor just setting up shop. The man sold small meat pies for one copper each. It would take two of the pies to make a proper meal, but that would use up two coppers, and Jax had decided that until he knew more, he would let caution rule all his moves. He pointed to one of the pies that didn't look more than a few days old. "I'll take that one."

When the vendor handed him the pie, Jax gave him a copper and asked, "How do I find the Boulevard of Commoners?"

"Keep going east," the man said, smiling and displaying a gap-toothed array of brown teeth. "You'll find it in about ten or twelve streets."

The Boulevard of Commoners was the one place outside the slums where the constables wouldn't roust a man of questionable means, as long as he kept moving. Jax walked north up the Boulevard for more than an hour until it ended and opened onto Crier's Square, a wide plaza in front of the Hall of Nobles. The posting boards outside the Hall were the one place in the district where the city constables expected to see a regular stream of common folk. The Council of Nobles posted important notices there for everyone to read, though since many of the city's residents were illiterate, the nobles employed criers to read the notices aloud throughout the day. Since he could read, it occurred to Jax he might find employment as a crier. But on that day he had other business to concern him.

The main notice boards displayed the important news, and in front of each stood a throng of people listening to a crier loudly reading the information written there. Jax made his way to the side boards which contained news of minor importance, news for people like Jax. It took him almost an hour, but he found what he was looking for. His father's funeral would take place the next morning, and Bartholomew Escher would be laid to rest on Widow's Hill, a cemetery reserved for the poorest of noblemen. Apparently, Julia had decided their father was not worth the money needed to purchase a proper burial plot.

On the east side of the square, the spires of the Witch Palace dominated the skyline. A wall about twenty feet high enclosed the palace yard, broken only by an imposing black iron gate. Atop the wall, Knights of the Witchguard patrolled its ramparts. Each wore a crisp, bright uniform of red and black, with silver piping, and everyone knew they were to be feared. Rumors constantly circulated through the city, stories of intrigues between the Witch and the High Noble Houses. Jax didn't understand most of it, but apparently the High Houses struggled relentlessly to gain ascendency over the Witch, and had never succeeded. Jax's father had told him lesser nobles were wise to stay clear of the constant strife.

Jax decided to head for Widow's Hill, just to make sure he could get there in time for the funeral. The cemetery lay just off the Boulevard of Commoners, probably a concession to those who might need to attend. It appeared the city paid a few workers to scythe the weeds that grew among the burial plots, but that was about all they did to keep the place up. He spotted two laborers digging a grave, and now knew where his father would lie.

He stopped in the middle of Widow's Hill and scanned the cemetery full circle. He and the two men digging his father's grave were the only people present on the entire hill. It occurred to him then that a cemetery was a very lonely place. And while people might come during the day to visit a grave, or to bid farewell to a recently deceased loved one, at night they probably avoided such a place. The city constables were likely of a similar mindset.

Jax now knew he had been a complete idiot to lie down in an alley, and had survived one night by pure luck. If those two boys had come across him in the dark of night while he lay in an exhausted sleep, or if they hadn't awakened him before bashing his head, he'd probably be floating face-down in the river. He vowed not to press his luck a second time.

As dusk settled over the city, Jax searched Widow's Hill. He found a secluded place hidden in a thicket of brush, and lay down for the night.

3

Farewell

IN THE MORNING, Jax returned to the Boulevard of Commoners. He bought a berry pie from a vendor for a copper. Again, it wasn't enough, but it quelled the most urgent pangs of hunger.

He didn't have a watch, something for which he chided himself. Had he been thinking clearly the day Julia threw him out, he would have stalled long enough to go through his own belongings and take anything of value. The watch would allow him to tell time until he needed to sell it to eat. And then he could have gotten enough to buy several days' worth of meals.

To ensure that he didn't miss his father's burial, he wandered through the crowds in Crier's Square. The clock tower above the hall allowed him to monitor the passing minutes, and when the time was right, he returned to Widow's Hill.

He found a spot in the dark shadow of a large oak, and from a distance he watched the small crowd gathered around the hole the two workers had dug the day before. He could only see Felix's back, but Julia stood on the other side of the hole, her lips held in a rigid, straight line. He held back and watched the short ceremony from afar, knowing Julia would probably react unpleasantly if she spotted him.

"Here now, young man."

Jax turned around to find that the two constables from the other morning had approached him. When they saw his face they both started, and frowned angrily.

The younger one said, "We warned you not to be disturbing the gentle folk."

The older one shook his head sadly. "We did warn you, lad. The magistrate'll not like you loitering around your betters."

Jax glanced over his shoulder and nodded to the small gathering of black-clad mourners. "My father. They're laying him to rest. I just wanted to say good-bye to him."

The younger constable grimaced and shook his head angrily. "That don't matter none. You can't be—"

The older one raised a hand to silence him. "Lower your voice and calm down a bit. We can let the lad pay his last respects to his da. But we'll wait here 'till the gentle folk are done, and see to it he don't hang about too long."

The two constables stood on either side of Jax, as if they feared he might try to break free and escape, or perhaps run forward and attack the gathering at his father's grave. It didn't take long for the mourners to finish the short ceremony and disperse. Jax's escorts led him forward, and released him only when they reached the hole.

Two workers had begun shoveling dirt onto the plain, wooden casket at the bottom of the rectangular grave. Jax lowered himself to one knee, scraped up a handful of dirt, and tossed it on top of the casket. "Good bye, father." A pang of sorrow and regret hit him in the gut, and his chest felt tight as if he might faint. But he controlled his emotions and stood silently, a tear in his eyes.

The younger of the two constables wanted to haul Jax before a magistrate for loitering. The older one said, "It ain't loitering to attend yer own da's funeral."

They saw him all the way back to the slums and released him.

On Widow's Hill, Jax had learned a valuable lesson about cemeteries. The cemetery in the slums didn't have an official name, but everyone called it Pauper's Walk. It had a wealth of trees and brush among which to hide, and it couldn't have been more deserted. Jax spent an entire day carefully searching every foot of ground in Pauper's Walk. He found an old, stone bench, hidden in a thicket surrounded by thick brush and covered by overgrown weeds. He cleared the weeds away from it, but took care to ensure it remained all but invisible from outside the thicket. The bench had been constructed from a solid stone slab resting on two stone supports. He could sleep on the bench, and remain unobserved, as long as he did nothing to reveal his presence.

••••

Each day Jax carefully counted the coins in his purse. He didn't really need to open the purse, spread them out, and tally them so precisely, because he knew exactly how many remained. But he counted them anyway because the exercise of reviewing the dwindling numbers gave him the impetus needed to adhere to his regimen of frugality. After two weeks on the streets, he had survived on the equivalent of about half a meal per day, and he had taken to tying a scrap of rope around his waist to keep his pants from sliding down around his knees. He now had one silver guinea and two coppers left, and he desperately longed for a real meal.

He had walked past the Angry Bear a number of times, a pub that appeared to be clean and well kept. It was situated on the edge of the slums in an area that wasn't expensive, but was close enough to the District of Nobles to boast of a lower crime rate. Jax pushed the front door open and stepped into the common room of the establishment. It was early evening, so there were only a few patrons seated at small tables haphazardly strewn around the room.

On the far side of the room an old man stood behind a bar, a few strands of wispy gray hairs atop his bald head visible in the light from a sconce. The fellow's hand gripped a rag that he slid back and forth as he polished the bar's surface. Jax's father's finances had forced him to always seek out inexpensive places like the Angry Bear, and under such circumstances he had taught Jax to look at the rag; if it was obviously dirty, "Turn around and walk out," his father had told him.

As Jax crossed the room, the old man tracked his progress with his eyes, and when Jax stopped at the bar the fellow smiled. "Welcome stranger. What can I be doin' for you?"

Jax glanced down at the rag. It appeared faded and threadbare, but clean. "A meal," Jax said. "I can't afford anything expensive, but I can pay."

The old fellow nodded, and the hand polishing the bar with the rag came to a standstill. "We got some stew, with thick, brown gravy, potatoes, and onions. The more you pay, the more meat you get."

Jax grimaced. "I can afford three coppers."

The old guy shrugged. "That'll get you a small piece of meat, but a plate full of potatoes and onions and gravy. Might even have a few carrots for you."

Jax couldn't hide his eagerness as he nodded. "I'd like that very much."

The old man smiled. "The name's Marcus. What'll you be drinking?"

Jax smiled back. "My name's Jax, and I'll just have water. That's all I can afford."

"Well then," Marcus said. "Take a seat anywhere, Jax, and me girl'll bring your plate. You can pay her when the food's in front of you." He spun about to a door behind the bar and pushed it open. Jax got a brief glimpse of an older woman working at a hot stove. The bartender hollered, "Bethy, a plate of stew. Three coppers worth."

Jax selected a small, unoccupied table on the far side of the room where he could sit with his back to the wall. A few minutes later the door behind the bar opened, and a young girl about Jax's age stepped through it carrying a clay plate in one hand, and a drinking mug in the other. The girl had brown hair that hung past her shoulders in a disarray of curls and ringlets. She wore a dress that exposed quite a bit of cleavage, though her breasts were not large. A heavy layer of kohl gave her eyes a dark, smoky appearance. She had badly overdone her lip paint and looked like a trollop, but her almond-shaped eyes were set in a strong face, and Jax found her rather attractive.

She crossed the room, walking with a confident gait, and stopped at Jax's table. "Eh! You order the stew?"

Jax smelled the heavy aroma of gravy laced with brown ale, and he swallowed hard as he nodded. "Three coppers worth."

"Aye," she said. "At's you, all right." She plopped the plate on the table, the handle of a wooden spoon protruding from the stew. She placed the mug next to it, and held out her hand.

Jax put three coppers in her open palm. She looked at them, closed her fist and jiggled the coins, then plopped down in a chair opposite Jax. "You don't sound like one of us."

Jax wondered why she chose to interrogate him. "I grew up in Val d'Ossa, just not in this district."

"You want to hire me?"

Jax scooped up a big chunk of potato that had turned brown from simmering in the gravy for hours. "Hire you for what?"

"I'm an ore. What do you think?"

She clearly was not a wooden boat ore, so Jax had to think carefully to glean her meaning. She had the most atrocious accent, dropped all her H's, and frequently added an extra half syllable to many words. *Whore* had come out more like *oh-er*. "You're a whore?"

Marcus looked up from the bar and shouted. "She ain't no whore yet, but she wants to be."

Jax couldn't believe what he was hearing. "Why do you want to be a whore?"

The look she gave him made it clear she thought he was the worst dullard she had ever met. "So's I can have nice things. And so's I can help me family. Me mum did it before me, and now it's me turn."

Back at the bar, Marcus shouted, "Her mum was a right good whore too."

One of the patrons at another table said, "By damn, I'll say she was. Bethy was one of the best. Hated to see her retire."

Marcus shouted, "But she don't want Maelleen being no whore like she was."

Jax asked, "You're Maelleen?"

"Aye," the girl said, standing. "You going to hire me or not?"

Jax shook his head. "I don't think I can afford you. But I would if I could."

"I figured as much," she said, winking at him. "Let me know when you can."

She turned, and he watched the sway of her hips as she walked away.

He focused on eating the stew, and only then realized he had told the truth when he'd said he couldn't afford her, and would if he could. A month ago he would never have considered such a liaison. He would have told her he didn't truck with whores, a claim he could no longer make.

••••

"Ten coppers."

The old fellow who owned the second-hand store eyed Jax with distrust, then he looked again at Jax's pistol resting on the counter between them.

Jax shook his head. "It must be worth three times that."

The shop owner coughed and hacked something up, then spit onto the dirt floor to one side. "It's only worth what I can sell it for, and it's used, and it ain't very big, and I still gotta make a profit."

Jax stood there with steam rising off his shoulders. It had rained the night before, the first of the winter storms. Since the bench in Pauper's Walk was a solid stone slab, he had tried sleeping beneath it, hoping it would protect him a little from the downpour. It had been a miserably, cold, wet night, and three hours after waking, his damp clothing still chilled him to the bone.

He tried one last time. "Twelve coppers."

The old man lifted the pistol off the counter and examined it one more time. Then he shook his head. "Ten coppers, and that's final. If you don't like that, then take it and leave."

Jax took the ten coppers, and when he stepped out of the shop he eyed the clouds in the sky. It would likely rain again that evening, and with the chill of winter approaching, he didn't relish another night shivering inside his soaking wet cloak.

He returned to his bench in Pauper's Walk, and deposited the coins in the purse he kept hidden there. He put four coppers in a pouch he carried with him, and left the cemetery with the intent of improving his small shelter.

On the streets he had heard talk of a garbage dump where the city deposited the daily refuse. The fellow who sold him the meat pies told him it was down-river from the center of the city, so Jax headed that way.

The smell of the place assailed his nose long before he reached it. He found it on the edge of the city where the filth of the slums drained into the river. Piles of refuse stretched for as far as the eye could see, and seagulls circled in the skies above, crying out to their companions in a constant din.

Jax spent a few hours scrounging through the garbage, looking for anything he might use to shield his bench from the rain. He found a board and three small sheets of tin, but as he carried them out of the dump, two young men about his own age confronted him. They both had a rough and surly appearance to them.

One of the two stepped forward with a confident swagger. "What you think you doing?"

Jax lowered the board and sheets of tin to the ground. "Just going about my own business." He wished he still had the pistol.

The other one stepped forward to stand by his companion. "Taking our stuff, are yuh?"

Jax shook his head. "It's a public refuse dump. It's not your stuff."

They both shook their heads and the first one said, "It's our stuff if we say it's our stuff."

The other one added, "And if you want it, you got to pay for it."

Jax slipped his hands into the pockets of the cloak as if trying to warm them. He gripped the handle of the dagger and lied. "I don't have any money."

The swaggering one grinned. "Then you don't get no stuff."

The two of them sauntered forward and Jax backed up a step. Then they charged. When they plowed into him, Jax's hand and the dagger were still tangled in the cloak, and he never got it free. One of them sat on top of him, pinning his arms, while the other pummeled him with his fists. Then they both stood over him, and with Jax curled into a ball, they kicked him and spat on him. When they tired of their sport, they searched him and found the small pouch containing a few coins. They took the coins and left the pouch, and he thanked the gods he'd had the foresight to only carry a small amount.

They left him lying on his side, coughing, choking, and groaning. His arms, legs, ribs and face hurt, and he thought his upper lip might swell badly. After some minutes he rolled over and sat up. They had gotten away with four coppers, but he still had the dagger gripped in his hand, and they had left the board and sheets of tin. He gathered them up and carried them back to the cemetery. He leaned the board and sheets of tin against the bench, then crawled beneath it. That night it rained again, and his little, make-shift shelter proved to be a bit more effective at keeping out the rain, but only a bit.

4

Desperate Need

"YOU CAN READ and speak good, eh?"

Jax nodded carefully, thinking he read and spoke a lot better than the man seated in front of him. "Yes, I was taught to speak, read and write properly."

"And where'd you learn your letters?"

"I was raised as a nobleman's son, but my father died and I've been disinherited."

He had come early that morning to the Hall of Nobles to inquire about getting a job as a crier. A guard had directed him to a factor in charge of the men who read the notices in front of the Hall. After three hours of waiting, he'd been called into this man's tiny office. The fellow had a small desk, behind which he sat in a simple wooden chair. The way the man puffed out his chest as he spoke, he probably thought of the chair as more of a throne. Jax decided not to point out that it was sadly lacking in cushions, and gilt, and all the other trappings of a seat of sovereign power.

The man slid a piece of velum forward and said, "Read this."

Jax picked up the page, and began reading aloud.

"No," the fellow said. "If you're going to be a crier, you have to read it loud so's people can hear, even if they're at the back of the crowd."

Jax raised his voice to a near-shout and started at the beginning. The fellow let him read for several minutes, then raised a hand and stopped him. "Enough," he said. "Two coppers a day. You read from one hour after dawn, to one hour before dusk."

One week later Jax's voice had grown so hoarse he could barely speak, and the man terminated his employment. At least he had earned fourteen coppers, which would keep him alive a little longer.

••••

Early that evening, Jax approached the street vendor who sold meat pies. He had decided to allow himself one pie, a ration he could barely afford. He recalled the pies Mrs. Dorton had cooked. The crust had been flakey, the filling a thick, dark gravy with tender meat, peas, carrots, onions, and potatoes. The pie he purchased from the vendor on the street did not compare at all, but it cost only one copper, and would fill his stomach, even if only briefly.

He gave the man a copper and the fellow handed him the small pie. But as Jax turned toward the busy street, a stranger bumped into him, knocking the pie out of his hands. It landed in the dirt of the street next to a pile of horse manure. Before Jax could react, a stranger walking past stepped on it.

Jax froze, wondering if he might salvage something of the pie.

The man who had bumped into him stepped back a pace and said, "I'm sorry, young man. That was clumsy of me."

Jax turned toward him, and only then took notice of the fellow. He stood a little taller than Jax, wore a tail coat, top hat, and shiny black riding boots that ended a little below his knees. He appeared to be about twice Jax's age, had kind, droopy eyes, a strong, handsome face, and by all appearances was a fine, young gentleman of excellent means.

"Let me make it up to you," the fellow said, turning toward the vendor. "I'll buy you another."

"No, good sir, that's not necessary," Jax said, surprised and horrified at his own words. His training as a gentleman had kicked in, and he had given the man a rote response. And now he had no choice but to follow through. "It was an accident, after all."

The man froze, turned back to Jax and looked at him curiously. "Will wonders never cease, a young boy on the streets who speaks with the diction of a gentleman."

Jax nodded. "Yes, sir, I was raised as a gentleman."

The fellow considered Jax for a long moment, his eyes narrowed in thought. "Well then, I'll do more than make it up to you. Come, I'll buy you something better than these horrid meat pies."

He threw an arm around Jax's shoulders. "My name's Andrew, young man. Come, let's find you something proper to eat."

A tall, broad-shouldered manservant accompanied Andrew as he led Jax to a nearby inn. "I have a room here," Andrew said. "Just for the night so I don't have to walk all the way back to my estate."

Andrew sat down with Jax at a small table, while the manservant stood nearby. Andrew then ordered them both a hearty meal. "And wine," Andrew said, slapping the barmaid on her rump. "Good wine so we can wash this down properly."

As they ate, Andrew questioned Jax about his circumstances. Jax didn't tell him the more sordid details of his new life, but gave him the basics.

"Your wine glass is dry," Andrew said, lifting the wine pitcher, and refilling Jax's glass.

In his previous life, Jax had drunk wine at dinner every evening, though never more than one glass, or perhaps a second on rare occasions. But during that meal Andrew refilled his glass several times, and insisted that Jax drink and enjoy the good wine he had purchased. When they finished, the room swayed as Jax stood, and he had to walk with some care.

As Jax retrieved his faded, old cloak from a hook on the wall, Andrew said, "Oh dear. It appears you've had a bit too much."

He leaned close to Jax, as if imparting confidential advice. "You don't want to go out on the streets with a wobble in your step. There are predators out there who would take advantage of you."

He straightened and spoke more loudly. "Come, you can relax for a bit in my room. At least until you're steady on your feet."

Jax shook his head. "I . . . I couldn't impose."

Andrew ignored Jax's protests, and he and his manservant helped Jax up the stairs. The manservant gripped Jax's arm so forcefully he would have had to make a scene to resist, and he didn't want to embarrass Andrew that way. But once out of the common room and on the second floor, the manservant locked both of Jax's elbows behind him in a painful grip, and hustled him down the length of a long narrow hall-way. Andrew produced a key, opened a door, and the manservant all but carried Jax into the room.

The room contained a minimum of furniture. Andrew and his man pinned Jax face down on the bed, and when Jax tried to protest, the manservant shoved a wad of cloth in his mouth and gagged him. They tied his hands to the headboard, and his ankles to the end of the bed, then yanked his pants down to his knees.

As Andrew took his pleasure all Jax could do was lay there and cry like a child, his protests muffled by the gag. When Andrew finished, he let the manservant have his turn. Jax tried to think of Mrs. Dorton's meat pies, and her berry pies. Her raspberry pie had been wonderful.

When the two men finished they quietly tidied themselves up. Then they walked out of the room, closed the door and left Jax tied to the bed. He cried himself to sleep, and a cleaning girl found him there in the morning.

"Oh you poor boy," she said as she untied him.

She helped him get his pants up, then retrieved his cloak from the floor and handed it to him.

He walked back to Pauper's Walk in a haze.

••••

When Jax finally ran out of money, he tried once more to be a crier, but the fellow in charge remembered him and would have none of it. After nothing to eat for three days, he started scrounging in alleys. He considered it a real treat when he found a chunk of raw potato. In several places sprouts had erupted from it, but he ate it any-way, and swallowed the sprouts as well. He spent that night vomiting until he had completely emptied his stomach.

He learned to eat almost anything, no matter how rotten or discolored it appeared, anything to fill his stomach, though he never again touched potato sprouts, and he never again came close to filling his stomach. One day he spotted a rat scurrying from one pile of rubbish to another, and considered trying to catch it. But he realized he had no idea how to do so, and would be a fool to attempt it. And if he did somehow manage to catch the thing, he had no way of cooking it, even if he knew how, though he thought he might soon be hungry enough to eat raw rat.

••••

In the kitchen of the Angry Bear, Maelleen grunted as she lifted the leather bucket of garbage. Working at the stove, her mother ignored her efforts. The two of them were not speaking.

The weight of the bucket forced Maelleen to take short, stuttering steps as she crossed the length of the kitchen to the back door. She hit the door's latch with her elbow, shouldered it open, and stepped out into the alley behind the pub. The dust cart wasn't due for another two days, and a fair amount of rubbish had accumulated against the back of the buildings that lined the alley.

A scuffling sound drew her attention. She looked down the alley, and saw a man with his back to her searching through some of the refuse. He found something, lifted it to his mouth and ate it.

"Eh," she said. "What you doing here?"

He started and spun to face her. His clothes were filthy, and her first thought was that he had unusually brown skin. But she noticed a lighter patch on his forehead, and realized a sheen of dirt and filth darkened his features. Something about him seemed familiar.

He frowned and squinted at her carefully, then his eyes widened. "Maelleen," he said, his voice little more than a croak.

She recognized that voice, and then she recognized the young boy. When he had eaten that meal in the common room of her father's pub, she had thought him quite handsome. She recalled that his dark hair had had a slight touch of curl to it, and his eyes, while bright and clear, had looked at her with a hint of sadness. But his hair now hung in lank, greasy strands, and taking in his appearance, her heart lurched.

Her father stepped out through the door behind her. He looked at the boy and spoke in a voice sharp with anger, "Who is this? What are you doing here?"

Maelleen felt a tear running down her cheek as she said, "It's that boy, da. Look at him."

Marcus took a step toward the boy and waved at him angrily. "Away with you. Be gone."

Pity welled up in Maelleen's chest as she grabbed her father's arm and said, "No, da, he's that boy. He bought some stew one night. And look at him now."

Tears now flowed freely down her cheeks. "Give the poor boy something to eat. Please, da."

It took a bit of pleading, and a fair amount of cajoling on her part, but Marcus finally consented to give the boy some leftovers from the bottom of the stew pot. The young man gobbled the scraps down like a starving animal, and when he left he looked at her, smiled, and said, "You're an angel."

••••

Jax had done everything correctly. He had been careful to be frugal and not squander the few coins he had. He'd avoided getting in trouble, except for that one incident at the dump, and that night with Andrew and his manservant. He had sold what he could to get more coins, and even worked as a crier until his voice gave out. When he finally tried to sell the valise, he quickly learned he couldn't give it away. He resolved not to sell the cloak, for that was all he had to keep him warm at night. He had done everything right, to the point of nearly starving, but each day his small fortune had declined by just a copper or two, until nothing remained. And somewhere along the line he'd lost the dagger.

After two months of living on the streets he found himself standing on a corner late one afternoon. The end of autumn heralded the coming of winter, and the nights had grown longer and colder. He hadn't eaten for several days, and had not a penny to his name, his only possession the clothing on his back, the cloak, and the canvas valise, which remained hidden under that bench in the cemetery. He shivered at the thought of spending another night on the cold ground there, and realized he probably wouldn't live through the winter.

A carriage pulled by two horses rolled past him, the animals moving at an easy walk. He paid it no heed.

He had to think of something, and he was running out of time, just as he had run out of food and money. At that moment, if Andrew had approached him, and offered to buy him a hot meal and let him sleep in a warm room in an inn, Jax couldn't be certain he would turn the man down, even if it meant he'd have to sleep with his hands and feet tied to the corners of the bed, and his mouth filled with a cloth gag.

"Boy."

Jax's stomach growled, hunger a painful emptiness in his gut. His resolve faltered and he considered selling the cloak, but he'd last longer without food than he would without some means of staying warm at night. He decided to wait a few more days. He could always sell the cloak later.

"You there, young man."

Among all the other sounds of the street, it took Jax a moment to realize that someone had addressed *him*.

"Young fellow."

It was a man's voice, and Jax turned slowly toward the sound of it. The carriage that had rolled by a moment ago had stopped a few paces past him. It had no markings or insignia of any kind, so it could be a hired coach. The coachman atop it wore no livery, just simple clothing, and he sat staring straight ahead, not paying Jax the least bit of attention. The door in the side of the carriage had an open window, though in the fading light of early evening Jax's eyes could not penetrate the darkness within.

A gloved hand reached out of the carriage's window and waved Jax toward it. "Come here, boy."

Jax approached the carriage cautiously and stopped a pace from the closed door.

From within the carriage the voice said, "Open your cloak. Let me see your clothing."

"Why?" Jax asked.

"Just do it. You won't regret it, and it'll probably be to your benefit. Trust me."

Jax opened the cloak slowly, not sure why this man wanted him to do so.

The man said, "You'll clean up well enough."

The door to the carriage creaked as it swung open. "Get in."

Again, Jax asked, "Why? What do you want?"

"My master wants to see you. You'll get a hot bath out of it, and some new clothes and a warm meal. Probably several warm meals, and most likely much better food than you've eaten in a long time. And you'll get to sleep in a nice, feather bed for a couple of nights, with a fire in the hearth to keep you warm."

Jax hesitated. Was this man's master another Andrew?

"It's your choice, boy. Just tell me one thing: If you don't get in, where are you going to sleep tonight? On the street? Shivering in the cold? It's getting colder each night, you know."

Jax shrugged. "I do know."

A feather bed, Jax thought, *and a warm fire, and a hot meal, and a hot bath.* At worst, this man's master might repeat Andrew's assault, or they might cheat him out of something, but he had nothing of any value they could take from him. And if the man proved to be lying about the bed, warm fire, and hot meal—well, Jax would be no worse off than now. He shrugged, climbed into the carriage, and closed the door.

That was Jax's second lesson, and years later it always amazed him how guileless and naive he had been back then.

5

A Warm Bed

SITTING IN THE dark interior of the unmarked carriage, Jax heard the coachman snap his whip. As the carriage lurched forward he asked, "Where are we going?"

"As I said," the man said. "To my master's estate. He wants to see you. And I guarantee you will be pleased with your reward."

Jax glanced out the window in the door of the carriage. After spending two months on his own, he'd learned enough of the streets to know they were headed out of the slums and into a wealthy suburb at the edge of the city. It was not the District of Nobles, but a place where many nobles had additional properties.

As his eyes adjusted to the darkness in the carriage, he began to discern the features of the man seated opposite him. The fellow wore a greatcoat, but no hat, and his dark hair had receded about half way back. He sat with his head cocked to the right, and there was something unusual about his left ear, as if it had been deformed in some way.

The interior of the carriage was warm enough to be comfortable. They rode in silence, so Jax leaned back, rested his head against the side of the coach, closed his eyes, and thought longingly of the hot bath the man had promised. He hadn't had a bath since leaving his father's house, though he recalled it was now Julia's and Felix's house, at least if they still owned the place. On the streets, the closest he'd come to being clean was when he'd wandered down to the river one day, then walked upstream far enough to get above the sewage from the city. He'd splashed water on his face and arms and dunked his head beneath the surface, though without soap the results were minimal at best. And it had been quite a hike, so he hadn't bothered to do that again.

Jax almost drifted off to sleep, but when they left the dirt streets of the slums and entered the better districts in the city, the carriage wheels made an unholy racket as they rattled noisily on the cobblestones. Nevertheless, Jax grew drowsy and had trouble keeping his eyes open.

When the carriage slowed it startled him and he came to full wakefulness. During the ride, night had enveloped the city, and with the horses now walking, the carriage made a sharp turn, pulled through the gates of a high stone wall and came to a stop in an enclosed courtyard.

The man seated opposite him leaned forward, hit the latch on the carriage door and popped it open. Light from a lamp spilled into the carriage, and for the first time Jax got a good look at the fellow. A nasty scar ran up the left side of his neck ending at his ear, where the ear lobe and the lower half of the ear had been chopped away long ago.

The man stepped out of the carriage and Jax followed him. He paused and looked around. They had pulled into a courtyard surrounded on three sides by high walls with battlements, ramparts and crenellations, and round turrets in the corners where the walls met. It was an old castle, obviously built centuries ago.

The man with the scarred ear looked up to the coachman still seated atop the carriage and said, "That'll be all for tonight, Carlos. You can stable the horses, get something to eat, and go to bed."

The coachman grunted something in reply, snapped the reins and pulled the carriage away slowly. Jax glanced about and was surprised to see he and the man with half an ear stood alone in the courtyard. For such a wealthy family, he would have expected to see footmen and night guards, and all sorts of servants rushing about.

"Come with me," the man said.

Jax nodded and followed him into the main building of the castle, then down a long hallway and into a sitting room far more elegant than anything his father might have afforded. As they entered the room, a beautiful woman seated alone on a couch raised her head from a book she had been reading and looked their way. She appeared to be in her mid-to-late twenties, with auburn hair and strikingly dark-blue eyes. In the style of the day she wore a dress with an empire waist. Cut low in front and back, it exposed her neck and shoulders, and a fashionable bit of cleavage. Jax thought her quite beautiful, though she would have been more so if her eyes hadn't appeared to hide some dark secret. But perhaps he read too much into the look she gave him.

Jax held back as the man walked forward, stopped a pace in front of her and bowed deeply. "Milady," he said, and Jax realized they were in the presence of the lady of the house.

The man straightened, turned to Jax, and said, "Come forward, boy,"

Jax walked forward, realizing that in front of such a beautiful and elegant woman, he should make a good impression. He recalled the manners he'd been taught, manners that had been of no use to him for the past two months. He bowed deeply and said, "Milady. I am honored."

When he straightened she lifted an eyebrow. "You speak rather well," she said, "for someone off the streets. And where did you learn to bow properly in front of a lady?"

Jax shrugged. "I did receive an education, and grew up properly. But my fortunes recently took a turn for the worse." He decided not to elaborate further unless pressed to do so, and then he might lie, because that had been the first lesson he'd learned when the constables had awakened him in the park that first day on the streets.

"Hmmm!" she said as she looked him up and down. If he hadn't known better, he might have thought she beheld him with hunger in her eyes.

She turned her gaze upon the man with the half-severed ear and said, "We may have more use for him than I had anticipated. My husband will be pleased, but perhaps I might find a use for him as well. You've done well, Lakorsa. Get him cleaned up, and see to his needs."

••••

The man with half his ear chopped away—Lakorsa was his name—led Jax to a room that contained a large metal tub filled with steaming water.

"Strip," Lakorsa said. "Get in and get cleaned up."

Jax was reluctant to undress under Lakorsa's watchful eye, but then anything was better than being thrown back out onto the streets to starve to death. And with the lady in command, he thought another Andrew-like rape most unlikely. He removed his clothing as instructed, folded it carefully, and placed it neatly on a chair.

Jax leaned on the edge of the tub and tested the water with a finger; it was gloriously hot. He stepped into it and savored the warmth as it sloshed around his ankles and shins. He lowered his body slowly into the steaming water, gasping as he did so. Once seated in the tub, with the water lapping against his chest, he slid down and ducked his head completely beneath the surface. He held his breath as long as he could, then came up for air.

Lakorsa had departed, and apparently taken Jax's old clothing with him, though he had left the worn and faded cloak. The loss of his old clothing didn't concern Jax; after all, the man had said something about new clothing.

Jax found a bar of soap on a little shelf on the edge of the tub. He scrubbed down meticulously, and took great pleasure in washing the grease and dirt out of his hair. Then he laid back and just enjoyed the warmth of the water for a time.

Lakorsa returned carrying a towel and new clothing. "It's time to finish up."

Jax stood and stepped out of the tub. The man handed him the towel, then placed the clothing on a dressing stand and said, "You can brush your hair and finish up here. I'll return shortly."

Jax dried off, brushed his hair and put on the new clothing. It was a bit large, but it fit well enough. Lakorsa had laid out a straight razor and shaving soap beneath a mirror on the stand. Jax looked at his image in the mirror. Hollows in his cheeks made the bones of his face stand out more prominently than he remembered. His dark-brown hair had grown out a bit, and he recalled that his father had told him he'd gotten that from his mother, along with his brown eyes. His hair was not exactly straight, with a faint touch of curl to it, which he'd gotten from his father. Earlier that year he had started shaving, though he didn't need to do so more than once or twice a week. But after two months on the streets he now had wispy tufts of unsightly hair on his cheeks and chin. He shaved quickly, then found a small bottle of men's cologne water that smelled of lavender, spice, and wood, so he dabbed some on.

Lakorsa returned and said, "Your dinner's ready, young man."

The fellow led Jax to a rather elaborately furnished bedroom, nothing like the kind of guest room he had expected. It had an enormous canopied bed, and at first Jax thought the fellow had made some sort of mistake. But his hosts had set up a table in a sitting room that adjoined the bedroom, and Jax's stomach growled as he caught the scent of roasted pheasant. The bird had been prepared in creamy gravy, with vegetables and small, delicate, little potatoes.

"Eat as much as you want," Lakorsa said.

Jax sat down and couldn't believe his great, good fortune. He resisted the urge to stuff the food in his mouth and gobble it down. The table had been set most properly, with utensils carefully arrayed next to the plate, so he forced himself to eat slowly using the manners he'd been taught. For a time Lakorsa stood silently by and watched him eat, then abruptly said, "My lady will be pleased you comport yourself at the table with proper manners." With that, he turned and left the room.

When Jax had first met the man on the street, Lakorsa had told him he might get several warm meals out of this, and he wondered what they wanted of him. He also wondered if he might make it last for more than just a few nights and a few meals. He really didn't want to return to the streets, not with winter coming and his purse empty.

When Jax finished and could eat no more, he sat back and felt drowsy and content. He sipped at tea while Lakorsa cleared the table, and Jax thought it odd that no other servants appeared to help him. The man seemed more like a valued steward than a footman or kitchen servant, and he'd be well within his rights to be miffed at such treatment, but he didn't seem to mind.

In the bedroom Lakorsa pointed to the enormous, canopied bed. "You can sleep there tonight." And with that, the man turned and walked out of the room, closing the door behind him.

Jax found a man's nightshirt laid out for him on the bed, so he removed his clothing and put it on. Then he climbed under the heavy comforter, and with a full stomach to aid him and a warm fire in the hearth, he quickly drifted off.

••••

Jax awoke the next morning with a full bladder demanding his attention. It had been the first time in two months he'd slept for more than a couple of hours at a stretch. In the chill of the night while sleeping beneath the bench in Pauper's Walk, his shivering had frequently awakened him, and it had often been a struggle just to get through the following day.

He threw off the heavy comforter, climbed out of bed, retrieved the chamber pot and relieved himself.

The room had a shuttered window on one wall. He opened the shutters and looked down on the courtyard below, the same courtyard where he had emerged from the carriage the night before. A high wall surrounded the court, interrupted by a heavy iron gate that closed it off from the street.

The door to his bedchamber opened, and Lakorsa walked in carrying more clothing. The previous evening the man had given Jax only a man's shirt, trousers and slippers, not much more than that of a simple servant. That morning he laid out the attire for a proper gentleman, spreading it out on the high canopied bed. It included cotton stockings and drawers, a white linen shirt, breeches, waistcoat, boots that ended a little below the knees, a single-breasted, velvet-accented tail coat, and a blue cravat.

Lakorsa looked at Jax with disapproval and said, "You'll be breakfasting this morning with her ladyship. See to it you're properly attired, and we'll learn if you really have the manners of a gentleman."

That sounded much like a challenge, and without another word, the man turned and walked out of the room.

A dressing stand contained a wash basin and a pitcher of water, with soap and shaving implements. Jax cleaned his face, combed his hair, and shaved, even though he wasn't sure he needed to. Then he carefully donned the clothing Lakorsa had laid out. Again, most of it was a little large, but not so that it was obvious, though if he wore the boots for more than a few hours, he might ask for another pair of stockings to fill them out. He then carefully brushed and arranged his hair to eliminate any appearance of the street-vagabond who had arrived in a carriage the previous night.

Out of curiosity, he checked the door to the bedchamber. It was locked, so he waited near the window looking out at the courtyard. The locked door made him consider what he might do if he needed to escape. The cobblestones of the courtyard were a good thirty feet below him, and there didn't seem to be any means of climbing down from the window, so he'd have to look for another way out and down.

About mid-morning a coach pulled into the courtyard and stopped at the front entrance of the house. A footman opened the coach's door, and out stepped a lady wearing a lavender dress, with an elaborate burgundy shawl. Looking down upon her from high above, a stylish bonnet hid her head and face, but Jax suspected she was the lady of the house. She had not spent the night in the house, possibly because with Jax present, that would be inappropriate if none of the men of the house were also present. And he had no doubt such a lady would adhere to the strictest rules of propriety.

Several minutes later the door again opened and Lakorsa took one step into the room. "Follow me."

The man led Jax down to a dining room with a table, chairs and a sideboard upon which an array of rolls, breads, butter and preserves had been placed. Trails of steam rose from the spout of a pot of tea, and from the delicious odor that touched Jax's nose, he guessed another pot contained hot chocolate.

Lakorsa left him there and closed the door. A few seconds later the door again opened, and in walked the lady with the striking, blue eyes. The lavender dress and burgundy shawl she wore confirmed his earlier suspicion that she had departed during the night and only just returned.

Not knowing her station or status, Jax executed a shallow bow, no more than a slight bending at the waist and a nod of his head. "Good morning, milady."

She smiled, and where the previous evening her eyes had appeared to hide some dark secret, that morning they were clear and bright. "Last night I didn't get your name."

He recalled the first lesson of the streets. "My given name is Felix." It gave him a certain childish pleasure to use his brother's name.

"And your house?" she asked.

He shrugged. "My father died penniless, and our house has been dissolved." If she pressed him on the matter, he'd give her the name Escher, because she could check on that.

He marveled at her eyes. They were a dark shade of blue, but in them a hint of grayish-silver seemed to light them on fire. Without question they were a prominent feature that drew one's attention.

"You're staring at me," she said.

He closed his eyes and bowed again with a nod of his head. "I do apologize, but your eyes are quite striking."

Her smile told him she clearly liked the compliment. "You're not the only man who has told me that."

He couldn't escape the sense that she was testing him. "Forgive me, milady, I did not mean the compliment in an inappropriate way."

She smiled again. "And I did not take it as such. Come, let us dine."

Jax wanted to eat everything on the sideboard. He wanted to fill a plate to overflowing and stuff it all into his mouth, but he limited himself to a roll, some butter and preserves. He chose to drink hot chocolate instead of tea, an extravagance he had thought he might never again experience.

They sat down at the table, and chatted while they ate breakfast. She didn't quiz him on his background, or question him in any way. Nor did he inquire as to why he had been plucked off the street, and she didn't volunteer the information. But they spent more than an hour at the kind of meaningless small talk appropriate for two strangers conversing over the breakfast table. When it ended, and Lakorsa escorted him back to his bedchamber, Jax had no doubt she had been testing him.

He recalled Lakorsa's earlier words. Had he demonstrated that he had *the manners of a gentleman?* The simple act of properly donning the formal day attire of a man of good means might have been a test in and of itself, and the formalities of dining would surely expose an imposter. But he couldn't escape the feeling there had been much more to it than that.

Yes, she had tested him, and he did hope he had passed.

6

Seduction

JAX SPENT A bored afternoon looking out the window at the courtyard, and wondering what the woman with the striking, blue eyes intended to do with him. Late in the afternoon Lakorsa brought him a meal of delicately poached trout, with small potatoes in an herbal cream sauce. A bottle of excellent, dry white wine accompanied the fare, and Jax decided not to question his good fortune. Again he went to bed early, and with a crackling fire in the hearth he fell asleep quickly.

Something woke Jax, some movement in the room … or rather, he realized, some movement in the bed with him. A lithe, warm body slipped under the sheets next to him, and he heard a soft sigh. He froze as a delicate hand reached out and touched his chest. It was a woman's hand with long fingers that traced a circle around one of his nipples.

He gasped.

"Don't be so frightened," she said, and at the sound of her voice Jax realized the beautiful woman with striking dark-blue eyes had climbed into bed beside him.

"I'm sorry," he said. "There must be some mistake. Lakorsa must have given me the wrong room. Please forgive me."

She reached out and pressed a finger to his lips. "Shhhh," she said. "There's been no mistake. You are exactly where I want you to be, as am I."

Her finger traced a line from his lips down to his chest, and again circled one of his nipples. Then it slid down further and traced a line around his navel. Not sure what to expect, nor what was expected of him, he reached out tentatively, ready to yank his hand back should the lady express even the slightest hint of displeasure. Under the sheets his fingers encountered a bare shoulder.

"Yes," she said. "Excellent. You are a most obedient young boy."

He slid his fingers across her shoulder to her neck, and encountered no nightgown. She took his hand in hers and slid it down her chest to her breast, then took one of his fingers and used it to trace the outline of her nipple. Her breathing quickened, and he responded as well. She gripped the back of his hand, slid it off her breast and down to her belly. He felt the muscles there tighten, and his breathing quickened to match hers. She pushed his hand farther down and pressed it between her legs. "For once, *I* intend to enjoy myself." She put careful emphasis on the word *I*. "This once, my husband can take his pleasure on another night."

She slid her hand down his stomach and into his crotch where she stroked him softly. Her touch sent a thrilling shock through him and he gasped.

"Ah," she said. "Clearly, you don't share my husband's proclivities."

He didn't understand that. "What do you mean, milady?"

"Milady?" she asked. "I think you can call me Stephanna. At least when we're alone . . . like this."

Jax's experience with women had been limited to a few stolen kisses with a young girl or two. And then the day he'd turned fourteen, his father had taken him to a whore house to ensure that he was properly educated in the ways of the fairer sex. He had enjoyed himself at the time, but this woman's touch was like nothing he had ever experienced before. He gasped again.

"You see," she said. "You're going to enjoy yourself too. We're both going to enjoy ourselves. And the timing is perfect for my greater needs, so there might even be a little bonus in this for me, an added benefit, shall we say."

She kissed him then, and as his tongue explored her mouth, he sensed in her a demanding and unrelenting hunger. In many ways they were alike. After starving on the streets for two months, his hunger had been just as demanding, though his need had been for food, whereas her desires were for something far more carnal.

In the whore house he had climbed on top of the whore, finished in a few minutes, then climbed off, but this woman would have none of that. She made him move slowly and carefully, taught him how to excite her, and excited him in a way that no whore could. That night he explored every inch of her body, and she his, and neither of them got much sleep. They spent the morning in bed as well, and never really got around to eating breakfast. He decided that if they wanted to give him food, clothing, and a warm place to sleep as compensation for doing to her what he was doing to her—well, he'd find some way to bear the heavy burden of that responsibility.

••••

Late in the morning after their first night together, Stephanna left Jax in his bedchamber. He checked the door and learned Lakorsa had not locked it that morning. It opened into a sitting room furnished and appointed in an elegant and expensive fashion. He crossed the sitting room to a door in the far wall and it would not open. With a little exploration he learned they had locked him into a small suite of rooms that included the bedroom, the sitting room, the room containing the bathing tub, and a private privy. Two hours after Stephanna left him, a coach pulled into the courtyard, a footman assisted her into it, the coachman cracked his whip, and the lady departed the premises.

He didn't understand why she had chosen him for her bedroom activities, and he didn't think for a moment she was drawn to him in any way other than for pure physical pleasure. In a day, or a week, or hopefully a little longer than that, he would end up back on the streets. This respite had given him a second chance, and he sat at the window looking out at the courtyard, thinking long and hard on how to make the best of it.

He had explored the place to learn the limits of his confinement. Now he explored it again, going through every drawer, closet, nook or opening. He quickly confirmed his first impression that the suite had been intended as the apartment of a lady of some means. He found several items of jewelry and coins in various drawers and small chests, so he concluded the suite probably had been her boudoir, at least until recently. Then again, he didn't need anyone to tell him he was just a temporary occupant. When she was finished with him, she would probably return to using it as her boudoir, at least when present in that residence.

He had the impression the old castle wasn't her permanent residence, that it was just a temporary place. He'd heard that many of the wealthy houses kept several places in the city, and often a villa on the coast.

She returned late that afternoon, again stepping out of the coach in the courtyard beneath his window. Jax had done his exploring wearing the boots, breeches and shirt from the expensive day suit she had provided. He quickly tied his cravat, donned the waistcoat and buttoned it up, then pulled on the tail coat. He finished by carefully brushing his hair, then prudently checking his appearance in a mirror.

A half hour later Lakorsa showed up. He looked Jax over carefully, then declared, "Good, you're properly attired. You'll be dining with her ladyship this evening."

Apparently, Jax had passed another test.

Lakorsa led him down to the dining room and left him there. A few minutes later Stephanna entered the room wearing a formal gown with a high waist, puffy little sleeves at her shoulders, and a low cut bodice that exposed the swell of her breasts in a way that excited Jax.

She smiled and said, "Good evening, Felix."

With Lakorsa present, Jax merely said, "Milady."

Jax escorted her to the table, held a chair for her as she sat down, and Lakorsa proceeded to serve them dinner. Jax again thought it odd that a staff of servants and footmen weren't present to see to the lady's needs.

As they ate their first course, she asked, "Tell me, Felix, where did you study?"

Jax told her the names of the schools his father had sent him to, and the tutors he had employed. And he realized he had forgotten the first lesson he had learned on the streets: he hadn't lied. He added, "They're probably not up to the standards . . . you might expect."

"No, no," she said. "They're perfectly adequate to give a young man a good education and train him properly."

She didn't seem at all put off by the truth, but he still resolved not to forget that first lesson again. She was a woman of incredible beauty, and the dress she wore drew his eyes to all the right places. At one point she caught him glancing at the swell of her breasts above the top of her gown. He looked away quickly, but he got the impression she found his attention flattering.

After dinner they retired to the downstairs sitting room where he had first met her. At her request he poured her a glass of chilled, sweet, after-dinner wine; for himself he poured a splash of brandy. They chatted for a while, then Lakorsa escorted him back to his suite of rooms. Ten minutes after Lakorsa left him alone, the door opened and Stephanna entered wearing that incredible dress, and looking at him with those captivating eyes.

Jax didn't know if the previous night had been a fluke, a whim, or something else he couldn't name. He recalled that she had said something about changing her plans regarding him, all done on the spur of the moment. But at the time he'd been so surprised and stunned, he now couldn't recall her exact words. He wasn't about to sweep her into his arms, only to learn he had offended her by doing so. But she crossed the room and stopped at an intimately close distance. She leaned forward on her tiptoes and kissed him gently on the cheek, and he responded by wrapping his arms around her and kissing her passionately.

When their lips parted, she said, "Slow down, darling. Pleasure, properly taken, is most pleasurable, when unhurried."

That night Jax learned it could take quite some time to properly undress a beautiful woman of her station. There were all sorts of straps and laces tied here and there, and pins elsewhere. He felt driven to plant kisses on every part of her as he exposed it, and she left no doubt in his mind she thoroughly enjoyed that, as did he.

••••

Twenty coppers! Maelleen looked at the coins in her hand and wanted to scream. She had given up her virginity more than a year ago in a groping fest with a young man of her choosing, and there had been some pleasure there, so it wasn't that. And for her first time as a whore, she had selected that good-looking lad from down the street. He was reasonably clean, and didn't yet have rotten teeth. But for his twenty coppers, he hadn't kissed her even once, had simply climbed on top of her, pounded in and out of her for a short bit, finished quickly, climbed off her, pulled up his pants, and walked away.

The experience had been far removed from the fantasy she had conjured, and she chided herself for being so foolish, so naive. And yet, she now had the twenty coppers. She could buy that pretty dress she had longed for. But she'd have to adjust her thinking on how she'd conduct her business as a whore. The money was good, but maybe she wouldn't whore as much as she had originally planned.

••••

Stephanna and Jax didn't talk much, not in the intimate way two lovers might share things. Without fail she left every day at mid-morning and returned every night, and every night they made love. She proved to be inventive in ways Jax could not have imagined, though he enjoyed her most in simple ways. One cold, winter night, they made love on a rug in front of a roaring fire in the hearth, then afterwards lay there naked, sharing a bottle of crisp, chill wine. She had laughed and poured wine on his chest, causing him to gasp as the chill liquid touched his skin, then she licked it off, and didn't miss a drop. But after a month, he had learned almost nothing about her. He had noticed that when he did ask regarding anything not trite or meaningless, she deftly avoided answering him, usually by diverting his attention with her body. She was rather adept at distracting him that way.

In the first week of his second month in the old castle, she arrived a little early and fully dressed. They kissed, and as he untied the straps of her gown, she said, "I think you've done quite well."

"How so?" he asked as he ran a line of kisses down her neck.

She lifted his blouse, and as she planted kisses on his chest she said, "I think you've given me that little bonus I had hoped for." She straightened and looked him in the eyes. "So tonight my husband is going to join us."

His heart skipped a beat and his gut clenched. "Your . . . husband. Won't he be jealous? Won't he be angry with me . . . and you?"

She traced a finger across his lips. "Oh no, darling. Not at all. In fact, he is quite grateful at what you've done for us."

"What exactly have I done?"

She didn't answer him, but instead reached into his pants, gripped his crotch and sent that thrilling shock through him. Only moments later they were in bed finding new places to kiss each other. As he reveled in the taste of her body, he wondered what kind of strange relationship existed between her and her husband that the man would be grateful another man had bedded his wife. But it got him a hot meal and a warm bed, and it got him Stephanna. It got him the touch of her flesh and the taste of her skin, so he didn't ask any questions.

Sometime later they were in the most passionate throws of lovemaking, when another body slipped into bed beside them. Jax froze.

"Darling," the woman said. "I'm glad you could join us."

"Yes, my dear wife," the man said. He leaned toward them and kissed Jax on the side of his neck. "So am I."

She said, "Do enjoy yourself, my dear."

He smiled. "I intend to."

Jax wasn't sure what to do. Were he and the husband supposed to share the woman? He had heard that some people called that kind of thing *sophisticated*. He wasn't sure if he could rise to that occasion, and he didn't want to share his Stephanna with any man. But he was stuck with the situation now, so he had to play along, at least for one night. He'd ask her about it in the morning after her husband had left, and try to gain some understanding, as long as she didn't divert him with her body.

They started with a lot of touching and kissing, but strangely enough the man never touched his wife, and she never touched her husband. And it was then that Jax realized it wasn't the two men who were supposed to share the woman, but the husband and wife who intended to share Jax.

He froze, trembling with fear. Were the two of them like Andrew and his manservant? He hadn't been able to overcome the manservant, but could he overcome the woman—did he even want to overcome the woman? He certainly didn't want to harm her, not his Stephanna.

Her husband raised up onto his hands and knees, looked carefully at Jax and frowned. Then he looked at his wife and said, "He's terrified. You said he's willing and able, and he clearly is neither."

Lying on her back, her bare breasts glistening with sweat and Jax's saliva, the woman shrugged. "I don't see that he needs to be willing, just able. He's here now, so enjoy him. I don't think he'll argue, or resist. And if he does, I'll have Lakorsa hold him down for you."

The man shook his head, climbed out of bed and said, "I'll not take a young man if he's not willing."

"That's a shame," she said. "I was hoping we could both enjoy him for another week or two. But I suppose it had to end sometime, darling. And he has done us an enormous favor. Why don't you just leave him with me and I'll clean this up?"

That was an odd way of putting it, but Jax was glad when the man took her advice and left the two of them alone. The woman and Jax sated their passion on each other well into the night, then she pleaded that she was sleepy and closed her eyes, so Jax closed his eyes and drifted off to sleep next to her.

7

Betrayal

JAX WOKE IN the middle of the night. It took him a moment to clear the dreams out of his head and realize Stephanna had awakened him while climbing out of bed. "Is something wrong?" he asked.

"No," she said, standing over him naked. "Nothing at all, darling. I'm just a little restless."

Jax sat up, reached out and touched her breast, caressing her nipple delicately. "I'm awake now, if that's what you want."

She hesitated, seemed to consider it for a moment, but then sighed and said, "I am tempted, but no, not now. I'm just restless. You go back to sleep."

She retrieved a dressing gown from where she had draped it across a chair, pulled it on and walked out of the room. Jax rolled over and closed his eyes, but could not return to sleep. Something in her words did not ring true, and it gnawed at him. He wasn't sure how he knew, but something within him told him to be careful. And it screamed at him that he must be wary.

He heard voices from the sitting room, muffled by the closed door, and he thought it might be a man and a woman speaking. A dim shaft of moonlight slanting through the window illuminated a faint square on the floor, but it didn't reduce the dark shadows in the rest of the room. He slipped out of bed, quietly crossed to the door and found it slightly ajar. Some instinct warned him he needed to hear that conversation. No light spilled beneath the door, so the man and woman were talking in the dark, and that too seemed odd.

He pried the door open just a little more, fearful that the hinges might creak or make some noise. If they did, he was ready to rush back to the bed, dive under the covers and pretend to be asleep. But luckily the door moved silently, creating a finger-wide gap through which he heard some of what they said.

"... done with him ..." That was Lakorsa asking a question.

"... minor nobleman's son ..." the woman said. "... loose end ... take chances ... tell tales ..."

The one clear thing he heard was Lakorsa's last sentence. "I'll take care of him like the others and dump him in the river."

She responded with, ". . . don't tell . . . husband . . . weak willed . . ."

Jax couldn't believe his ears; he liked the lady very much, though he had never fooled himself into thinking anything might come of their relationship. But he thought she at least had some feelings for him. To hear her speak so callously hurt in a way he'd never experienced before.

With his heart pounding in his throat, he crushed those feelings, eased away from the door and moved quickly. He'd have to escape somehow, and money or valuables would help him stay alive on the streets. He carefully opened a drawer where he'd found a small chest during his earlier explorations. He recalled that it contained some jewelry and coins. He opened it and didn't waste any time sorting through its contents. By touch, he retrieved the coins and the jewelry, then closed the chest and returned it to the drawer. He crossed the room and slipped the coins and jewels into his boots where he'd left them on the floor. Then he climbed back into bed and pretended to be asleep.

It was Lakorsa who came through the door. "Wake up, boy. We're leaving."

Jax sat up in bed and rubbed his eyes as if he'd been awakened from a sound sleep. "Where are we going?"

"I'm returning you to the slums. My master is done with you. Get up, get dressed, and be quick about it."

As Jax climbed out of bed, Lakorsa turned and walked out of the room, saying over his shoulder, "I have to make arrangements for the carriage. I'll be back shortly."

Jax found a small handkerchief and tied his fistful of jewelry and coins into it in a tidy bundle. He dressed quickly, donning the expensive day suit and boots she had purchased for him, and he noticed they no longer seemed too large; he had filled out in the month he had been with her. He tied the bundle to the waist of his pants, then shoved it down inside his breeches where it hung in his crotch. He checked carefully to be sure the bundle of jewelry and coins didn't produce a telltale bulge. He didn't want Lakorsa to notice he'd taken the expensive clothing, so he pulled on his old, faded cloak.

Lakorsa arrived a moment later and escorted Jax down the stairs.

Out in the courtyard of the old castle the coachman waited standing next to the carriage. It was the first time Jax had seen him at eye level. He was a burley fellow with broad shoulders, and a pistol tucked into his belt. He reached for the latch on the carriage door, but Jax beat him to it and opened the door. He thought he might need to know the feel of that latch and how it worked, if he wanted to survive the night.

Jax climbed into the carriage and sat down. Lakorsa followed and sat opposite him. The coachman snapped his whip and the coach pulled away. It was just past midnight, so the streets of Val d'Ossa were dark and deserted.

Jax wondered how they intended to *dump him in the river*. What would they do to him first: hit him over the head with a cudgel, shoot him with the pistol, or perhaps the burley coachman would just hold his head under water until he drowned? Jax and the coachman stood about the same height, but the man outweighed him by a considerable amount and had broader shoulders, so Jax had no delusions about being able to resist the fellow. And if Jax had any doubts about their intentions, his suspicions were confirmed when they skirted the edge of the slums and headed for the river.

The carriage slowed, then pulled off the street and into a park where couples picnicked on warm spring days, but on that winter night they had the park to themselves. The coachman drove the carriage through the park, and as it slowed further, Jax saw the moon glint off the flowing waters of the river. He glanced up and luck was with him; the moon was no more than a sliver low on the horizon. A full moon could have made it impossible for him to elude the two men, and might have meant he wouldn't survive the night.

As the carriage slowed even more, Jax didn't wait for it to come to a complete stop. He lunged out of his seat, hit the latch on the door and threw his shoulder against it. It sprang open and he tumbled out of the moving carriage, hit the ground painfully and rolled.

"Stop!" Lakorsa shouted. "Stop the carriage."

Jax stumbled to his feet and ran like the devil was on his tail. A hundred paces distant the river glinted in the dim light of the moon. As Jax zigzagged toward the water, he heard the pop of the coachman's pistol and a musket ball hissed past his ear. The crack of another pistol sounded and something stung his upper arm. He stumbled and went down, realizing Lakorsa must have had a pistol hidden in his cloak.

"Get him," Lakorsa shouted. "Don't let him get away."

Jax struggled to his feet and ran on, but now he heard the thud of the coachman's booted feet behind him. Jax ignored the burning pain in his arm and mentally told himself to *Run, run, run!* as the coachman narrowed the gap between them.

He reached the bank of the river and jumped, using his momentum to arc out over it in a long, flat dive. He hit the chill water and gasped. The heavy cloak prevented him from slicing gracefully through the water and brought him to a stop not far from the bank. He imagined the coachman following him, and recalling the man's heavily muscled shoulders, there'd be no contest in the dark water.

Jax's head broke the surface, but no coachman landed on top of him to drown him. Two dark silhouettes stood on the bank of the river about twenty feet away. As the current carried Jax downstream, Lakorsa shouted, "Go after him."

"I can't," the coachman said in a thick, common accent. "I don't know about swimming."

"Then reload your pistol, by damn."

As the current carried Jax further away from the two men, the coachman turned and sprinted back to the carriage. Jax managed to keep his head above water and get out of the heavy cloak, though he held on to it because he'd need it later if he survived this.

The current carried him around a bend in the river and he lost sight of Lakorsa and the coachman. He treaded water and let the current carry him farther, fearing that at any moment the two men would appear on the bank with reloaded pistols. He drifted further into the city, and when one of its bridges loomed above him, he swam hard and dragged himself up onto the river bank beneath it. He crawled up under the pilings of the bridge, wrapped the soaking wet cloak about his shoulders and hid in a shadow. Realizing his shivering and gasps might give him away, he tried to calm his breathing and his shaking shoulders.

With his fingers he probed the wound in his arm, was relieved to find no musket-ball hole, only a nasty tear in the skin and blood soaking the torn cloth of his shirt and coat. He'd end up with a bad bruise and a scar, but he could live with that.

After about an hour he thought he'd hidden long enough, but the same thing that had warned him to listen to the conversation between Lakorsa and Stephanna, now told him to wait just a little longer. A moment later he heard the clatter of a carriage's wheels on the cobblestoned street, and he knew that thing inside him had again saved his life. The carriage stopped on the bridge above him. He heard the carriage door open, then boot heels clacking on the stone of the bridge surface.

"Blast," Lakorsa snarled. "We've lost him, you idiot."

"Weren't my fault," the coachman said.

They argued for a few seconds, then Jax heard the door of the coach open and close. He heard the coachman grunt as he climbed up into the coach box, and a moment later the carriage pulled away.

Jax waited another hour crouched under the bridge, and he thought of that thing inside him that had saved his life twice that night. It had always been there, an instinct that had guided him at times. But never before had his life been on the line as it had that night. Never before had it spoken so vehemently to him, and so he had not recognized it as something special. After that night he would always think of it as his *instinct*, and never again would he fail to heed its warning.

When he finally emerged from his hiding place beneath the bridge, he felt an uncomfortable lump in his crotch. Somehow, throughout the night's ordeal, he hadn't lost the little bundle of jewelry and coins.

••••

Jax returned to the stone bench hidden in the thicket in Pauper's Walk. To his relief, even after more than a month, the board, sheets of tin, and his valise remained undisturbed. Winter's grip on the city would continue for another two months, but he only needed to survive through the night. He had no idea how many coins he'd stolen from Stephanna's boudoir, and couldn't count them now in the dark, but he was certain he had enough to give him a second chance on the streets. Only a few hours remained before sunrise, so he curled up in a ball beneath the bench in his wet clothing, and shivered until dawn.

The winter day began without a cloud in the sky, and as long as the wind didn't blow, the sun warmed him. He pulled off the cloak and tail coat, and spread them across a bush where they could dry in the sun. He yanked off his boots and stockings and placed them on the bench so they could dry as well. Then he retrieved the make-shift pouch from his crotch, and spread its contents on the bench before him.

His haul amounted to four gold sovereigns, six silver guineas, a hand-full of coppers and pennies, a jeweled silver broach, and two gold rings containing precious stones. He suppressed a shout of joy, for in his wildest dreams he couldn't have hoped for more.

Would Lakorsa be out searching the streets for him? Whatever the woman and her henchman had been up to, their desire to murder him simply to silence him made it clear he must move carefully. He didn't include her husband in their conspiracy. "I'll not take a young man if he's not willing," the man had said. He had also refused her offer to have Lakorsa hold Jax down so he could take him the way Andrew had. No, her husband was probably innocent of anything beyond the need to satisfy the urges dictated by his body. Many people considered his desires unnatural, but Jax's own perspective on such matters had shifted considerably in the last few months.

By noon his cloak had dried, as had his boots and the expensive day suit, though his swim in the river had left it badly wrinkled and it no longer looked so expensive. He put the jewelry and most of the coins in the small purse he'd carried out of his father's house the day Julia had thrown him out onto the streets. It had been empty for a couple of months now, and he placed it back in the valise.

Leaving the valise hidden in the thicket, he headed for the edge of the slums closest to the District of Nobles, carrying with him only four silver guineas, several coppers, and some pennies. Staying close to the border between the districts, he wandered the streets, keeping his eyes and ears open, and stepping into a shadow or alley any time he heard a coach approaching. It didn't take long to find what he was looking for: a sign advertising an apartment for rent.

An old widow named Mrs. Beamish owned the small building, and kept it clean and clear of infestation. That close to the District of Nobles, the only crime he might encounter were pickpockets and petty theft, which were of no concern as long as he exercised some caution. Mrs. Beamish kept the one-room flat tidy and clean, and after careful examination Jax determined there were no vermin in the sheets of the small bed. He gave the woman three month's rent in advance.

Mrs. Beamish also proved to be adept with a needle and thread. For a few pennies, she repaired the bullet holes in his tail coat and shirt, and as a bonus carefully pressed them with a hot iron. Jax left her building looking every bit a young gentleman of modest means.

Jax bought a new dagger to replace the one he'd lost. It included a sheath that he tied to a strap inside his old cloak. That kept it out of sight, but close at hand.

He returned to the stone bench in the cemetery to retrieve his valise and his ill-gotten gains from that woman's boudoir.

••••

Two months on the streets had taught Jax many things. He had occasionally heard the name Rondo whispered here and there, but never thought he might need the services of a middleman to whom he could sell stolen goods. In the slums, his newly refurbished day suit labeled him as an outsider, so he took care to keep it hidden beneath his old cloak while he made a few judicious inquiries. Late that afternoon he turned down an alley, stopped at the last door on the right, and knocked.

After several seconds the door opened a crack. The darkness of the room beyond hid its occupant from view. "What do you want?"

"I'm looking for Rondo."

"What do you want him for?"

Jax had thought carefully about how he might broach the subject. "I've come on hard times . . . and have some merchandise I need to sell."

"Why come to him?"

At that point Jax was fairly certain he was speaking to the man himself. He shrugged. "I need to sell it discreetly."

"How'd you get his name?"

Jax caught the glint of an eyeball in the dark crack of the open door. "I've been on the streets long enough to hear a name or two."

The eyeball glanced down to Jax's boots, then back to his face. "You don't look or sound like you're from the streets."

"I wasn't, until recently. But as I said, I've come on hard times."

"You a constable or something?"

Jax shook his head and didn't try to hide his exasperation. "Do I look like a constable?"

The eyeball stared at him in silence for several seconds, then the door creaked further open, but only enough for Jax to edge through it sideways. "Get in here."

Jax slipped into the room, wondering if he'd get a knife in the back, but nothing of that sort happened. In the dark he heard footsteps, then Rondo struck a match and lit a candle. The man had crossed to the opposite side of a heavy oak table, the only piece of furniture in the room. He stood just shoulder high to Jax, with a fat belly that protruded from a tattered tail coat, and the light of the candle glistened off a greasy sheen on his face. "What have you got?"

Jax stepped forward to stand at the table. He reached into his cloak and retrieved the small pouch he carried. From it he produced the broach and two rings, placed them on the table, then slid them toward the fat little man. Rondo carefully picked each of them up one at a time and closely examined it.

"You didn't get the likes of this through some smash-and-grab."

Jax wasn't familiar with the term, but it seemed rather self-explanatory. "That's because I don't do smash-and-grab."

"Second story man, eh?"

Second story man wasn't self-explanatory, so all Jax said, "Hmm."

"You're new. Why haven't I seen you before this?"

Jax had to think quickly to answer that. "As I said, I've come on hard times, and I recently had to take on . . . a new profession."

Rondo appeared to like that answer. "I'll give you five silver guineas for the lot."

Jax didn't know what a good price for the jewels might be, but he shook his head. "I can throw away the stones and melt the metal down, get the equivalent of a gold sovereign or two from the two rings, and several silver guineas from the broach."

Rondo shrugged. "I gotta split them up and sell the stones separate anyway. These pieces are too recognizable."

They haggled back and forth for a few minutes, then settled on two gold sovereigns.

As Jax stepped out through the door into the alley, Rondo said, "Good merchandise, kid. Let me know when you get more."

Until that moment, Jax had thought he would simply sell what he'd taken from that woman, and never see the little fence again. Rondo's parting comment made him reconsider. His limited plans for his future had been rather hastily thought out, but he now had the resources to take his time and consider all the possibilities. The lack of a long-term plan for survival had bedeviled his thoughts, and the fat, little man might have just given Jax a possible solution.

8

The Harlot

JAX HAD UNFINISHED business at the Angry Bear, so he headed straight there. Again, the faded, old cloak allowed him to blend in with the denizens of the slums and avoid their distrust of outsiders.

Marcus remembered him. "Last time I seen you, you wasn't doin' so well."

"No," Jax said, "I wasn't. But I've rectified my difficulties."

Jax ordered a plate of the stew he remembered with such fondness, but this time he paid four coppers and got a healthy chunk of meat. And instead of just water, he ordered a mug of ale to wash it down.

This time Maelleen's mother brought him the food. Bethy stood as tall as her daughter and had clearly been a beauty in her time. There could be no doubt Maelleen had inherited much of her beauty from her mother, but age and a hard life had dimmed Bethy's girlish charms.

Jax wanted to see Maelleen again, and had hoped she would be the one to bring the plate of stew to his table. The last time he had seen her, he'd been rummaging through the garbage in the alley behind the Angry Bear, and she had coaxed her father into giving him a free meal. It had only been scraps from the bottom of the stew pot, and to Maelleen it had probably been just a meal, but to Jax, it had been a kindness beyond imagining, an act he would never forget, an act he must repay in some way. He had sworn then he would always remember the angel who had given him such a boon, the girl with brown hair that hung past her shoulders in a disarray of curls and ringlets.

He finished the stew and was musing on that memory, when Maelleen plopped down into the chair opposite him. She was every bit as pretty as he remembered, though as before she had overdone the makeup and looked like a trollop. "Eh, you look a lot better than last time I seen you."

He smiled. "I am doing better."

She leaned forward and lowered her voice. "What'd you do, rob the old Witch? Or maybe you burgled the Witch Palace, come away with yer pockets full of gold, eh?"

He knew she wasn't serious and laughed at the thought. "No, nothing like that. But I am financially better off. I've overcome my difficulties."

That wasn't completely true. He had accumulated enough of a fortune to live comfortably for a year, maybe more if he acted with care. But to survive beyond that, he'd have to think of something else. And recalling Rondo's parting words, perhaps he already had.

"Lots of money, eh?" she asked.

"No," he said. "Not lots, but I don't think I'm going to end up destitute and on the street again, at least not for some time."

She leaned to one side to look at his boots, then slowly scanned him and took in his entire appearance. "You're looking quite the fancy gentleman, ain't yuh?"

"The nice clothing was a gift," he said, "something I couldn't afford myself." For all intents and purposes he had spoken the truth, though, in fact, he'd whored himself to that woman every bit as much as Maelleen wanted to whore herself to men.

Recalling the kindness Maelleen had shown him, he felt he owed her a great debt, and if he could repay her in no other way, he would at least hire her for her services. "Last time we sat here, you wanted to be a whore. Did you ever do that?"

She wrinkled her nose with distaste. "A couple of times. It makes ends meet, makes it so's I can buy me a few nice things, and makes it so's we can hire a girl to help, and maybe me mum don't have to work so hard in the kitchen."

Jax nodded. "Then I'd like to hire your services."

She flinched. "You mean . . . you want me as a whore?"

No, he didn't want her as a whore, but that was probably the only way he could ever have her. "Yes, if that's all right with you."

Her eyes hardened as if he'd done something to anger her. "Sure, it's all right."

She stood rather stiffly. "Follow me."

She turned and marched away across the common room. Jax had to hurry to keep up. He followed her through the door into the kitchen, and her mother gave him a disapproving frown as he passed her. Maelleen led him up the back stairs to where she and her parents obviously lived above the pub, and into a small room with a bed.

She closed the door, lifted her skirts to expose undergarments that looked like a pair of loose pantaloons, then slid the pantaloons down to her knees. Holding her skirts up, and naked from her knees to her waist, she lay down on her back on the bed, and spread her legs. She propped herself up on her elbows and spoke with a sharp note of anger in her voice. "Twenty coppers, it'll be. And you pay first."

All Jax could say was, "Uh."

She gave him a hard look. "Have at it. I don't have all night."

Jax shook his head. "What . . . what are you doing?"

"Come on," she said. "Climb on and get it done."

Jax moved slowly, leaned over, gripped the top of her pantaloons, and slid them up to her waist.

She frowned. "What are you doing?"

He took the hem of her skirts out of her hands, and pulled it down to her knees.

"What are you doing?" she asked again.

He took her hands and forced her to stand, facing him. "First, you tell me what you're doing."

"I'm a whore," she said, spitting the words in his face. "I lays meself down, spreads me legs, you climbs on top, and gets your business done."

Jax put his arms around her waist and pulled her against him. He recalled the words the woman with striking, blue eyes had uttered to him, and repeated them now. "Pleasure, properly taken, is most pleasurable, when unhurried."

Her eyes narrowed with distrust. "Ain't no pleasure in what I do."

He smiled and ran a line of kisses down her neck. As he did so he felt some of the stiffness come out of her spine. He kissed her earlobe and whispered, "Let's see if we can change that."

Jax would have said he had learned nothing of value in the boudoir of that woman, but that night he realized he had learned quite a bit. And while he would never think of himself as an expert in such matters, Maelleen clearly enjoyed herself as well.

••••

A knock on the door woke Jax. Maelleen lay next to him, her eyes shut. At the sound of a second knock her eyes opened. "Come in," she shouted. "Stop knocking and come in."

The door opened and Bethy stuck her head in, a grin on her face. "From the sounds that came out of here last night, I thought you two might be so tired you'd sleep all day."

Maelleen blushed, and Jax wanted to kiss her. But he felt his own face warming also.

As Bethy marched into the room carrying a small tray, Jax hurriedly covered himself. Maelleen didn't bother, and sat up next to him, her bare breasts bouncing as she did so.

Bethy placed the tray on the end of the bed. "You let him stay the night."

Maelleen shrugged. "He's nice."

Bethy considered that for a moment, then nodded. "Your da needs you downstairs in an hour or so, but not right away."

She leaned close to Jax and winked. "Old Marcus and me like knowing a man's treating our girl proper like."

He recalled the unhappy look she had given him the night before. Clearly, something had changed.

She turned toward the door but paused half way through it and looked back at them. "Dear, you can take the hour to say a proper good-bye to Mr. Jax here." The grin returned. "Just don't make any noise doing it. We got customers now."

Maelleen blushed again, and Jax felt himself doing the same.

The tray contained a breakfast of sliced peaches and toast. Maelleen sat on the bed next to Jax, not in the least concerned that she wore absolutely nothing.

As they ate and talked, he learned she had whored a couple of times, and had been disappointed at the experience, though the money had been good.

"How did you survive?" she asked him. "You disappeared a month ago, and we thought you was dead or something, maybe face down in the river."

He couldn't tell her the truth, for the truth was so unbelievable even he had trouble accepting it. He told a half lie. "I worked as a crier at the Hall of Nobles, made a few coppers a day."

She cocked her head and closed her eyes, squinting and clearly thinking on his words. Then she opened her eyes and lifted one eyebrow. "But how can you be a crier. You have to know letters to do that."

He shrugged. "I do know letters . . . and numbers as well."

She shook her head. "You can't know letters, not good enough to be a crier."

"Why not?"

She waved her hands as if the answer were self-explanatory. "You're here in the slums with the rest of us."

"But I'm not originally from the slums."

He carefully explained how he'd been born to a very minor nobleman, but a nobleman nonetheless. He told her how he'd been educated, taught to ride a horse, fence with a rapier, and comport himself properly in polite company. As he spoke, the look on her face morphed slowly into something calculating, and he could almost see her thoughts racing ahead with each new revelation.

When he finished, she gripped his arm and said, "Can you teach me?"

"Teach you what?"

"Letters," she said, "and numbers, and how to talk like a fine lady. I could get meself a rich husband. And me da and ma could maybe even retire, and not work their hands to the bones until the day they die."

Jax's mind raced ahead of her, because she obviously didn't understand the magnitude of her request. "You'll have to learn more than letters, numbers, and how to talk. You'll have to learn what subjects are appropriate for the moment, and proper table manners, and you'll have to wear your makeup and hair different, and different clothes, and which fork is the right fork for which course at the table."

She clearly didn't believe him. "A fork's a fork. And what's a course?"

He tried to make her understand. "In a proper setting, food is served one dish at a time, and there's an array of table utensils, and you have to use just the right one, or maybe two, for each dish." He shook his head. "I don't know. It'll take a lot of time and effort."

A sly look crossed her face. She leaned forward and lightly kissed him on the lips. "A lot of effort, eh? Well I'm willing to try if you are. You make the effort to teach me all those fancy things, and at night I'll make the effort to keep you a happy man. And you won't have to pay me none for it, neither."

Jax's thoughts raced, and he decided that if that's what she wanted, he'd try to give it to her. He owed her at least that much. "Very well, I'll try."

Her eyes brightened. She kissed him on the lips, then on the cheek. "Oh," she said, "there's one more thing. Can you teach me what you did to me last night? That'll come in handy as well."

••••

As night enveloped the city, Jax's father's estate remained quiet and still. The properties of lesser nobles were rarely walled and enclosed, which made Jax's job easier. He listened carefully to his instinct, and it told him he could move without fear. At a gap between gas lamps he crossed the street and paused in the dark shadow of a large elm. He waited, and listened, giving his instinct a chance to work, but it said nothing to him.

He rushed in a crouch to the side of the house and paused there. A rumble broke the stillness of the night. The wheels of a carriage rattling on the cobblestones of the street made an awful racket as it approached. He waited as the sound rose to a crescendo, passed by in the street, then dwindled into the distance.

He sought a particular window on the ground floor at the back of the house. It had a broken latch that might fool an unknowledgeable intruder. If he tried to simply lift the window, it would stick and appear to be locked. It was for that reason Felix had not bothered to have it repaired, a frugal choice on his part. But Jax knew that the casing was slightly loose, and if he edged the window just a fraction of an inch to one side, it would slide open easily.

Jax had purchased a broad brimmed hat to cover his face in shadows during the day, then wearing his good day suit, he'd walked past the property several times to determine its present owners. Sure enough, Julia and Felix had yet to sell the estate, and he wondered how they had managed to scrape by without doing so.

He paused beneath the window and listened to his instinct. Five times now he'd attempted this foray, and each time his instinct had warned him off. Julia, or Felix, or both of them, had probably been present in the house, so he'd never gone beyond the window with the broken latch. But that night his special talent told him he could proceed.

It took a few seconds and a bit of effort to edge the window to one side in the casing, but then it slid open with almost no effort. He climbed in, taking care to make no sounds. Just to be certain his instinct had led him true, he checked all the bedrooms and his father's office, now Felix's office. The place was empty, and he was free to move about without hindrance.

He quickly answered the question of how they'd managed to scrape by without selling the place: much of the furniture was gone, probably sold at auction to pay the taxes and bills. But they'd soon be out of furniture, and that source of income would end.

His father had not had a proper safe, but had kept what coin he possessed behind a false panel hidden beneath a particular drawer in his desk. Jax went straight to it, and to his great delight, Felix had followed their father's example. Jax found ten gold sovereigns and a number of silver guineas there. With his take from that woman's boudoir he didn't need the money, but he had imagined again and again the looks on Felix's and Julia's faces when they found it gone. They would suffer the same panic and fear he had gone through, and probably end up on the streets like he had. He wondered how Felix would feel if Andrew were to assault him the same way he had assaulted Jax, and thinking of that his heart lurched.

He stood there for an unknown length of time, reliving the horrors of his months on the streets, and he couldn't find it in him to be the architect of his sibling's destruction, even though they so richly deserved it. Oddly enough, he now didn't need the money and they did. It was in that moment that he decided to never harm those like him, simple people stuck in a life of quiet desperation. He put the money back behind the false panel, and returned everything to its proper place so there would be no evidence of his visit. Then he exited through the back window.

As he walked back to his small flat in Mrs. Beamish's building, he decided that if he wanted to do this burglary thing properly, he'd need to learn how to get through locked doors. His present finances allowed him a grace period of about a year to learn the necessary skills. Rondo could arrange for almost anything, and in response to a discreet inquiry from Jax introduced him to a locksmith who was happy to divulge the secrets of his trade—for the right price. Jax studiously practiced and became adept at picking locks.

He started small, a minor noble's property that was more practice than anything else. He came away from it with a couple silver guineas, and some experience. But the first two years plying his new profession as a thief proved to be stressful. Twice, while burgling a house, the owner discovered him and chased him off, both times with a musket ball hissing past his ear. And another time he barely eluded the constables by disappearing into a city park. For two hours they searched the park, and several times came so close to him he could hear them whispering. But that night he learned to depend on his instinct as never before, and eventually escaped from the park exhausted and hungry.

Those first few years he barely scraped by, but from his close calls with the constables and musket balls, he learned to be cautious. He adopted the strategy of thoroughly reconnoitering each target property until he knew the owner's routine. And he carefully avoided the richer houses that employed guards to patrol their properties at night. His resolve to never prey on those less fortunate than him, and to never take more than his victims could afford, further limited his opportunities, but he was happy with that strategy.

Occasionally one of the more aggressive denizens of the slums emerged as a crime boss, usually a young man who made a living by depending more on muscle than stealth. Each invariably espoused the benefits to everyone of organizing the criminal elements of the district. Jax noticed that part of their vision always included a tax on the profits of illicit activities to be paid to the crime boss, a piece of the action as it were. They taxed everyone, including the prostitutes, whose professions were not illegal. Interestingly enough, none of them ever lasted more than a season or two. Two of them simply disappeared without warning or trace, and another three ended up with their heads impaled on a pike mounted on the walls of the Witch Palace. From that, Jax learned that discretion, a low profile, and modest aspirations were the best way to stay alive long enough to enjoy the spoils of his thieving.

While Jax developed his skills as a thief, Maelleen worked hard at her lessons to become a fine lady. After five years of his tutelage, she became reasonably literate. But as with everything, *reasonably* literate wasn't good enough for her. She demanded perfection of herself and wanted to develop her new appearance and manner so there could be no chance of a mistake. He never did tell her he had become a thief, though that was one of the few secrets he kept from her.

Carefully working his way up to more profitable targets, and always using his special instinct to warn him away from danger, Jax quickly became one of Rondo's most valued suppliers. Then nine years after Julia and Felix had disinherited him, Rondo wanted him to do a special job.

9

The Witchguard

THE ADDRESS THE stranger had given Jax was somewhere in the District of Nobles, and not on its outskirts where the most minor of the lords lived. But other than that it meant nothing to Jax. Standing on the other side of Rondo's dimly lit room, the stranger waited impatiently for him to respond to the offer.

Next to Jax, Rondo leaned in close and whispered in his ear. "What do you think? Are you going to take the job?"

Jax and Rondo had worked together now for nine years, a profitable relationship for them both. The fat little middleman couldn't hide his anxiety. Rondo wanted Jax to take the job, because Rondo wanted his commission. Rondo didn't need to concern himself with breaking into a large and well-guarded mansion to steal a valuable figurine, or with getting out of that mansion alive. That was rather short-sighted of him, because he wouldn't get a commission if Jax didn't succeed. But then again, Rondo wouldn't be the one hanging from a gibbet if Jax failed. Rondo and people like him had no qualms about risking Jax's life. That was one of the many lessons Jax had learned from his years on the streets.

The only window in the room had been shuttered to keep the bright afternoon sunlight from illuminating the interior of the small space, then covered with a piece of cloth to ensure that no light leaked past the cracks in the boards. Their prospective client stood in the shadows on the opposite side of the dark room, with a heavy oak table separating them. The flame of a single candle, stubbed onto the middle of the table, cast a wan, flickering light. It produced shadows that danced around the room, allowing them all to maintain their anonymity. Like Jax and Rondo, the client wore a hooded cloak that hid his features.

The fellow was most likely an important factor in one of the noble houses. He probably wasn't lying about the monetary value of the figurine, but why would a wealthy house need to steal an expensive piece of artwork from another wealthy house? It was certainly possible that some of the more affluent houses weren't as prosperous as they put on. But if their objective was truly financial, as the client had implied, jewels, precious metals, or coins would be far easier to unload. Even a unique and artistic piece of jewelry could be broken down into gold, silver and individual stones. But the value in a precious figurine stemmed from the prestige of owning it, or the ability to resell it, both of which were highly unlikely with a piece of easily recognizable stolen property.

The client's story didn't ring true. Possibly the figurine had some hidden value, or there could be a political aspect to this job. Jax doubted the fellow would reveal the true nature of the figurine's value, so the decision to take the job would depend on who he stole from, and who he stole for.

Jax had honed his instinct now for nine years, and it helped him understand such things. He didn't want anything to do with the politics of the noble houses. It was much too dangerous, but it could be just as dangerous to turn one of them down when they made such a request. He decided not to make a decision until he had more information.

He considered his options carefully. Rondo still didn't know Jax's real name, and Jax had concocted a fake history to satisfy the fat little fence's curiosity. The client hadn't seen Jax's face, nor had Jax seen the client's face, which was an important consideration. The fellow would be more likely to simply drop the matter if he felt confident he couldn't be identified.

Jax shook his head. "Before I can commit, I'll have to check out the address you gave us, determine if it's even feasible. And of course . . . all of these factors will influence price." He'd added that last bit because the client would expect something like that.

"Yes," Rondo said, the greed in his voice obvious. "The degree of difficulty is always an important consideration."

The client nodded with a slow, calculated tilt of his head. "How long will that take?"

Jax shrugged. "No more than two days."

"Very well, two days." The client turned and walked to the door. Knowing what to expect, Jax tensed and prepared not to cringe and squint. The fellow opened the door and the harsh glare of the afternoon sunlight spilled into the room. The client stepped out into the alley beyond, then turned to one side to walk down its length, pulling the door shut behind him. In that instant, Jax caught a momentary glimpse of his face in profile, half of it hidden by the hood of his cloak. The fellow had sunken cheeks, a nose with a prominent arch, no facial hair, and snow-white eyebrows.

As the door clumped shut and the room darkened again, Rondo said, "This could be good money."

"Yes," Jax said, "it could." At this stage he wasn't going to confuse the middleman by voicing his doubts.

Rondo prattled on about the money as he opened the shutters on the window. Jax didn't want to squint blindly when he stepped out into the street, so he kept his eyes open to allow them to adjust to the light. He also didn't want to leave following the same path as the client. If the man waited on the street to see who emerged from the alley, he could identify Jax and that wouldn't do. Jax walked to a door that led deeper into the building and opened it.

"You'll get back to me?" Rondo asked.

Jax didn't look back as he said, "Two days."

He walked down a narrow hallway, then through a large room where Rondo stored a lot of stolen goods before disposing of them. At the far end of the room he opened a door and stepped out into a different alley from that the client had used. He glanced up and down the alley and was glad to see nothing more than a mongrel dog sniffing through garbage piled against the buildings. It was late afternoon, and the light of the sun would soon begin to dim.

He walked with an unhurried pace to the mouth of the alley, then onto a street teeming with pedestrians, mounted horses, and the occasional carriage. He stopped, glanced both ways and saw nothing out of the ordinary. But as he stepped out into the flow of pedestrians, he noticed a young boy up ahead standing on a street corner. The lad appeared to be in his mid-teens, with curly, blond hair. He looked hungry and tired, and a rip in the elbow of his shirt made it clear his clothing had seen better days. The young fellow reminded Jax of himself nine years ago.

A two-horse carriage had stopped on the street in front of the boy. The carriage had no markings or insignia, and the coachman atop it wore no livery, just simple clothing. The young boy gestured with his hand, his lips moved, and Jax realized he was talking to someone in the carriage. But because of the distance and the slanting angle of Jax's view, he saw only darkness through the window in the door of the carriage.

The door opened, the boy stepped forward, and Jax's heart leapt. "No," he shouted and ran forward, waving frantically. "Don't get in that carriage."

The boy glanced his way briefly, but ignored him and stepped into the carriage. The door closed, the coachman snapped his whip, and the carriage pulled away.

Jax came to a stop and recalled the day he had accepted Lakorsa's invitation and stepped into a similar carriage. For the boy's sake, he hoped he was wrong. It could be the same carriage, but then again there must be a hundred such simple, unmarked coaches on the streets of Val d'Ossa. Could it really be the same one, after all these years? Jax couldn't deny that he might be overreacting, but he decided to check the river every morning for a couple of days anyway, see if any commotion occurred down near the water.

Another carriage rattled by and he had to move quickly to keep from being run over. Someone nudged him as they walked past, and he realized everyone seemed in a hurry to get somewhere, everyone but him. He glanced up and down the street and noticed that, other than him, there was only one other person not moving. A man stood looking at something in a shop window, then glanced Jax's way, noticed Jax looking at him, and looked away quickly. *Now that was odd,* Jax thought.

Jax looked away and walked on, conscious of the man behind him.

At the intersection of another busy street he turned right and glanced over his shoulder. About thirty paces behind him the fellow walked his way, though he wasn't looking at Jax, and he wasn't hurrying to catch up. As Jax continued walking, the corner of a building hid the man from view.

Jax wondered what had drawn his attention to that particular fellow. Had it been his instinct, his special talent?

He tried to recall the man's appearance, and nothing about him stood out as unusual. The sword strapped to his side looked to be no better than the kind of blade a common soldier might carry, and thankfully the man had no pistol tucked into his belt. He wore loose breeches that were better than homespun, but not by much, with the pant legs tucked into calf-high boots that appeared to be well-made, but not expensively so. The leather jerkin he wore over a modest cotton blouse had been made from simple cowhide, without embellishment or anything else that might draw attention to him. Jax thought he might be an off-duty guard for one of the noble houses.

At the next intersection Jax turned left, and again glanced over his shoulder, spotting the fellow still about thirty paces behind him. Jax looked away from him and continued walking, thinking that the man's simple attire seemed all wrong. For some reason Jax thought the fellow belonged in a red and black uniform with silver piping, or perhaps even armor, with red, black and silver embellishments.

Jax stumbled as he missed a step and stopped in his tracks. Why had he pictured the fellow in the uniform of a Knight of the Witchguard?

His instinct had definitely spoken to him.

••••

Once Jax understood that he was being followed, and that he needed to do something about it, he had no trouble losing the fellow. With the man keeping a steady distance of thirty paces behind him, Jax turned at an intersection onto another busy street. During the few seconds in which the building on the corner hid him from view, he broke into a run and sprinted to the next intersection.

"Here now, be careful," a man shouted as Jax raced past him.

Jax turned down the next street and continued running. He made a series of random turns onto streets he knew well, then halted and stepped into the shadow in the doorway of a clothing shop. He waited for several seconds, but saw no sign of his pursuer and breathed a sigh of relief.

He returned to the small flat he rented from Mrs. Beamish and changed out of his lurking-in-the-shadows clothing. Then, as evening approached, he wandered down to The Angry Bear. Old Marcus treated him well, partly because the fellow regularly employed Jax in his legitimate day-job, and partly because of Jax's relationship with Maelleen.

When Jax stepped into the common room of The Angry Bear he saw no sign of her. Marcus stood behind the bar pouring a cup of ale for a patron Jax didn't recognize, the top of the old fellow's bald head glinting in the light of a lamp hanging from the rafters. A small fire burned in a large hearth—in early summer a meager blaze was more than enough to remove the chill from the room. There were only a half-dozen customers seated at tables located on the floor between the door and the bar, but Jax knew the place would fill up as the evening progressed.

Marcus spotted Jax and nodded.

Jax crossed the room and stepped up to the bar.

"Jaxon, me boy," Marcus said. "What'll you have?"

The man for whom Marcus had just poured the ale tossed a coin on the bar, lifted his cup, and walked away. Jax nodded toward him and said, "A cup of that ale."

Marcus retrieved the man's coin and frowned. "Thought you preferred wine?"

Jax shrugged. "I do, but my purse is a bit thin right now, and I need to save enough for dinner."

Marcus retrieved a cup, and as he poured the ale he said, "We got some good boar tonight, in nice, thick, brown gravy, with onions, carrots and boiled potatoes."

"That sounds good," Jax said. "I'll have a small plate."

Marcus spun about and stepped into the kitchen, then returned a minute later carrying a clay plate of food that made Jax's stomach growl. Marcus handed the plate to him and said, "I'll put it on your tab."

Jax carried his cup and plate to a small table in the corner and sat down. The only thing he'd eaten all day was a single slice of bread in the morning, and the boar, gravy and vegetables tasted quite good. He had just finished eating and was sipping the last of his ale when the door to the kitchen swung open, and tall, curvaceous Maelleen stepped into the room. In the nine years Jax had known her, her bust line had expanded, her curves had grown curvier, and the eyes of every man in the place followed her as she crossed the floor, her hips swaying invitingly.

She stopped at Jax's table, leaned forward and placed her hands flat on the tabletop next to his plate, purposefully allowing the top of her blouse to billow outward, giving him an unobstructed view of her ample bosom. At the look on his face Maelleen grinned and spoke, her voice low and sultry. "Like what you see?"

Jax smiled. "I always like what I see when I'm looking at you."

"I know," she said, slowly wetting her lips with her tongue. "That's one of the things I like about you."

"Are you working tonight?" he asked.

Her grin widened. "Not on my back, if that's what you mean. What did you have in mind?"

After nine years of Jax's tutelage, Maelleen could pass as a fine lady of good repute. That allowed her to be more selective regarding her clientele, and she only *worked on her back* once or twice a week.

He stared openly at the view she offered. "What I had in mind shouldn't be voiced in polite company."

She gave him a predatory smile. "Well it's just you and me, so there's no polite company present, is there?"

She leaned a little farther forward, exposing even more flesh. "But I do have to work tables for an hour or so. After that I'm free—for whatever you have in mind."

Openly glaring at her, he said, "I'm not sure I can wait an hour."

Again, she ran her tongue across her lips. "Well you'll just have to, especially since, after an hour of watching me work tables, you'll be ready for what you're going to have to do to me later."

He grinned. "I guess you're going to end up on your back anyway."

She pouted. "Maybe not. Maybe I'll ride you, and you'll end up on your back."

"I've been there before," he said, "but it'll still be my pleasure."

She took her hands off the table and stood up. "Of course . . . and mine, as well."

He just smiled, and ordered another cup of ale to bide his time. But he couldn't put that carriage out of his mind, and the young boy who'd disappeared into its dark interior.

10

The Thief

SEATED IN THE Angry Bear, Jax thought back to that beautiful woman all those years ago, recalling her striking dark-blue eyes. He decided the coach he'd seen the young boy step into that afternoon couldn't be the same one. Nevertheless, it wouldn't hurt to continue checking the river.

A young minstrel showed up, set up in a corner, played tunes on a mandolin, sang a few songs and told a few tales. But the main attraction at The Angry Bear was always Maelleen. The common room slowly filled up and she worked the crowd mercilessly, brushing her hip against one man as she walked past his table, leaning over in front of another a little more than necessary so he could see down her blouse. As the night progressed, the eyes of every man there followed Maelleen covetously, and she fueled their imaginations with ruthless intent.

None of these people knew of Jax's illicit nocturnal activities—his night job, as he thought of it. To them, he was merely the impoverished, youngest son of a minor nobleman whose father had had a weakness for drink, and done a poor job of managing the family's limited finances. Jax didn't really resent Felix and Julia for keeping what little their father had left them. He made a little money here and there keeping accounts for people like Marcus, and writing the occasional letter for those too illiterate to do so themselves. It wasn't enough to sustain him—hence, the nighttime work that might get him thrown into prison—but it provided a nice cover for what he did make from those special jobs, and it supplemented his night work.

Maelleen controlled the crowd in the common room like a maestro leading an orchestra. When the hour was up, she walked to the kitchen door and opened it. She held it for a moment, looked back at Jax, and gave him an inviting smile. Then she stepped through the door and closed it. Jax could almost hear the hush of disappointment from all the men in the room.

Jax finished the last of his ale, stood, and was about to cross the room when the front door of the pub opened and a man wearing simple, unadorned clothing walked in. Jax's instinct shouted at him that it was another Knight of the Witchguard, though it was not the same man he'd encountered earlier that afternoon. Standing near the hearth at the far end of the room, Jax stepped closer to the wall so his face fell into deeper shadow. The Witch Knight scanned the room and his gaze passed over Jax without any reaction. Then he edged his way through the crowd to the bar.

Jax crossed the room quickly, walking behind the Witch Knight as the fellow approached Marcus, and keeping his face turned away from the man. When he followed Maelleen through the door into the kitchen, old Marcus gave him a quick nod.

Jax encountered Bethy working the stoves, and she smiled at him as he crossed the kitchen to the back stairs. At the top of the stairs the door to Maelleen's room stood open. He found her standing in front of a polished brass mirror, running a brush through her hair. Trying not to think of the Witch Knight in the common room below, Jax walked up behind her and put his arms around her waist. The brush in her hand stilled and she leaned her head to one side. He ran a line of kisses down her neck and a breathless grumble escaped her throat. And with Maelleen in his arms, he had no trouble forgetting the Witch Knight.

She put the brush down, turned around in his arms and looked in his eyes. She stood taller than most women, but still had to look up to meet his eyes because he stood a little taller than most men. She pressed her lips against his, and their tongues fought a pleasant little war that she always won, though sometimes she allowed him a small victory of his own. As their lips parted, he tugged at the straps on the back of her blouse and the knots that secured it loosened easily.

"You're good for me," she said. "I don't mean I love you or anything like that, but you make me feel good. If you weren't so poor I'd give up my search for a rich husband and make you marry me. I'd even settle for just *well-to-do*, instead of wealthy."

He regretted that he had to admit, "My prospects aren't very solid right now."

He ran his lips lightly down her neck. She sucked in a quick breath and said, "I guess we'll just have to take it one . . . very solid . . . development at a time."

••••

Lying next to Maelleen as she slept soundly, Jax spent a restless night wondering why a Knight of the Witchguard would follow him through the busy streets of Val d'Ossa, and why another would show up at The Angry Bear that evening. He'd been ready to ignore his encounter earlier that afternoon as simple happenstance, but two such events in the same day couldn't be coincidental. On the other hand, if the knights wanted him, they could simply scoop him up and take him to the Witch Palace, then do whatever they wanted with him.

The Witch ruled all of Val d'Ossa, and maintained her supremacy over the noble houses using strange and incomprehensible magical powers—at least, that's what everyone believed. It was said she owned the souls of the Witchguard, and that they would die happily at her feet if she commanded them to do so. Rumors circulated constantly of sorcerous incantations and demon manifestations at the Witch Palace.

But Jax had never met anyone who'd actually witnessed such events, and he suspected the stories were heavily embellished in the telling.

Jax eventually slept, and Maelleen woke him in the morning. They shared a small breakfast of toasted bread and apple slices, and as they ate they talked. "The sad part is," she said, "I know I'll eventually find my wealthy husband."

Maelleen could now read, write and do simple math. She could sit at table in the most elegant of settings among the wealthiest of nobles, and not a person there would know she was a harlot from the slums. Jax knew nothing about applying a woman's makeup, so he hadn't taught her anything there, but he told her when she *looked* like a prostitute, and she had learned by imitating the makeup she saw on fine ladies. She now frequented some of the nicer establishments where her favors commanded a much higher price, and focused on a more limited and exclusive clientele.

They were sitting on her bed with their legs crossed and the small plate of food between them. She wore a loose robe, and with the front of it open she was all but naked. She held her hands out to the sides, palms up, and said, "Surely, rich, old men can't resist me. I mean, look at me."

He leered at her. "I am looking at you."

She grinned and said, "Even your eyeballs have an erection."

"Well, that's your fault, isn't it?"

"Yes," she said proudly, "I guess it is. But as I was saying, I probably will find that wealthy husband, and he'll be a rich old fart, with gas, bad teeth, and even worse breath. He'll make me wealthy, and I'll make him happy. But I doubt he'll keep me happy between the sheets. So you'll have to continue at that task even after I've married him."

Jax leaned forward and kissed her shoulder. "A most challenging responsibility, but one I'll gladly perform."

She winked at him. "You've spoiled me, you know."

They finished breakfast, he dressed, gave her a parting kiss—a very passionate kiss—and with the loose robe half open he couldn't resist touching her, just to remind him of the feel of her soft skin. One touch led to another, which led to another kiss and he didn't make it to the door, at least not for another hour. But when they finished, and he dressed again, and he turned to leave again, she said, "By the way, if you ever do get rich, please let me know right away. I'll get rid of the old gas bag and marry you."

Jax grinned, nodded and headed downstairs. In case there were Witch Knights prowling about and keeping an eye on Marcus's tavern, Jax left through the back door that opened onto an alley. He returned to his flat, and once there he stripped down, shaved, washed his hair, then combed it carefully into place. He kept it cut in the shorter style popular among young noblemen, which just hid the tops of his ears. He polished his best boots to a bright shine, stepped into a pair of fitted breeches, then pulled on the knee-high boots and tucked the legs of his pants into them. He donned a good linen blouse, then over that his best waistcoat, and over that his best tailcoat, though his impoverished *best* wasn't great by most standards. He strapped on a light rapier, which was purely for show, then hid a dagger up his sleeve. If he must defend himself, the dagger would be of much more use than the rapier. That had been one of the harshest lessons he'd learned on the streets. In close quarters gentlemen fought with rapiers, but survivors fought with a dagger, knife or short blade.

The noble estates were all located within the District of Noble Houses, with the Witch Palace at its center. He needed to fit in, and proper attire was a necessary prerequisite. Any nobleman who looked closely at his clothing might recognize that it was cheaply made, but he wasn't planning to get close to any of them. And if anyone did notice, they'd probably assume he was the son of some minor nobleman, with nothing approaching the wealth of the High Noble Houses, which actually had an element of truth to it.

He set out for the address Rondo's client had given him, but first made a detour to the river. Walking along the river bank proved to be a bit out of his way, but he had to be certain. He saw no commotion there, no constables discussing an unpleasant find in the shallows, no crowd of bystanders eagerly looking on.

It took a good hour to walk across the city, and by the time Jax got there his boots were covered with a fine sheen of dust. He passed a constable and the fellow didn't give him a second look, which meant his appearance passed muster. He knew the area rather well, mainly because he'd broken into, and stolen from, a number of the residences there. But that had all been freelance work: get in and get out quickly, and on the way steal a few bits and pieces worth something, though never anything so valuable it might gain him a reputation and force the constabulary to get serious about hunting him down. He'd never before hired out, and considered it now only because he didn't want to risk the ire of someone who might be quite powerful.

His target was near the center of the district, not far from the Witch Palace and the Hall of Nobles. He turned down the street that contained the address the client had given him, and slowed his walk to a casual stroll. He couldn't just stop and loiter about to examine the place in detail, gawking through the front gate like some country bumpkin. He'd have to keep walking, but by maintaining a slow pace he'd have enough time to get an initial feel for the place, then return that night to study the layout of the residence much more carefully.

The street was a broad, cobblestoned avenue with plenty of space for two carriages to pass going in opposite directions, and flagstone sidewalks on either side, nothing like the narrow lanes in the slum where he lived. The residences were all hidden behind walls about the height of a tall man, and from the spacing of the gates that opened into each, they occupied an enormous amount of frontage on the street.

He found the address on the south side of the street facing north, with a wrought-iron gate at its main entrance. It was one of the larger noble houses, a two-story stone structure set back from the street by a large yard about thirty paces deep, with balconies on the second floor. He didn't see any guards stationed about the premises, but that would probably change with the coming of night.

He noted that a small day park had been constructed on the north side of the street directly across from the residence in question. It wasn't large, but it contained a couple of benches that would be shaded from the sun by the branches of some broad elm trees. That his target was situated directly across from the park probably meant it was the most expensive property on the street. And it bothered him that he saw no emblem or crest to identify the owners.

Every bit of information he gathered about this job only raised more questions, and his unease grew. He was beginning to think he wanted nothing to do with this client, no matter how good the money might be. But to make that decision he needed to return that night and complete a more thorough inspection of the grounds.

Jax reached the end of the mansion-filled street and headed toward his apartment. As he walked away from the center of the district, the houses and properties grew smaller and less opulent. Near the edge of the district, while walking past the least powerful of the noble houses, he heard a rumble in the distance. As the noise grew he recognized the pounding of horse's hooves and the clatter of a carriage's wheels on the cobblestones. He stepped into the shade of a narrow alley and waited in the shadows. There were a number of other pedestrians nearby, and they too scurried out of the way, like prey sensing a large predator close at hand.

As the thunder of the horse's hooves grew to an ear-splitting roar, a troop of about twenty mounted Witchguards came into view escorting an enclosed carriage that bobbed and swayed as it hit the ruts in the street. The knights all wore uniforms of red and black cloth with silver threaded embellishments, the sun glinting off brightly polished insignia. They had swords strapped to their sides, with pistols and muskets holstered on their saddles, and several carried lances with their points raised to the sky.

From the shadows in the alley Jax watched them pass by, the knights' eyes locked straight ahead, their backs rigid. An emblem decorated the side of the carriage: a closed fist crushing a bolt of lightning, the symbol of the Witch's rule. He saw nothing through the windows on the carriage doors because the dark interior hid its mysterious and never-seen passenger. He wondered if she could use her sorcerous powers to sense him standing there, and if she could strike out from within the carriage and render him dead with nothing more than a whim. Or perhaps she would cripple him, or blind him, leaving him at the mercy of the more predatory denizens of the streets.

Until the previous day, he'd never before seen one of the Witch Knights in simple garb; they'd always worn at least the uniform he'd just observed, and sometimes heavier armor. *Why now?* he wondered. *And why me?*

He waited until the thunder of the hooves dwindled into the distance before stepping out into the street, and saw that the other pedestrians had done the same. An hour later, and several blocks short of his flat, his instinct drew his attention to another pedestrian. The fellow was neither of the men he'd seen the previous day, but one very much like them. He wore ordinary and plain clothing, though not ragged or dirty, and it reminded Jax of the others. And again, Jax's instinct told him the man should be wearing the raiment of a Knight of the Witchguard.

This fellow only followed Jax for a few blocks, then Jax lost him and went his own way. Still, he took a circuitous route back to his flat.

11

High House Carkoska

THAT EVENING JAX pulled on dark breeches and dull, black boots that wouldn't reflect the glare of a lamp. He put on a dark blouse, and over that he draped the black, hooded cloak he'd worn to the meeting with Rondo and his client. Then he retrieved his special kit, the canvas valise that had been one of his few possessions the day Julia and Felix had thrown him out onto the streets. It contained the tools he needed, all carefully padded with cloth so they wouldn't clink together and give him away at an inopportune moment. He threw the valise's strap over his shoulder and started across the city for the mansion.

Once in the District of Noble Houses, he moved much more cautiously. He never walked openly, but dashed furtively from one shadow to the next. He halted in each, looked up and down the street for movement, and listened for any sound, which allowed his instinct the time it needed to speak to him.

The streets were well lit by gas lamps and carefully patrolled. He wasn't surprised when his instinct told him to freeze in place. Pressed against a wall just within an alley, he heard the creak of leather, and the clump of boots on the cobblestones.

"Me wife's madder'n hell at me," a gruff voice said.

Two constables approached, walking casually up the street. Armed with short swords and cudgels, they could be dangerous. At least they weren't carrying muskets or pistols.

"She catch you out whoring again?" the gruff one's companion asked.

They weren't expecting anything, so they didn't poke into every dim patch of darkness. And since nothing ever really happened in that district, other than the occasional drunken nobleman, their boredom lulled them into a sense of complacency. They walked past Jax's shadow, swinging their cudgels casually, not looking either right or left. After they walked out of sight, and Jax's instinct told him he had nothing to fear, he moved on. He never did learn if the guard's whoring had caused his wife's ire.

There were also plenty of establishments that catered to men with too much money in their purses. But only high-end establishments were allowed in that district, the kind where Maelleen now plied her trade in search of a rich husband. From the shadow of the doorway of a closed shop, Jax watched one group of young men pass, comparing notes on the prostitutes they had just enjoyed.

"I'm in love," one of them said.

Another asked, "How can you fall in love with a whore?"

The fellow clearly didn't know Maelleen, for if he did, he would never have asked such a question. A little later, from a dark alley Jax watched a group of older men walk by grumbling about their poor luck at the gambling tables that evening.

When Jax reached his target, he slipped into the day park across the street from the mansion, selected one of the broad elm trees closest to the street, stopped behind it and didn't move for several minutes while he listened. Warm, still nights that at first seemed silent, were actually filled with all sorts of informative sounds. Above him the leaves of the tree rustled softly in a light breeze then calmed. He heard the creak of leather, then someone cleared his throat. He couldn't make out the words, but he heard two men across the street speaking in soft tones. Just standing there in the dark and listening was almost enough to understand completely the schedule the guards followed as they made their rounds on the grounds of the nearby estates.

He couldn't reach the lowest limb on the tree, so he retrieved a rope from his kit, tied one end around the canvas bag's strap, then tossed the free end of the rope over the lowest limb above him with enough slack that it dangled within easy reach. He secured the end to the trunk of the tree with a knot. Careful not to grunt with effort or make any sound, he climbed up and onto the limb, then used the rope to hoist his kit up. He tied it to the limb, retrieved a small telescope from it, then climbed up to the next limb. He now had a nice view over the wall and into the yard of the target house, obscured only by a few branches and leaves.

The telescope hadn't cost much, but had proven invaluable time and again. He put the glass to his eye and surveyed the property for more than two hours, watching and listening until he knew the rhythm of the night guards' rounds.

It bothered Jax that the occupants of the mansion didn't display a crest or provide any other evidence of their family name. The lesser noble houses were quick to identify themselves as a matter of prestige. The guards that patrolled the grounds all wore some sort of emblem on the breast of their tunics, but it was small, and the combination of distance and dim lighting thwarted Jax's attempts to make it out clearly. Then one guard stepped directly beneath a lantern at the front gate. Jax got a brief glimpse of the emblem on his tunic through his telescope, and he came away with the impression of a hand extended upward, palm open, with something wrapped around its wrist. He'd seen something like that before, but couldn't place it, and he resolved not to take this job until he did.

When he was satisfied he'd learned all he could, he climbed down to the lowest limb and repacked the telescope in his kit. He lowered the valise back to the ground, then climbed down the rope to join it. He coiled the rope and returned it to the kit.

He needed to do a little research regarding the crests of the noble houses. He didn't like what he'd seen, and if his suspicions proved correct, he'd quote Rondo a price so extreme, the client would turn it down and go to someone else. Rondo and the client wouldn't be happy, but more importantly, Jax wouldn't find his neck stretched at the end of a rope.

••••

Jax still had several hours before dawn, so he took a detour before returning to his flat. He kept to the shadows and moved slowly, and half an hour later stopped at the end of a street of mid-level nobles. Manicured shrubs lined the avenue on both sides and none of the properties were hidden behind walls.

The shrubs didn't provide much cover so he had to trust his instinct. When it told him to go, he bent into a crouch, stayed close to the bushes and moved quickly. Midway down the street he turned onto a property under construction and crouched behind a pile of stone blocks. The place had been vacant for several years, then recently purchased. The new owners were having it extensively renovated, and they had yet to move in. The front entrance was just a gaping hole with no doors, so Jax stepped into the place without the need to pick a lock or break in.

Moving carefully, he climbed the stairway to the second floor and made his way to one of the rooms at the front of the house. Hidden in the darkness, he looked out a window at the house across the street. He'd been watching the place for several weeks now. It was one of a number of potential targets he regularly checked on, and he instantly realized that something had changed.

The house's owner had been successful in the merchant trade, which allowed him to purchase an insignificant title and a nice property in the District of Noble Houses. If his wealth continued to grow he might climb higher in the ranks of the nobility, but for now he and his neighbors were forced to pool their resources and could only afford a single night guard to patrol three properties. The guard was an old pensioner who made his rounds like clockwork in a dangerously predictable pattern.

Jax didn't have to watch the house long to realize what had changed that night. The windows of a room on the ground floor and one on the second were illuminated by light from within. But on his previous visits the house had started out each evening with several rooms well lit, and as the night progressed the lamps were extinguished one by one until the house became completely dark. Once, one lamp had remained lit until close to midnight, but never had light shown from any of the windows in the wee hours of the morning.

It was an old ploy: when the entire family left the house empty, the night guard lit a few lamps and kept them burning through the night to make the house appear occupied. They thought it discouraged thieves, when, in fact, it did just the opposite, and would prove to be useful for Jax.

Jax watched the night guard make the rounds of the merchant's property, then move on to one of his neighbor's houses. He hefted his valise and moved quickly, climbing down the stairs and out the front entrance, where once again he crouched behind the pile of stone blocks. When his instinct told him it was safe to cross the street, he sprinted all the way to the target house and around the side to a servant's entrance he'd spied earlier. In the dark he had to work by feel, but he'd used the same pick set for years, knew his tools well, and had no trouble picking the lock. He stepped inside and closed the door.

It was possible he'd erred in his analysis of the situation and the house was occupied. The owner might have fallen asleep in a chair near one of the lit lamps, and had not extinguished it before retiring for the night. Jax left his valise on the floor near the servant's entrance so he could easily grab it if he needed to make a quick escape. Then he moved carefully and checked each room in the house, confirming that he had the place to himself. The old pensioner never entered the house, but if one of the lamps began to dim he might do so to replenish its oil. Jax checked both lamps to be sure he had more than enough time.

He started with the lady's boudoir, which was attached to the master bedroom on the second floor. In a dresser drawer that contained a woman's undergarments he found a little, wooden chest hidden near the back. The chest didn't have a lock, and he was pleased to learn that the merchant was wealthy enough that his lady didn't take all her jewelry with her when they left on an excursion.

He carried the chest to the room at the front of the house where the guard had placed one of the lit lamps, staying low so he didn't cast any shadows visible from the grounds below. The lamp had been placed on a small table, and sitting on the floor beneath it he carefully examined the contents of the jewelry box. He thought it ironic how much the lamp helped him steal from them, because without it he'd have had to work by touch in the dark.

The chest contained some jewelry with stones that he thought might be cheap, colored glass, but there were several that appeared to be valuable. He took a small, gold ring with a red ruby and two small diamond studs, plus a little broach with a bright green emerald at its center. He stayed away from the large pieces because the lady of the house would instantly notice them missing. There were also six gold sovereigns. He took only two.

The lady might not notice that anything was missing for some time. And if she did, she would assume that a thief would take everything. She would probably think she'd miscounted the coins and misplaced the jewelry, and the few bits he stole would not impoverish them. He could keep that promise he had made to himself years ago, and never harm those of limited means like him. If the worth of the jewelry matched his estimate, he could live for half a year on what he'd pocketed that night.

Jax returned the jewelry box to the back of the drawer, then sat in the dark of an unlit room on the second floor at the front of the house. He watched the night guard make his rounds again and waited until the fellow moved on to the adjacent property. Then he climbed down the stairs, retrieved his valise, and slipped out the servants' entrance. He carefully relocked the door before disappearing into the night.

••••

Jax thought again of the young boy he'd seen step into the unmarked carriage, and he recalled the nights he'd spent with that beautiful woman. Had she not betrayed him in the end, he'd have only fond memories of desire and pleasure.

That morning he put on his young-nobleman's disguise. He detoured again to the river, and found no commotion or excitement, so he continued on and walked across the city to the Hall of Nobles. He glanced briefly at the spires of the Witch Palace on the east side of Crier's Square, and prayed that he never came to the attention of that evil old woman.

He could have done without the disguise because a number of residents from the slums were always gathered at the posting boards. Jax had no interest in the notices, but at the top of each, the name and crest of the House that sponsored it were displayed for all to see. He looked at the postings carefully without actually reading them, and on the fifth he saw what he was looking for: a crest containing a hand extended upward with the palm facing forward, a snake intertwined between the fingers, both ends of its body wrapped around the wrist, its fangs buried in the center of the hand's palm. Next to it was written the name Carkoska.

Jax's heart went cold. He turned and hurried away from the Hall of Nobles.

••••

"One thousand gold sovereigns," Rondo shouted. "You're insane. They'll never pay that. And if I quote them a price like that, it'll only anger them."

Jax had arranged to meet Rondo, and he wasn't surprised at the fat little fence's reaction to his quoted price. He didn't raise his voice in return when he said, "Do you even know who they're targeting?"

"A noble house," Rondo shouted. "It won't be the first one you've broken into, and I'd wager it won't be the last."

Jax continued to speak calmly. "It will be if I break into this one. It's not just any noble house—"

Rondo interrupted him. "I don't care."

"—it's High House Carkoska."

"I said I don't care. I—" Rondo abruptly froze with his mouth open. He paled visibly, and his next words came out in a whisper. "You said . . . Carkoska?"

"Yes, I said Carkoska."

"Are you sure?"

"You know how careful I am."

Beads of sweat formed on the fence's upper lip as he dropped into a chair and fanned his face. "By the gods! Carkoska, highest of the High Noble Houses and second only to the Witch herself."

"Exactly," Jax said. "And I want nothing to do with this."

Rondo frowned. "Are you sure? It's good money, and I could ask for even more than they're offering—not a thousand gold sovereigns, but certainly more than their original price."

Jax shook his head. "I won't even consider it, and don't ask again."

Rondo didn't try to hide his disappointment. "I'll have to tell them we know who it is, and that frightens us off. It'll be better to tell them we don't want anything to do with it, than to quote them an outrageous price."

"I'll have to trust your judgment on that." The one thing Jax had going in his favor was that the client had to work through Rondo, and didn't know how to contact Jax directly. And the only information Rondo had on Jax was all fictitious.

Jax walked to the door, opened it, and stepped out into the alley. He'd keep an eye on Rondo from a distance, and if the little man suddenly disappeared, either on his own initiative, or otherwise, Jax would do the same.

12

Loose Ends

JAX TOUCHED THE scar on his arm and recalled that night so long ago when he'd escaped from Lakorsa and the coachman Carlos. The jewelry and coins—and his instinct—had kept him alive through that winter. Had he had more experience, he could have gotten far more for the jewels than he did, but back then he didn't know how to properly value such trinkets. Another lesson learned on the streets of Val d'Ossa.

Each morning he walked near the river, and one day he came across a little commotion there. The city constables had fished the body of a young boy out of the shallows beneath a bridge. Jax joined the crowd of onlookers, and while the corpse was bloated and had been chewed on by something in the water, he had no difficulty recognizing the young boy who'd stepped into the unmarked carriage on the busy street corner several days ago.

The guards bundled up the body and carried it away. The boy came from the slums, and any number of bodies washed up on the river's banks every year, so they were unlikely to investigate further.

A week after Jax turned down the Carkoska job, nothing unusual had happened. During that time Jax kept an eye on Rondo, and the fat little man didn't wash up dead on the banks of the river, or disappear without a trace. Rondo liked to drink at The Thirsty Miller, a sleazy place that offered cheap prices for watery ale, and even cheaper prostitutes. It was located in a section of the city where the streets were haphazardly lit, so late one evening Jax stepped into the darkness of an alley across the street from the pub.

Jax had never gone to the place, and as he waited and looked on, the front door of the establishment swung open and a large man stepped out with a young girl on his arm. He escorted her to an alley next to the pub and they disappeared in its shadows. A short time later they both emerged, he retying the laces of his breeches, and she straightening the folds of her skirt.

For the next few hours Jax watched a continuous stream of prostitutes and customers enter and leave the place, many making use of that same alley, some walking away to more private accommodations. A quickie in the alley probably cost less than taking a girl up to a room, especially since the girl could finish more quickly and move on to the next customer.

Near midnight Rondo emerged, a middle-aged prostitute on his arm, and as they disappeared into the alley across the way, Jax glanced up and down the street. It was empty, so he moved quickly, wrapped his dark cloak tightly about him and crossed to the other side. Near the mouth of the alley he stepped into the shadow in the recess of a doorway.

"Ten coppers," he heard Rondo say. "You ain't worth ten. I'll give you five."

The prostitute spoke with a hoarse, throaty voice. "All you get for five is me hand."

They haggled back and forth for a few minutes and settled on eight coppers. Then there came a brief period of grunting—it sounded as if both of them enjoyed themselves to some degree, or maybe the woman just faked it—probably better for business if she did. It didn't take long for Rondo to get his money's worth, then the prostitute emerged, took a second to straighten her skirt, and headed back to The Thirsty Miller. As she walked away Rondo stepped out of the shadow of the alley, retying the laces of his pants. Jax waited until the woman reentered the pub, with Rondo still working on his laces.

"Rondo," he said.

Rondo started, gasped, and turned to face Jax.

Jax stepped out of the shadow in the doorway and tossed the hood of his cloak back.

Rondo's shoulders relaxed and he said, "Ah, it's just you, Felix."

Jax still took a certain amount of pleasure in using his older, half-brother's name as the nom de guerre for his thief persona. After all, Felix and Julia were the reason he had resorted to such a nefarious means of survival.

"Scare a man half to death," Rondo said. "What are you doing lurking around here?"

"Just wanted a quick word with you," Jax said. "How'd the client take the news?"

"You mean that we didn't want to do his job?" Rondo shrugged. "He shrugged it off, said he'd go elsewhere. It's a shame. Could have been good money. You sure you won't change your mind?"

Jax shook his head. "The money's no good if you're not alive to spend it."

Rondo grimaced. "Always are the cautious one, aren't you. Let me know when you got something worthwhile to sell."

The fat little fence turned and headed back into The Thirsty Miller.

••••

Jax laid low for a few more days. Rondo remained among the living, so he relaxed a little.

The proceeds from the job the other night would tide him over for a while, but he'd learned to never take the coins in his purse for granted, so he wandered down to the open market in the center of the district. The density of the crowds there made it possible to acquire a few coins with a little pickpocket work. He did well and was happy with the morning's take. Thinking he might go to The Angry Bear that evening and look up Maelleen, he glanced over his shoulder and spotted a Knight of the Witchguard easing his way carefully through the crowds in the dusty market. Jax would have been happy if the fellow had been in uniform, but once again he'd encountered a Witch Knight dressed inconspicuously.

"Buy or move on."

Jax turned toward the sound of the voice: a woman standing by a portable stall displaying fresh fish from the morning's catch. Greasy tendrils of hair hung lankly past her shoulders in twisted and knotted clumps, and her face and arms were smeared with dirt and mud. She probably smelled as bad as she looked, though, thankfully, he wasn't close enough to confirm his suspicion.

She grinned at him, displaying a mouth full of brown teeth, with several gaps where she'd lost a few. "If yer not buying, then yer gettin' in the way of me customers who are."

Jax nodded politely. "My apologies, madam."

She grinned, again displaying the ugly teeth. "Ain't you full of fancy talk?"

He turned, choosing a direction away from the knight, and walked casually. He hadn't spotted one of them since turning down the job to burgle High House Carkoska, and for just a moment he wondered if the two were connected.

If he broke into a run, or repeatedly glanced nervously over his shoulder, he might alert the fellow to the fact that he had seen through his disguise. He paused briefly and turned to look at the wares on display in a fruit vendor's stall, an excuse to turn far enough to glance back without being obvious. He didn't recognize the fellow, so he wasn't one of the others he'd spotted before. Perhaps the man wasn't following him and was just there through pure coincidence. As Jax turned and walked up the street, he recalled that he didn't believe in coincidences. Another lesson he'd learned on the streets.

At an intersecting street he turned right, glanced over his shoulder and saw the fellow behind him. At the next intersection he turned left, glanced again, and the knight had considerably closed the gap between them. If the man intended to simply follow Jax, he would have maintained a constant distance behind him, just as they'd all done before. It was time to lose his pursuer, so at the next intersection he turned right, and was careful to walk casually as long as he was within sight of the knight. But he had resolved that as soon as the corner of the building blocked the knight's view of him, he would break into a sprint. He was about to do so when he came face-to-face with another inconspicuously dressed Witch Knight. They both halted, the knight looked him up and down, and the fellow's lips spread into a broad, satisfied grin.

"Got you now," the knight said. "Don't we?" Jax recognized him. He was the first knight Jax had spotted several days before.

Jax looked left, saw another knight standing there blocking that avenue of escape. The fellow grinned and shook his head.

Jax looked right, and a third knight stood there grinning.

Someone grabbed Jax's arms from behind, and in short order four Knights of the Witchguard had him pinned face-on against a stone wall. They removed the dagger and sheath from his sleeve, and the one from his boot. They didn't tie his hands, but held him pinned there as one of them raised a small horn to his lips and blew on it. It made a sharp, whistling sound, nothing like a horn, more like the cry of a hunting hawk.

They waited in silence for a few seconds, then Jax heard the thunder of hooves, and the rattle of carriage wheels on the cobblestones of the street. His four assailants turned him around as everyone else in the market scattered right and left. And exactly as had happened that day when leaving the District of Noble Houses, a troop of mounted Witchguard rode up the street at a gallop, escorting that same enclosed carriage, lances aimed toward the sky, muskets and pistols glinting in the cavalry holsters attached to their saddles. The emblem on the side of the coach mesmerized Jax, the closed fist crushing a bolt of lightning. The mounted Witchguard slowed, the carriage slowed with them, then stopped directly in front of Jax about two paces from him. The windows of the carriage were black openings beyond which he could discern nothing. His knees felt as if they might give out, and he stood there trembling.

One of the four knights who had trapped him stepped forward, reached up to the latch on the carriage's door and turned it. The door's hinges squealed softly as he opened it. With two of the knights gripping Jax's elbows tightly, they marched him toward the black chasm of the open doorway, but they stopped just short of it.

Would the Witch strike out now with her sorcerous powers, perhaps send his soul to some hell where he'd spend eternity suffering the flames of infernal damnation? Or maybe she'd turn him into a toad, or some other base animal.

One of the knights said, "Step up inside, take a seat to the right, and behave yourself. You don't want to make her angry."

They released Jax, though the four knights remained in a tight semicircle around him, leaving him no choice. With his heart hammering in his chest, he reached up, gripped the edges of the doorway and climbed up into the dark abyss of the carriage's interior. Having just stepped out of bright sunlight, he could see nothing within, so by touch he found the padded seat on his right and sat down. He waited silently, not sure what to expect, ready for a bolt of magical lightning to rip his still-beating heart from his chest.

A female voice crackling with age spoke from the darkness. "Well now, young man. We finally meet. What am I going to do with you?"

••••

Jax sat in the darkness frozen with fear. As the coachman cracked his whip and the carriage lurched forward, the old voice said, "I asked you a question, young man, so answer me, and be quick about it."

Jax said something to the effect of, "Ummm . . . Uhhh . . . Ummm . . ."

A pleasant young voice said, "Mother, I think we've frightened the poor fellow."

The old voice snapped, "Well he should be frightened. I'm rather upset with him right now, so I just might turn him into a toad or something."

"Yes," the young voice said. "There is that. But you really should do a better job of controlling that temper of yours."

"I'm an old woman, dear, so I get to have a frightful temper if I want to."

"Oh, don't be an evil, old witch."

"But I am an evil, old witch. And don't forget, an *all-powerful*, evil, old witch."

"Why do you always have to remind me of the all-powerful thing?"

"Because you're impertinent, dear."

"I'm sorry, mother. I'll try to do better. But it does get tiresome, and the poor fellow is trembling like a frightened rabbit."

The old voice demanded of Jax, "You're not going to piss your pants and foul my lovely coach, are you?"

"Oh," the young voice said. "I certainly hope he has better control than that."

As the coach swayed and rocked down the street, Jax's eyes slowly adjusted to its darkened interior. The windows were covered with some sort of diaphanous material that reduced the brightness of the sun's glare considerably, but still allowed some light to pass. He could just make out two figures seated opposite him, though as yet he couldn't discern much more than their silhouettes. To Jax's left, where the younger voice had come from, a slender woman sat looking his way. She appeared to be wearing a stylish bonnet, with locks of dark hair peeking out from beneath it. Next to her, on the right, sat a woman in a dress with heavy skirts, her head and features hidden in the folds of a hooded cloak.

"Now, young man," the old woman said. "What do you have to say for yourself?"

Jax tried to think quickly, but all he could do was imagine the many horrible fates he would suffer at the hands of the Witch of Val d'Ossa. "I . . . um . . ."

"Oh come now," the she said. "You're an educated young man. Your father was a drunken fool, but you've obviously not inherited his failings. Surely you can be more articulate than that."

She was right, but Jax wasn't sure if he was up to the task. He tried to suppress his fear and steady his nerves. "No . . . I'm not at all like my father."

"Are you proud of that? Do you hate him, that he would squander the family's fortune and leave you penniless?"

Jax would have been less off-balance if the Witch of Val d'Ossa had been a screaming, maniacal terror with flames in her eyes, finger-long fangs protruding from her mouth, venom dripping from the fangs, and ram's horns sprouting from her head.

He waited for his instinct to aid him, but this calm, reasoned interrogation had completely shut it down. "I am grateful I don't suffer from his weakness for drink. But I don't hate him, and I did love him. He was good to me, though I don't know if he was generally a good man or a bad man."

"Probably neither," the younger voice said. "It's likely he was just a weak man."

The rickety old voice said, "You still haven't answered my question. What do you have to say for yourself?"

She clearly knew about his family and his upbringing, and probably knew that Julia and Felix had thrown him out onto the streets at the age of sixteen. She might even know that he'd used his education to eke out a meager living among the illiterate. Hopefully, she didn't know that he augmented his income with profits from stolen goods. He said, "I . . . haven't . . . done anything wrong . . . have I?"

His eyes had adjusted enough to see the old woman cock her head to one side. "You haven't done anything wrong? I suppose you think there's nothing wrong with breaking into High House Carkoska and stealing their property."

"Mother," the young voice said. "He didn't break into High House Carkoska. He turned the commission down, which I think was rather admirable of him."

"Admirable!" the old woman said. "There was nothing admirable about it. He turned it down because it frightened him. He turned it down to save his own neck. If it hadn't been one of the High Noble Houses, he would have accepted the offer without another thought."

Jax wanted the young voice to continue arguing in his favor, but instead she said, "Yes, I suppose you're right about that. He isn't really the admirable sort, is he?"

"But," Jax said, "I—"

The old woman interrupted him. "He considered breaking into High House Carkoska, considered it seriously, put on that disguise and walked down that street in broad daylight. That was clearly a reconnaissance foray. And he's burgled any number of the lesser noble houses."

She hesitated and cocked her head to one side, obviously considering him. She hadn't mentioned the nighttime foray, or sitting in the elm tree watching the guards make their rounds of High House Carkoska. And there'd been nothing at all about Maelleen, Marcus and The Angry Bear. All-powerful implied all-knowing; he wondered if there were limits to her abilities, and if he could use that to his advantage somehow.

The old woman said, "I should have him beheaded, or better yet have him eviscerated while he's still alive, let him stare at his own guts for a few days while he dies slowly."

No, Jax almost shouted, but he managed to keep his mouth shut, knowing than an outburst like that would only anger the old woman further.

"Mother, you're so bloodthirsty. You should be more kind."

Yes, Jax wanted to shout, but he forced himself to say nothing.

The young voice continued, "Just have him executed quickly, without all the gore."

Jax desperately tried to think of some argument that might save his life.

"The blood and gore is a good lesson for the rest of them," the old woman said. "Trust me, dear, after you've had to deal with enough of these situations, you'll look upon it differently."

At that moment the carriage lurched to a sudden stop, tossing the young woman forward out of her seat. She landed in Jax's arms with one of her breasts pressed against the palm of his hand. His eyes had adjusted more to the dim lighting, and he found himself face-to-face with a pretty young woman. She had hazel eyes, a dark complexion with an oval face, straight black hair, and soft, delicate skin.

"Are you groping at my breast?" she demanded.

"No," he said, pulling his hand away. "It was an accident."

She pouted and said, "Well that's a shame."

"Dear, please don't throw yourself at the young man. If you want to bed him, just say so and I'll give him to you. You can have him for a couple of nights before we execute him."

The girl smiled, extricated herself from Jax's arms and returned to her seat. "He is rather handsome."

"Don't be a brazen hussy, dear."

The way the old witch took the incident so casually, Jax suspected the young woman hadn't accidently tumbled out of her seat into his arms. It occurred to him that everything these two women did was a test of some sort, though he wasn't sure what they hoped to learn with their little games.

The old woman leaned forward, and for the first time Jax saw her face, a mask of wrinkles, with wispy-gray eyebrows. But her eyes were her most commanding feature, coal black and completely colorless, as if something haunted her soul.

Those eyes bored intently into him as she spoke. "The question still remains, young thief. What are we going to do with you? And how is it that you can look at a very ordinary man on the street ... and so easily recognize that he's one of my knights incognito?"

13

The Witch Palace

THE CARRIAGE DOOR creaked on its hinges as someone outside opened it and bright sunlight spilled into the interior. The Witch of Val d'Ossa nodded toward it and said to Jax, "You go first."

That was clearly not a polite request, and he suspected she didn't want to turn her back on him.

Jax rose, bent to clear the top of the door frame and stepped down onto the cobblestones of a large courtyard. A group of about a dozen Witch Knights surrounded the carriage, all dressed in their red and black uniforms. Two of them immediately accosted him, each gripping an arm and pulling him to one side. With the two men holding his elbows tightly, they had him as confined as if they'd locked him in hand and leg irons, which, he suspected, they would do shortly.

A wall about thrice the height of a man enclosed the courtyard on three sides, with a building four stories high completing the enclosure on the fourth. In the taller structure windows, balconies and trellises overlooked the courtyard. Jax would have never believed he'd one day stand on the cobblestones inside the walls of the Witch Palace, or that he would ride there in a carriage with the Witch herself.

One of the Witch Knights approached the open door of the carriage and placed a small stepping stool just beneath it. He had more emblems and brightly glinting decorations on his uniform than all the rest. He held out his hand, and from within the carriage a hand on the end of a slender, delicate arm reached out and gripped it, then the young woman emerged and stepped down onto the cobblestones.

He said, "Mistress Venessta."

She greeted him by smiling and saying, "Captain Darganna."

She appeared to be about Jax's age, or perhaps a little younger. She stood average height for a woman, which meant she was considerably shorter than Maelleen. But where Maelleen was all vivacious curves and wonderfully rounded bits of female, Venessta was downright petite, with a slight, almost boyish figure. She was pretty, and had nice curves of her own, but nothing like Maelleen's. Maelleen's curves were just . . . curvier.

She caught him looking at her and smiled, as if seriously considering the Witch's offer to give him to her for a few nights. He wasn't sure he'd survive a few nights with her.

Captain Darganna extended his hand again, and an arm draped in lace and embroidered brocade reached out from the dark interior of the carriage. The Witch of Val d'Ossa put one foot down onto the stepping stool and paused for a moment to catch her breath. Darganna extended his other hand, and she gripped it so that she held both of his hands. He carefully helped her down to the cobblestones, and greeted her with, "Mother."

Now that was odd, Jax thought. He had assumed Venessta was the old witch's daughter because she had addressed her as *Mother*. But if they all addressed her as Mother, perhaps it was just a title. He looked again at Venessta and caught her looking his way, though he got the impression she was appraising him, and the look on her face clearly showed distaste.

He'd been right about the two women's attire. Venessta wore a simple, yellow summer dress with an empire waist, and short, puffy sleeves at the shoulders, a bonnet atop her head protecting her face from the sun. In the fashion of the day the dress was cut low in the front and back, exposing her neck and shoulders and the swell of her small breasts above the top of it. A pretty shawl modestly covered most of the exposed skin. The old witch wore a sleeveless, hooded cloak open down the front, a gown with full skirts, a high collar and long lacy sleeves. She walked with a little difficulty, supporting herself with an elaborate cane on one side, and with the arm of Captain Darganna on the other.

She casually pointed at Jax. "Lock him away securely. But treat him well and don't harm him. I don't want to limit our options yet. If he's not cooperative we can always torture and kill him later."

••••

Regardless of what the Witch had told her knights, Jax fully expected them to toss him into some hellish dungeon where he'd spend the last of his days eating gruel and suffering unimaginable torment at the hands of some smelly and unclean torturer. But to his surprise they escorted him to a room more elegant than anything in his limited experience. It was on the fourth floor with a barred window overlooking the courtyard, furnished with a small table and chair, a table near the window with a pitcher and wash basin, a nice wingback chair near the window so one might sit there comfortably and read by natural light, and a plush feather bed. He hadn't slept in a feather bed since that last night long ago with that murderous woman, a thought he had tried to forget. The room also had a private privy.

When he considered it more carefully, his little prison was actually quite functional for their purposes. He'd done his share of second-story work in his night job, but even if the window hadn't been barred, attempting to descend a sheer wall, from four floors up, was a good way to bash his brains out on the hard cobblestones of the courtyard below. The room only had one way out, a heavy oak door with a lock that required a very large key. And when he pressed his hands against the inside of the door, he suspected a Witch Knight stood guard just on the other side of the heavy wooden planks. He wouldn't be going anywhere unless the Witch wanted him to.

They brought him dinner, a plate of stewed beef with carrots and potatoes, plus a tankard of good ale to wash it down, and a sweet, crisp apple for dessert. Then they left him alone to eat, which gave him time to consider his situation. Chewing on a piece of meat, it occurred to him that when the knights had apprehended him on the street, and one of them blew that horn, the Witch's carriage had arrived in a matter of seconds. They had carefully orchestrated his arrest, with the two women waiting near-by.

They had him nicely imprisoned. They were so confident he couldn't escape, they'd even left him a sharp knife to slice the beef while eating. Clearly, the Witch wanted something from him, which was obviously the only thing keeping him from torture and a most horrible death. Whatever she did want, he couldn't imagine that it would be worse than that, so he decided he should probably find out what she want-ed, and give it to her as soon as possible. On the other hand, when she got what she wanted, would she then consider him superfluous and have him executed anyway? He had no delusions about the gratitude of noble personages.

Escorted by two knights, a servant came to take away his empty dinner plate, and the knights were careful to take the sharp knife. The servant also turned down his bed for the night. He'd never had a servant prepare his bed before, and if it weren't for the looming possibility of an unpleasant death, he might have even enjoyed his stay in the Witch Palace.

Oddly enough, he slept rather well. The next morning they woke him an hour af-ter dawn and brought him a light breakfast, though again he ate a lonely meal. Then a servant refreshed the pitcher and wash basin, the knights gave him a razor, soap, and a comb, and told him to freshen up.

One of them said, "Later this morning you're scheduled for an audience with the Witch of Val d'Ossa and her apprentice. Try to look presentable."

Jax considered the man's words carefully. He had said, ". . . her apprentice." Could that be Venessta? Interesting!

••••

With the razor and soap they also provided a small, polished brass mirror, so shaving didn't turn into an ordeal of blood and soap. Afterwards, he stripped down and took a whore's bath, then spread his clothing out on the bed and examined it for any spots or stains. His pants and blouse had been fresh and clean the previous morning, so he could look reasonably presentable in them for a few more days. He dressed, combed his hair, and sat down to wait.

In the carriage the previous day his instinct had completely abandoned him. He wondered now if the Witch had done something to him with her powers, or if being thrust into her presence had simply befuddled him. And if the former, he hoped that she hadn't completely extinguished his odd little talent. He didn't think he'd be much of a thief without it, or at least not as successful as he'd been with it. But some minutes later his instinct warned him a few seconds before the lock in the door ratcheted with a metallic chunk, and that allayed his fears. The door opened and in walked four Witch Knights.

One of them said, "Your presence is required."

Thankfully, they didn't pin his arms to his sides as they'd done the day before, but allowed him to walk unrestrained among them—surrounded by them, actually. They escorted him down two flights of stairs to the second floor, then into a comfortable sitting room furnished with expensive couches and delicate little tables. A hearth in the middle of one wall remained unlit. The knights left him there alone and closed the door. He didn't need his instinct to tell him not to waste his time trying the door; if he could open it, there would undoubtedly be a Witch Knight or two waiting on the other side.

Curious, he walked over to the only window in the room. It looked out onto the grounds of a formal garden, with pretty little pathways of crushed white stone that meandered haphazardly among trees, beds of flowers, and other plants. Not far from the window, a Knight of the Witchguard stood in the shade of a tree watching him. He was probably going to have to get used to that. He certainly hoped he'd live long enough to get used to it.

He heard the door open behind him, so he turned around. Venessta entered the room accompanied by an older man of average height. The fellow had pale white hair and eyebrows, with his chin clean shaven, and for some reason something about the man sparked a memory that Jax couldn't place.

Again, Venessta wore a summer dress with an empire waist that exposed her neck and shoulders and a slight bit of cleavage, though today she'd chosen a gown of a pale blue color, with long sleeves that extended down to her wrists. And she had her hair pinned atop her head in a stylish coif. The blue of the dress contrasted with the slight darkness of her complexion. Just like the first time he'd seen her in the courtyard, Jax got the impression she might be a year or two younger than him, and he tried not to find her attractive.

"Your name is Jaxon," she said. "Is that what I should call you? Or should I call you Felix, the thief?"

He found it interesting that they knew so much about him, and yet there seemed to be little gaps in their information. He decided the best thing he could do was pull out all the manners he'd been taught as a young man and speak plainly, but politely. "Jax will do."

"Well then, Jax,"—she glanced at the man accompanying her—"this is Master Nathaniel. He is Mother's most valued counselor."

But not her apprentice, Jax thought.

The fellow gave Jax an unfriendly, appraising look. "You're the thief," he said, no kindness in his voice.

Jax shrugged. "That's not how I prefer to be known, but I guess there's no use denying it." He couldn't put away the thought that somewhere he'd encountered this man before.

The door opened again and the Witch walked into the room leaning on the arm of a Witch Knight. Nathaniel turned toward her, the knight handed her off to him, then turned and walked out of the room, closing the door. But in that moment Jax saw the counselor's face in profile, and only then did he realize that the man had sunken cheeks, a prominently arched nose, and show-white eyebrows. He recalled the moment Rondo's client had stepped out into the bright sunlight of the alley, and his brief glimpse of the fellow's partially hidden profile.

Jax started, and might have given himself away had any of them been looking, but they'd turned their attention wholly on the Witch.

"Mother," Venessta said, and Jax heard true affection in her voice. "The hip appears to be bothering you a little less, today."

"Yes, dear," the old witch said, "thanks to your ministrations."

Venessta helped Nathaniel get the old woman seated comfortably on a couch. She sat down next to her, and Nathaniel stood over them both. Then the three of them turned their attention to Jax: the Witch, her counselor, and her apprentice.

The Witch asked, "You're being treated well?"

Jax's mind raced. Nathaniel had tried to hire Jax to break into High House Carkoska. Was the counselor playing some game of his own, double-crossing the Witch of Val d'Ossa, or had he been carrying out her orders? If simply doing the old woman's bidding, that would explain why they knew so much about the Carkoska job.

In answer to the Witch's question, Jax said, "No torture or dismemberment so far."

The Witch chuckled. "You have a sense of humor, young thief. That's good, because you're going to need it."

Jax decided to play the Nathaniel card. Whether the man was double-dealing or working for the old woman, either way he'd get some sort of reaction that should tell him something. And hopefully that wouldn't lead to his demise.

"You make me wonder why I'm going to need a sense of humor," Jax said. "May I ask a question?"

The old woman waved a hand at him impatiently. "By all means, ask away, though I may choose not to answer."

Jax considered his words carefully, then said, "Why does the Witch of Val d'Ossa want to hire a thief to break into High House Carkoska and steal a valuable figurine?"

Nathaniel's eyes narrowed angrily, Venessta's eyes widened, and the old witch merely smiled. Unfortunately, their reactions hadn't answered the question of whether the counselor was working for himself, the old witch, or someone else.

Venessta blurted out, "How did you know?" and Jax had his answer. She might be near Jax's age, but she certainly hadn't learned the same level of caution. He'd have to remember that. Perhaps he could put that to use.

"My dear," the Witch said. "You shouldn't have spoken. You just clarified the entire situation for him."

The young woman said, "I don't understand."

Nathaniel explained. "Until that moment he was off balance. He didn't know if I was working for Mother, or double-crossing her, either for my own gain or someone else's."

The counselor crossed the room and stopped a few paces from Jax. "How did you know it was me?"

Jax had no desire or need to enlighten the man. "A lucky guess."

Nathaniel shook his head. "I don't believe you."

Jax shrugged. "Believe what you like."

"Well," the Witch said. "I'm glad to see you're not stupid. But then we knew you have some wits about you. You wouldn't have been so successful at thievery, had you been a fool."

He looked at her pointedly. "You tried to hire me, I refused, so you had your Witch Knights follow and arrest me. I take it that means you still want me to steal this figurine for you, and you're going to force me to do so regardless of the risk."

The Witch smiled. "I would think you'd find the risk preferable to the certainty of torture and death."

Jax shook his head. "The word risk implies at least some possibility of success, but if I break into High House Carkoska, I'll not get out of there alive. And I'd bet they'll use the same methods of torture and dismemberment that you have in mind."

Nathaniel turned around to look at Venessta and the Witch. "I hadn't considered that. If he is captured and tortured, and they can prove to the other High Houses he's working for you, that might create some serious complications. That's not really a chance we can take."

They had finally decided to take the situation seriously. The Witch remained silent for a long moment, and her black eyes appeared to be focused on nothing. After several seconds she lifted her chin and looked at Jax. "So, thief, you've burgled any number of noble houses with uncanny success. Why are you so certain you'll not succeed with Carkoska?"

The three of them waited for Jax to answer. He'd gone this far, so he decided he might as well go all the way. "I choose my targets carefully, minor houses that can't afford a continuous guard presence, or don't need one because they don't have anything of truly great value. I only steal what I need, and never enough to impoverish them. More often than not, they don't even realize they've been burgled. I go in only at night, and only when the house is empty—perhaps they're attending a party, or vacationing on the coast for a few days."

Venessta shook her head. "I've been in House Carkoska a number of times. It's never empty, and the only time they don't have guards about is during the day."

Jax didn't like the way the Witch sat staring at him, and only him.

"Well," the old woman said, "I guess that means you're of no use to us. So we might as well just torture and kill you."

Venessta said, "Oh Mother, does that mean we're back to the evisceration and guts thing?"

Jax knew he had to come up with something right then and there. And apparently, the old witch thought the same thing because she sighed dramatically, looked at Venessta, and said, "I'm afraid so, dear, unless"—she turned her gaze upon Jax and smiled—"our young thief here can come up with a better idea." She raised a questioning eyebrow.

Jax asked Venessta, "You've been in House Carkoska?"

She nodded.

"And you know exactly where this figurine is?"

She shook her head. "No, but I think I can guess where. High Lord Carkoska has an office on the second floor that he keeps locked at all times. Samuel, his youngest son, showed it to me last year. He was only fifteen at the time, had a terrible crush on me, and was upset that his father didn't trust him with a key. I was very sympathetic and got him to show me where the office was located. But again, that he keeps the figurine in the office is only a guess on my part."

Jax would not have believed that Venessta had it in her to play the femme fatale. She had probably contrived some way to fall into the poor young man's arms the same way she'd done to Jax in the carriage. And no doubt she had ensured that the fellow accidentally cupped a breast in his hand as well.

She continued. "Apparently, only Carkoska and his guard captain possess keys, and no one enters that room unless they're under his watchful eye. He even watches over the maids when they clean, then shoos them out and locks the door behind them."

"Can you draw the layout of the house, draw me a map?"

She grimaced and shook her head. "Perhaps, but when I was there I didn't know I needed to memorize the place. I'm not sure I'd be entirely accurate, and it would certainly be incomplete."

Jax's options had quickly run out.

"I've got an idea," the Witch said. She spoke like a schoolgirl planning a party. Jax looked into her coal black eyes, and she clearly knew he was ready to jump on anything. She said, "We'll get you an invitation to High House Carkoska, so you can go there and look it over yourself. You do know how to dance, don't you?"

14

Dance Lessons

THE OLD WITCH was actually serious about getting him an invitation to House Carkoska. She and Nathaniel put their heads together and started making plans, something about a dress ball, with Jax and Venessta in attendance.

Venessta stood and crossed the room to Jax. "You didn't answer her question about dancing. You can dance without stepping all over my toes, can't you?"

Dance lessons were a part of the training for all sons and daughters of a nobleman, even a minor one such as Jax's father. "Yes, I do know how to dance, though it's been quite a while. There isn't much need for dancing in the thief business, so I'm a bit rusty."

She smiled and gave him a coquettish look. "Do you know the new style of dance called the waltz? It's all the rage among the younger set."

"It's not that new," Jax said. "And yes, I do know how to waltz."

She extended her arms out to each side and said, "Then prove it."

"Ummm . . ." he said, ". . . but we have no music."

She reached out and grabbed his right hand, pulled him toward her and put his hand on her hip. She wrinkled her nose in a sneer, as if tolerating an unpleasant smell. "We don't need music for you to prove you can dance. Just walk through the steps."

She put her right hand in his left, then rested her left on his shoulder. "Now, show me that you can dance. Or was that just idle bragging?"

Since his continued existence apparently depended upon proving he could dance with this troublesome young woman, he took a tentative step and she followed. While they walked slowly through the steps of a simple waltz, he lifted his right hand off her hip and raised it higher on her back, almost to her shoulder, the way he'd been taught.

She stopped, pushed his hand back down to her hip and said, "No, that was the style some years ago. It's a little more intimate now."

She emphasized the point by pulling him closer, actually pulling him tightly against her. As they walked through the steps he asked, "It's that intimate, is it?"

"No," she said, giving him a snotty smirk. "But I'm having fun, aren't you? This is certainly better than torture and impending death."

From across the room the Witch asked, "Can he dance?"

They stopped walking through the steps of the dance, but Venessta didn't release him, and kept him there held tightly against her. She looked into his eyes like a predator examining its next meal, and didn't look the old woman's way as she said, "Yes, he can, though I don't think he knows the latest steps. I suppose we can introduce him as a distant cousin from Lieudess. They're all provincial bumpkins there."

Still holding him tightly, Venessta put a hand behind his head and pulled, forcing him to bend his head down, bringing his lips toward hers. He thought she might kiss him, but she stopped with her lips a hair's breadth from his. Under other circumstances Jax might have enjoyed holding a pretty, young woman in his arms that way, but at that moment, all he could think was that Venessta was nothing but pure trouble. And he couldn't put the evisceration and guts thing out of his mind, though he had a little trouble putting *her* out of his mind as well.

With her lips brushing lightly against his, she said, "I think I might take her up on that offer to give you to me for a couple of nights."

Jax wasn't sure he'd survive a couple of nights with Little Miss Trouble.

"Dear," the old witch called out. "The two of you are getting rather lurid. If you're going to seduce him, at least take him up to a room."

Venessta gave him another predatory smile, then put the palm of one hand against his chest and slowly pushed him away. Jax gulped hard as she stepped out of his arms, and was relieved she ended their embrace, though a little piece of him would have liked to continue holding such a pretty young woman that way.

She turned, walked back to the Witch and her counselor, and as she did, he whispered under his breath, "Trouble!"

She halted, turned, and looked at him. "What was that?"

"Nothing important," he said, though it came out in a hoarse whisper.

She smiled knowingly, turned and continued across the room. Jax followed her.

"This is going to work nicely," the Witch said as they approached.

Jax couldn't believe what he was hearing. "I don't understand. How are you going to get them to throw a ball and invite us in there?"

She waved a hand at him dismissively. "High House Carkoska hosts a dress ball in mid-summer every year. That's what I had in mind when I mentioned dancing. The invitations went out some time ago and it's only three weeks away."

"You have an invitation?"

"Of course. After all, I rule Val d'Ossa. I always get an invitation."

"Do you usually go?"

She gave him a look of distaste. "No, of course not."

"Well, you can't just suddenly go this year. It'll look suspicious."

She rolled her eyes, as if he had missed the obvious, though there was nothing obvious about these women. "I don't intend to go."

Venessta said, "Last year she sent me in her place, so if I go again this year it won't be at all suspicious. And I can certainly bring my cousin from Lieudess. You'll be—let me think—Roland, we'll call you. I'll spread a rumor or two that we're lovers. We can be"—she gave him a big, flashy grin—"kissing cousins."

"I've never been to Lieudess," Jax said. "I don't know anything about it. What if they start asking questions I can't answer?"

The Witch dismissed his concerns with a casual wave of her hand. "I'll see to it you're briefed on some of the particulars so you're not completely ignorant. But it doesn't really matter. They're all going to assume you're not who I say you are anyway, simply because I am the Witch of Val d'Ossa and I rarely tell anyone the truth. So it won't matter if they catch you in a lie or two. Since they've never heard of you before, and you're my guest, they'll probably assume you're a wizard of some sort, with all sorts of mystical powers. It's amazing what those people can come up with when they let their imaginations run amok."

She looked thoughtful for a moment, then said, "It occurs to me it might be wise to spread a few rumors to that effect, keep them guessing, as it were."

"I like that," Venessta said. "We might also spread a rumor that he's actually from Palvestra, and that we *are* lying about Lieudess."

"That's absolutely brilliant," the Witch said, looking smugly at Jax. "Spread enough contradictory rumors and they'll never guess that you're just a simple thief from Val d'Ossa who's only a heartbeat away from losing his head and having it displayed on a pike above my walls."

"One more thing, Mother," Venessta said. "It occurs to me that you should attend this year. If Jax and I are going to be sneaking about during the ball, it might be helpful if you're present. And we can get away with the change, because this is my dear cousin Roland's first time in the city, and you'll want to introduce him personally."

The Witch beamed. "Another good idea, my dear."

Venessta looked at the old woman. "Last year the ball was a terrible bore, but I think this year might be a lot more fun. I've never been a thief."

Fun for Venessta, Jax thought. It was just a game to her, and like Rondo, if it didn't work she wasn't the one who would end up with her neck stretched on the end of a rope.

••••

Jax had no intention of going through with a break-in at High House Carkoska. Nathaniel had made it clear that it would be disastrous if Carkoska could prove to the other High Houses that the Witch was complicit in a crime against one of them. Even if Jax got away with the figurine, he knew better than to trust the Witch of Val d'Ossa or her apprentice. He knew full well how the High Nobles thought. Just like his murderous lover from nine years ago, they wouldn't want to leave any loose ends around, like a young thief who might be induced through torture and evisceration to provide damning evidence. The only good news was that the Witch's knights probably wouldn't torture him. They'd want the damning evidence disposed of as soon as possible, so in all likelihood they'd just quietly garrote him and dump his body in the river, or perhaps take him down to the coast and throw him off the cliffs there.

He'd always worked alone before, so for the actual theft from House Carkoska, he could make a good case that if they wanted any chance of success, they dare not saddle him with a watchdog-partner. They'd have to cut him loose in some way, and he felt confident that in the dark he could break away and get lost. Then he'd disappear, maybe move to Lieudess. He could pursue his night job just as easily there, and maybe even more so, without the Witchguard in the way. He'd miss Marcus and Bethy, and especially Maelleen and their little trysts. But he'd come to place a great deal of value on remaining alive, and not having little bits and pieces of him cut off by some sweaty torturer in a dark dungeon. There would probably be rats scuttling around everywhere, eating the little pieces of him they dropped to the floor.

The Witch brought in a tailor, saying, "Can't have you going to one of the High Houses looking like you acquired your wardrobe by picking through their rubbish."

Jax was more insulted by that than anything else he'd heard. He thought he'd done a rather nice job of putting together his young-nobleman's disguise, though he had to admit that he had been operating on a very tight budget.

They brought the tailor up to his room. The Witch and Venessta joined them and gave the man instructions to make a couple of day suits and an elegant evening suit for the ball. As the tailor knelt behind him taking measurements, Jax looked askance at the two women and said, "Day suits?"

"Yes, cousin," Venessta said. "We talked it over, and we feel it's necessary to introduce you to Val d'Ossan society before the ball. Three days from now we're going to an afternoon soiree at High House Tray'enall. You do know how to behave yourself at a soiree, don't you?"

"Of course," he said, only then realizing how out-of-hand this had gotten. He resolved to keep his eyes open for any opportunity that might present itself. Perhaps he could somehow escape even before the ball. But if he did, he'd have to get out of the city immediately. He had no doubt the vindictive old woman would turn the city inside out looking for him.

The Witch stood over the poor tailor and said, "You can deliver the day suits by then, can't you?"

The man kept his eyes locked on the floor. "Certainly, Mother."

The Witch also brought in four musicians and had them set up in her sitting room with the pretty couches and little tables. When not being fitted for his new wardrobe, or planning how they would get him tortured and killed, he and Venessta worked on updating and improving his dancing, but now to music.

Venessta hadn't lied when she'd told him the dancing style had become more intimate, but couples really didn't dance anything as close as she had demonstrated that first time. She'd simply been teasing him, though he had to admit he did enjoy holding her inappropriately close. The present style of dance dictated that they maintain about a hand's breadth distance between their chests, and it was now acceptable for men to rest their right hand on the small of the lady's back just above her hip.

Their first session with the musicians went rather well. Jax picked up the new steps quickly, and felt he demonstrated that he had been educated properly, even if not by the most expensive tutors. But after about an hour of practice, Venessta abruptly said, "Now, we're going to dance the way I want to dance."

Little Miss Trouble pulled him toward her, pressing herself intimately against him in a scandalous disregard for propriety, and they danced that way, though most of the waltz steps didn't work at all well when they were that tightly embraced. A couple of the musicians blushed bright red, while all of them focused intently on their sheets of music.

Jax had to admit he really didn't mind holding a pretty young woman that close, if only she didn't portend his imminent demise.

As they danced, he said, "You enjoy making people uncomfortable, don't you?"

She stopped dancing and he stopped with her, though the musicians continued to play. She rose up on her tiptoes as if to whisper in his ear, when in fact she brushed her lips lightly along his neck. "Now why ever would you say that?"

"Because you do."

"Not really," she said. "It's only *you* I enjoy making uncomfortable."

She ran her tongue along the side of his neck just under his ear. "You taste rather nice," she said. "I think I'd like to taste more."

Jax felt a stirring in his crotch, and with her pressed tightly against him he wasn't sure he hid his reaction from her.

She made it clear he hadn't when she whispered in his ear. "And I can tell you're starting to enjoy yourself." Her lips curled upward in a self-satisfied grin.

The musicians started missing a lot of notes, and they had to end the practice session. After that, Little Miss Trouble proved to be Little Miss Tease as well, and she saw to it that every practice session ended with the musicians red-faced and missing notes, and Jax struggling to maintain his composure.

It bothered him the way she frequently spoke of taking the Witch up on her offer to give him to her for a few nights, as if he was nothing more than a possession to be used at her will. He knew he had no say in the matter, but he didn't like having his nose rubbed in it with such casual indifference. It didn't bother him that he'd whored himself to the murderous woman with striking, blue eyes, but the thought of being nothing more than a piece of property completely unnerved him.

••••

Jax had helped Maelleen assemble an outfit they called her *fine-lady* clothing, and that morning she carefully donned the attire. The dress had been more expensive than anything she had ever purchased, but still affordable. It didn't expose any cleavage, but it also didn't hide the fact that she had an ample chest, which she hoped would help her attract that rich husband. She carefully applied her makeup, doing so sparingly with only a slight touch of kohl to shadow her eyes a bit, a little rouge on her cheeks, and delicately applied lip paint. She then donned a hooded cloak and left the Angry Bear through the back door that let into the alley behind the pub.

It took about twenty minutes to walk to the edge of the District of Nobles where Jax rented the apartment from Mrs. Beamish. Maelleen climbed the steps at the front of the small building, then used the brass knocker to rap softly on the door. Several seconds passed, then the older woman opened the door—she obviously couldn't afford servants for such tasks. She wore her gray hair in an attractive bun, and smiled pleasantly at Maelleen. "Mistress Maelleen, what brings you here this time of morning?"

Mrs. Beamish knew Maelleen as Jax's fiancé and a young woman of good repute but modest means. To solidify that persona, Maelleen and Jax frequently donned their best attire, ate dinner near his flat at a pub that catered to people of *good repute but modest means*, then spent the night in his apartment. During such forays, Jax insisted that Maelleen stay in character at all times, which helped her grow comfortable with the assumed identity.

Maelleen didn't try to hide her concern. "I haven't heard anything from Master Jaxon for more than a week, and I'm hoping you might tell me I shouldn't worry."

Mrs. Beamish's lips slowly curled downward and the smile disappeared. "Oh dear, I assumed he was with you."

Maelleen's gut tightened and fear clutched at her chest. The streets of Val d'Ossa could be dangerous. "You've heard nothing of him? I was hoping perhaps he'd taken a minor illness and was just feeling a bit under the weather."

The old woman shook her head. "No, nothing now for about a week. Do come in, dear." She stepped to one side to admit Maelleen. "Please come in."

"No," Maelleen said, trying to think of a small lie. "I have a few other places I want to check."

In Val d'Ossa there were many ways someone might simply disappear, and Maelleen walked back to the Angry Bear fearing she might never see Jax again.

15

To Remain Human

THE TAILOR DELIVERED the suits as promised, and Jax endured a last fitting. He had to strip down and carefully put on each suit, taking care not to tear a seam if it was too tight. The tailor tested the fit and marked the cloth, then helped Jax strip out of that suit and into the next. When they'd finished with the last suit he undressed down to his small clothes. Naked from the waist up, he turned away from the tailor and happened to be facing the window and the wingback chair near it. The chair had been upholstered in a brocade cloth that had an intricately busy pattern to it. But at that moment something about it struck him as odd.

He squinted, took a step forward, and thought he saw the outline of a person sitting in the chair, though the person would have to be painted completely from head to toe with the same pattern as the brocade cloth to blend in so invisibly. The outline became more distinct, and took on the shape of a slender young woman sitting there in a simple dress. The pattern covered her completely, the dress, the skin of her face, arms and chest where the low-cut gown exposed a little cleavage. Then the pattern dissipated and he recognized Venessta sitting there looking at him, a satisfied smirk on her face.

He'd just seen his first demonstration of real witch-magic.

When she saw the look on his face, the smirk turned into a triumphant grin.

"How long have you been sitting there?" he asked.

Her grin turned lurid. "Long enough to thoroughly enjoy myself watching you put on and take off your clothing."

She rose and slowly crossed the distance between them. She reached out and traced a finger lightly along the ripple of his abdominal muscles. "You stir something in me. I think I will have her give you to me, and for more than just a few nights."

Time and again she had demonstrated that he was nothing more than an object, a piece of property she could toy with at her whim. They intended to use him, get their hands on their precious little figurine, then discard him like an old piece of clothing. Intense anger boiled up from his gut, his jaw muscles tightened, and to maintain control he spoke through gritted teeth. His voice came out in a low growl, like that of an enraged animal. "Get out."

Her brow wrinkled and she tilted her head slightly to one side. "What . . ." She shook her head and the lurid grin disappeared. "What did you say?"

"I said get out. Leave now, before I kill you. I know I probably can't, but I'll at least die trying."

She took an involuntary step back. "I . . . Um . . ."

He leaned toward her and shook with anger as he said, "Have the decency to grant me some privacy and just . . . get . . . out." The last word came out in a ragged shout.

Her eyes blinked rapidly for a moment, and he thought he saw the hint of a tear there. But no tears came, and he realized that none would ever flow from those heartless eyes. He gave her a hard, unyielding look. Her eyes widened for a moment, she hesitated, then the startled look disappeared and the proud, young woman emerged. She acknowledged his rejection with a nod, and with her chin held high she turned and walked out through the door, closing it without another word.

He heard rapid breathing behind him and realized he'd forgotten the tailor. He turned about. The poor fellow stood there as pale as a sheet, his eyes wide and his mouth open in a big, round O.

Jax's voice trembled as he said, "I'm sorry you had to see that. Please accept my apologies."

Jax retrieved his simple, poor-man's clothing and put it on while the tailor gathered up the suits and his tools. The tailor left, scurrying out of the room like a fearful rodent.

Jax sat down in the wingback chair where Venessta had sat invisibly spying upon him. He seethed with anger and could find no calm in his soul. He couldn't deny that he found her physically attractive, and she elicited a very male response from him. But he resolved to never forget that she and the Witch held his life in their hands, and that he was just a thing to them, a tool to be used for their purposes, then discarded when no longer needed.

He sat there for some time and managed to slow his pounding heart somewhat. But just as he started to find calm, the door to his room burst open, arcing around on its hinges and slamming against the wall with an earsplitting thud. The Witch stormed into the room, fury radiating from her like heat from a blazing hearth. She screamed, "What did you say to my little witch? What did you do to infuriate her so?"

Jax's gut tightened with dread, but his fury with Venessta warred with his fear of the old woman and won out. He refused to stand, refused to face her and let her intimidate him.

She had always appeared to be ancient and old beyond imagining. But now she seemed younger, perhaps in her sixties, and while Jax feared her to the core of his soul, obstinance drove him to foolishly defy her. Somehow he managed to speak calmly. "It's not a question of what I did to infuriate her, but rather what she did to infuriate me."

The Witch hesitated, frowned, her eyes widened a bit, she took a breath and said, "Oh, now that's an interesting development." She now appeared to be in late middle age. "Tell me what she did to anger you so."

"No."

"I command it."

"No."

She smiled, and appeared to approve of his defiance. Her brow furrowed in thought as if trying to figure out some way to break through his obstinacy. "Oh, she must have really crossed some line to anger you enough to defy me."

"She did."

The Witch gave him an appraising look, and now she appeared to be even younger, perhaps in her thirties, and there was no sign of the cane or the infirmity. "You know, little thief, you made Venessta cry. How did you do that?"

"Ask her."

"No."

He shrugged. "Then you'll have to remain ignorant."

"Very well."

His heart pounded in his throat as he waited for her to incinerate him with lightning or some magical power, but as always, the woman perplexed him completely. "Just like that? No torture and evisceration. No dismemberment, just a simple 'Very well' is all you have to say?"

The Witch smiled, and she now appeared to be a vibrant young woman in her late twenties, only a little older than Jax. Her breasts stood up firm and strong, her back straight, her skin smooth and fair. She had off-blond hair with a slightly brownish tint to it, and would have been beautiful had her eyes not been colorless black orbs, like the eyes of a demon from one of the hell-pits. Looking at Jax, she nodded and raised one eyebrow. "I need her to be more human. She's spent too much time with me and other beings that are not truly mortal, and she's forgetting what it's like."

"And you're . . . not human?"

"I started out human, and I still am—for the most part—but my . . . chosen profession tends to change a person, and that's acceptable at my age. But for a young one like her—let's just say too much of that at an early age is not a good thing."

She pursed her lips and put a finger to them. "Hmmm. It hadn't occurred to me that you might be helpful in that respect."

The old woman had brought Jax's anger to the fore again. "I don't see how I can."

She walked closer and stood over him. "But you helped enormously today. We're witches—"

He interrupted her. "I had figured that part out."

Her eyes flashed with anger and he realized he'd gone too far. "Don't be impertinent." Oddly enough, she smiled warmly.

He winced. "Sorry."

The smile turned into a grin. "No, you're not, but you are a good liar, an asset that makes you even more valuable to me. But as I was saying, most of the strange and unusual creatures we must interact with don't experience any human emotion, and that can rub off on one a bit. Today you made her feel anger, hatred, fury, sorrow and shame. In a single hour you've done more to rekindle her humanity than I could have done in years."

"Shame?" He would not have guessed that of Venessta.

"Yes. Whatever she did, she knows it was *very* wrong. Shame is a powerful emotion. And fear, let's not forget fear."

"What does she have to fear?"

"That you might abandon her."

He lifted one eyebrow, and made a point of looking at the walls that imprisoned him.

"Of course you can't physically abandon her. After all, you're my prisoner, and I would hunt you down and hang you outside the palace walls. No, she's afraid you might abandon her emotionally."

"To abandon her, I would have had to embrace her first, and I can't stand the little tease."

The Witch leaned close to him and he tried not to cringe. "I've noticed that you seem to enjoy holding the little tease in your arms, so you must not hate her too much."

She straightened, turned around and paced slowly across the room, clearly lost in thought. "We'll have to see if we can trigger some jealousy." She turned back to him. "You're doing a good job with lust, so I won't worry about that, but jealousy really stirs the heart. I'll have to think on that."

He recalled the hint of a tear he'd seen in Venessta's eye. It had only been there for a heartbeat. "You said I made her cry?"

The Witch cocked her head to one side and regarded him. The smile disappeared and she turned thoughtful. "Yes, cried like a little girl who's lost her first puppy. No one's made her cry like that in a very long time."

He considered his own feelings in the matter. "I'm trying to feel some remorse, but I'm having a difficult time doing so."

The smile returned to her face. "Good. Stay angry. Don't yield to her easily. It'll be all the better for her when you do finally capitulate."

She turned and started toward the door. In a step the vibrant twenty-something woman had aged to thirty, in another step forty, and in another fifty. By the time she reached the door she was bent with age. A cane appeared in her hand and she leaned on it heavily. She stopped in the open doorway, glanced back over her shoulder, and again said, "Good."

She stepped out of sight into the hallway beyond. A Witch Knight reached in, grabbed the door handle and closed it. The lock ratcheted with the all-too-familiar metallic chunk.

Jax let out a long, slow sigh, and tried to calm his heart. Somehow he had survived that encounter, and he decided he'd be a damn fool to ever press the Witch again that way.

••••

Jax had to admit that the day suit was far better than anything he could have afforded: a tightly fitting, dark brown tailcoat with tan trousers, pale waistcoat, white shirt and cravat. After Julia and Felix had thrown him out onto the streets, his only concern for clothing had been the need for something to help him hide in shadows in the dark of the night, or a proper disguise to blend in with the residents of the District of Nobles. The Witch had also brought in a cordwainer and had expensive footwear made to his exact measurements. The knee-high black boots he wore now were stylish, fit better than any shoes he'd ever owned, and went well with the new suit. He also had expensive shoes for formal evening wear. He thought it a shame that he would probably have to pay for it all with his life.

His instinct warned him a moment before the door to his room opened. A Witch Knight entered and said, "We're ready."

As usual, four knights escorted Jax down to the main floor, but on that occasion he followed them out to the cobblestoned courtyard; it was the first time he'd been outside since being imprisoned in the Witch Palace. A troop of Witch Knights waited there with their horses and the carriage. There was no sign of the Witch and her apprentice, so Jax stood to one side and waited. A short time later the old woman emerged from the palace proper, leaning on Captain Darganna's arm, with Venessta following close behind them. The young woman glanced at Jax and her look hardened, producing crow's feet in the soft, youthful skin around her eyes.

Captain Darganna helped the Witch up into the carriage where she took the rear seat in the coach. Jax decided to at least be a gentleman, even if he didn't like the little snot. He held his hand out to assist Venessta, but she looked at it coldly and sneered at him. She turned to Captain Darganna and held out her hand. "Captain, if you don't mind."

He smiled and said, "Certainly, Mistress Venessta."

He assisted her up into the coach, but when she turned to sit beside the old woman, the Witch pointed to the forward seat and said, "No. Today you'll sit facing me."

With a look of surprise, Venessta sat down. Jax didn't know what to expect as he climbed into the carriage, but the Witch made her wishes clear. She pointed at the spot on the seat next to Venessta and said, "You're sitting next to her." The tone in her voice made it clear she was not happy.

Jax sat down, the coachman cracked his whip, the carriage lurched forward, and they pulled out into the streets of the city.

"Now you children listen to me," the old woman said, clearly in a foul mood. "I will not tolerate any more of your sniveling, nasty little fight. The two of you have a part to play, so stop acting like babies with shit in your pants and play it."

Venessta's eyes widened as the old witch pointed at her. "You will continue to tease him coquettishly, with those little knowing smiles you're so good at. Do all those little things where you rub against him and toy with him. I liked that bit where you licked his neck just beneath his ear. Do you understand me?"

Venessta's eyes widened even further. "I—"

The Witch interrupted her. "If he doesn't look a little frustrated, I'll know you're not doing your job."

She turned the finger on Jax. "And you, you're going to continue to be the poor befuddled fellow who's not sure if I'm going to execute you for seducing her, or for not seducing her. So do your perplexed mumbling, and when she's not looking, continue to give her those little surreptitious looks where you admire her pink, little bottom. Do you understand me?"

Jax said, "I—"

She interrupted him too. "Because if the two of you don't do this right,"—she looked at Venessta—"I'm going to lay you over my knee and spank you like I haven't done for a long time."

She looked at Jax. "And you'd better deliver as well, or we'll accelerate the schedule on that torture and evisceration thing."

After that they rode in silence to High House Tray'enall.

When they pulled into the courtyard of the noble house, Jax stepped out of the carriage first. He helped Venessta out of it, and she looked at him uncertainly. When he helped the old woman out of the carriage, the strength of her grip surprised him. She straightened her skirts, took Captain Darganna's arm, then looked at Jax and Venessta, her eyes narrow with anger. "Take her arm, young man. And both of you look like you're enjoying yourselves."

Venessta gave him a self-satisfied smirk. "So he likes to steal looks at my derriere, does he?"

Jax ignored her and held out his arm. She looked at it for a moment, then reached out and pulled it tightly against her. He looked down at it and raised an eyebrow. She smiled unpleasantly and said, "Just obeying orders. But that's about as close as you're ever going to get to really doing anything about it."

The Witch turned about and gave Venessta a look. "I heard that, young lady. If you make me give you that spanking, I'll bare your pink, little bottom and let the young man watch. I might even let him participate."

Venessta responded by raising her chin proudly.

Jax tried not to think about it, but it occurred to him that Little Miss Trouble's complexion had a slight olive hue to it, so he didn't think her pink, little bottom was actually pink.

She didn't turn her head to look at him, but her eyes glanced his way for an instant. "What are you thinking about?"

He grinned. "Your pink, little bottom."

She blushed intensely.

The Witch looked over her shoulder again and said, "That's better. And if you're a good boy, you may get to do something with her pink, little bottom other than spank it. Then again, perhaps she's hoping you'll do exactly that."

Jax could almost see the storm clouds forming in Venessta's thoughts. As they walked into the vestibule of High House Tray'enall she looked straight ahead, refusing to acknowledge him in any way.

16

A Soiree

THE WITCH LEFT Captain Darganna in the vestibule and proceeded on her own. She'd also left the cane in the carriage, and walked now with no sign of her infirmity. Jax and Venessta followed her into a large sitting room filled with people. It appeared that the soiree had been under way for some time.

"Are we late?" he asked Venessta.

"Only fashionably so," she said. "Since the Witch rules Val d'Ossa, and is above the highest of the noble houses, we always arrive last, and leave first. The old woman was once miffed at the High Noble Houses, and refused to leave for hours just to punish them. No one could leave before her, and that didn't happen until late in the evening. For them it was a stressful bore."

"And for you?" he asked.

She looked him in the eye. "At times they grow tiresome. It was her way of spanking their pink, little bottoms without starting a war."

"And it didn't fatigue her to stay so late?"

Venessta flashed an unpleasant smile. "When she's angry, she has more stamina than any ten of us combined."

Recalling the way the Witch grew younger as her anger blossomed, Jax didn't doubt that.

Lord Tray'enall was a tall, imposing man, with broad shoulders, piercing eyes, salt-and-pepper gray hair, and a neatly trimmed goatee. Lady Tray'enall stood at his side, a pleasantly plump woman with streaks of gray running through her brown hair.

"Lord and Lady Tray'enall," the Witch said, "how good to see you."

Lord Tray'enall bowed, and his wife bobbed a slight curtsy. "Mother," he said. "It's always a pleasure. And you're looking well."

"No, I'm not," she said. "I'm looking old."

She turned and looked back toward Jax and Venessta. "You know my little witch Venessta. Dear, come forward and introduce your cousin."

As Venessta led Jax forward she released his arm a bit so she no longer held him so tightly. In front of Lord and Lady Tray'enall, Jax stepped aside and Venessta dropped into a deep curtsy. She did it with a flourish, and the Lord and Lady bowed and curtsied in return. Then Venessta straightened and turned to Jax, "May I introduce my dear cousin Roland?"

Jax and the Tray'enalls did their bowing and curtsying.

Lady Tray'enall leaned toward Venessta and gushed. "Your cousin is quite the handsome young fellow. He's certainly going to have trouble fending off all the young women."

Venessta's eyes blinked as she considered that, and she seemed none too happy.

"I'd heard you were in Val d'Ossa, Roland," Lord Tray'enall said. "From Lieudess, eh?"

The man had a slightly sardonic look on his face, as if he didn't care to hide the fact that he knew all the information released about Roland had been fabricated by the Witch and her minions.

"Yes," Jax said. "And now that I've seen some of Val d'Ossa, I confess my home city is clearly not as urbane."

"What brings you to our city?"

In that moment it occurred to Jax that if he couldn't escape the Witch's clutches, and he had to go through with this idiotic fiasco, it would help if he saw the insides of a few more noble houses.

"I have some financial interests here," Jax said. "And I'm thinking of relocating to Val d'Ossa to manage them properly."

The Witch raised an eyebrow and gave him a distrusting look. Lady Tray'enall beamed at him like an immature schoolgirl and said, "That would be wonderful."

Lord Tray'enall's eyes brightened with interest. "If you're in the market for residential property, I know of a few you might be interested in."

"Thank you, Lord Tray'enall," Jax said. "If I do decide to relocate, I'll let you know right away."

The Witch waved a hand and said, "You children go and meet some of the other young people, while Lord Tray'enall and I discuss a few matters of some importance."

Venessta took Jax's arm and led him away. "You know," she said, speaking softly, "Lady Tray'enall is not the vapid twit she pretends. She can be quite shrewd, but she likes to disarm people by hiding behind that pretense."

They met the Tray'enall offspring, a boy about fifteen, and a girl a few years older. Venessta led Jax through the crowd, introducing him to a lot of people whose names he wouldn't remember. Her attitude toward him seemed to have softened a bit.

To Jax's great surprise, he spotted Julia across the room standing in the midst of a group of young men. Something about her seemed different, as if she was not the woman from his memories. She smiled pleasantly at one of her companions, and only then did Jax realize he had never seen such a look on her face. Jax remembered only derision, or distrust, and not just directed at him, but to everyone she met. The intervening years had been kind to her, and she still looked attractive, but the tightness around her eyes had disappeared and softened the lines of her face. She laughed at something one of the young men said, and at that moment she happened to glance Jax's way. Their eyes met and his heart skipped a beat, though either she didn't recognize him, or she hid it well.

He leaned close to Venessta and whispered. "We're in trouble."

Venessta perked up. "Oh, really! How so?"

"My half-sister is here and she's just seen me. She'll tell them who I really am."

Venessta leaned close to his ear and whispered. "She won't recognize you. Mother has placed a glamour upon you. Nothing dramatic, mind you, but it alters your features just enough so people who know you won't recognize you. And don't forget, your half-sister hasn't seen you in nine years. I'm sure you've changed quite a bit since then. After all, you were just a sixteen year old boy."

She took his arm and said, "Let's test the glamour."

"Are you sure?"

"No, not really, but you're the one who'll get tortured and killed if I'm wrong, so why not?"

She led him across the room to the group with Julia. Venessta knew one of the young men and greeted him warmly. He introduced her to the rest, then she introduced Jax as Roland. Julia curtsied deeply, and Jax realized that as a member of the Witch's retinue, his station had been elevated far above that of his half-sister, even if only temporarily.

A handsome young man joined them carrying a small cup of punch. He handed it to Julia, saying, "Here it is, my dear."

She beamed at him, accepted the drink and turned to Jax and Venessta. "And let me introduce my husband," she said. "Lord Ephram Tercees."

Jax thought he did a rather good job of hiding his surprise. After their father's death, they'd all had to find ways to survive. Julia must have curbed her sharp tongue to find a husband, though Jax thought it likely the barbs had returned once the marriage vows were complete and the wedding consummated. But from the happy and joyful way she looked at the fellow, who appeared to be a few years younger than her, it occurred to Jax that he was possibly being unfair. If she had found happiness, he would not begrudge her that.

As Venessta led him away from the group, Jax asked her, "Tercees. I'm not familiar with that house."

"It's a minor house," she said, "but apparently up-and-coming."

Little Miss Trouble leaned close to his ear again and brushed her lips across his earlobe. "When Mother told me about the glamour she intended for you, I wanted her to make you really ugly so the other women wouldn't find you attractive. But she wouldn't hear of it."

Jax recalled that the Witch had spoken of inducing jealousy in Venessta. "You sound jealous. I thought you were angry with me."

"I am, but I made that request before I knew how much I dislike you."

Pretending to whisper in his ear, she traced her tongue along the edge of his cheek. "In any case, I have my marching orders, and I'm a very obedient girl."

"Why do I find that hard to believe?"

The Witch accosted them at that moment. She introduced him to High Lord Carkoska, a man of average height with a mane of golden hair and considerable girth. High Lady Carkoska was not present that day.

Once they completed the formalities, Carkoska said, "Glad to meet you, young man."

To Venessta he said, "You are coming to our summer ball, aren't you?"

She smiled at him coquettishly. "I wouldn't miss it for the world, Your Lordship."

Carkoska beamed and looked at her breasts. He nodded Jax's way and said, "And I'll see to it your young man gets an invitation tomorrow. I assume you want him to accompany you."

She smiled. "That will be most kind of you, Lord Carkoska."

As the afternoon progressed Jax met many of the other lords and ladies of the Higher Houses, and many of their offspring. Venessta took every opportunity to obey the old woman's orders and torment him mercilessly.

"I told you I'm an obedient girl," she said.

"And I told you I don't believe that for a second."

Late in the afternoon she steered them toward the vestibule. "Last to arrive, first to leave." They found the Witch waiting for them.

The old woman leaned close to Venessta and whispered, "Well done, my dear. If you'd tried a little harder, you might have even produced an unsightly bulge in his pants."

Venessta gave Jax a snotty smile and said to the Witch, "I wouldn't want to embarrass the poor fellow."

Jax said, "I would never allow that to happen."

Venessta shrugged, nodded, and said, "I must concede that he pretends rather well at being a gentleman."

The old witch smiled. "Are you sure you don't want him, just for a night or two?"

"No. He's not worth it."

The two of them locked arms and walked out of the vestibule. Jax followed, knowing full well their banter had been meant to goad him into anger.

••••

As they stepped out of the carriage back at the Witch Palace, the old woman asked Captain Darganna, "Did all go well?"

He nodded. "Yes, Mother."

"And she's here now?"

"Yes, Mother."

"How is she?"

He shrugged. "As you instructed we tried not to frighten her, but she is fearful at the moment, though otherwise unharmed."

"Did you get her cleaned up?"

"Yes, Mother. We assigned one of the maids to help her and see to her needs. And we gave her some new clothing, though we didn't have anything that fit her exactly."

"Is she at all dangerous?"

"No, Mother. She's complacent, but that might be because she doesn't yet know what's going on. She seems intelligent, so I'd recommend we watch her closely."

"Very good, Captain. I'll leave the details to you."

Darganna bowed and backed away.

To Jax and Venessta, the old woman said, "Come, I have something I want the two of you to see."

The Witch had retrieved her cane from the coach, and with his curiosity aroused, Jax provided an arm for her to lean on as they climbed the stairs, Venessta following close behind. But when they reached the fourth floor, instead of turning toward Jax's room, they turned the other way down the hall. Jax noticed several doors much like the one to his rooms, but up ahead only one had a Witch Knight standing guard outside of it. The fellow bowed deeply to the Witch as they approached.

"Please admit us," she said.

The knight retrieved a large key from his belt, inserted it into the lock in the door and turned it. It made that ratcheting chunk Jax had come to recognize, and the knight swung the door inward. The knight preceded them into the room, Jax helped the Witch across the threshold, and Venessta followed just behind them.

The room had been furnished and laid out identically to the one Jax occupied, and like his prison cell it had a single barred window. As they entered the room, a tall woman stood at the window with her back to them looking out at the courtyard below. Her brown hair hung past her shoulders in a disarray of curls and ringlets, and Jax saw something familiar in the line of her waist and the curve of her hips.

••••

Maelleen stood at the barred window looking down at the courtyard below, her heart pounding with fear as she tried to control her breathing. She had been walking alone down a street on her way to the market square when the Witch Knights accosted her, bundled her into a carriage, and spirited her away. There had been no witnesses other than strangers on the street, so she didn't think any of her family or friends knew she had been arrested and taken to the Witch Palace. What did they want of her? And why her? Would she now disappear like Jax? And did this have anything to do with Jax's disappearance?

At the Witch Palace they had forced her to strip, bathe, then don a low-cut, green, brocade gown. It fit her reasonably well with one exception: it was a little too small in the chest, and bunched her ample bosom at the top of it, displaying an enormous amount of cleavage not unlike one of the prostitutes that worked the streets.

A racket in the courtyard below drew Maelleen's attention. A carriage escorted by mounted Witch Knights rumbled through the main gate. The driver swung it around and pulled it close to the palace proper, which put it out of sight of her limited view from the window. She heard horses neigh and a male voice shouted a few unintelligible commands. Then all went silent.

Several minutes passed. She was so intent on trying to see something through the window she almost missed the ratcheting chunk of some mechanism behind her. But at the sound of voices she turned and saw that a Witch Knight had entered the room. Behind him came Jax with an old woman supporting herself on his arm. The look on her lover's face told her he rather liked the way the gown was too small to accommodate her breasts properly.

"Jax," she said, "we thought you were dead."

A young woman stood a little behind Jax and slightly to one side, as if she feared Maelleen. She wore an expensive looking gown with an empire waste, had a slight olive hue to her complexion, and a sharp, unhappy look on her face. In that moment the improper fit of Maelleen's dress embarrassed her, and that angered her.

The old woman released Jax's arm and leaned heavily on a cane. Maelleen started toward Jax, but the knight stepped in her way, held up a hand and said, "Hold it right there, young lady." The man looked to the old woman for guidance.

"Yes, dear," the old crone said. "Please go sit down."

Maelleen felt like a caged animal. "Who are you?"

With an uncomfortable grimace, Jax said, "She's the Witch of Val d'Ossa."

Maelleen's heart climbed up into her throat.

••••

Jax watched Maelleen absorb the information that she stood in the presence of the Witch. And then he watched the expression on her face change from fear to calculation. Maelleen was better than him at finding advantage in a bad situation. But she didn't fully understand their predicament, so he said, "Please do as she says. I don't think you'll be harmed."

The Witch looked at him and shook her head. "You don't *think*? Come now, young man, we're not barbarians here."

He shrugged, "I do have to keep in mind the whole beheading and evisceration thing."

"Oh yes," she said, "there is that."

He added, "And I do assume that option is still on the table."

She grinned. "Of course it is, dear."

She turned back to Maelleen. "In any case, young lady, please sit down. We're going to have a little chat, and I don't want you getting hysterical."

Jax said, "She's not the type to get hysterical. In fact, she's pretty level-headed."

"Very well," the Witch said. "Then I think *I'll* sit down while we have that chat."

As the old woman hobbled across the room, Venessta looked at Maelleen as if examining spoiled meat in the marketplace. "Who is this woman?" she asked, her tone frigid and filled with distaste.

The Witch sat down in the wingback chair, adjusted the folds of her skirt and said, "She's a prostitute."

Venessta's lip curled upward, the way one might grimace after tasting sour wine. "Oh," she said, and took a step back as if prostitution might be contagious. "Why is she here?"

The Witch smiled triumphantly. "She's also his lover."

The look Venessta gave Maelleen could have chilled wine on a hot summer day. "His . . . lover?"

At Venessta's reaction the Witch's smile broadened a little, and Jax realized she was thoroughly enjoying the young woman's discomfort. "Yes, she's quite beautiful, isn't she? Downright voluptuous, I'd say, and incredibly sexy. I can see how attractive she must be to men, though I'm much too old to even think about that kind of thing anymore."

"Well," Venessta said. She refused to look at Jax, and apparently couldn't take her eyes off Maelleen. "I suppose . . . she does have . . . certain charms."

"Yes," the Witch said. "And they're most visible, aren't they? All sorts of little round curves that men just love, and some not so little as well."

Maelleen's eyes darted back and forth between one women and the other. "What's . . . What's going on here?"

"Jax," the Witch said. "I think introductions are in order. We know who Maelleen is. And you've introduced me. So please introduce Venessta."

Jax said, "Venessta is her apprentice."

Maelleen looked at Venessta and her eyes narrowed, then she walked toward her. Jax had completely forgotten about the Witch Knight, who had remained near the door unmoving. As Maelleen started toward Venessta the fellow tensed, but the Witch silently shook her head and he froze.

Maelleen stopped one pace from Venessta, close enough to tower over her. "You're a pretty one," she said.

At the compliment, Venessta smiled.

Maelleen continued, "Too skinny to make any money on the streets, but still rather pretty. I'd have you eat more, put on a little weight, which, hopefully, would fill out those breasts a bit. They're so small. You'll never attract a man."

Venessta's eyes blinked rapidly as she took an involuntary step back.

Maelleen asked, "And you're studying to take over for the Witch, eh?"

That was one of the things that Jax liked about Maelleen: there wasn't a woman alive who could intimidate her, not even the Witch of Val d'Ossa, or her apprentice.

The Witch said, "Yes, she is studying to replace me. And she's also practicing the ancient magic art of raising a bulge, aren't you dear?"

Venessta blushed, and there was no question that Maelleen noticed it. Jax prayed he wouldn't have to explain that one later.

Maelleen turned back to the Witch. "Why is Jax here? Why am I here?"

The old woman was positively enjoying this. "Jax is here because we've enlisted his aid to help us with a little project."

Maelleen looked from the Witch to Jax, then back to the old women. "You want him to steal something for you, don't you?"

Jax flinched, which drew Maelleen's attention. "Of course I know," she said, snapping the words at him. "I've always known. I don't bed a man for pleasure, unless I know what he does at night when I'm not around."

"You bed him for pleasure?" Venessta asked. "But you're a whore."

Maelleen's eyes sharpened and she gave Venessta a big grin. "Not when I lay under him. He makes me feel like I'm not a whore. You should try him some time. I'll bet he can make even you feel like a woman, even with those boyish hips and tiny breasts."

Venessta blushed.

"As I was saying," the Witch said, "he's agreed to help us with our little project, but he's somewhat reluctant. And he certainly has a devious mind, so it occurred to me he might be thinking about finding a way to disappear on us. Once we let him loose to do his thieving, we won't have much control over him, will we?"

Maelleen nodded. "And that's why I'm here."

"Exactly," the Witch said. "If he wants you back when this is done, he'll have to complete the job properly."

Jax knew the Witch wasn't being entirely honest. The old woman also wanted Maelleen present to fuel Venessta's jealousy.

"And what is it you want him to steal for you?" Maelleen asked.

The Witch glanced at Venessta before answering. "A valuable figurine."

Maelleen didn't let up. "What does this figurine look like?"

"Small," the Witch said. "Probably of a size you could easily hold in one hand. Fired clay, perhaps glazed, perhaps merely painted, it should be the figure of a woman wearing a cloak, and holding a small box."

Maelleen nodded, and Jax could see her carefully considering what she'd just heard. "And why is it so valuable?"

The Witch hesitated. "Its value is . . . purely artistic."

Jax heard the lie in her words, and clearly, so too did Maelleen.

Maelleen rocked back on her heels, frowned, and put her hands on her hips. "So you want him to steal something you've never seen, and you aren't even certain what it looks like?"

"Yes," the old woman said. She stood. "And I think we're done here now."

She crossed the room to Venessta, took her by the arm and said, "Come, my dear. Let's go. I'm sure Jax and Maelleen have much to catch up on."

Venessta's eyes widened. "You're going to leave him here with her?"

"Yes, dear, why not?"

Venessta's upper lip curled in distaste. "She's a whore."

"Of course, dear. After all, they're lovers. And we're all whores. She just gets to do her whoring on her back."

Maelleen frowned and shook her head. "I don't do all my whoring on my back."

The Witch rolled her eyes and spoke carefully. "Metaphorically speaking, she does her whoring on her back, and we get to do our whoring standing up."

Maelleen's frown deepened. "I've whored standing up as well."

The Witch said, "Stay with the metaphor, dear."

Maelleen lowered her eyes. "Yes, Mother."

Venessta hesitated and asked Maelleen, "Is that fun, standing up?"

Maelleen smiled and gave Jax a lascivious look. "With the right lover, it can be."

The Witch said. "I don't think it's a metaphor anymore." She held her arm out to Venessta. "Now help an old woman down those awful stairs."

As Venessta helped her to the door, the Witch leaned on her more heavily than she had on Jax. At the last instant Venessta glanced over her shoulder at Jax, then at Maelleen. Then she and the old woman stepped out into the hallway beyond. The knight closed the door and locked it.

Maelleen rushed across the room, wrapped her arms around Jax's neck and kissed him. "I thought you were dead."

He grimaced. "It's a long story, and I still may end up dead, and probably in a very unpleasant way."

She frowned thoughtfully. "And what's this about magical bulges?"

17

A Harlot With Manners

WITH HER ARMS wrapped around Jax's neck, Maelleen said, "We all thought you were dead. I'm so glad you're not."

He nodded. "Me too."

Jax wanted to talk, but she kissed him again, and he enjoyed holding her in his arms. Not until sometime later did they get around to talking.

As Maelleen lay naked on her stomach on the top of the sheets, Jax traced a finger down the length of her spine and over the curve of her buttocks.

"What's going on here?" she asked. "There's something in play here way beyond stealing a valuable figurine."

Jax was not surprised Maelleen had picked up on that. And when Venessta had described Carkoska's office, he'd grown even more suspicious of the whole affair. If the figurine was merely a valuable piece of artwork, the Lord of High House Carkoska would have it on display, perhaps with guards and other protections, but not hidden behind a locked door.

He kissed the back of her thigh. "I've been thinking about that, and I don't think I should tell you."

She glanced over her shoulder and gave him an unhappy look.

He planted a kiss in the small of her back. "Don't worry, I trust you. It's them I don't trust. I'm not sure I'm going to get out of this mess alive. And if you know too much, they might not free you even if I do complete the job successfully. There's some High Noble House politics involved, and I don't yet know what."

She rolled over and sat up, then crossed her legs in front of her. "Do you really *want* to know what?"

"I didn't at first, but I've been thinking about that a lot. If I'm forced to do this job, I'm beginning to think that to have any chance of surviving, I may need to understand exactly what they're up to."

"And I've been thinking too," she said. "The pretty, little skinny one . . . what's her name?"

He sat up, crossed his legs and faced her. "Yes, the apprentice, Venessta. The old witch refers to her as her *little witch*."

Maelleen took his hand, held it to her cheek, then kissed his palm. "When she learned I am your lover, the air grew thick with her jealousy. I could almost taste it."

Jax recalled the Witch's words about human emotions, and her desire to see Venessta experience jealousy.

Maelleen batted her eyes at him. "Have you seduced her yet?"

That caught him off guard. "No."

"Have you tried?"

"Not really. Why?"

She looked at him as if speaking to a dim witted child. "Get the little witch in bed, give her pleasure, and when she's exhausted and sated, you never know what you'll learn. Pillow talk can be very informative."

"She's a child," he said.

Maelleen dismissed that argument with a shake of her head. "She's clearly close to our age, and if younger, only by a little."

She didn't understand. "You're the only woman I take pleasure from."

She smiled, leaned forward and kissed him on the cheek. "I can tell that you find the little witch attractive. She is certainly pretty, and I won't begrudge you taking pleasure from her. Bed her, learn what you can, and enjoy yourself."

"I made her cry," he said.

"Did she deserve it?"

Every time he thought about that incident, his fury at the little witch returned. He told Maelleen about the Witch's offer to give him to Venessta, and how the apprentice had threatened to take her up on it. He explained the magic he'd seen, and the way Venessta had blended into the pattern of the fabric of the chair until she'd been virtually invisible, and the way he'd felt violated and used.

Maelleen's lips tightened into an angry pout. "That nasty little witch!"

He told her how the old witch had confronted him, and the way it seemed that her anger had returned her briefly to her former beauty, and how, as her anger had dissipated, her age and infirmity returned. He described what he'd learned of their constant struggle to remain human.

"Interesting," Maelleen said. She leaned forward, pulled him toward her and planted a delicate kiss on his lips. "So you'll bed the little witch?"

"I'll think about it," he said. "But right now I'm thinking more about bedding you."

She looked down at the sheets they were sitting on, and the feather bed beneath them. "You've already got me in bed. Now finish the job."

••••

The Witch allowed Jax and Maelleen the entire night together without interruption. He thoroughly enjoyed every curvaceous little piece of her, though it bothered him that she had become entangled in his problem.

The next morning four knights escorted him back to his room where a hot bath awaited him. The only time he'd had a hot bath since escaping from Lakorsa and his murderous employer had been when he and Maelleen occasionally shared one, though bathing had never been their priority when doing so. For a moment he considered asking the Witch to allow Maelleen to bathe with him, but he really didn't want to have that discussion with the old woman.

The tailor delivered two more day suits and Jax went through the rigors of a final fitting. The tailor kept glancing toward the wingback chair, and a couple of times Jax walked over to it and patted the cushions just to be sure. When the tailor finished, Venessta didn't magically appear sitting there with a smug smirk on her face. Given that Jax had sent her away in tears, she had hopefully learned her lesson in that regard.

That afternoon, Jax donned one of the new day suits, and dressed like a well-to-do gentleman. Then four knights escorted him to the sitting room where he found the four musicians setting up. A moment later Venessta and the Witch arrived.

"I really don't think this is necessary," Venessta said as they entered the room. "His dancing is adequate. There's no need for more practice."

"Nonsense, my dear," the Witch said. "Even you admitted he doesn't know all the latest steps."

Jax stood next to the musicians, and the five of them watched the women argue.

As Venessta helped the old woman cross the room, she said, "He doesn't need to know *all* the latest steps. You said it yourself: no one's going to believe anything we tell them about him anyway."

The Witch sat down in her usual place on one of the couches, adjusted the folds of her skirts and said, "But the harder we make it for them to find inconsistencies, the more it will confuse them."

Venessta opened her mouth to rebut, but the Witch cut her off. "In any case, the ball is still more than two weeks away, so we have the time. I insist. Please make an old woman happy, dear."

Jax walked out into the middle of the room where they had cleared a small space. Venessta crossed the room to join him, a pout on her face. She stopped in front of him and tried to look bored as she held her arms out. He rested his right hand on her hip, took her hand in his, and adjusted his position to the proper distance. She reached around to his right hand, took it off her hip and carefully lifted it to the back of her shoulder. Then she adjusted the distance between them so at least two broad hand-spans separated their chests. Apparently, they were going to dance in the less intimate style that had fallen out of favor.

The musicians began playing, and the two of them danced rather stiffly. Jax noticed the Witch trying to hide a smirk by raising a hand to her lips as if covering a yawn.

"So," Venessta said. "You and that whore are lovers. How long has that been going on?"

"Nine years."

"She's so . . . attractive. Do you love her?"

Jax had to think about that for a moment, but regardless of how he felt about Maelleen, he was not going to divulge his inner feelings to this young woman. "No, and she doesn't love me. We do like each other a lot, though."

Venessta looked him straight in the eyes in a challenging way. "How did you meet her?"

"I met her in her father's tavern."

"But how?"

"I hired her."

"For what?"

Jax gave her a sardonic look and raised one eyebrow. She frowned for a second, and he watched her think it through. Then her eyes widened and she said, "Oh."

She looked down and focused her eyes on his chest. "So you hire her, and she gives you pleasure."

"No, only that one time. After that it became a mutually beneficial relationship, no money involved; just pleasure. We do enjoy each other a lot."

"So you give each other pleasure?"

"That's pretty much the idea, isn't it? But there's more to it than that. As I said, we're friends, and I tutor her in etiquette."

Venessta frowned and looked up into his face. "Why?"

"She wants to marry a rich man, and the best way for her to catch one is to not look or act like a prostitute. When she wants to, she can act quite the noblewoman."

At that moment Jax could see the Witch over Venessta's shoulder. The old woman perked up and cocked her head as if listening intently to every word the two of them spoke.

Venessta's eyes brightened. "So she's going to marry someone else?"

"Yes, of course. I'm certainly not rich."

The music ended. Jax and Venessta separated. The musicians started another tune, Jax stepped in and reached for her, assuming she still wanted to maintain the non-intimate distance. But she said, "No," and placed his hand on her hip. "This tune calls for the more intimate style of dance."

They danced that way through that melody. Then on the next tune she pulled him tightly against her, and by the end of that, he saw by the smug grin on her face that she knew she'd had an effect on him.

"That's enough for today," the Witch said. She patted the couch next to her. "Come, my little witch, sit beside me. And I have a question for the young man."

Jax wondered what that meant as Venessta sat down beside the old woman and straightened the folds of her dress. He remained standing in front of the two of them. The old woman smiled at him, a devious glint in her soulless eyes.

"You have a question for me?" he asked.

"Yes," she said. "Did I hear you say you've tutored your young harlot in manners?"

He shrugged. "She wants to catch a rich husband. What's wrong with that?"

"Nothing," she said. "Nothing at all. So what have you been teaching her?"

"Diction, for one thing, and manners, both when at the table and when not. How to properly use the dining utensils in both formal and informal settings. Things like that."

"I hadn't realized it," she said, "but she really doesn't sound or carry herself like a whore. It appears you've done a good job. Anything else?"

"I've helped with her reading a bit."

The Witch's eyes widened. "She's literate? A prostitute who can read?"

"Yes. She stumbled over a lot of words when we first met, but she's improved considerably since then. She's ambitious, and works very hard at it."

The woman's eyes appeared to focus on nothing for a moment. "A literate whore who can carry herself like a noblewoman. Interesting!"

She perked up. "Well, that's neither here nor there."

She turned to Venessta. "Dear, would you ring for the servants. I think I'd like a cup of tea."

"Certainly, Mother," Venessta said. She stood and crossed the room to a bell-pull.

The Witch leaned toward Jax and whispered, "Both jealousy and envy all wrapped up together, such a wonderful combination of human emotions. You're doing a very good job, young man."

••••

After the dance practice, as the knights escorted Jax up to his room, he passed Maelleen going the other way, accompanied by two knights. Again, she wore the dress that didn't properly fit when it came to her expansive chest. She flashed her eyes at him warmly and he smiled. He wasn't sure if they would be allowed to say anything in passing, so he kept his mouth shut. It did occur to him that the knights were foolish to think she needed an escort of fewer knights than him just because she was a woman. Maelleen could be formidable and calculating, and though he'd never had to experience it, he thought she could be dangerous as well.

The next morning the knight guarding the door to his room admitted the Witch's counselor, Nathaniel. With his usual blunt demeanor, he asked, "Do you know how to sit a horse?"

Wondering why the fellow asked, Jax shrugged. "I was reasonably good as a youth, but I haven't been on a horse in nine years."

"You won't have forgotten," the counselor said, casually dismissing Jax's concerns, "and I'll tell the stable master to select an animal that isn't too spirited."

"What's this about?" Jax asked.

"If we're going to pretend you're a gentleman, then you'd better know how to ride, hadn't you?"

Clearly, in Nathaniel's mind, the key word was *pretend*. In his first days in the Witch Palace, Jax had quickly learned that the counselor rarely gave up any information not absolutely required, and no amount of questioning could induce him to be more forthcoming. So Jax let it go without pressing the matter.

"Come with me," the counselor said. "I want to see if your definition of *reasonably good* is anything close to mine."

Out in the hallway, with the four knights surrounding him, they passed a woman accompanied by two maids and carrying several bolts of cloth. The maids led her to Maelleen's room and the knight at her door admitted them. They'd brought in a seamstress. *Good*, he thought. Maelleen might as well get something out of this, if nothing more than a few nice dresses. After this was over, if they survived, and if they let her keep them, dresses of a quality that neither he nor she could afford would certainly help her catch that rich husband.

Jax hesitated. It had never before occurred to him that she would actually be successful in that endeavor. And now that she might, he wondered how he felt about that. He had to suppress a pang of jealousy.

Jax and the knights followed Nathaniel down to the stables. The counselor gave orders to the stable master, and the fellow walked down among the stalls, then led a sleek mare out to the courtyard. A groom saddled her, then handed the reins to Jax.

Another test, he thought. *Always another test.*

He gripped the saddle horn, stuck his left foot in the stirrup, climbed up and swung his right leg over the mare's rump. As he settled in the saddle, she snorted, neighed and sidestepped, but he quickly got her under control.

Nathaniel said, "Take her around the courtyard a couple of times."

Jax nudged her flanks lightly with his heels and she walked forward. He kept her at a walk through one full circuit of the courtyard, which allowed him to gauge her nature. Then he nudged her flanks again and she broke into a trot.

He noticed that the main gate of the courtyard was wide open to the city beyond. If he spurred the mare into a gallop just as he approached it, he could be out the gate in an instant. There were no mounted knights in the courtyard, or any horses readily at hand. He'd be well into the warren of streets around the palace long before they could give chase. But then the open gate was probably another test, and they undoubtedly had guards on the wall with muskets, and he'd end up with a large hole in his back and his brains splattered on the cobblestones of the street. In any case, he couldn't abandon Maelleen that way.

After two circuits of the courtyard he reined the horse back to a walk, completed another circuit, then brought her to a stop near Nathaniel.

"Good enough?" Jax asked.

"Adequate," the counselor said.

As Jax dismounted an important consideration occurred to him. "It occurs to me I haven't done this in a tail coat in a long time, and especially not in a greatcoat. Mounting and dismounting can be difficult with all the extra material swinging around. Perhaps I should try this a couple of times in full regalia before going out in public."

Nathaniel nodded but frowned, as if the idea that Jax could produce an intelligent thought gave him pause. "Good thought. I'll arrange it."

Jax handed the mare's reins to the groom. As the knights led him away, Nathaniel called out, "You'll be dining this evening with Mother and Venessta. Dress appropriately for dinner."

18

Little Witch, Little Thief, Little Harlot

THAT EVENING THE knights escorted Jax down to the ground floor of the Witch Palace. They admitted him to the dining room through a set of tall double doors; he was the first to arrive.

He'd eaten a number of meals in his room upstairs, but he'd never *dined* in the Witch Palace. He expected to be admitted to a giant hall with a massive table stretching its entire length, with hundreds of carefully arranged place-settings, and chandeliers overhead providing dim, intimate lighting. Instead, the knights admitted him to a relatively small room, with a table at its center that might seat a dozen, though it only contained four elaborate place-settings. One candelabrum in the middle of the table provided some lighting, with two more on side tables against the walls.

Behind him the door opened and he turned as Maelleen entered the room, but it was a different Maelleen. They had pinned her hair up in an elaborate style on top of her head, and there was something different about her face.

"You look stunning," he said.

She smiled, clearly enjoying the compliment. "You're just looking at my breasts again."

"No, I'm not. Well, they are something to look at, and I did look at them, repeatedly, and will continue to do so, but not at this moment. You just look . . . great."

She pouted. "You said stunning. I like stunning better than great."

"Well that too. You're definitely stunning."

She smiled happily and crossed the room. "They had a lady's maid set my hair and apply my makeup. I think I've learned a few things. I'm going to get that rich husband yet."

One more step closer to her goal, and there again Jax felt that pang of jealousy. He brushed that thought aside and put his arm around her waist, but she pushed him away. "No," she said. "Who knows who's going to walk into the room, and when. And I don't think it would be wise to fuel the little witch's jealousy any more than we already have."

She was right about that, a point made clear when a few moments later the doors opened and in walked the Witch leaning on Venessta's arm. Jax bowed and Maelleen curtsied; he'd never before seen her curtsy.

The Witch said, "Excellent, excellent. I see you've been practicing your curtsies, my dear."

Venessta rolled her eyes and gave Jax a critical look. "Thankfully, we learned about that deficiency early enough. Why didn't you teach her to curtsy?"

Jax said, "I don't know how to curtsy. It's not really something I do terribly often, so how would I have taught her that?"

The Witch nodded. "He does have a point, dear."

Venessta led the old woman to a seat at the table, and Jax held the chair for her. The two younger women waited as she sat down. He then seated Venessta, and following that, Maelleen.

"Good," the Witch said to Maelleen. "You know enough to wait for a gentleman to seat you."

Venessta said, "If only there were a gentleman present."

The Witch leaned forward and gave her a sharp look. "Don't forget the pink-little-bottom thing, my dear."

The old woman turned to Jax. "If you like, I can bare it for you now, and you can administer the spanking."

Maelleen leaned toward Venessta. "A spanking. I suppose that could be fun." She turned to the Witch. "Is that the kind of thing she likes?"

The Witch snapped, "You'd think so, the way she keeps begging for it."

Venessta lowered her eyes.

As the older witch glared at the younger, Maelleen leaned back and gave Jax a conspiratorial smile. Clearly, she still thought he should seduce Venessta.

Servants brought in the first course, and they began the meal. The two witches seemed more interested in watching Maelleen and Jax eat, and it was at that moment he realized this was just another test. It didn't surprise him that the two witches might want to confirm he had been trained properly, but what difference did it make if Maelleen had learned her lessons well? The Witch and Venessta had something sneaky in mind, and Jax hoped Maelleen would drop a plate on the floor, or get roaring drunk and puke all over the table. But throughout dinner she proved that she had absorbed his tutoring nicely. Jax wanted to put Maelleen over his knee and spank her pink, little bottom. And he knew for a fact that her derriere was truly pink.

After dinner they retired to a sitting room furnished much like the one where he and the little witch practiced dancing. The Witch had cordials brought in: a snifter of brandy for Jax, and something lighter for the women. Jax and Maelleen were then tested on their ability to hold a pleasant conversation about meaningless drivel while sipping their drinks.

"By the way, dear," the Witch asked Maelleen, "how are the dancing lessons coming?"

"It's really not that difficult," she said. "In fact, I'm rather enjoying it."

Jax couldn't hide the anger in his voice as he asked, "Why does she have to learn to dance?"

Both witches smiled, probably thinking they were being pleasant, when all Jax saw was a couple of conniving women. "Don't worry about it, little thief," the Witch said. "We'll discuss it in the morning after you finish dance practice with my little witch."

The two witches turned and walked out of the room. The old witch had no trouble moving quickly when she wanted to.

He turned on Maelleen. "Why are they teaching you to dance?"

"I don't know," she said, clearly lying.

Before they could talk further, the Witch Knights entered the room and separated them. And as they escorted Jax up to his room, he couldn't escape the unmistakable feeling that all three women were hiding something.

••••

The next morning, before Jax and Venessta began dancing, he demanded, "Why are you teaching Maelleen to dance? There's no need to teach her that."

The old woman said, "Won't it be nice for her to know the proper steps when the two of you dance in that tavern you spoke of."

"In The Angry Bear?" Jax asked. "No one dances like that in a tavern. If anyone dances in a tavern it's a jig, not a waltz."

The two witches shared a look, then the old one glanced at the musicians and said, "We'll have to wait until after dance practice is concluded to discuss this further."

They couldn't discuss anything meaningful in front of the musicians, so Jax didn't argue with her. Venessta was all business that day, no teasing or intimately close dancing. Jax rather liked holding her in his arms, and almost regretted that she didn't force him to dance intimately close. As the musicians were putting away their instruments, the knights escorted Maelleen into the room. Venessta sat down next to the Witch, and a few minutes later, Jax was alone with the three women.

"So what is this about teaching Maelleen to dance?" Jax demanded. "She's not involved in this."

The Witch looked him straight in the eye and said, "She asked if she could help, so she is involved. And I think she might be useful."

Jax turned on Maelleen. "You asked if you could help?"

She rolled her eyes. "Yes. That'll be better than passively sitting in this palace while you get yourself killed."

"I thought we agreed it was too dangerous for you to get involved."

"No," she said, shaking her head. "We agreed we can't trust the two of them,"—she nodded toward the two witches—"but only you agreed I shouldn't get involved."

Maelleen looked at the other women and said, "He is such a man."

They responded by raising their eyebrows and nodding in silent agreement.

Looking at Maelleen, Venessta said, "I think he's trying to protect you, even at the cost of his own life. That appears to be . . . admirable. He must love you."

"Of course he loves me," Maelleen said, "but he's not *in love* with me. He and I come from a place where we don't get to be . . . *in love*." Maelleen raised an eyebrow and added, "And so do you, little witch."

Venessta started and leaned back, her eyes blinking rapidly.

"Why?" Jax demanded. "Why get her involved? We can do it without her."

Maelleen ignored him. "As you pointed out, he is trying to protect me. We both learned long ago that for the nobility, truth is a somewhat flexible concept. He believes that if I know too much, even if he fulfills his end of the bargain, you'll kill us both anyway, just to clean up any loose ends. So if I don't know anything, maybe you won't kill me. On the other hand, I think it won't matter one way or another. Regardless of what I know, I'll still be just another loose end . . . won't I?"

Venessta shook her head vehemently. "That's absolutely not true."

The Witch grimaced and said, "Well, my dear . . . I can't guarantee anything when—"

"Mother," Venessta gasped, a horrified look on her face. "You lied to them?"

The Witch held her hands up in a placating gesture. "Dear, I have days when not a single truth crosses my lips. But in my own defense, more often than not, those days are when I'm dealing with the High Nobel Houses."

She looked carefully at Jax, and then at Maelleen. "The only thing I can truthfully say is that if we don't succeed, you two will not likely survive. On the other hand, if we do succeed, then I will try to treat you fairly. But sometimes my options are limited in such matters, so I can't guarantee anything."

"Darling," Maelleen said to Jax. "I think we have no choice but to play the odds, even if they are heavily stacked against us."

She was right; they were stuck with the situation. "Okay," he said. "So how is Maelleen going to help us?"

Venessta stood and walked over to Maelleen. "Please stand."

Maelleen stood and towered over the young woman.

Venessta said, "Jax is a little taller than the average man, and she's certainly taller than the average woman. She can be his sister, Katrina. And she doesn't have to know all the politics of Val d'Ossa because she's just another bumpkin from Lieudess."

She spun toward the old witch. "We could spread some rumors that there might be a hint of incest among our relatives from Lieudess. They are, after all, rather provincial."

"Excellent idea, my dear," the old witch said. "That'll put them off a bit."

"Yes, they won't know if it's true or not."

The old woman shook her head. "No, dear. I'm afraid they will know."

Venessta's brow wrinkled. "But how?"

"The way he looks at her, dear. It's not the look a young man would give his sister."

Maelleen grinned and said, "Sometimes he is rather obvious about it, isn't he?"

Jax cringed. "Would it help if I denied it?"

Venessta looked at Maelleen, and Jax could almost see the jealousy smoldering beneath the surface of her thoughts. He wondered if the old woman was pushing the jealousy thing a little too far.

Maelleen put her fists on her hips and asked, "So what did you have in mind for me?"

The Witch looked pensive for a moment. "I'm reluctant to ask a woman to spread her legs for a man."

With her fists still on her hips, Maelleen cocked her head to one side. "I am a prostitute, you know."

The two women looked at each other for a long, silent moment, then the Witch said, "But you'll have to do this willingly."

Maelleen said, "I am a willing prostitute, you know."

"So you like being a whore?" the Witch asked, a look of distaste on her face.

Maelleen didn't respond immediately, but stood there with her fists planted firmly on her hips and a matter-of-fact look on her face. She stood so still she could have been a statue made of stone. Then the look on her face slowly darkened and her eyes hardened. She lowered her hands to her sides and walked slowly toward the Witch, stopping only when she towered over the seated old women. Jax thought the look of alarm on Venessta's face mirrored his own, as they both held their breaths in anticipation of what Maelleen might do.

With her voice barely above a whisper, Maelleen said, "I like not starving to death, you hateful old woman. I like not sleeping on the street. I like not freezing to death during the winter. I like not living in filth. And I like making love to Jax."

The two women faced each other for the longest moment, then the Witch closed her eyes, and gave one, slow nod of her head. When she opened her eyes she looked at Maelleen with sadness. "I do apologize, my little harlot. That was . . . terribly insensitive of me."

"Apology accepted," Maelleen said, and Jax could breathe again. He noticed Venessta carefully exhale.

Maelleen stepped back from the old woman and said, "So what do you have in mind for me?"

The manipulative old crone grinned happily. "High Lord Carkoska; I'm thinking you could seduce Carkoska himself."

The thought of Maelleen seducing a High Lord frightened Jax. "That could be dangerous. What will that accomplish?"

"Perhaps nothing," the Witch said. "Then again, she might learn something useful. Or perhaps we'll need him dead at some point, and she'll be in a position to help our assassin gain entry and kill the fellow. Or, he'll become so enamored with her, he'll have his wife murdered, and then our little harlot will have found her rich husband."

"Or," Maelleen said, looking at Jax, "I'll be in a position to help *you* gain entry to High House Carkoska when it's time to steal the figurine."

"She's quite intelligent," the Witch said. She stood up. "So we're agreed. She'll be your sister from Lieudess. It's settled. We have a team." She looked at each of them in turn. "My little witch, my little thief, and my little harlot."

She leaned toward Maelleen, who towered over the older woman. "This weekend, my dear, we'll take the air in Samanski Park where we'll meet High Lord Carkoska. How soon do you think you can have him in bed?"

Maelleen frowned as if the old woman had asked a ridiculous question. "Not as soon as you might think."

The Witch returned the frown and Maelleen continued, "I can probably get him in bed rather quickly if I want to, but I don't. You see, the more he wants me, and the longer he can't have me, the more he'll want me."

The old witch smiled happily and nodded. "I'm so glad we have a professional handling this."

She turned to Venessta and held out her arm. "Come, my child. It's time for us to retire."

Venessta helped the old woman out of the room. As the door closed behind them, Maelleen grabbed Jax, pressed him against the wall and kissed him passionately. He would have enjoyed it if his mind wasn't focused on keeping the two of them alive.

She finished the kiss, then ran a line of kisses up his neck and stopped at his ear. She whispered, "Make the little witch want to keep you alive," and he understood that the kiss had been a ruse so they could speak privately, "then hopefully she'll make the old witch want to keep you alive. Then make the little witch want to keep me alive, then hopefully she'll make the old witch want to keep me alive as well. It's our only chance. You have to seduce the girl. And you have my permission to enjoy yourself when you do."

The door creaked open and a knight said, "Here, now, enough of that. At least try to *act* like decent people."

19

A Little Disagreement

JAX WAITED IN the courtyard wearing one of his day suits, with riding pants and tall, black boots that ended a little below the knees. He held the reins of the mare and patted her nose to keep her calm. Nearby, two coachmen waited in the box of an open carriage drawn by two black horses. It had seats that faced each other from both front and rear, with a large chest strapped to the back of it.

Escorted by Captain Darganna and several knights, the Witch, Venessta and Maelleen walked out of the palace proper. The Witch wore a gown with full skirts, a high collar and long sleeves, which was not uncommon among older women. The two younger women wore more stylish gowns with slim lines and empire waists. All three wore high, peaked bonnets to shield their faces from the sun.

Venessta had opted for a low-cut dress that exposed her neck and a tiny bit of cleavage. She wore long gloves that extended up past her elbows and ended just short of little puffy sleeves on her upper arms. She had carefully draped a shawl over her shoulders in a way that didn't hide any of the exposed skin, and she carried a parasol to protect her from the sun.

The Witch said to her, "Take care, child, not to get too much sun on that delicate complexion of yours."

Maelleen had chosen exactly the opposite, a pale blue gown with a high collar and long delicate sleeves. It completely covered her chest right up to the neck and exposed nothing, deemphasizing her ample bosom. It surprised Jax to realize that she was just as sexy with nothing but her hands and face exposed to view. But there was something different about Maelleen, and it took Jax a moment to understand exactly what. She and he had worked hard on her lessons so she could pretend to be a noblewoman, but to transform her from beautiful to elegant had taken a combination of lady's maids and the two witches; a woman's touch.

Captain Darganna helped the Witch into the back seat of the carriage. Then he helped the two young women into the front seat so they sat facing her. Jax climbed into the mare's saddle, and the Witch said to the coachmen, "Samanski Park, though we're not in any hurry."

Samanski Park had been constructed in the middle of the District of Noble Houses. Broad, tree-lined avenues snaked through the park separating lush, grassy meadows with intimate little pathways meandering through opulent gardens. Jax had long ago explored it carefully and knew it well. He'd hidden in it a couple of times to elude pursuit when a night job had gone bad in one of the nearby mansions.

As they pulled out of the palace courtyard, a troop of eight mounted Witch Knights joined them, four in front, four behind. They rode through the city at a brisk pace, but when they pulled into the park, the Witch instructed the coachmen to slow to an easy walk, while Jax, on his mare, trotted beside the open carriage. They moved down a broad avenue paved with finely crushed gravel. Tall elm trees lined both sides of the avenue and their branches formed an arch overhead, shielding them from the heat of the late morning sun.

The summer day proved to be comfortably cool, and Jax found the ride in the open air refreshing. The two young women seemed to enjoy themselves, and so did the old witch, but Jax had come to realize that she remained ever on guard.

The Witch said, "I rarely take the air in the park, so our presence here should draw a bit of attention. I've let it be known that I'm doing so today because Katrina has just arrived from Lieudess, and I want to show her about. I've also had my knights spread some rumors about her exquisite beauty. Everyone will be most curious to see Venessta's stunning cousin."

Maelleen asked, "How do you know he'll be here?"

The two coachmen were within hearing, so they couldn't speak openly about Carkoska and many other things.

The Witch said, "He always takes the air on the weekend, frequently with his sons, and never with his wife or daughters. It's an ideal setting for your first meeting."

Maelleen nodded and smiled.

Everyone in the park took notice of the Witch's carriage. Ladies in carriages going the other way on the broad avenue nodded their bonneted heads politely, while mounted noblemen reached up and touched the bill of their top hats in a gracious gesture of respect. High Lord Samatain, riding in the opposite direction, actually reined his horse around, reversed course, and pulled up beside the Witch's carriage. He touched the bill of his top hat and said, "Good morning, Mother. It's good to see you about."

The Witch introduced Jax and Maelleen, then she and Samatain chatted politely for a bit. Jax got the impression that besides their actual words, they were having some sort of unspoken conversation as well. Then Samatain excused himself, reversed course again, and spurred his horse into a trot to catch up to his ladies and their carriage.

Up ahead Jax spotted Carkoska mounted on a white stallion, riding toward them on the other side of the broad avenue. He recognized him immediately because of his golden mane of hair and his girth. Beside him rode a couple of younger men, both fashionably dressed. When they came abreast of the Witch's carriage, they executed the same maneuver as Samatain, and pulled their horses up beside the carriage. Carkoska greeted the Witch and her apprentice with, "Mother. Mistress Venessta." Then he looked at Maelleen and said, "But I don't believe I've had the pleasure of meeting this lovely creature."

Jax watched Maelleen turn on her seductive charms as she batted her eyelashes shyly and blushed like a maiden schoolgirl. Maelleen never blushed, so somehow she had done that on purpose, a thoroughly impressive performance. Watching Carkoska respond to her, Jax now understood what Maelleen had meant when she'd told him even his eyes had an erection.

The Witch made the introductions, finishing by pointing out Jax. "And, of course, you remember her brother, Roland, from that Tray'enall soiree last week."

Jax could see by the look on Carkoska's face that he didn't remember, but he lied. "Of course, young man. Of course. Good to see you again."

Carkoska introduced his two sons to Jax and Maelleen. Martin appeared to be a few years younger than Jax, while Samuel appeared to be about sixteen, and was obviously the boy who had shown Venessta the locked office. Both had inherited their father's looks and wavy, blond hair, and by the way the buttons on their waistcoats puckered from the strain of their bellies, Jax guessed they would also develop his girth as they grew older.

The Witch said, "We were just about to stop for a little lunch. Would you care to join us?"

"We'd love to," Carkoska said. He couldn't take his eyes off Maelleen. "That's most gracious of you, Mother."

At the Witch's instructions, the coachmen pulled the carriage off the avenue and stopped near a grassy knoll where other small groups had spread blankets. Jax, the Carkoskas, and the knights dismounted, and two of the knights took charge of the horses. While the coachmen and a couple of the knights hefted the large chest off the back of the carriage, Jax helped the ladies step down out of the coach.

They spread a blanket in the shade beneath a large oak tree. From the chest, the coachmen produced three wooden folding chairs, chilled wine, delicate little sandwiches, sweets, cheeses and fruits. They opened the folding chairs for the ladies, Carkoska's sons sat down and lounged on the blanket, while Carkoska stood next to Maelleen's chair. Jax leaned against the trunk of the oak tree to watch her performance.

They spent about an hour eating while Maelleen played Carkoska like a finely tuned harp. She batted her eyelashes at him, paid rapt attention to his discourse on the politics of Val d'Ossa, laughed at all his jokes, even blushed when he told one slightly off-color, though he'd been careful not to push the bounds of propriety when doing so. Jax noticed that when the ladies were not looking Carkoska's way, his eyes invariably focused on Maelleen's chest, then returned quickly to her face when any of the ladies turned their attention to him.

••••

If Maelleen had found Carkoska unattractive she would have soldiered on and seduced him anyway. His girth bothered her a bit, but he had a strong jaw and attractive features, and he appeared to take his personal hygiene seriously, so she could enjoy herself with him, especially given his apparently vast wealth. But his preoccupation with her breasts made it clear his thoughts had focused on a quick, one-time romp in bed, and she needed to steer him toward the idea of a more sustained relationship.

She purposefully surprised him by abruptly standing. "I feel like a little walk." She pointed to a narrow pathway. "Perhaps among those roses over there."

She asked Venessta, "Would you care to join me?"

It wouldn't be appropriate for her to ask one of the men, Roland being the only exception since he was auspiciously her brother. And as she and Venessta had planned earlier, the girl shook her head. "I shouldn't get too much sun, so I think I'll stay here in the shade."

One of Carkoska's sons started to rise, but the older man beat him to it and stepped forward. "I'd be happy to accompany you, young lady." He turned toward the Witch. "If Mother approves, of course."

As propriety demanded, Maelleen looked to the old woman for permission.

The Witch waved a hand impatiently. "Go. Enjoy yourselves. And you'll be visible on that path, so there's no need for a chaperone."

Carkoska held out his arm and Maelleen took it. They headed down the gravel-strewn path that meandered among carefully tended roses. As the Witch had pointed out, the path never took them out of sight, though it led them far enough from the group that no one could hear their words.

As they strolled, Carkoska asked, "What is your impression of Val d'Ossa, Mistress Katrina?"

She feigned indifference. "It is certainly less provincial than Lieudess."

He paused and for once looked her in the face. "You sound bored."

She shrugged. "Not bored, exactly, but the old woman and Venessta can be tiresome company, if they're all one has."

Still focused on her face, his eyes narrowed thoughtfully. "I begin to think you're not the flighty young woman I thought."

She smiled knowingly, the way one might give a close confidant a private glance. "Propriety dictates so much of our behavior." She reached out and touched his shoulder in a proper and polite way, but still a gesture that hinted at the possibility of more intimacy. "At least when in public, does it not?"

"Yes," he said, nodding, still looking into her eyes. "Propriety."

She could almost see his thoughts racing.

They continued their stroll, and she steered the conversation back to the politics of Val d'Ossa. He didn't reveal anything of significance, but now he spoke of more serious matters, not the humorous vignettes of some nobleman's foolish indiscretions. When they returned to the larger group, Maelleen knew the High Lord's interest in her had increased considerably.

The coachmen repacked the chest and tied it to the back of the carriage. Jax, Venessta, Maelleen, and Carkoska's sons gathered near the carriage, while the Witch and the High Lord held back and spoke privately for a moment. Then the two older people joined them at the carriage and they said their good-byes. Carkoska kissed the hand of each lady as he helped her into the carriage. He kissed Maelleen's last, then held it for a long moment while looking into her eyes. She took care not to beam at him like a young schoolgirl, but gave him a touch of smile with one eyebrow slightly raised, a look he would know was intended only for him. His eyes sparkled with desire.

The Carkoskas rode away, Jax and the knights mounted up, and the coachmen pulled the carriage back out onto the broad avenue going back the way they had come.

They rode in silence for a minute, then the Witch leaned forward, her eyes focused on Maelleen. "He wants to throw a small, afternoon soiree later this week. He feels obliged to introduce you properly to Val d'Ossan society, so you'll have made some acquaintances before the ball. And of course, I gave my permission. The invitations will go out tomorrow."

Venessta looked at Maelleen and said, "I think I have a lot to learn, and I don't mean witchcraft."

The old witch leaned back in her seat and steepled her fingers in front of her. She locked eyes with Maelleen and frowned. "Are you sure you're not a witch?"

Maelleen thought it best to answer her with a simple smile.

••••

Jax had noticed time and again that the Witch had uncanny hearing. When practicing dance steps, and holding Venessta in a close embrace, he'd tested that conclusion by whispering something provocative in the young woman's ear, keeping his voice low. Anyone else, seated across the room near the Witch, with the musicians playing nearby, would have heard nothing. But more than once, the Witch had immediately commented on his words, sometimes with one of her offhand, acerbic remarks. And a couple of times now, when Jax had posed a question to Venessta, hoping to gain some valuable information, the Witch had intervened, deflecting the question like a seasoned politician. Jax had concluded that if the Witch was in the room, she heard every word uttered regardless of volume, distance, or background noise. He hadn't yet figured out how to determine if she had some magical ability to hear every word spoken in the entire Witch Palace. He was forced to assume there must be some limits to her ability.

He was pleased that morning when Venessta showed up for dance practice arm-in-arm with Maelleen, and no Witch of Val d'Ossa present. Perhaps today he could learn a thing or two from the younger woman. "Where is Mother?" he asked.

He didn't like referring to the Witch in that way, but such things were required, so he complied.

Maelleen wore one of the dresses the seamstress had made for her, which contributed to her transformation to an elegant noblewoman. The cheap dresses she'd worn in her father's pub showed considerably more flesh, and yet, without all that exposure, she still exuded a sexuality few women could match. "Yes," she said. "Where is the old witch?"

Venessta shrugged. "She has some business with High Lord Naesmyth."

Jax had met Carkoska, Tray'enall, and Samatain, but had yet to meet Naesmyth, the fourth and final Lord of a High Noble House. Carkoska was reputed to be the most powerful, Samatain the least, with Tray'enall and Naesmyth somewhere in the middle.

Venessta deposited Maelleen on the couch where the old witch normally sat, then walked out to the center of the room where Jax waited. The musicians began playing, he took Venessta in his arms, and they danced.

Venessta had a certain look in her eye that day. Jax wasn't sure what to expect, but it made him wary. Then he noticed that she kept throwing furtive glances Maelleen's way, and it occurred to him that it was the first time he and she had danced in front of the harlot. Venessta was planning something, though if she hoped to compete with Maelleen, she didn't stand a chance.

At the beginning of the third dance Venessta pulled him into the intimate embrace that made a waltz almost impossible. Jax really didn't mind if she wanted to show off in front of Maelleen. He never begrudged a pretty woman who wanted him to hold her inappropriately close, and he always enjoyed embracing Venessta that way.

The little witch had occasionally blurted out an indiscreet answer before considering her words, so in the old woman's absence, Jax hoped he might finally learn a thing or two. He waited until half way into the dance, then whispered, "I've been wondering about this figurine I'm supposed to steal."

She tilted her head back a little and looked him in the eyes. "Yes, what about it?"

"Well, you and the Witch have never seen it before. And Carkoska keeps it locked away, hidden in a room where no one ever sees it. That seems odd to me."

"Why is that?"

Jax smiled, bent his head down and brushed his lips lightly along the side of her neck. Her breathing quickened a little. "A valuable piece of artwork like that," he said. "Carkoska strikes me as the type of man who displays his wealth for all to see. And yet, he hides away this incredibly valuable figurine behind a locked door. To me, that seems out of character for him."

She stopped dancing, stepped back, and demanded, "What are you saying?"

"There's something about this figurine you're not telling us." He shrugged and held up his hands in a placating gesture. "And that bothers me greatly."

Venessta's lips tightened into a pucker and her eyes narrowed. She turned and marched toward Maelleen like a soldier on a field of combat. The tune the musicians were playing dwindled, then died on a few misplaced notes.

Venessta stood over Maelleen. "Come, whore, let's see you dance with the thief."

Maelleen smiled and lifted one eyebrow. She stood and crossed the room to Jax, and as she did so she poured her sexuality into the room the way a footman pours wine delicately into a lady's glass. Neither Jax nor the musicians were immune to her when she did that, and while the musicians didn't miss a note, their eyes followed her every move.

The musicians played, Jax took her in his arms, but held her at the appropriate distance, and they danced. She clearly enjoyed herself. "I think I'm beginning to understand this ancient magical art of raising a bulge."

"Oh no," Jax said, returning her smile. "You advanced beyond the beginning stages long ago. And you women speak as if it's actually visible, but I know it's not, because I do have better control than that. There is no bulge."

She gave him a satisfied smile. "There is in your eyes, darling."

He shrugged and lifted an eyebrow. "I forgot about that."

They danced two more dances, then Venessta suddenly stood and said to the musicians, "We're done here. You may go."

The music ended abruptly. Jax and Maelleen stopped dancing and separated. The musicians quickly packed up their instruments and left.

Venessta said to Jax and Maelleen, "Good day." Then she walked out the door, leaving the two of them momentarily alone.

Jax pressed Maelleen against the wall and planted kisses up her neck, stopping at her ear, using the same subterfuge she had used to whisper in his ear. He spoke softly, "I challenged her on the figurine: they've never seen it and it's locked away. None of it adds up."

"I know," she said.

"I didn't get anything out of her."

"Don't worry, darling, I'm sure you'll get something when you seduce her."

Behind him, Jax heard Venessta gasp, "Oh."

Jax released Maelleen and turned around. Venessta had reentered the room with their escort of knights behind her. She raised her chin and gave Jax and Maelleen a haughty look. "I suppose we should lock the two of you in a room so you can rut. What's your going rate, whore?"

Maelleen started, and Jax watched her strain to contain her anger. She always presented a tough, matter-of-fact exterior to the world, but Jax knew she could be insulted and hurt just like anyone, and woe to the fool who touched a nerve. Venessta had put such venom into the word *whore* that Jax wanted to cross the room and slap her, though he thought Maelleen might do that for him. But she stiffened, and quickly hid whatever feelings roiled beneath her exterior calm.

She stepped past Jax and walked up to Venessta. "Dear," she said, "you should try rutting with him yourself. Let me assure you you'll be pleased with the result. Sometimes I can hardly walk for a day or two afterwards."

Venessta's eyes widened and blinked rapidly. Maelleen had exaggerated just to irritate her.

Jax tensed, waiting for the two women to start hissing and scratching at each other, like two feral cats in an alley.

Maelleen reached up and traced a finger along Venessta's cheek. "I can see you've thought about it. I'll bet you've fantasized about him, haven't you? Well trust me, dear, the real thing is a lot more satisfying than whatever you're using now, and much, much larger."

Maelleen left her standing there with her mouth open, eyes wide, her face a bright, scarlet red.

20

Talents Exposed

JAX LEARNED FROM one of the servants that the Witch Palace did have an enormous dining hall with a massive table, just as he had imagined. But that evening the knights again escorted him to the smaller, more intimate dining room in which they'd dined previously. Maelleen had preceded him, and the Witch and her apprentice joined them shortly thereafter.

Jax went through the ritual of seating each of the ladies as a gentleman should. Just as he and Maelleen practiced dancing almost daily, he guessed that they would now practice dining as well, and the art of polite conversation—and polite evasion, and polite back-stabbing, all the things required of young nobles.

The Witch seemed to read his thoughts. "I can't let you become complacent. Mustn't have you giving us away with some little slip."

"I was raised this way," Jax said. "We were certainly not this wealthy, and we didn't live this elegantly, but we did live properly."

The Witch nodded toward Maelleen. "But she didn't. And how much need did *you* have for proper manners while living in the slums for the last nine years?"

"I concede the point," he said, though he felt a bit insulted that she thought he might have forgotten his manners.

"Thank you," the Witch said. "For the next several weeks, you two are going to live the life to which you're pretending. Thinking and acting properly must become reflex, instinct, mundane. You'll speak of nothing controversial at the dinner table, nor afterward when chatting amiably with your contemporaries—I suppose I should say, your *pretend* contemporaries. You can broach a sensitive subject when speaking one-on-one with an intimate, or with a small, but select, group, but caution is required even then."

They chatted politely while they ate. The Witch corrected Maelleen on only a few minor things.

Jax hadn't made a lot of friends in the slums, but he recalled one or two boisterous dinners in The Angry Bear with Maelleen, Marcus and Bethy after the tavern had closed for the night. And after they'd eaten, he and Maelleen had enjoyed each other's company in a more intimate setting. He thought he rather preferred the louder conversation when eating in the pub. And he realized that that now made him just as much of an imposter as Maelleen.

After dinner they retired to the sitting room. The women sat down demurely, while Jax stood at the hearth nearby. Maelleen had completely turned off her sexuality and appeared to be a shy, young noblewoman not unlike Venessta. It amazed Jax the way she could switch it off like blowing out the flame on a candle. Servants brought them cordials, and as soon as the last of the help left the room, the Witch said, "About this figurine."

"Yes," Maelleen said. "About this figurine."

The Witch aimed her comments at Jax. "You had some questions that you posed to my little witch yesterday."

Jax said, "As I recall, I didn't pose any questions, but I did make a few observations."

"And those were?"

He raised one finger. "Neither of you have ever seen this figurine before. Why is that?"

The Witch smiled unpleasantly. "That wasn't merely an observation. You also asked a question."

He couldn't help but admire her masterful ability at evasion. "Yes, I did."

She sat in silence for several seconds, and he wondered if she would answer him at all. She seemed to come to a decision. "It's very old, and until recently had been lost for quite some time."

He raised a second finger. "You've never seen it. So how do you know what it looks like?"

Again, she hesitated for a long moment before answering. "It is described in some old texts, but with only a simple written description, no sketches or drawings, so our understanding of its appearance is limited."

"How old are these texts?"

"Very old."

"So the figurine is as old as, or even older than, the texts?"

"Older. They were written centuries after it was originally made."

He raised a third finger. "The figurine really has no monetary value, does it?"

The Witch's eyes narrowed with distrust as she answered. "No, it does have some monetary value; quite a bit, in fact."

Since she had finally agreed to answer some questions, Jax decided not to stop until she refused to go further. "But its real value to you is not monetary?"

He watched her think about her answer carefully. He already knew the answer to that question, so if she spoke truthfully, nothing would change, but if she lied, he'd trust her even less. Apparently, she came to the same conclusion. "I think it's rather obvious I don't need the money."

"Thank you," he said.

"You're welcome."

"So I must conclude that the figurine's real value to you has something to do with witchery."

She cocked her head and looked at him like a magistrate examining a felon. "I'm always wary of an intelligent opponent. But it heartens me to see that the two of you"—she glanced at Maelleen, then back at him—"are far more intelligent than I had first assumed. It gives me greater hope we will succeed at this enterprise."

"Must we be opponents?" he asked. "Why not allies?"

She smiled and nodded. "I think we're slowly working our way toward that kind of relationship, though a rapport of that nature requires time to develop. It also requires trust, and we do need to work on the trust issue."

"There is that," he said. "I assume you don't trust us any more than we trust you."

She raised both eyebrows, conceding the point.

Jax's instinct warned him a second before the door opened and he glanced toward it. The door opened and Captain Darganna stepped into the room. He stopped just within the threshold and said, "Mother."

She said, "Thank you, Captain. You may go."

Darganna stepped back out of the room and closed the door.

Jax's thoughts roiled with confusion at Darganna's meaningless entry and exit. Maelleen gave him a perplexed look that probably mirrored that on his own face. The Witch and her apprentice both shared a satisfied smile.

Venessta said to the old woman, "This time you saw it too, didn't you?"

The Witch didn't respond. She stood, shed about twenty years of age, and Jax recalled that as she grew angry, she grew younger. She took a step and dropped a decade of age, another step and another decade. By the time she reached Jax she had transformed into the beautiful young woman he'd seen once before, and she marched at him with no hint of her infirmity. Jax stepped back, but he hit the wall and dropped his drink. As the glass shattered on the floor, Maelleen's eyes grew wide with fear, again, probably mirroring the look on his own face.

The Witch stopped with her chin only a hand's breadth from his. She spit words in his face, her anger an overwhelming presence in the room. "That was a little test, my little thief. You glanced toward the door an instant before it opened."

"I . . ." he said. "I heard something that drew my attention."

"No you didn't," she snarled. "I put that test together very carefully, and you fell for it nicely. You have a special little ability, don't you? That's why you've been such a successful thief all these years; never been caught, jailed, or imprisoned. And except for my little harlot, none of your friends have ever learned the truth about you."

She turned away from him and returned to the couch. By the time she reached it, her years again hung heavily about her shoulders, and she eased herself down carefully.

She looked at Jax, and the satisfied smile returned. "So, my little thief. I've answered your questions, now you're going to tell me about this little talent of yours."

As Jax stood with his back still pressed against the wall, his heart pounding in his chest, he saw the look on Maelleen's face change from fear to curiosity.

Venessta maintained her smug, self-satisfied look and said, "I saw it first, and alerted Mother."

Jax didn't think Little Miss Trouble would appreciate the expletives that came to mind.

The old witch just stared at him, waiting for him to say something.

Jax swallowed and managed to calm his racing heart. "It's just . . . instinct, nothing special."

The Witch leaned forward, lost about ten years of age and pointed a shaking finger at him. "Don't forget who you're talking to, little thief. Lie to me again, and I will turn you into a toad. Or better yet, we'll start cutting little bits off of you."

The look on Maelleen's face slowly changed from curiosity to thoughtful calculation. "I think he is telling the truth, Mother. At least, as he believes it to be."

She stood, and he watched her switch on the sexuality, just the way a full moon on a cloudy night suddenly appears from behind a dark cloud, lighting up the entire landscape in an instant. The change in her was so dramatic, the Witch and Venessta must have seen it as well, because they both gave her a curious, questioning look.

Maelleen walked slowly toward him, saying, "I don't think he's truly aware of it. What is it that you are aware of, darling? Tell me. Please."

"I just have an instinct," he said, wondering if he should fear the harlot's sexuality even more than the Witch's power. "Sometimes I just have a feeling and take a guess, like when to step out into the street, or when not to. But when the feeling comes to me I know with absolute certainty it is right."

She stopped at an intimately close distance, reached up and traced a finger along the line of his jaw. "Did you ever have that feeling when we were making love? Did you ever anticipate my next desire?"

With the effect she had on him at the moment, he could only answer her truthfully. "To be honest, when I'm with you I'm always too preoccupied to think about it, so I really wouldn't know."

At that moment, all Jax could think about was all sorts of sordid things he wanted to do to Maelleen right then and there. And he was ready to do those things on the floor in front of the two witches. He leaned forward, brushed his lips across her cheek, moving slowly toward her mouth. Maelleen switched off her sexuality, and all his desire disappeared. Well, almost all of it.

She gave him a thoughtful, knowing nod. "I understand. I'm always just as preoccupied while you do to me what you do."

She turned around to face the two witches. "I think he's telling the truth. I think he's only vaguely aware of what he's doing."

She walked across the room and sat down next to Venessta, then she leaned close to the little witch and said, "I never realized it before, but when I think back on it, whenever we made love and one of those moments came when I was about to think there was something I'd particularly like him to do to me, he did it to me just as the thought occurred, almost every time."

The little witch's eyes widened.

Still leaning close to her, Maelleen added, "It makes the pleasure so much more intense."

The Witch said, "There's an element of prescience to that, which could be powerful."

The little witch turned to the old woman. "Do you think he's a witch?"

"Oh dear," the old witch said. "I begin to wonder if they might both be witches."

••••

During the ride to the soiree at High House Carkoska, the old witch sat Maelleen next to her on the rear seat, with Venessta and Jax facing them on the front seat. As the carriage jostled and swayed down the cobblestoned street, she said to Maelleen, "Now, dear, remember that Lady Carkoska knows full well her husband is a philanderer. She's aware he maintains a mistress somewhere, sometimes more than one at the same time. But never turn on the full extent of your charms in her presence. Our young thief here was ready to rape you on the sitting room floor right in front of us."

"It wouldn't have been rape," Maelleen said. "It would have been fully consensual, and I would have certainly enjoyed myself."

"Right in front of us?" Venessta asked, her nose wrinkled with distaste.

Maelleen said, "Oh posh, don't forget I am a harlot. And I'll bet you would have enjoyed the show, and probably learned a thing or two as well."

Venessta blushed. She clearly didn't control her blushing the way Maelleen did.

"In any case," the Witch said. "Your charms, in full blossom, are much too . . . effective, and should you allow Lady Carkoska to witness them, she'll have you murdered in short order. She's not known for her charity and kindness, so keep it toned down in her presence."

Maelleen said, "I'll do absolutely nothing. I'll just be a pretty, vapid, naive bumpkin from Lieudess. But even then, I guarantee you he'll be longing for me before the afternoon is done, and he won't be able to put me out of his thoughts after we leave."

Venessta asked, "How do you do that?"

Maelleen spoke with obvious pride. "Practice."

The Witch leaned toward her and patted her wrist. "My dear, I have the utmost confidence in you. You are a consummate professional, after all."

Venessta said, "And let's not forget that Lady Carkoska has had a string of lovers as well, and her husband is certainly aware of them. She prefers younger men"—she looked Jax's way—"about your age, in fact."

Venessta's eyes widened and she said, "Oh, I just had a thought. Should we have Jax seduce her as well? Maelleen can bed Lord Carkoska, while Jax beds his lady wife."

Jax's instinct hit him strongly, and without thinking he snapped, "Absolutely not."

Maelleen raised an eyebrow at his reaction. Venessta's eyes narrowed and the Witch asked, "Is that your instinct speaking?"

Jax nodded.

Maelleen said, "I think we should trust Jax's instinct. And in any case, that would be an unnecessary complication. His particular talents in the bed don't really have an effect until he's already got you on your back . . ." She smiled wistfully for a moment. ". . . or in any number of other wonderful positions."

Venessta blushed again.

Jax said, "You know, I'm sitting right here."

Venessta ignored him. "But if his instinct helps him anticipate what you'd like in bed, perhaps he can learn to use it to anticipate what a woman wants to hear, and that might help him get her there."

Maelleen shook her head, and the Witch said to Venessta, "Lady Carkoska can be quite dangerous, usually more so than her husband. Let's trust the harlot, and Jax's instinct."

"Yes, Mother."

The Witch turned back to Maelleen. "Something to keep in mind, dear, is that if Jax is unable to acquire the figurine during the ball, he'll have to break in to High House Carkoska at some later time. And we'll need you there to help him get in. So I think you should try to get that fat, old fart to bed you in his own house the first time. He's done it before, and discreetly enough that Lady Carkoska didn't have the young woman murdered. But he's going to want to get his penis out of his pants in short order."

Maelleen said, "I do hope his penis isn't in short order."

The old woman gave her a sharp, unhappy look.

Maelleen lowered her eyes and said, "Sorry, Mother."

The Witch ignored the interruption and continued. "And we did spread a few rumors about incest. That'll keep him a little off guard, but it'll also give him hope that you're approachable. Just keep in mind that you're going to have to keep him interested, and fend him off at the same time, until we can orchestrate the right opportunity."

Maelleen waved a hand dismissively. "I shouldn't have any trouble doing that."

The Witch smiled contentedly.

As the carriage pulled through the main gate of High House Carkoska and into the courtyard in front of the house, Jax wondered if he and Maelleen would survive the afternoon, let alone this entire fiasco.

21

Reconnaissance

PASSING THROUGH THE main gate and onto the Carkoska property in broad daylight was an opportunity Jax couldn't waste. So at his request he'd been seated on the left side of the carriage, knowing that the coachman would pull the right side of the carriage up to the house. When the carriage stopped, Jax stepped out the door on the left, while the women exited on the right with the aid of footmen. The front yard of the house stretched out before Jax, and it gave him an opportunity to examine it carefully without having to specifically walk around the carriage to do so.

A broad driveway paved in crushed stone stretched from the gate to a large turnaround in front of the house, with a tall fountain in the middle of the turnaround. The wall that separated them from the street stretched for more than a hundred feet on either side of the gate. He didn't see a stable and carriage house, but there had to be one and he guessed it must be somewhere near the back of the property. There might be other outbuildings as well.

Jax walked casually around the back of the carriage and joined the women just as they stepped into the house. The Witch leaned close to him and asked, "Learn anything?"

"Not much," he said, "though I didn't expect to. But one never knows. And it was helpful to get a look at the front gate from the inside."

The Witch escorted Venessta into the soiree, and behind them Roland escorted his sister Katrina. Word had gone out that Venessta's beautiful and vivacious cousin from Lieudess would be introduced to society, and all eyes followed her as they crossed the room. Maelleen didn't need to turn on her sexuality to have every man in the place hungering for her favors, and possibly some of the women as well.

A line of minor nobles waited to be received by Lord and Lady Carkoska, but it parted as the Witch approached with her retinue. Lady Carkoska stood beside her husband, a tall middle-aged beauty, with blond hair that had yet to show any gray. Even at her age the skin of her face—and the skin in the cleavage exposed at the top of her gown—remained smooth and unwrinkled. Her beauty easily rivaled that of the younger women in the room, and Jax's instinct told him to stay away from her.

Venessta could be girlish trouble, but something told him Lady Carkoska would be lethal trouble.

As the two witches greeted their hosts, Maelleen leaned close to Jax and whispered, "The Witch said she is dangerous, and looking at her now, I don't doubt it."

Jax nodded. "She frightens me."

The Witch introduced them, and Lord Carkoska said, "Master Roland and Mistress Katrina, good to see you again."

Lady Carkoska smiled warmly. "A pleasure to meet both of you." When her eyes passed over Jax she paused for a moment and looked him over from head to foot.

Jax kissed the lady's hand, then stepped aside.

When Maelleen curtsied, Jax got no hint of animosity in Lady Carkoska's demeanor. Maelleen wore the gown that exposed no skin below the high collar at her neck, and Jax had to look twice to realize he was staring at his Maelleen. Somehow she'd taken her sexuality in the other direction, and seemed almost plain. Jax had to admit that was quite a feat.

As they spoke in a small group, Lord Carkoska carefully avoided paying too much attention to Maelleen. But Lady Carkoska kept glancing Jax's way, and when their eyes met once or twice, she smiled warmly, coquettishly. She certainly carried herself well and had much to attract a man's eye. Under other circumstances Jax might have considered the invitation he saw in her eyes, but his instinct kept warning him off.

He caught Venessta giving him a nasty look. When the time came to move on and allow their host and hostess to greet others, Lady Carkoska took Jax's hand. She wrapped his hand in both of hers and caressed it warmly. "It's been a real pleasure meeting you, Master Roland. Perhaps you'd like to call on me some time . . . for afternoon . . . tea." Her manner made it clear she really meant afternoon *everything but tea.*

When they left the Carkoskas to mingle with the other guests, Venessta pulled him aside and hissed at him, "Are you doing that thing to her?"

He didn't have the vaguest idea what she was talking about. "Doing what thing?"

"Doing that thing where you know exactly what to say to get her in bed."

"No, you're the one who came up with that idea. I don't even know how to do that. And you've heard everything I've said to her this afternoon. I'm not trying to get her into bed. I don't want to get her into bed."

"Afternoon tea," Venessta spit. "She didn't mean afternoon tea. She clearly had a lot more in mind than just tea."

"I know that. And anyway, we all did agree I wouldn't get near her."

"You didn't agree. You may have said no at first, but only we women agreed."

"Well I'm agreeing now. And anyway, she's not my type."

"What is your type?"

"It certainly isn't dangerous older women."

"I'm beginning to think your type is anyone with breasts."

Venessta didn't storm away in an obvious huff. She'd been too well trained to make such a scene. But every time he caught her eye that afternoon, she gave him a hard, cold look.

Someone grabbed his elbow, and he turned to find the old witch there. She pulled on his arm, forcing him to lean over so she could whisper in his ear. "And an afternoon filled with even more jealousy. You're doing a wonderful job with my little witch, young man. But watch out for Lady Carkoska. She's had a string of lovers, but they don't last long. And when she's done with them they frequently die of some strange and unknown cause. It's most unusual."

••••

Jax and Venessta had one important task for that afternoon: she had to show him where that locked office was located. The Witch reminded them both of that by pulling them aside and hissing, "Put your jealousy away, little witch. You have a job to do, so do it."

Venessta pouted as she spoke. "I'm not jea—"

The Witch silenced her by pressing a finger against her lips. "Do your job, child, while I keep Lord and Lady Carkoska occupied."

The old woman turned away from them, and the crowd of guests parted to allow her to pass. She crossed the room to the Carkoskas and the three of them walked to the side of the room, put their heads together, and began speaking in what was clearly meant to be a private conversation. No one would dare interrupt them.

Venessta took Jax's hand. "This way."

She led him out of the room through a side entrance that opened into a hallway. She actually started tiptoeing, but Jax put an end to that.

"No," he said. "Walk like you own the place. We'll get there faster, we'll get this over with sooner, and if someone catches us, we're not so obviously trying to sneak around. And try to think of some excuse for why we're lost if we do run into anyone."

She straightened and led him down the hall toward the back of the house. She started up a flight of stairs, but he halted her. "Where are we going?"

"At the top of the stairs," she said, "there's another hall. I think it's the fourth door on the left. It opens on a combination library and vestibule. The locked door to the office is in there."

"You wait here," he said. "If someone comes along and starts up the stairs, cough loudly. If you have to return without me, do so. I'll find my own way back."

She said, "But I—"

"Don't argue," he hissed. "I'm the one here who knows thieving."

He didn't wait for an answer, but turned and raced up the stairs, taking the steps three at a time. At the top he found a dark hallway exactly as she had described. There were no windows, so even during the day the hallway was lit by gas sconces spaced evenly along the wall, though they remained turned down and provided minimal illumination at best. At the fourth door on the left he gripped the latch, took a deep breath, and decided that if it was the wrong door and he encountered anyone, he'd pretend to be drunk. It wouldn't do much for Master Roland's reputation, but he'd deal with that later if necessary.

He turned the latch and stepped into the room without hesitation, staggering a little to reinforce the excuse of drunkenness, but there was no one else present. The room had been furnished with a cushioned chair and a small writing table. Two sconces on the walls remained unlit as well as a lamp on the writing table. He always carried matches when doing his night work. He'd have to remember to bring a candle as well when he came back, because he couldn't count on the lamp being there in the future. Books lined the walls on either side, with a closed door in the middle of the wall opposite him.

Leaving the door to the hallway open so he had some light, Jax crossed the room quickly, grabbed the latch on the second door, and prepared to use the same excuse if it opened and he encountered someone. It was locked.

He retrieved the lamp from the small table, lit it with a match, then closed the door to the hallway. He bent down and carefully examined the lock mechanism on the office door. He had seen its type before and thought he could pick it, but he needed the right tools. He straightened, extinguished the lamp, returned it to the writing table, then stepped up to the hallway door and put his ear against it. He heard no voices or other sounds, so he slowly opened it and glanced up and down the hall: nothing. He raced down the hallway, stopped at the top of the stairs and peeked down to the landing below. Venessta stood there nervously tapping her foot. He raced down the stairs, took her hand, and they returned to the soiree without incident.

Back in the room with all the guests, she breathed an enormous sigh of relief. He asked her, "Why did you let young Samuel take you up there?"

She smiled unashamedly. "I let him take me up there to kiss me. The vestibule outside the office is a rather private place."

"He's a bit young for you, isn't he?"

"Well of course he is. I wasn't enjoying myself."

He doubted it was even possible for Little Miss Trouble to enjoy herself.

She looked at the doorway through which they'd just come. "Before we do this the next time, we'll have to think it through more carefully."

He shook his head and said, "I'm going alone the next time, so there won't be a next time for you."

She gave him a condescending smile. "Oh yes there will."

She refused to say anything further.

••••

The coachman snapped his whip; the carriage lurched forward and charged out through the main gate of High House Carkoska.

"Well?" the Witch said, aiming her question at Jax.

He shrugged. "There's a vestibule that leads to a locked door. I'm familiar with the type of lock so I'm reasonably confident I can pick it, but what lies beyond that, we won't know until I do."

Venessta said, "Samuel told me it's his father's private office, and he was terribly infatuated with me at the time, so I'm sure he didn't lie to me."

Again Jax shrugged. "He may not have lied to you, but his father might have lied to him, and the office is elsewhere. Or his father told him the truth, but the figurine isn't in the office. Or the figurine is in the office, but there are other protections or complications I can't overcome. There are just too many things we don't know."

He let that hang without further comment.

The Witch considered him for a moment. "Your points are all well taken, little thief. We won't know until we try. Can you try during the ball?"

Jax considered that the ideal time. "I don't see why not," he said. "I'll bring the proper tools to pick the door lock, and we'll see what happens."

Venessta added, "And I'll accompany him when he sneaks up there."

Jax could feel his temper rising as he leaned forward and pointed a finger at her. "And I've already told you that's not going to happen."

"But what if you do get the figurine?" she asked. "How are you going to hide it, stuff it down your pants? That'll be a bit obvious, won't it? And you won't be able to pretend that's the kind of bulge Maelleen produces in men."

He shook his head. "I'll figure out something before then." He knew he sounded unreasonable.

Venessta ignored him and looked at the old witch. "Mother, you know as well as I that, at these nighttime affairs, any number of young couples sneak away from the ballroom for a little tryst."

"Yes, dear," the Witch said. "And your point is?"

Venessta looked at Jax and gave him a nasty smile. "If Jax is discovered sneaking about by himself, it'll be obvious he's just sneaking about and he'll be in trouble. Conversely, if Jax is discovered sneaking about hand-in-hand with me, we're just an attractive young couple sneaking off for a little tryst. If we're discovered we'll tell them that."

The Witch turned her attention back to Jax. "She's got a point."

Maelleen intervened. "But no young couple would admit to an unchaperoned tryst. It could damage the young woman's reputation, so they'd come up with some other excuse. If you are discovered, he should throw you against a wall and kiss you passionately. Show, as they say, don't tell. Then after you're discovered, no one will think it odd that your denials ring false."

The Witch looked at Venessta and waited.

The young woman said, "Well, I can see how that would be more effective than just trying to talk our way out of it."

Maelleen added, "And he'll have to visibly fondle your breasts."

Venessta's back straightened. "I think that's going just a bit too far. I don't think that's at all necessary."

The Witch turned her attention on Maelleen and waited.

Maelleen said, "I am the professional in this kind of thing."

The Witch turned her look slowly back to Venessta. "You heard her."

"But, Mother, that's—"

The Witch sliced her finger through the air like a knife and pointed it at the young woman. "If you're discovered, he'll throw you against a wall, kiss you passionately and fondle your breasts. And I'll not listen to any argument about it."

Venessta pleaded, "Perhaps he might just *press* me against a wall as opposed to *throw* me there."

"I don't care if he presses you, throws you, or slams you. I don't care if it's against the wall or on the floor . . ."

Jax couldn't believe what he was hearing. Maelleen was doing everything she could to get him in bed with the little witch, and she had trouble concealing a smile as the Witch tore into Venessta. If he ever got Maelleen alone again in a room he decided to have a long talk with her.

While the two witches argued, Maelleen threw a surreptitious wink Jax's way. The wink seemed to say, "If I'm just a whore, then you're just a whore too."

Jax looked her in the eyes and said, "If you're just a whore, then I'm proud to be a whore too."

She gave him a smile that said the next time she got him alone, she would make him a very happy man. He hadn't realized there could be anything more she might do to make him happy, but then he was dealing with Maelleen, after all.

The Witch finished upbraiding the little witch, the younger woman lowered her eyes and said, "Yes, Mother."

The Witch swung the finger toward Jax. "And you, little thief, you're going to kiss her and fondle whatever you have to fondle to make sure you're not exposed for what you are, including fondling your own personals, if that's what it takes. Do you understand me?"

The Witch's fury had blossomed into a complete rage, but apparently not enough to turn her into the younger version of herself. Jax lowered his eyes and said, "Don't worry, Mother. I'll make sure she enjoys it."

The Witch frowned and hesitated. The little witch looked at Jax suspiciously, as if trying to understand what he'd meant by that. Maelleen grinned like a satisfied cat. Jax was beginning to think he needed to turn Maelleen over his knee, bare her pink, little bottom and give it a good spanking. But that wouldn't do any good, because if he did that, they'd just get distracted, and end up pursuing other activities.

After a brief pause, the old witch calmed, the heat left the carriage, and she said, "Well, I guess we've settled that."

She turned her attention to Maelleen. "And how did it go with Lord Carkoska?"

Maelleen said, "I paid more attention to his wife than him, and made sure she was always close when I came near him."

The Witch lifted a skeptical eyebrow. "Was that wise?"

"She and I get along nicely," Maelleen said. "I think she rather likes me, which will make it easier when I bed him; easier for me, him and her. Oh that's right, *he's* going to bed *me*, not vice versa. I'll have to keep that in mind."

The Witch said, "Little harlot, I felt you turn off your considerable charms like extinguishing a candle flame. How did that go?"

Maelleen smiled and nodded. "That's what made Lady Carkoska so comfortable with me."

"And Lord Carkoska?" the Witch asked.

"Trust me," Maelleen said. "Sometimes, all it takes to inflame a man's desire is the way you run your tongue across your lips to wet them. And such things are easily done in an instant when the lady is not looking. Right now High Lord Carkoska can think of nothing but me."

"Good," the old witch said. "Jax and Venessta will try to steal the figurine during the ball. And if that fails, you're our backup plan. Take whatever time you need to properly seduce the fat, old bastard."

The subject had clearly ended. But then the Witch said, "There is another factor we should consider."

She turned her gaze pointedly on Jax. "It was clear that Lady Carkoska would gladly allow you into her bed."

"No," Jax shouted, surprised he couldn't control his voice better. "I'm not getting near that woman."

Maelleen said, "I agree with him. She's dangerous. And let's not forget Jax's instinct in the matter, which is apparently quite accurate."

Even Venessta came to his defense. "And I too agree, Mother. She's poison, and I'm not willing to sacrifice one of us to her."

Jax sat there stunned. The little witch had said, *one of us*, as if he and Maelleen were actually part of this whole fiasco, not just hired help—*coerced* help, he reminded himself.

Apparently, the little witch saw the look on his face. She leaned toward him and said, "Don't worry, little thief. I can't let you be killed before I've allowed you to properly seduce me."

22

No Justice

THE WEEK LEADING up to the dress ball at High House Carkoska proved to be quite busy. It started with an argument with the old witch in her sitting room. Jax, Venessta and Maelleen were practicing their dance steps, though with both young women present, dancing seemed to have turned into a contest between the two of them to see who could torment Jax the most.

Venessta started it by pulling Jax out into the middle of the room, pressing herself tightly against him and insisting they dance that way. The Witch smiled, clearly pleased with the situation.

Jax danced next with Maelleen, who showed off by *not* pressing her body tightly against him. Jax could see in Venessta's eyes that Maelleen's casual indifference challenged her more than flaunting her assets would have. When the dance ended, Maelleen leaned close to him and said, "I'm sorry, darling, but the old woman expects me to fuel the little witch's jealousy."

He frowned. "That doesn't make life any easier for me."

She grimaced. "I know, but we have to keep the old woman happy."

He danced with Venessta next, then with Maelleen after that.

"Enough of this," the Witch said. "Can't you two have a little mercy on the poor fellow?"

Venessta said, "I don't know what you're talking about, Mother."

Jax didn't point out to the old woman that she had been the architect of the little contest between the two younger women.

The Witch dismissed the musicians with a wave of her hand. "We're done with the dancing. You may go."

They packed up their instruments and left.

It was time to broach an important subject. With the three women seated, Jax stood in front of them. "I need my tools."

"Tools?" the Witch said. "What do you mean by tools?"

He feared she wouldn't understand. "If I'm going to pick that lock, I need my tools to do so."

"What kind of tools?"

"A pick set and tension tools."

"And where are these tools?"

"At my flat."

She dismissed him by shaking her head. "We'll make new tools for you."

Jax tried not to let his exasperation show. "It's not that simple. It's a complete set of carefully formed picks and tools made from fine stainless steel. It could easily take more than a week to replicate them, and then I'd find myself in that room, trying to pick a lock with untested tools that I'm not familiar with."

"He has a point, Mother," Maelleen said. "That does sound like a recipe for failure. Can you get his tools for him?"

The Witch clearly didn't like where this was going. "I'll send some men to get them."

"And how will they gain entry to my flat," Jax asked, "identify themselves to my landlady as Knights of the Witchguard? Don't you think word of that will spread quickly, and do you really want to make that kind of connection to an impoverished nobleman's son who lives in the slums?"

From the look on her face, he'd cracked the surface of her confidence a little. He pressed his case. "Or they could simply break in. How good are your Witch Knights at thievery? And my tools are hidden—they have only one purpose, after all, which might be somewhat incriminating if the wrong people discovered them. So your knights will have to tear the place apart to find them."

He held his silence while he let her think it through. "Very well," she said. "I'll send you there with an escort."

"That'll work nicely," Jax said, putting as much sarcasm into his words as he could muster. "A troop of mounted Witch Knights escorting me to my flat in broad daylight. That certainly won't draw any attention, or start any rumors circulating through the slums."

The Witch did not look at all happy. "So what do you propose?"

"Two of your knights, dressed in simple clothing, accompany me to my flat, at night, on foot. No noise, no fuss, no muss. Two of them should be more than enough to handle me, don't you think? And you do have Maelleen. You know I'm not going to abandon her."

The Witch narrowed her eyes with distrust. "When?"

"Tonight."

She took a deep breath and considered his proposal for a moment, then nodded and said, "I'll have Captain Darganna assign the men to you."

He asked, "May I do one additional thing?"

Her eyes narrowed suspiciously. "And what might that be?"

"I'd like to stop at The Angry Bear and tell Maelleen's parents that she's okay, that they shouldn't worry. I won't give them any details, and your men can listen to everything I tell them to be sure of that."

Maelleen gave him a warm smile, and so did the Witch. Even the little witch's face softened.

"That won't be necessary," the Witch said, "because I've already taken care of that. I sent Nathaniel some time ago." She gave Jax a smug look.

Maelleen's eyes widened in surprise as the old witch turned to her. "He told them you're spending a month with a wealthy admirer at his villa on the coast. They're hoping you've found you're rich husband. And I gave them some small compensation since you won't be around to help at their little establishment."

Maelleen said, "That was kind of you, Mother."

The old witch gave Jax a self-satisfied smile, and he wasn't sure if she'd done such a thoughtful thing out of real kindness, or just to pull it out at a moment like this to remind him she was always one step ahead of them.

"I should still make some sort of appearance," Jax said. "Let them know I'm still alive. It's a dangerous coincidence that I disappeared just as Roland appeared."

The Witch's eyes narrowed suspiciously, and she clearly thought he'd devised some ploy to angle for advantage. But Jax's concern was genuine, because if he had to go through with this lunacy, then to save his own neck, and Maelleen's, he needed to eliminate even the slightest complication.

The Witch shook her head. "I doubt anyone will make the connection. And in any case, when Maelleen told us everyone thought you dead, I had Nathaniel spread a little false information through some of his agents. Maelleen's parents and the riffraff that haunt their tavern think you've found temporary work in Del Fransika, while your more nefarious friends think you're doing some sort of illicit job there. And that Rondo fellow, he believes you're just staying out of sight for a while because of your concern about turning down the Carkoska job."

Maelleen intervened. "Nevertheless, it would still be good if Jax made an appearance. He could reinforce that misinformation."

Jax added, "And I've stayed alive by never taking anything for granted."

The Witch looked thoughtful for a moment, then said, "Very well. But my knights will stay close by your side at all times. And if you elude them somehow . . . well, we'll do the evisceration and guts thing with your dear Maelleen."

Jax decided to go for broke. "And I should pay my rent so I don't lose my flat."

The Witch gave him another self-satisfied smile, this one even broader than the last. "Already taken care of, dear. You're paid up two months in advance."

••••

While the Witch, the little witch, and the little harlot dined in more formal circumstances, Jax ate a quick meal in his room, then changed into the clothing he'd worn the day the Witch Knights had abducted him. He'd just finished dressing when Captain Darganna arrived with the knights who would accompany him. He recognized the two fellows because both had been, at one time or another, dressed incognito and following him on the streets. They both wore loose-fitting brown pants tucked into calf-high black boots, a leather jerkin over a faded, gray shirt, and a sword strapped to their side. They would have been identical, except one had black hair and sported a goatee, while the other had brown hair with a clean-shaven chin. Both stood rigidly erect with the aura of guardsmen about them.

Jax said, "This won't do, Captain."

Darganna scowled at him. "How so?"

"They look like palace guardsmen."

Darganna looked at the two men carefully and shook his head. "No they don't. They look like disreputable hooligans, just like you."

Jax took a deep breath, let it out slowly and tried to remain calm. "They look like guardsmen, they act like guardsmen, and they walk like guardsmen. Look at their stiff backs. They look like they're standing at attention. You might as well give each of them a halberd and put them in a uniform. They look like the kind of men I would never associate with."

Darganna stared at him angrily for a long moment, then rolled his eyes and said, "I think we need to consult with Mother."

He turned to the uniformed knight who guarded Jax's door. "Please ask Mother if she'll meet us downstairs in the vestibule at the main entrance."

The fellow saluted the captain, turned and marched out of the room.

Darganna and the two disguised knights escorted Jax down the three flights of stairs. They waited in the vestibule for about half an hour, then the Witch arrived with Maelleen and Venessta in tow. "Captain, what is so important that you must interrupt our dinner?"

"Forgive me, Mother," he said, "but the thief dislikes the way these men appear. He says they look too much like guardsmen."

The Witch eyed the two men carefully, a perplexed look on her face. "They look like riffraff, to me."

Maelleen said, "Mother, with all due respect I must disagree. They look almost identical, like they're wearing a uniform. The people on the street that they need to fool will see right through that."

Venessta said, "She has a point."

Surprised that Venessta saw what Darganna couldn't, Jax said, "Dirty them up a bit, though just a smudge here and there will do. Put a few small tears in their clothing and get rid of the sabers. Give one a cudgel and the other a short sword. And have them stuff them in their belts, not buckled neatly to their sides in sheaths."

The Witch gave Jax an unhappy frown. "But you don't look like that."

"These men are carrying weapons," Jax said. "That makes them thugs. I'm not a thug. In fact, I don't associate with thugs so why don't we just get rid of the weapons altogether? A small knife tucked into the belt, or in a sheath—that's okay—but they don't need the real weapons."

Maelleen said, "And have them slouch a bit. They're standing so stiff and straight. No one but a guardsman carries himself like that."

Once they managed to get the two knights dirtied up and looking the part, they and Jax left the Witch Palace. It took them an hour on foot to reach the slums and Jax's small flat. There, they ran into Mrs. Beamish.

"Jax," she said. "I was so glad to hear you hadn't fallen to some misfortune."

"I found a little work in Del Fransika," he said, continuing the Witch's lie. "But I had to leave quickly, or miss the opportunity."

He and the two knights trudged up to his flat, and when he opened the door, one of them barred his way and said, "The pick set; where is it?"

Jax kept his voice neutral. "Come, I'll get it for you."

He tried to step past the knight, but the fellow refused to budge, shaking his head. "No. You tell me where it is and I'll get it."

Jax knew without doubt the Witch would not allow him to keep his pick set in his room at the Palace—he just might pick locks he wasn't supposed to. And that night he had hoped to have a second or two with his tools hidden from the knights' view by his body, during which he intended to palm a medium sized pick and tension tool. If he ever did need to escape from their clutches, it would be good to have a slight advantage hidden away. But to his disappointment, the knights made him show them the set's location. Then one of them retrieved it, opened it, carefully examined its contents, and shoved it into his coat. Jax took great care to show no disappointment.

The two knights proved to be useful as more than just guards to watch over him. Jax retrieved his canvas valise with his other tools, and bundled up his lurking-in-the-night cloak and clothing, along with his second-story clothing and tools. The two knights were strong fellows, and they had no trouble carrying it all.

They left his flat and walked to The Angry Bear. He convinced the two knights to agree to pretend they didn't know him. So by prior agreement he went in alone and closed the tavern's door. Old Marcus saw him and gave him a nod. Jax started across the room and was half way to the bar when the door opened and the two knights entered behind him. As he leaned on the bar Marcus said, "We was all glad to hear you wasn't dead. Got some paying work, I hear."

"Yah," Jax said. "In Del Fransika." He needed to support the old witch's lies, so he looked around the room and asked, "Is Maelleen about?"

"Sorry," Marcus said. He leaned on the bar close to Jax and spoke in a confidential tone. "She's with some rich fella at his place on the coast. I hear he's loaded."

Jax gave him a wide-eyed look. "She found her rich husband?"

Marcus nodded. "That's what we're hoping. Maybe old Bethy and me can finally retire, sit back and relax a bit. And it would be nice if Maelleen didn't have to work so hard to help us out."

Jax ordered a mug of ale. Standing at the bar a few paces away, the two knights also ordered mugs, and did a good job of fitting in.

Jax finished his ale and left, and as he and the two knights returned to the Witch Palace, while walking down a street a hearty laugh drew his attention. It was a voice he'd never forget.

Across the street two men had stepped out of an inn and stood beneath the light of a single gas lamp.

"A pleasurable night," Andrew said.

His broad-shouldered manservant nodded. "Yes, my lord."

Jax's heart pounded up into his throat, and his vision clouded with rage.

••••

Jax was blind to everything else around him, and could see only Andrew standing there outside the inn laughing with his manservant. He had marched half way across the street before he realized what he was doing, and then he didn't care. He glanced down to his hand and didn't recall drawing his dagger. He held it close to his side to keep it concealed. If he moved quickly, he could bury the blade in Andrew's heart before the manservant beat him to death. He would die a happy man.

A hand caught his elbow and spun him about, stopping him in his tracks facing one of the Witch Knights. The fellow's companion gripped both of Jax's elbows from behind, and he could not have moved to save his own life. They quickly disarmed him, then the man in front of him leaned close and hissed, "What do you think you're doing?"

Jax spoke through his rage, his teeth gritted sharply, his voice like the growl of an angry animal. "I'm going to repay a debt."

"Here now," Andrew shouted, stepping up nearby. His manservant stood a little closer to them, ready to protect his master. "What are you two ruffians doing with this young man? Do I need to hail the constabulary?"

The Witch Knight facing Jax flashed something silvery in his hand toward Andrew, some sort of pendant or badge. "This is the Witch's business, Lord Maricone. She will be displeased if you interfere."

Andrew's eyebrows rose and his manservant backed up a step. "My apologies," Andrew said. "You must understand how it appeared."

The Witch Knight nodded. "We do, Your Lordship. Your reaction was most natural, and admirable. And Mother will not be displeased if you go your own way now."

The two men turned and walked away.

Jax demanded of the knight, "Do you know what he and his man do?"

The knight's lips tightened into a knife-sharp line and his eyes hardened. "There are rumors, but only rumors, and he is the heir to a powerful house."

Jax looked at the door to the inn from which Andrew—Maricone—and his man had emerged. "Let go of me and I'll show you more than a rumor."

The knight nodded and the man behind Jax released his shoulders.

Jax marched across the street and through the door of the inn. It opened into the common room, with a bar against the left wall, and stairs on the back wall leading upward. Jax walked to the bar and approached the innkeeper standing behind it.

"The man who just left," Jax demanded, making no attempt to hide his anger, "with his manservant. Did he rent a room?"

The innkeeper polished a tin cup with a rag while he eyed Jax warily. "Well now, young sir, I don't discuss me patrons with just—"

One of Witch Knights stepped up to the bar beside Jax and flashed that pendant. "Tell him."

The innkeeper's eyebrows rose. "Aye, he did."

Jax didn't want to spook the innkeeper, so he tried to keep the fury out of his voice. "Take us to it."

The innkeeper led them up the stairs to room number three. He unlocked it and started to enter, but Jax grabbed his arm and hauled him back into the middle of the hallway. "You stay out here."

The room contained a small table with two chairs, plus a rickety bed with a thin mattress. On the bed a young boy lay face down. His hands and feet had been tied to the corners of the bed, his shirt shoved up to expose his back and his pants pulled down to his knees. The boy's shoulders heaved with sobs. Red welts on his back and legs would turn black and blue by morning. Jax had forgotten his own bruises and welts, because there was so much else that clouded his memories of that night, but he remembered them now.

The knight out in the hall told the innkeeper. "Go down and see to your customers."

Jax knelt down beside the bed and placed a hand on the boy's shoulder. He started and looked at Jax, his face clouded by fear, his eyes puffy and red. Jax thought he couldn't be more than fourteen or fifteen years old. As the knights cut the ropes binding his hands and feet, Jax said, "We're not going to harm you. Who did this to you?"

"Lord Andrew," the boy said, and he would say no more.

They helped the boy pull his clothes back together. Jax gave him all the coins he had on him, which wasn't much, and they sent him on his way.

Jax turned to the two knights. "There are laws against this, aren't there?"

They both grimaced, and the more senior of the two said, "Aye, laws against sodomy. But they're rarely enforced, and never against the heir to a powerful noble house."

"But he's done this for years," Jax said, "time and time again. How many boys does he have to rape before someone stops him?"

The knight shrugged his shoulders. "He picks his victims carefully. If he harmed a child of another powerful house, they might declare vendetta against him, but most likely his family would simply pay some reparation."

The fellow's companion shook his head. "If he did it to a son of one of the High Noble Houses, he and his man would be found floating face-down in the river. Everyone would know what actually happened, but they'd all pretend the two men were the victims of street thugs."

"He's protected?" Jax asked. "You allow him to do this again and again, and nothing happens to him? I want to know his full name."

Both knights frowned, and the more senior of the two said, "You can't go after him."

If Jax could take Andrew's life, he'd have no regrets paying for the privilege with his own. But Maelleen was still a captive of the Witch, and he couldn't abandon her, even that way. Jax lowered his voice and tried to speak calmly. "I know. I just want to know his full name."

The two knights shared a look, and then the older one said, "Lord Petra Maricone."

23

Afternoon Tea

AFTERNOON TEA AT High House Carkoska proved to be a complete bore for Maelleen. She, the Witch, and Venessta attended without Jax because they all agreed Lady Carkoska appeared to view Jax as a meal of which she'd like to partake, and they didn't want to tempt fate. When they arrived, the first words out of the woman's mouth were, "And where is young Master Roland?"

The old witch smiled. "He's feeling a bit under the weather today."

Lady Carkoska lifted a skeptical eyebrow. "I do hope it's nothing serious."

The Witch shook her head. "A few days of rest should see him back to normal."

Maelleen, the Witch, and Venessta hoped to find some way to get Maelleen alone with the Lord of the House, but the Carkoska's had invited Lord and Lady Rellman, a young, attractive couple about Maelleen's age.

Venessta leaned close to Maelleen and whispered, "Lord and Lady Rellman are sworn to House Carkoska, so be careful what you say in front of them."

When the Carkoska's introduced them and Lord Rellman kissed Maelleen's hand, he smiled in a friendly way, but his eyes regarded her with cold indifference. As they sipped tea and dined on delicate sandwiches and scones, the look in the man's eyes only warmed when he spoke to one of their hosts, and his wife fawned over Lady Carkoska in a most irritatingly obsequious way. With the Rellman's present, Maelleen feared there was little hope of getting Lord Carkoska alone that afternoon. Then Venessta proved that she could be calculating when the need arose.

She leaned toward Lord Carkoska. "I've been telling Maelleen about your rose garden. It's magnificent, and I know she'd love to see it."

They had discussed no such thing, but Maelleen played along. "Yes, Venessta has piqued my interest. I'd very much enjoy that."

Carkoska stood. "I'd be most happy to show it to you."

Venessta stood and addressed the Witch. "Do you mind if we take a stroll with Lord Carkoska?"

The old woman shook her head. "Go, enjoy yourselves."

Lady Rellman stood, dashing Maelleen's hopes. "I'd love to see those roses as well."

Lord Rellman stood also. "May we join you?"

Maelleen would have liked to see some disappointment in the look Carkoska gave the young man. She had hoped that the High Lord might also seek an opportunity to get her alone, but he didn't appear at all displeased as he said, "By all means."

The five of them left the Witch and Lady Carkoska and walked out to the rose gardens behind the main building. As they walked along carefully tended pathways, and Carkoska extolled on his roses, Maelleen wished that Lady Rellman would trip and smash her face into the ground. They paused at a gazeebo that offered cool shade from the warm sun. Maelleen stepped into it, and Lord Carkoska followed her. Standing alone in the gazeebo with him, she heard Lady Rellman say, "Mistress Venessta, there's a wonderful display of wildflowers nearby. Let me show it to you."

She heard the voices of Venessta and the two Rellmans dwindle as they strolled away, and it all fell into place. The Rellmans had orders from the High Lord to help him get Maelleen alone, which could be considered a scandalous breach of propriety. But they'd done so with a subtle ploy that anyone would consider an innocent accident.

Maelleen turned and found Carkoska standing between her and the gazeebo's entrance. He stepped forward and closed the distance between them.

She lowered her eyes and said, "We should . . . join the others."

She could have easily stepped around him and walked out of the gazeebo, as propriety dictated, and that she did not was a clear message to him of her mindset.

He reached out and took her hand in his. "I've wanted to speak to you alone, and this . . . accident of circumstance is perhaps not a bad thing."

"I really should join the others," she said, and she saw the disappointment in his face. But then she added. "But I believe you're right. Perhaps this accident is not a bad thing."

His eyes flashed with victory and desire. He put his arm around her waist, pulled her tightly against him, and kissed her. He tasted good, with a hint of the fragrant tea they had been sipping. No, his girth would not get in the way of taking pleasure from him, and he didn't try to grope at her, so it was time for her next move.

She ended the kiss, pressed the palms of her hands against his chest, and slowly pushed him away. She gave him a frightened look and said, "I shouldn't be here. It's too indiscreet. I must join the others."

She stepped around him, then out of the gazeebo and into the sunlight, and there she waited. He followed only a pace behind her, and as he stepped into the sunlight she looked into his face and gave him the most inviting smile she could produce.

He nodded and smiled. "Yes, it is too indiscreet. Perhaps sometime we can remedy that, but for now, let's join the others."

••••

It had been a while since Jax had needed to pick a lock under pressure, and he had to assume that during the ball he couldn't just take his time. To refresh his skills he picked locks on every door he came across in the Witch Palace. He also found a couple of doors with locks similar to the one he had seen on the door to Carkoska's office. He spent several hours picking them again and again until he could almost do it blindfolded. The Witch Knights didn't say anything overt, but from a few comments here and there, it became obvious they were none too happy that all their precious locked doors might no longer keep Jax out when he should be out, or in when he should be in.

After the three ladies returned from afternoon tea at High House Carkoska, Maelleen told him of her dalliance with Carkoska in the gazeebo.

He frowned as he said, "Don't you think you overdid the blushing maiden ploy a bit?"

She flashed a big grin. "No. He'll remember the kiss and the passion. And right now he's thinking of what more awaits him if he seduces me properly, as opposed to pinning me against a wall like some whore on the street. Trust me, he'll make another try."

The next day Lord Carkoska came to the Witch Palace to pay his respects to the Witch. The three woman made sure he had a chance to get Maelleen alone for a brief moment.

When he left, Venessta demanded, "Well?"

Maelleen said, "He apologized for his indiscretion yesterday, asked if he might make it up to me, perhaps with a ride in the park. We're going to do that tomorrow, though he doesn't realize I'm going to bring a chaperone so he can't make any moves."

She said to Venessta, "If you don't mind, dear, that'll be you."

Venessta smiled and said, "It'll be fun watching the old fellow chafe."

Maelleen said to the Witch, "At the ball, while Jax and Venessta are doing their little thief thing, you and I should divide and conquer Lord and Lady Carkoska. Can you keep the lady occupied, while I allow him to maneuver me into some private place? This will be an important test. If he kisses me again, and again doesn't try to go further, we'll know he wants more than a simple romp in the sheets."

Jax had to endure the final fitting for the formal evening suit he'd wear to the ball. The dance practices continued, the four of them dined together every evening in the same formal circumstances, then reviewed their strategy over after-dinner drinks in the Witch's sitting room. One evening the women kept planning in circles, trying to eliminate any possibility of failure or discovery.

Jax had long ago learned he couldn't anticipate everything, and he tried to intervene. "I think we're over-planning. You know what the generals say: the best of battle plans don't survive first contact with the enemy. And it's not any different when thieving."

The three women were nervous and on edge because none of them had ever thieved before, and they didn't want to hear that. That started a real squabble, with all three of them ganging up on him. Everyone went to bed that night thoroughly upset, and the next morning at dance practice, both Venessta and Maelleen refused to speak to the Jax. They danced stiffly, like automatons produced by an untalented clock maker.

Venessta danced without a word and refused to make eye contact.

When dancing with Maelleen, Jax tried to break through her anger. "Surely, *you'll* speak with me."

All he got for his efforts was, "Humph!" At least she looked him in the eyes to emphasize her disapproval when she said it.

"Little harlot," the Witch snapped angrily, startling them both. "Come here this instant."

The Witch had stood, a rare occurrence during the dance sessions, and she'd lost about two decades in age. With a startled look on her face, Maelleen walked toward the not-so-old woman hesitantly.

The Witch looked at the musicians, pointed to the door and said, "Out."

Rushing desperately, they packed up their instruments and scurried out like frightened hens.

Jax retreated to stand by the hearth as the Witch sat the two young women down on the couch and stood facing them. By that time she'd lost another twenty years in age, the significance of which was clearly not lost on the two young ladies. They sat like prim little girls, with eyes wide and hands folded demurely on their laps. Never before had Jax seen Maelleen look demure.

With her fists on her hips, the Witch leaned forward and said, "He's right, you know."

That startled even Jax.

By that time the Witch had become the youthful, blond beauty he'd seen before, which didn't bode well for the two young women at the focus of her wrath. "And what upsets me most," she snapped, "is that I refused to listen to him as well, and was just as stubborn last night as you are right now. He's right, because he's the thief, he knows what he's doing, and we're the amateurs. Now you're going to listen to him, and heed what he says, because if you don't, I may just turn the two of you into toads instead of him." She paused and straightened.

Both young women took that as their cue. They spoke in subdued tones as they simultaneously said, "Yes, Mother."

The Witch turned around slowly to face Jax, a blond beauty that could steal any man's heart, except for the damn coal-black eyes. "You were trying to tell us something last night, my little thief. Today, I'm going to be more receptive to your words, and I'm sure the little witch and the little harlot will do so as well." She hadn't grown any older, so her anger continued to boil within her.

Jax spoke carefully. "All I meant to say is that we can't plan for everything and we can't count on anything. We have to be prepared for the unanticipated, or for a random factor to come into play. If we try to fool ourselves into believing we have anticipated everything, then we won't be ready to react if the unexpected does arise, and that could spell disaster."

The Witch smiled, looked at him as if she was about to devour him. "We'll take that excellent advice to heart,"—she didn't look back as her voice hardened and she snapped—"won't we?"

On cue, both young women again said, "Yes, Mother."

The Witch considered Jax for a long moment, her black eyes examining every inch of him. Then she walked toward him at a slow, stately pace, and his gut tightened. She remained the blond beauty as she stopped just a hand's breadth from him. He couldn't say why he chose that moment to glance down at the swell of her breasts above the top of her gown, but some irresistible force compelled him to do so. Her breasts were larger than Venessta's, but smaller than Maelleen's, and for some reason he now wanted to touch them, to caress them.

The Witch leaned toward him, her tongue lashed out and licked the side of his cheek. It was forked, like that of a snake, and her eyes remained coal-black pits of chaos. To his own horror, he got an immediate erection.

She gave him an evil grin. "Just a small demonstration, my little thief. If I decide to pleasure you, I'll make the little harlot look like an inexperienced schoolgirl."

In an instant she transformed back into the wrinkled, ancient, old woman.

He swallowed hard and said, "Yes, Mother."

••••

The knights convinced the Witch that they should hold onto Jax's pick set when he wasn't using it. They no longer walked into his room unannounced, but had adopted the practice of unlocking the door, then knocking on it and waiting for him to answer. It was a concession to privacy that he appreciated. That evening, in response to a knock, when he answered the door, Maelleen stood there with her hands folded in front of her and her eyes downcast.

"I'm sorry," she said. "She's right. We should have listened to you. We've talked it over and we're all going to try to be ready for anything. It's just that none of us have ever done this thieving thing before, and we're all a bit nervous about it."

She looked up and met his eyes. "May I come in?"

He stepped back and to the side. "If you're allowed to, of course."

She walked past him and he closed the door.

When he turned away from the door toward her, she put her arms around his neck. "Since tomorrow night is the ball, I asked her if she'd let us have this night together, and she was kind enough to grant my wish."

It occurred to him that since it was his last night before the ball, perhaps the Witch had allowed Maelleen to come to him in the way a condemned nobleman sometimes received a last meal. If this was his last meal, it would be a delectable one.

As he put his hands around her waist, she pressed her body against his and whispered in his ear, "We're going to survive these witches, you and I. Somehow, we'll find a way."

Like her, he whispered, "The old witch has a forked tongue, you know, like a snake."

"Really!" she said, an odd look of curiosity in her eyes.

He added, "At least when she's angry and turns into the blond, young beauty. I saw it."

She leaned away from him a bit, ending their whispered conversation. She looked him in the eyes and spoke more openly. "We treated you badly, so I intend to make it up to you, my poor, little, mistreated thief."

Jax and Maelleen had never fought before, so they had never had to make up. She did make it up to him, and he learned a few new things that night.

24

At the Ball

JAX PULLED ON his trousers then his shoes. He carefully positioned and tied his cravat, then pulled on the square cut waistcoat and buttoned it up. Over that he pulled on the tail coat and shrugged it into place. The top hat the women had chosen for him for the ball seemed a bit extreme, but in nine years living in the slums he'd lost all but the most rudimentary sense of fashion, so he deferred to their judgement. In any case, the Witch had paid for it all, so he didn't care. He hoped that after this was over he could keep the day suits. Of course, that wouldn't mean much if he got to keep one simply because they needed something in which to bury him.

He retrieved the soft, leather wallet where he stored his pick set, tension tools, a couple of matches, and a small, thin candle. At his request, the Witch had had one of her seamstresses sew a special pocket into the lining of his tailcoat, and he slipped the wallet into it. The wallet and tools were nicely flat, so it didn't create an unsightly lump on the breast of his coat.

He knocked on the door to his room, the lock made a loud chunk as the knight disengaged it, and the fellow opened the door. They escorted him down to the waiting carriage, and the women joined him a moment later.

The old witch had surrendered to the dictates of fashion, and like the two younger women wore a dress with an empire waste, though hers had long sleeves and a high collar. As usual, Venessta's gown was cut low, exposing her neck and shoulders. Maelleen had chosen not to completely cover her assets this time, nor to show a lot of flesh for the world to view. Her gown exposed just a little hint of cleavage, which seemed to promise that there was much more hidden than visible. Venessta caught him looking at Maelleen's cleavage, and she gave him a sharp look.

He and the three women rode in silence to High House Carkoska. They'd done all the planning they could, and though they were all nervous, Venessta appeared jumpy.

In the vestibule at Carkoska, as the women handed their cloaks to servants, Jax leaned close to Venessta and said, "Don't worry. You'll do fine. Just follow my lead and everything will work out."

She gave him a grateful smile, but his words didn't seem to calm her.

This time, servants led them to a grand ballroom, and as they entered, Maelleen took the old witch's arm, and Venessta took Jax's. They were greeted by the lord and lady of the house with the usual formula of bowing and curtsying. Lord Carkoska struggled visibly to keep his hands and eyes off Maelleen.

Jax danced with Venessta. He danced with Maelleen. Maelleen danced with Lord Carkoska, and with a few young men. Jax danced with a few young ladies, but he kept an eye on Venessta. Her nerves were visibly frayed, so he made sure he got the next dance with her.

He took her out onto the dance floor, and as the musicians began the next tune, he held her at an appropriate distance and they danced. He decided to tease her a little. "We're not going to dance in that intimate style you taught me where you press yourself against me?"

She hissed at him. "Be quiet. You know no one really dances that way. It would be . . . scandalous."

He smiled. "I know. You were just teasing me."

She lowered her eyes. "I'm sorry."

"Don't be. I like the way you tease me. I like holding you scandalously close when we dance. I do hope you won't stop doing that at our practice sessions."

She frowned. "After tonight there won't be any more need for practice sessions."

He grinned and gave her an openly lascivious look. "Well let's keep at them anyway, you and me."

She blushed and regarded him curiously.

"By the way," he said, "it's all right to be nervous. In fact, a little bit of it sharpens the senses, makes us more aware of the dangers around us. You'll do just fine."

Across the room he spotted Lord Carkoska approaching Maelleen, who stood alone at the edge of the room. She saw Jax looking her way and gave him a slight nod before Carkoska got to her. Jax scanned the edge of the room and saw the Witch looking his way also. At that moment she was talking with Lady Carkoska, who had her back to him. The Witch didn't nod, but she smiled. The smile was meant for him, but if Lady Carkoska noticed it she'd think it just a polite acknowledgment of her words.

He leaned close to Venessta and brushed his lips lightly along the side of her neck, just under her ear.

"What are you doing?" she asked, though no anger sounded in her voice.

"Time for us to go to work."

••••

Jax led Venessta to the refreshment table. They both sipped at a little champagne for a few minutes, and pretended to be talking intimately. Then they put the glasses down and slipped out through one of several doors on the periphery of the ballroom. Since he'd been there before, Jax had a good sense of position and direction.

They found themselves in a long, narrow gallery where Carkoska had a lot of artwork on display. They were not the only couple strolling down its length. Jax paused briefly at a large painting on the wall, then leaned close to Venessta as if discussing it. He whispered, "I told you Carkoska is the type to display his wealth openly."

"Yes," she said. "He most certainly is."

He glanced up and down the gallery. "We're near the northeast corner of the house. The stairway you led me to the other day is at the back of the house near the southeast corner. We just have to go to the end of this gallery and we should be somewhere near that hallway that leads to the stairs."

She leaned away from him a little and gave him an appraising look. "You do know what you're doing, don't you? I'm completely turned around."

He grinned. "I've had a bit of practice. Let's stroll down to the end of the gallery and admire the artwork on the way."

He held out his arm and she took it, saying, "I'd love to, Master Roland."

They did stroll casually, but they didn't waste any time stopping to admire paintings or sculptures. At the end of the gallery Jax noticed a young man with his back to them partially hidden in a dark recess next to a statue on a pedestal. The fellow seemed to be moving in an odd way, but then Jax saw the arms of a young woman around his neck and realized his silhouette hid her from view. He had his arms around the girl, and his movements were consistent with kissing her passionately.

Venessta leaned close to him. "I told you so."

On impulse, Jax put his arm around her waist and pulled her tightly against him. Her eyes widened as he leaned toward her and kissed her. She didn't resist, but responded stiffly, as if unsure of herself.

When the kiss ended he continued to hold her there, their lips almost touching. She asked, "Why did you do that?"

He smiled. "We're supposed to be two lovers who have snuck off for a tryst. It's important we play the part. Just part of the act, you know."

"Oh," she said, and she seemed relieved.

He released her and she took his arm again. They stepped out of the gallery and Jax had to choose to go left or right. His instinct told him left. A few moments later they found the hallway that led to the stairs. They were now alone.

He whispered, "We have to be careful from here on."

This time he took Venessta up the stairs with him, moving slowly and cautiously. The hallway at the top of the stairs was also empty, so he led her to the fourth door on the left. Before opening it, he wrapped his arm around her waist and pulled her against him.

"What are you doing?" she hissed in a whisper. "Are you going to kiss me again?"

"When I open this door, if there's anyone in there, you'll be in my arms. You'll giggle for a moment, then we'll both be embarrassed that we've been caught sneaking in there."

With a little awe in her voice she said, "You are rather good at this. I would have never thought of that."

"Practice makes perfect," he said. "Ready?"

She nodded.

Jax opened the door and swung her through it, holding her tightly in his arms. He looked past her into the room. Light from the hallway sconces spilled into it, enough that he could tell they were alone.

"All right," he said. "Go back into the hallway and wait at the top of the stairs. If you hear anyone coming, come back into this room, close the door and warn me. We'll take it from there."

Venessta fluttered her eyes. "That would be the passionate kissing and fondling thing?"

He gave her a lecherous look. "Mother said I could fondle anything I wanted."

Her eyes flashed angrily. "Including your own personals, as I recall."

He smiled. "There's a piece of me that really hopes we *will* be discovered."

Jax didn't know how to interpret the look on her face as she stepped out of his arms and slipped out the door.

He leaned out into the hallway and whispered, "One more thing."

She looked back his way. "What?"

"I lied," he said.

Her eyes flashed angrily. "About what?"

He grinned. "It wasn't necessary to kiss you just to play the part. I kissed you because I wanted to."

She frowned, put her fingers to her lips and said, "Oh."

He left her standing there, retreated into the vestibule and closed the outer door to the hallway.

Luck smiled on him; the small lamp he'd seen the other day remained on the table. Jax retrieved his wallet from the pocket in his tail coat, took a match from it and lit the small lamp, then knelt down at the office door. He selected the pick and tension tool he thought would work best. His practice back at the Witch Palace paid off, and after a few minutes the door's lock clicked. Before opening the door he turned down the wick on the lamp to keep it low just in case the office had a window to the outside. It wouldn't do for someone to see strange shadows and lights through the window of a room that should be empty. He turned the door's latch and swung it inward.

It occurred to him now, that it hadn't occurred to him earlier, to consider the possibility that someone waited within on the other side of the locked door. As the door swung open his heart pounded for a second until he saw that the office was unoccupied.

There was a window to the outside. The back wall of the room had a steep pitch to it, and the window appeared to be in a shallow dormer embedded within it. Jax kept the lamp turned down and lowered it to the floor, crossed the office and looked through the window to the grounds below. The gardens there were well lit for the ball, with decorative lanterns hung from tree limbs, and several groups and couples strolling about. He tried to memorize what he saw in case he had to return and attempt to gain entry through the window. He also took careful note of the window's latch. On the second floor, above carefully guarded and patrolled grounds, the latch hadn't been designed to provide maximum security, just ensure that the window didn't flap open during a gusty storm. He thought he could jimmy it from the outside with the right tool.

He turned away from the window, retrieved the lamp and used its limited light to scan the room. To his surprise the figurine sat in plain sight on a pedestal in the corner like a trophy mounted for all to view. He put the lamp on the floor again and examined the statue closely; a woman wearing a hooded cloak that hid her features. Her hands were raised to about mid-torso, and in them she held a small box as if offering it to someone. The statue looked to be fired porcelain, no paint, glaze or color to it. The box she held was rectangular in two dimensions and fairly flat in the third. Based on the height of the little woman, it would be about the size of Jax's hand when pressed flat against a hard surface, and about an inch thick.

Could it be that easy? Just reach out, grab it and run? His instinct screamed *No* at him, but why? And why display it like a trophy in a room Carkoska never allowed anyone to enter, an obvious presentation that no one would ever see. Did Carkoska just sit here by himself, admiring it and taking some sort of strange pleasure in owning it? Too many things about the figurine in front of him simply didn't add up.

He reached out slowly, but his instinct warned him away from it, and the closer he moved his hand, the louder his instinct shouted. Perhaps the statue rested on some sort of spring-loaded alarm that would alert the guards. He pulled his hand back carefully.

A heavy wooden desk in the center of the room drew his attention. His instinct pointed him to it.

He stopped and stared at the desk for a moment, then approached it. He sat down in the chair behind the desk and tested a drawer. It wasn't locked. He opened each drawer, and to his disappointment, found a lot of items that belonged in a desk drawer, though nothing out of the ordinary. But on closer examination, he realized the bottom drawer on the right appeared shallower on the inside than its exterior dimensions indicated.

There were some books in it so he carefully noted their position, then lifted them out and placed them on the desk. Beneath that he found a plain, wooden slat consistent with the way the bottom of a drawer should be constructed. He tapped it lightly with a finger nail, it sounded hollow, and his instinct said, *Yes.*

With a little experimentation he learned that pressing on the far edge lifted the near edge a bit, which allowed him to remove the slat completely. Beneath the false bottom a hidden compartment contained a small strongbox about the right size in which to store the figurine. His instinct didn't warn him off, so he tried to lift the strongbox out of the compartment, but it appeared to be solidly affixed there, possibly with bolts of some kind.

Shielding the lamp with his body so it didn't flash out the window, he turned it up a little to examine the lock on the strongbox. *Could it be?* he wondered. If the figurine on the pedestal was attached to some sort of mechanical alarm, he could understand why his instinct warned him off, but why lead him to the strongbox?

"Jax, someone's coming."

His heart skipped a beat and he almost shouted as he looked up to find Venessta standing in the open office door. She had remembered to close the outer door to the hallway.

Realizing that to rush or hurry might be their undoing, he tried to keep all his movements calm and steady as he turned the lamp down, replaced the false bottom, then returned the books to the drawer, carefully repositioning them as he had found them. He slid the drawer shut, stood and came around the desk carrying the lamp. Her eyes wide with fear, Venessta backed into the vestibule as he stepped out of the office and closed the door softly. He relocked the door and quickly replaced his picks and the wallet in his coat, then placed the lamp back on the writing table. He left it lit but turned down low.

"Quickly," Venessta said. She grabbed him by the lapels of his jacket, put her back against the wall and pulled him toward her. "Kiss me passionately."

He pressed his lips against hers and she shoved her tongue in his mouth. Venessta felt stiff and unyielding in his arms, like someone forced to carry out an unpleasant task, her back unnaturally rigid, her shoulders tense. Her tongue probed at the inside of his mouth like the point of a pike piercing the heart of an opponent in battle, nothing close to the pleasant little war of tongues he and Maelleen frequently shared, and nothing like the passionate kiss he and Venessta had shared earlier.

Their lips parted. Her eyes fluttered and she panted breathlessly, obviously terrified. "You're supposed to fondle my breasts. Mother'll be upset if you don't."

She grabbed his hand, lifted it and clamped it against her breast. They kissed again, and he should be enjoying this: a beautiful young woman in his arms kissing him passionately while he caressed her breast, but all he could think about was a Carkoska guard bursting through the door behind him and impaling him on the point of a sword. "You know," Venessta said between kisses, "when you fondle a woman's breast, you should caress it softly, not knead it like a glob of lumpy dough."

"Sorry," he said. "I'm usually better at this. The thing about being discovered and killed has me off my game."

"Just try to do better."

She pulled his face toward her and kissed him again. He concentrated on the young woman in his arms, tried to think of that and not the door behind him. The material of her dress was thin and insubstantial, and through it he felt the soft contour of her flesh. As he ran the tip of his finger lightly around the sharp point of her nipple the tension left her shoulders, she relaxed and melted into his arms. Her tongue stopped rigidly probing his mouth so he ran his tongue across her lips and pinched her nipple softly. She gasped.

He leaned down and brushed his lips across the soft swell of her breasts above the top of her dress.

"You know," she said. "You're pretending rather well."

He had trouble whispering. "It doesn't feel too much like I'm pretending right now."

She kissed him again, and he continued to caress her breast softly. "Yes," she said. "I think we stopped pretending a while ago. I hope they hurry up and discover us."

Breathing heavily, he said, "And I hope they don't."

"Oh," she said. "I hadn't thought of that. I've been waiting for you to seduce me, and you really should, you know."

"Any particular reason?"

"You could learn all my secrets, or something like that. Isn't that what a thief is supposed to do, seduce the innocent, unsuspecting young woman?"

He brushed his lips lightly across hers. "Maelleen said something like that. But you're neither innocent nor unsuspecting, and somehow I don't think you're the kind of woman to cry out all her secrets while in the throes of ecstasy."

"No, I'm not. But I wouldn't mind the throes-of-ecstasy part."

He kissed her again, and he realized that pretending wasn't helping, and not pretending would make it appear all the more real to whoever discovered them. So he decided to stop trying to pretend and just enjoy himself. And with her body pressed against him, he sensed that she did the same.

The latch on the door behind them clicked, then the door slammed open. "Who's there?"

The thin, lithe body in his arms tensed. One of her hands had reached his buttock and squeezed it a couple of times.

The light from a lantern splashed across them. "What are you doing in here?"

Jax released Venessta and stepped away from her. In the glaring light she looked horribly disappointed, then quickly straightened the top of her gown where he'd wrinkled it a bit. Neither of them had trouble looking sheepishly guilty, though Jax couldn't see past the glare of the lantern

"Oh," the voice said, and the man chuckled. "You shouldn't be in here." He was clearly having trouble holding back a laugh.

Jax thought it sounded like Carkoska. The man confirmed it when he said, "Oh, it's you Master Roland, with Mistress Venessta."

Shielding her eyes from the light with a raised hand, Venessta said, "We were just . . . talking."

Another man had accompanied Carkoska and he spoke in a voice Jax didn't recognize. "Yes. Talking. We can see that. And it appeared to be a rather heated discussion, because you're both quite flushed."

Carkoska chuckled again. "You children should return to the ballroom before your discussion gets even more heated. Mother might not approve."

Jax recalled the Witch's orders to press her, throw her, or slam her, and to fondle whatever he needed to fondle. *No,* he thought. *Mother would approve.*

Jax and Venessta stepped past Carkoska and the other man. Out in the hall, Venessta took his arm and stuck her chin out proudly as they walked away. Behind them Carkoska chuckled again, and his companion said something in a lowered voice. Both men were gentlemen and didn't insult them by openly laughing. Neither Jax nor Venessta looked back.

By the time they reached the gallery outside the ballroom, Jax had calmed down but Venessta still remained flushed. They passed the small alcove where earlier they'd seen a couple kissing in the shadows. The two young people had departed, so he led Venessta into the alcove. He turned to face her but she wouldn't meet his eyes.

"I thought we might take a moment to . . . recover. Are you all right?"

She looked up at him and said, "No." Then she put the palms of her hands against his chest and pushed, forcing him to step back against the wall.

She threw her arms around his neck and kissed him, and this time there was no pretending from either of them as she pressed her body against his. He was really starting to enjoy himself and didn't want the moment to end. He slid his hand up the side of her dress across her ribs, but she ended the kiss suddenly and stepped back from him.

"What was that for?" he asked.

She threw his own words back at him. "We're supposed to be two lovers who have snuck off for a tryst. It's important we play the part. Just part of the act, you know."

"It didn't feel like an act," he said.

She ignored him, walked past him out of the alcove, and refused to speak of it further.

25

Those Striking, Blue Eyes

WHEN JAX FOLLOWED Venessta out of the alcove, she took his arm and made him escort her to the end of the gallery and back out onto the dance floor. He spotted the Witch standing next to Maelleen. Both were looking his way, so he shook his head slightly from side to side to let them know he had failed.

They didn't congregate to discuss their failed attempt at the figurine, which would be lunacy anywhere in High House Carkoska. A young man asked Venessta for the next dance. Jax knew he should appear to enjoy himself, so he approached one of the young women he'd danced with earlier. She agreed to dance with him and he escorted her out onto the floor.

She had heard he had come from Lieudess, and while they danced she asked him about it. At the Witch's orders, he had been thoroughly briefed on the foreign city, but he'd sound odd if he spewed a stream of data and facts, so he told her just a bit here and there. The young woman in his arms was saying something about her father's villa on the coast when, at that moment, on the far side of the ballroom, he saw a woman with striking, dark-blue eyes and auburn hair. She stood in a small group at the edge of the dance floor chatting amiably with someone. He still remembered the touch of her delicate flesh and taste of her skin, and he recalled how he'd felt betrayed when she had planned his murder.

"Is something wrong?"

He'd stopped flat-footed in the middle of the floor without realizing it.

His dance partner said, "You're white as a sheet."

"I'm sorry," he said. "I thought I saw someone I knew,"—he made up a quick lie—"a friend who died last year. But it's clearly not her."

She turned to follow his gaze. "Who?"

He nodded toward the group. "The lady with the auburn hair, and the striking, dark-blue eyes."

"Oh," she said. "That's High Lady Naesmyth. Isn't she beautiful?"

"Yes," he said, "she is." He recalled the softness of her skin beneath his lips when he'd kissed her neck and shoulders, and he recalled the coldness of her resolve when she had instructed Lakorsa to murder him.

At that moment the music ended, so he escorted the young woman off the dance floor.

He didn't dance again that evening, but got a small glass of champagne and stood on the periphery of the dance floor. Wherever Lady Naesmyth went, he carefully found a place where he could spy on her from a distance, though he took great care to be discreet about it.

Jax's memories of his murderous lover were vague and shrouded in the mists of the past. So much of their time together had been spent groping each other in the dark of her boudoir. They had dined together any number of times, but they had never talked the way lovers do. He didn't really know that woman from his past, and now he wondered if the lady standing on the other side of the ballroom was the Stephanna of his memories. There were differences, but those could be attributed to aging and the passage of time, though she still claimed beauty that any woman would envy. Or perhaps nine years had clouded his memory and the lady of High House Naesmyth was not the woman who had been his lover and ordered his death.

Throughout the evening she frequently held the arm of a tall and handsome man about her own age, and Jax concluded the fellow must be her husband. Lord Naesmyth had dark, curly hair and an aristocratic chin. Jax's only recollection of his murderous lover's husband was a shadowy figure in bed in a darkened room that one night, so he had no memory to compare with Lord Naesmyth's handsome face.

"Lovely couple, aren't they?"

Jax started, and found that the Witch had stopped beside him. She had an uncanny ability to appear at his elbow without warning, and at the most inopportune moment.

"Who?" he asked.

"Lord and Lady Naesmyth," she said. "Quite striking, aren't they, the envy of every couple in the city, she the most beautiful and he the most handsome."

She looked at him pointedly and frowned. "I don't believe you've met them yet, have you? Come, I'll introduce you."

He had trouble focusing on the Witch's words as he shook his head. "If you don't mind, I'd rather not. Not tonight."

She misinterpreted his reticence. "Had a trying evening, have you?"

"Yes."

"I understand. Another time, then."

By the time the Witch was ready to leave, Jax had concluded that he was wrong about Lady Naesmyth; she was not his murderous lover from long ago. At the time he'd only been a sixteen year old boy, not yet wise in the ways of the world. He couldn't really trust his memories, not after so much time had passed.

As they gathered in the vestibule waiting for their carriage, Lord and Lady Naesmyth walked in behind them. They exchanged a few kind words with the Witch, but thankfully, Jax didn't have to interact with them because the Witch's carriage arrived quickly. They stepped out into the cool night air, and as Jax helped the three ladies into the coach, another carriage pulled up behind it. Lord and Lady Naesmyth walked out of the vestibule and approached it. Two men sat in the coach box above them. One of them climbed down and helped the Lord and Lady into the carriage. The fellow had a nasty scar that ran up the left side of his neck ending at his ear, where the ear lobe and the lower half of the ear had been chopped away long ago.

••••

In the carriage on the way back to the Witch Palace, Maelleen said, "I take it we failed."

"Yes and no," Jax said, trying to pull his thoughts away from Lady Naesmyth. "There's something else going on, and I need to think about it a bit."

"Then think away," the Witch said calmly. "We'll talk when we get back to the palace."

Jax should have spent the time thinking about the figurine, but he couldn't put that woman out of his mind. He tried not to think of the taste of her skin, but her blue eyes haunted every thought. It was close to midnight when they arrived at the Witch Palace, and Jax was still trying to digest what he'd seen and experienced in Carkoska's office, as well as whom he'd seen on the dance floor that evening. His thoughts kept skipping back and forth between the two disparate subjects, and he couldn't make any progress with either.

As they stepped out of the carriage the Witch looked at him and frowned. "You look like you could use a strong drink, young man." Turning to the other two women, she added, "I think we all could."

In her sitting room the Witch rang for a servant, and as the three women settled themselves on couches, she gave the fellow instructions. He returned a few minutes later with a silver tray containing a pitcher of chilled water, four small glasses, a bottle of cognac, and four glass snifters. As the servant left the room the Witch said, "Jax, will you do the honors?"

No one expressed any interest in the water so Jax poured a healthy splash of cognac in the snifters, then carried them to the ladies and handed one to each of them. Jax sat down in a large chair and swirled the cognac in his glass, trying to recall every detail of Carkoska's office, and wanting to forget Lady Naesmyth.

The Witch said, "Something clearly disturbed you, my little thief. Tell us about it."

Jax focused on the issue of the figurine and not the woman, though he found it exceedingly hard to do so. He described the office and told them how he'd checked out the window, looked out it and tried to memorize the grounds below. Then he told them how he'd found the figurine displayed openly, which surprised him greatly. "Just sitting there," he said, "out in the open on a pedestal for display. And yet it's locked away behind that office door so no one will ever see it."

"Describe it to me," the Witch said.

He did, and tried to be concise about details. "Based on the scale of the statue, the box she's holding would be about the size of my hand pressed flat, and about an inch thick."

"That sounds like the figurine we're after," she said. "Why didn't you take it when you had the opportunity?"

"It bothered me the way he had it on display."

"How so?"

Jax had to think carefully about his reaction to the presentation of the little statue. "Like a shrine, or a grand exhibit, a trophy on display to which you might invite people for a special showing. But why display it so in a locked room into which no one is ever allowed to go?"

The Witch's eyebrows rose and she nodded thoughtfully. "That is curious. Did you try to take it, or touch it?"

"I tried, but my instinct told me not to, warned me off before I touched it."

"Ah, your little ability comes into play."

"In fact," he added, "the closer I moved my hand to the figurine, the louder my instinct shouted that touching it would be a mistake."

Venessta said, "I don't understand."

The Witch came to the same conclusion Jax had when standing in Carkoska's office. "Perhaps it was rigged to some sort of mechanical alarm."

Jax went on to tell them how his instinct had drawn him to the desk, and then to the bottom drawer with the concealed compartment. "It contained a strongbox just about the right size to hold the figurine. I couldn't lift it out because the strongbox is attached to the drawer in some way, perhaps bolted down, but my instinct kept pushing me to it, and didn't warn me off at all."

The Witch said, "That does seem odd. I can understand why your instinct might warn you off if the figurine was attached to some sort of alarm, but why lead you to the strongbox?"

That was the question Jax had asked himself as he'd sat at the desk looking into the concealed compartment.

Maelleen said, "Perhaps the statue, openly on display, wasn't rigged to an alarm, but was just a fake."

Jax nodded. "Or both."

The Witch leaned toward him, her eyes narrowed, and she gave him an intent look. "Why do you say that?"

He'd been struggling with those disparate facts with every thought that didn't focus on Lady Naesmyth, and he thought that maybe he now had it figured out. "For the sake of argument, let's assume the figurine on display is a fake, a decoy, and it's attached to some alarm, with the real one hidden away elsewhere. If a thief does a quick grab-and-run with the false one, that protects the real one because he ignores it, and doesn't even look for it. And at the same time, by grabbing the false one he sets off the alarm and alerts them to his presence. Carkoska probably has a whole box of cheap imitations tucked away somewhere."

Venessta said, "They could eliminate a lot of thieves that way, one right after the other."

"Well I'm glad our Jax didn't get eliminated," Maelleen said. When he looked at her, she added, "I still have plans for you, darling."

The Witch sipped her cognac and looked thoughtful for a moment. "We'll have to get you back into that office somehow so you can see what's in that strongbox."

She looked at Maelleen. "And you, little harlot, are going to have to bed Lord Carkoska so we can do that. Did he try anything tonight?"

She grinned. "He got me alone briefly. We kissed most passionately, but he didn't try to take it further." Her eyes focused in the far distance for a moment as if lost in thought. "He wants me in his bed, and right now can think of nothing else."

••••

Jax spent a restless night thinking about the young boy who'd stepped into that coach on the street, and later washed up on the bank of the river. Jax had been lucky because he'd had his instinct, though that night long ago had been his first experience with it, and he hadn't truly understood it back then. How many other boys had lost their lives so that Lady Naesmyth and her husband could sate their desires for a few nights? And while Lord Naesmyth clearly had his own appetites, he'd refused to force himself on an unwilling partner. Jax certainly knew what it was like to live a life of which others did not approve, so he couldn't fault the man for the needs that drove him. But was he also a willing participant in murder? Jax struggled to recall the little snippets of whispered conversation he'd overheard that night. He couldn't deny that the husband participated willingly in their *sophisticated* life style. But Lady Naesmyth had said something to Lakorsa about her husband being weak willed, so was he no more than a dupe?

Jax slept poorly, and woke the next morning feeling tired and fatigued. He struggled to find any enthusiasm as they gathered for dance practice. With both Venessta and Maelleen present, the Witch announced, "I noticed a few mistakes at the ball last night, one or two in the dance, and one or two in manners and etiquette. Nothing to be embarrassed about, or that might tarnish one's reputation, but still, I expect perfection. So we're going to live the way all three of you must comport yourselves in public. We'll continue to practice dance, etiquette, and manners, and I want you to act like young nobles day and night, even here when no one is watching you."

Venessta raised an eyebrow, and gave both Maelleen and Jax a self-satisfied smile.

The Witch turned her ire on her apprentice. "And don't look so smug, little witch. They can get away with a little more because they're supposedly bumpkins from

Lieudess. But it was not just the little thief and the little harlot who made those mistakes. Yes, she's new at it, and yes, he's out of practice, but I think you've lived a rather sheltered existence here in this palace, always under my wing."

Venessta didn't see it, but the Witch finished by giving Jax a calculating look. He hated it when she gave him those looks. They usually portended some sort of machination that pitted Venessta against Maelleen, with Jax in the middle.

As Jax and Venessta paired off for the first dance, she pulled him into the intimately close embrace. He recalled the way she'd kissed him after Carkoska had discovered them in his office vestibule, and he didn't mind the embrace.

"Stop that," the Witch said. "That's probably why you made those mistakes. Dance with him now the way you should dance with a young man in polite company."

Venessta stepped unhappily away from him and they danced with their chins about a hand's breadth apart, though as time progressed she drifted closer, and Jax had to repeatedly readjust the distance to stave off further rebukes from the old woman.

Venessta smiled at him and blushed. "You forgot yourself last night."

"How do you mean?" he asked.

"In the vestibule," she said, "outside Lord Carkoska's office, when you kissed me, you forgot yourself and stopped pretending."

He shook his head and said, "No, I didn't."

"You did too stop pretending."

"I did stop pretending," he said, "but I didn't forget myself. I decided that if I allowed myself to enjoy pinching your nipple that way,"—she blushed—"it would only make it appear more real, and more convincing when we were discovered, so I allowed myself to enjoy it; a conscious decision."

"So you did enjoy it?"

He leaned close to her and momentarily broke the Witch's rule about maintaining proper distance. "Of course I did, though I have to admit the fondling-the-breast thing certainly helped. Next time I'm going to kiss it, maybe bite it a little."

She blushed again and her eyes widened. "There's not going to be a next time. You're not going to get another chance at that."

"Stop dancing so close," the Witch snapped.

Jax gave Venessta a lascivious smile. "I wasn't the only one who stopped pretending."

"What do you mean?"

"I do recall that hand of yours caressing my back side, squeezing it rather passionately."

"Children," the Witch barked, and Jax leaned away from her.

For once, Venessta seemed to be at a loss for words, and remained that way for the next few minutes until the dance ended.

Jax then danced with Maelleen, but the Witch dragged her off to talk about something, so he finished the practice session with Venessta. While the musicians put away their instruments Jax walked over to the window. As always, a Knight of the Witchguard stood in the shade of a tree watching him; different day, different knight, same tree, same shade.

What was Carkoska up to? he wondered. But more than that, what was it about the little statue that made it so much more valuable than its monetary worth? Why did the Witch want to acquire it so badly? Why did Carkoska keep it hidden away, but on display? And were the other High Houses involved? If the figurine displayed on the pedestal in his office was a trap, that certainly implied they were. Those questions were the key to his survival and Maelleen's, and he needed to find answers to them.

"Little thief."

At the sound of Venessta's voice Jax turned around. She had approached him and stood only a pace away. The musicians were gone, leaving the two of them alone in the room.

"I did forget myself," she said, though she seemed to have some trouble getting the words out.

"So did I," he said. "It's easy to do when you get to hold a beautiful woman in your arms and kiss her passionately."

She frowned, clearly considering his words, perhaps wondering if they contained some hidden insult. Her eyes brightened, she turned around, and as she walked to the door she had a little extra bounce in her step. She called the knights to escort Jax back up to his room.

That evening, when they escorted him down to dinner, Venessta was the only one in the small dining room.

She looked at him suspiciously. "Where are Mother and Maelleen?"

He shrugged. "I wouldn't know."

"They're rather obvious, aren't they?"

"What are you talking about?"

She looked at him as if addressing a naive child. "Mother and the little harlot; haven't you noticed the way they keep finding opportunities for you and me to be alone in a room together? Purely by happenstance, of course."

Now that she mentioned it, he recalled several instances like that, though he'd been too preoccupied to notice. "Why are they doing that?"

"They want you to seduce me."

"Why?"

"I'm not sure about Mother, but I'll wager Maelleen hopes I'll reveal all our secrets while crying out in ecstasy."

He rolled his eyes. "I think we already established you're not the type to cry out in ecstasy."

She shook her head carefully and stepped a little closer. "No, I'm not the type to reveal all our secrets, but crying out in ecstasy is another matter."

"Ah, then you do cry out in ecstasy?"

"I wouldn't know," she said.

The door opened and Maelleen and the Witch walked in.

They ate dinner, practiced their etiquette and manners, and throughout the evening Jax wondered at Venessta's words.

26

Secrets Revealed

NOW THAT VENESSTA had pointed it out to him, Jax noticed the way Maelleen and the Witch created one opportunity after another for the little witch and the little thief to be alone together. They'd leave early, arrive late, or sometimes not show up at all. He should have seen it himself. He wanted to ask Maelleen about it, and intended to press her on the matter, but he hadn't gotten her alone since before the dress ball at Carkoska.

Maelleen's relationship with Lord Carkoska progressed nicely. He invited her to dine at High House Carkoska one evening, and when she arrived, to her surprise, she learned that she and he had the entire estate to themselves. Lady Carkoska and their two sons were spending a few nights at their country estate outside of the city.

At the Witch Palace the following day Maelleen told Jax, Venessta, and the Witch of her evening with the High Lord. "Had I been a proper young woman, I would have insisted that I immediately return here, but I didn't. We dined, and afterward he wanted to show me some new artwork he'd acquired. It just happened to be temporarily stored in a sitting room on the second floor about as far from Lady Carkoska's boudoir as one can get. I could probably reside there for weeks, and never run into the lady of the house. We kissed, and both became inflamed with desire, so he lured me into an adjoining bedroom and seduced me there. I was terribly embarrassed that I was such a weak-willed young woman, but I couldn't help myself in the presence of such a powerful and commanding man."

Apparently, the Witch had spies all over the city, which didn't surprise Jax or Maelleen. Somehow she had learned that Lady Carkoska was making plans to spend a few weeks at their villa on the coast to breathe the sea air. She had to clear up certain responsibilities in the city first, so she wouldn't leave for several days. And Lord Carkoska couldn't clear his calendar at all, so he'd have to remain in Val d'Ossa.

"In fact," the Witch said, "Lady Carkoska intends to spend the time at their villa with one of her lovers,"—she looked pointedly at Maelleen—"and I'll venture that Lord Carkoska intends to spend the time in the city with his."

The old woman's analysis proved to be correct. The next day Lord Carkoska invited Maelleen to join him in House Carkoska while his wife was away. After dinner, Jax and the three women assembled in the Witch's sitting room to do some planning.

"This is our opportunity," Jax said. "With you inside, and the lady gone, it's almost ideal."

"Why only *almost?*" Venessta asked.

"It would be good if he and his sons were out of the house as well."

The Witch smiled happily. "The three of them dine at his club two nights a week like clockwork. They conduct a lot of important business there, so I doubt he'll stop doing so just because Maelleen is waiting and available."

Maelleen said, "And I'll encourage him to continue doing so. He'll quickly learn that he can have a wonderful evening with his cronies at the club, then finish it in bed with me. I'll be his dessert. I'm so weak; I just can't help myself in his virile presence."

Jax said, "It will be even better if you can learn the daily routine of the servants, and exactly where their quarters are. But how will we get that information from you?"

"I don't think that'll be a problem," Maelleen said. "Like any man, after the first day or two, he won't want to spend every hour of the day with me, so I should have no trouble getting free. Especially during the day."

Venessta perked up excitedly. "You and I can meet for lunch. I know a stylish, little café frequented by young women like us."

"Start now," Jax said. "Before she takes up residence there. Establish a pattern that won't be something new."

The Witch said, "And you can do a little shopping afterwards. That would certainly be in character."

Jax asked, "And when Lady Carkoska returns?"

"We should have this finished by then," Maelleen said, "and I'll move back here."

Jax still needed more information on the Carkoska property. "One more thing, I need to reconnoiter that property again, at night." He described how he'd done that once before, and how that had convinced him not to accept the job Nathaniel had offered him through the middleman Rondo.

The Witch said, "I'll ask Captain Darganna to assign the same two men to you."

Jax grimaced and didn't try to hide his disapproval. "How good are they at sneaking about at night?"

The Witch dismissed his concerns with a wave of her hand. "I'm sure he has men who are good at operating covertly."

Jax shook his head. "This isn't a nighttime military assault. How good are they at skulking and thieving?"

Venessta wrinkled her nose. "Probably no better than they were at pretending to be street ruffians."

Maelleen leaned toward the Witch and placed a hand gently on her wrist. It was an intimate gesture that spoke volumes about the relationship developing between the old woman and her little harlot.

"Mother," Maelleen said, "you're going to have to start trusting us, at least to some degree. And you'll have me here to ensure Jax's return, so let him go alone."

The old woman sighed dramatically. "Very well. When?"

Jax tried not to sound relieved. "Tomorrow night."

The knights escorted Jax up to his room. He pulled off his tail coat and tossed it on the bed, and was unbuttoning his waistcoat when the ratcheting chunk of the door lock drew his attention. It was followed by a polite knock that sounded nothing like the commanding rap the Witch Knights usually produced. He assumed Maelleen had come to see him.

He walked over to the door, opened it, and to his surprise he found Venessta standing there looking at him uncertainly. A knight stood behind her, one eyebrow lifted in an unasked question.

"Venessta," Jax said, unable to hide his surprise. "What can I do for you?"

"I want to talk. Won't you invite me in?"

He stepped aside. "By all means."

She walked past him and the knight tried to follow her, but she turned back to him and said, "Please wait out in the hallway. Master Jaxon and I have something private to discuss."

"But Mistress Venessta," he said. "My duty—"

"He's not going to harm me," she said. "And if he tried, don't forget that I'm a witch. I'll turn him into a toad or something."

The knight reluctantly nodded his acquiescence.

"Thank you," she said. "I'll knock when I'm ready to leave. And please don't disturb us until I do."

The knight nodded again, Jax closed the door, but he didn't hear the lock engage. The fellow was being cautious. He didn't want to waste time with keys and the lock should he need to rush into the room to rescue the young woman from a brutal assault by the disreputable thief.

Venessta turned away from Jax and began a circuit of the room, walking slowly and examining everything carefully. Jax followed a pace behind her.

She stopped at the wingback chair and ran her fingers along the brocade fabric. "It's identical to Maelleen's room."

"Yes," he said.

She glanced over her shoulder. "I'm sorry about the day I spied on you from this chair. It was . . . thoughtless."

He smiled, trying to put her at ease. "Apology accepted."

She grimaced. "Thank you."

She turned and continued the circuit of the room, stopped at the barred window and looked out at the night, and the dimly lit courtyard below.

He asked, "Why are you here?"

She turned to face him, and appeared to carefully consider her words for a moment, then blurted out, "I think it's time you lure me up to your room and seduce me."

Her words sounded hollow and forced. He stepped toward her and stopped with his face only inches from hers, though he didn't touch her. "Since you're already here, the luring part isn't necessary."

She wouldn't meet his eyes. "But the seducing part is?"

He couldn't hide a frown as he looked at her carefully. "Why now?"

"The gods know Mother and the harlot want you to seduce me. And you said I'm beautiful, and that you forgot yourself when you kissed me."

She sounded petulant, not like a young girl thrilled and excited at the prospect of satisfying her desires with a passionate liaison. More like a young woman who must reluctantly carry out an unpleasant task. He reached out and put his hands around her waist. "It was easy to forget myself with you."

"Thank you."

He recalled their conversation when they'd found themselves alone just before dinner. "You once implied that you've never really . . . enjoyed yourself."

Her eyes lost their focus, as if recalling a memory. "When it was time for me to . . . give myself to a man . . . the Witch arranged it: a young fellow from a good house, though a minor one, to minimize any possible complications. I don't think he was terribly experienced. There was some pleasure but it was . . . mechanical, little better than pleasuring one's self. There've been other times. But still, at best, they were only a little less mechanical, and not much more pleasurable."

"No passion," he said. He gently pulled her toward him.

"No," she said. "No passion. Is that really important?"

He smiled and said, "You tell me."

He kissed her, and she responded, but without heat or desire—no passion. It felt as if she tried very hard to be something she thought she should be. He ended the kiss. "You don't really want me to seduce you, do you?"

She wouldn't meet his eyes. "I don't know."

"No," he said. "If this was your desire, you would know."

She stepped out of his arms. "I don't think you really want to seduce me."

He shrugged. "I do and I don't. You're a beautiful woman, and I could enjoy myself greatly with you. But . . ."

She reached up and gently traced a finger along his jaw. "I've seen the way you look at Maelleen. She only sees the lust in your eyes, but I see something else there when you look at her."

He shrugged again. "Maelleen . . . is Maelleen."

She turned around and walked to the window, stood there looking down at the courtyard. "Mother and Maelleen won't let up until you and I wind up in bed together."

She was right. Those two conniving women were set on seeing to it the little thief got between the little witch's legs. Jax wished Maelleen would spend more time trying to get herself in his bed. He had to figure out something to get the pressure off the little witch. "I have an idea."

She turned away from the window and looked at him. "An idea?"

"Trust me," he said. "We'll make them think I seduced you. Take off your clothes and get into bed. And throw your garments about the room, as if I tore them off in the heat of passion." He turned his back on her. "I won't look. And I won't touch you."

"You promise you won't look?"

"Well," he said. "I might peek just a little. You are, after all, a beautiful woman."

She giggled. He heard the rustle of material, punctuated by a few more giggles. Then her dress landed atop his head. He left it there and waited. More giggles, then he heard the rustle of the bed sheets. He glanced over his shoulder and caught a glimpse of her little bottom as she climbed under the covers. As he suspected, it wasn't really pink. He looked away and heard the bed creak. "I'm ready."

He tossed her dress to one side and turned about. She lay in the bed with the sheets and covers pulled tightly up about her neck.

He tossed his waistcoat to one side, and as he unbuttoned his trousers, she asked, "Should I not look?"

He paused and considered that for a moment. "As I recall, you've already seen everything—" He nodded toward the wingback chair. "—from that chair."

She grimaced. "Not absolutely everything."

He continued removing his clothing. He was, after all, a whore. "Look, or not, I don't care."

She didn't look away as he finished undressing. Then he extinguished the gas sconces on the walls, leaving only a single candle to illuminate the room with a flickering light. But when he climbed in bed beside her, she spoke in a panicked hiss. "What are you doing?"

"If they check on us, it'll look like we've made love. But don't worry, I won't touch you."

She giggled, and they talked, though they spoke of unimportant things. When she grew drowsy, she rolled onto her side, and slid her rear up against him. "You can touch me, but not in that way."

He rolled onto his side, facing her, and wrapped an arm around her. It was difficult lying in bed with a naked woman and doing nothing about it, but he kept his promise. They fell asleep that way.

At some time during the night he awoke to the sound of the door creaking open. The candle still cast its flickering light across the room. The door closed.

"You were right," she whispered. "They did check on us."

Jax fell asleep with a beautiful young woman in his arms.

••••

When Jax awoke with a soft, delicate body in his arms, he had a moment where he thought he was lying next to Maelleen; more out of habit than anything else, because he hadn't slept with another woman in a long time. Then he recalled the previous night, and Venessta.

She lay on her side with her back to him, the sheets tangled around her waist. He took a moment to admire the slight olive hue of her skin, then edged up on one elbow and traced two fingers along the line of her neck and down her shoulder.

She started and tensed. "Am I lying where I think I'm lying?"

"Yes."

"You didn't touch me?"

"I would hope if I had touched you, in that way, you would remember, though I must admit, it's rather difficult to lay in a bed with a beautiful, naked, young woman in my arms, and not . . . do something."

"Thank you."

"You're welcome."

From above and behind her he could see the side of her face as her lips curled up into a smile.

He leaned down and put his lips close to her ear. "By the way, I confirmed last night that your bottom is not pink. It's got a slight olive—"

She abruptly rolled over, facing him and laughing. Then she looked down and her eyes widened as she realized that, with the sheets tangled around her hips, she was naked from the waist up. She tugged at the sheets and pulled them up to her neck. Maelleen would have shrugged, sat up and tossed the sheets aside, not in the least concerned about her nakedness.

He smiled and said, "I did peek, couldn't help myself."

Venessta looked under the sheet at her own naked body, but she still wouldn't abandon the sheet. "Last night, you said my previous experience . . . was not . . . as pleasurable as it should have been because it lacked passion. What did you mean?"

"Heat," he said. "Fire in your soul, a desire for the other person so intense, you have to force yourself to slow down so you don't simply rut like a couple of animals, a need for their touch, the smell of their skin, their sweat, anything. I don't think I'm describing it that well, but when you feel it you know it. And you've never felt anything like that?"

She looked thoughtful for a moment. "Almost . . . once . . . about fifteen years ago."

Jax had to replay her words carefully in his mind to process that. He would have guessed her age at something close to his twenty-five years, maybe a few years short of that. Fifteen years ago she would have been a pubescent pre-teen. "Fifteen years ago?" he asked.

Her eyes widened again, but now with fear, and they both realized she had just revealed a secret, but he wasn't sure what.

"How long have you been with the old Witch?" he asked.

Venessta hesitated. "I first apprenticed to her when I was nine?"

"How long have you been with the old Witch?" he asked again.

He watched her think carefully, watched her consider lying to him, then watched resignation flood her face with sadness. "A little over thirty years."

"Thirty . . . years . . ." he said. "You're close to forty years old? How can that be?"

Venessta's eyes glistened with tears, but she didn't shed any. "We witches . . . those of us who are most powerful . . . we . . . age slowly. My aging slowed down considerably once I apprenticed to Mother."

In thirty years with the Witch, Venessta had aged less than half that. She was close to forty and yet, looked his age. The Witch herself looked to be absolutely ancient.

When he realized where that thought had taken him he sat up. "How old is Mother?"

Venessta sat up also, still clutching the sheets tightly to her chest. "I don't know. Very old."

He demanded, "Take a guess."

She flinched and lowered her head as one tear slid down her cheek. "Four . . . or five hundred years—I don't know for sure."

As he sat there, trying to absorb the enormity of what he'd just heard, another tear slid down her cheek. He reached out and wiped it onto the tip of his finger, then he touched it to his tongue and tasted the salt in it. It was a very human tear.

She wouldn't meet his eyes as he reached out and hooked a fingertip over the top of the sheet where she had it clutched against her neck. He tugged downward, and she resisted, so he stopped and retracted his hand.

Without warning she released the sheet and buried her face in her hands. "I'm not a monster," she said. She didn't make any noise, no gasps or sobs, but tears dripped between the fingers of both hands.

The sheet had dropped to her lap, fully exposing her breasts. He looked at them now, small, delicate, and so very human. He looked at her shoulders, also small, delicate and human.

He watched a tear slide down her chest and stop when it reached the swell of her breast. He leaned forward, bent down and licked the tear off her skin, leaving a soft kiss in its place.

She gasped. "What are you doing?"

He looked into her eyes. "You're very human, and not a monster, and I hope someday you find that passion. You deserve it."

She smiled.

He slid out of bed and stood. "Let's get dressed. And again, I promise not to look, but I'm a consummate liar, so like last night, I'm probably lying about that too."

27

Who Seduced Whom?

JAX WAITED FOR night to settle fully over the city before setting out to reconnoiter the Carkoska property. A moon, only two nights from full, rose with the setting sun, and in a few more hours would sit in the night sky directly overhead. He'd learned long ago that his night job sometimes benefitted from a large, bright moon on a clear night. The enhanced illumination increased the chance that someone might spot him, but the added brightness darkened the moon shadows in the city, turning them into intense, black splotches of safety in which to hide. And because of the added advantage of his instinct, he faced little danger of discovery. He donned his lurking-in-the-shadows outfit and cloak, threw the strap of the canvas valise over his shoulder, and slipped out of the Witch Palace into the night.

The Palace's location made it an ideal base of operations for this job. Located in the heart of the District of Nobles, it was only about a ten-minute walk to High House Carkoska. But since Jax was lurking from shadow to shadow, it proved to be a twenty-minute lurk.

He squatted in the shadow of a large shrub at the far end of the street and waited. All of the properties on that street were walled, which meant that, with the exception of the small day park across from Carkoska, and each main entrance, he had uninterrupted walls running the length of the street on both sides. Their heights varied a little from property to property, but not much. The almost-full moon illuminated the street brightly, but cast a deep, black shadow at the base of the wall on the Carkoska side. Moving in a crouch, one cautious step at a time, Jax slipped into that shadow and started down the street.

The blackness of the shadow concerned him because he might not see a twig before he stepped on it. If it snapped and made any noise whatsoever, his life could be forfeit. So he tested each step carefully before putting weight on his foot. He also paused at the boundary between each property and the next. He waited and listened quietly to the night and its sounds, and didn't proceed until he knew the rhythm of the night guards patrolling the next property. Some, like Carkoska, were more heavily guarded than others.

Jax's first real obstacle was the main gate on the first property. Like all of the main entrances on the street, a high wrought iron gate blocked entry to the property, and it cast no moon shadow other than a few dark lines from the iron bars. To cross the space in front of it meant he'd have to step out of the shadow beneath the wall. He listened carefully to his instinct, and when it told him to go, he moved quickly across the distance to the other side. He slipped into the shadow at the base of the wall there and froze. No cries of alarm broke the stillness of the night; no guards rushed to investigate furtive movement near the gate. He breathed easier and continued on.

When he reached the main gate at the front of High House Carkoska, he paused in the shadow near its hinges. Through the wrought iron gate he had a slanting view of the grounds, the driveway beyond the gate, and the fountain in the turnaround. The near-full moon outshone pools of illumination from dimly lit lamps. The shadows beneath trees and shrubs were so deep they could hide almost anything, including any number of guardsmen. He listened carefully for several minutes and confirmed that the rhythm of the night guards had not changed since his last visit.

He crossed to the other side of the gate to get a view from a different angle, and didn't learn anything new from that. He listened to his instinct, and when the time was right, crossed to the day park on the north side of the street. Once again, he climbed up into the elm tree, secured the canvas valise on the lowest branch, retrieved his telescope, and ascended to the perch from which he could see the Carkoska grounds.

Now that he'd visited the property and been inside twice, the configuration of the building and the layout of the grounds made a little more sense. The main building was a square, two-story structure with a flat roof hidden behind a knee-high, stone balustrade. It faced north where the street ran in front of it. The window to Carkoska's office was on the back of the house, and though he couldn't see it, he recalled that it was near the west corner overlooking an expanse of ornamental gardens. He saw what he thought might be a carriage house built against the west wall near the back of the property, but the distance was too great for him to make out any detail. A wing on the east side appeared to have been added sometime after the initial construction, turning the house from square to L-shaped. The addition also had a flat roof and decorative balustrades. The original structure had been situated at the center of the property, so the addition had considerably narrowed the gap between it and the east wall. From Maelleen's description, Jax guessed Carkoska had seduced her somewhere near the back of the later addition, and that was probably where he would house her while Lady Carkoska spent time with her lover on the coast.

Jax needed to see that office window on the back side of the property, so he climbed out of the elm tree, shouldered his canvas valise, and worked his way back to the end of the street. He headed south one block and turned down a street running parallel to that containing High House Carkoska. The properties on the north side of that street abutted the rear of the properties he'd just observed. From the spacing of the main gates, they appeared to be smaller, and some were not as heavily guarded. But only when Jax reached the back wall of the Carkoska property did he truly understand the layout.

The depth of the Carkoska property stretched the entire block, and its back wall ran along the street behind it. Some properties on either side of it were merely a quarter its size, only half as wide and half as deep. They were probably minor houses aligned with, or bearing allegiance to, Carkoska. It occurred to Jax that these *minor* houses were minor only in comparison to Carkoska, and were far above the minimal status his father had attained. His father's property had been a terraced row house near the edge of the District of Nobles, with a small enclosed garden at the back, and attached stables. He hoped that Julia and Felix had somehow managed to keep it.

Jax crossed the street to put a little distance between him and the back wall of House Carkoska. He stepped into the shadow at the base of the wall there, and from that vantage he saw several windows on the second floor at the back of the house. Using the small telescope, he noted that his earlier assessment when inside the office had been correct. The window was built into a shallow dormer embedded in a steeply pitched slope of stone work or slate tiles. At that distance and under the dark of night he couldn't be certain, but he thought the stone work around the dormer had some texture to it. It was a decorative touch he'd seen on other buildings, and it would considerably lessen the difficulty of climbing from the window up to the roof.

He counted six windows across the back of the house on the second floor, all identical and evenly spaced. He thought he could pick out the office with the figurine, but any lack of certainty might get him killed. Maelleen would have to pin that detail down if he chose to enter through that window.

He crossed the street again to the back wall of the Carkoska property, then continued down the street to investigate the rest of the minor houses there. To his surprise, when he stopped at the property next to Carkoska to listen to the night sounds, he heard nothing like the small noises he would expect to hear from guards patrolling the grounds. He waited a few more minutes and still heard nothing. He continued on and stopped at the property's main entrance, waited there for some minutes and still heard nothing. For some reason that small property employed no night guards, a property adjacent to the southeast corner of High House Carkoska. That interesting little bit of information needed more investigation, and he made a mental note to learn why the property stood unguarded at night.

Jax had seen more than enough, so he shouldered his canvas valise and headed back to the Witch Palace. As he approached it, a couple of incognito Witch Knights stepped out of a shadow. They took up positions on either side of him, matching his pace. One of them said, "Weren't sure you'd come back."

Jax shrugged as he walked. "You have someone who's important to me."

"Aye," the fellow said. "I'd come back for that whore too."

Only then did Jax realize that when he'd mentioned someone important, he'd been thinking of both Maelleen and Venessta.

When he stepped into the palace proper, uniformed knights took over, escorted him up to his room, and locked him in. He lit a single candle, stripped off his clothes and tossed them over the wingback chair near the window, then blew out the candle. To his pleasant surprise, when he climbed into bed, his hand encountered a soft, bare thigh. A lithe, naked young woman lay asleep in his bed. He slipped under the covers next to Venessta.

She stirred and spoke, her words a groggy whisper. "You're back."

He said, "You're here."

Still groggy and only half awake, she said, "Thank you."

He wrapped an arm around her. "You're welcome."

They fell asleep that way.

••••

A few days later, for the second time in Jax's experience, without warning the door to his room swung all the way around on its hinges and slammed against the wall. The Witch stormed in, so angry and worked up that she'd already assumed the aspect of the beautiful, twenty-something blonde with coal-black eyes. She screamed at the top of her lungs, "What did you do to the little witch?"

He recalled Venessta's tears when he'd discovered her age, but he thought they'd moved past that, and he wondered if he'd done something else to make her cry. "I didn't make her cry again. I'm sure I didn't."

She pointed a finger at his nose. "You seduced her."

He backed away from her with his hands held up between them. He and Venessta had agreed they would maintain the lie of her seduction. "It was more like she seduced me. She pretty much demanded it. She's not crying again, is she?"

"No," the old woman shouted, wagging her finger at him. "You seduced her."

"What's wrong with that? You made it awfully clear you wanted me to, did everything but print invitations."

"But not like that."

"Not like what? The physical act is pretty straight forward, when you get right down to it. There are a few minor variations—" At the look on the Witch's face, Jax decided it might be wise to shut up.

She put her fists on her hips. "She's walking around all mooney-eyed and gaga. I can't get her to pay attention, I can't get her to focus on her lessons. All she talks about is how nice you've been to her, and how much she likes it when you're nice to her."

Jax's ego got a pleasant little boost from that, but he really hadn't done anything to make Venessta react that way, and that bothered him.

The Witch jabbed her finger into the middle of his chest hard enough to hurt. "I can see exactly what you're thinking. Wipe that smug look off your face right this minute."

"But what am I supposed to do?"

"Stop being nice to her."

"Just like that?"

"Yes, just like that."

She spun on her heel and marched out of the room. No knight needed to reach in and close the door. As she passed it, the door swung shut of its own accord, as if sucked closed by a whirlwind swirling violently in her wake. It slammed shut with a loud crash, and a moment later the lock ratcheted into place.

••••

At dinner that evening only two places had been set, and they'd been positioned at opposite ends of the table. The Witch and Venessta did not appear, so Jax and Maelleen had the small dining room to themselves. It was the first time they'd been alone together in some time. Jax repositioned his chair and moved his place setting to sit close to her.

"So," Maelleen asked, toying with the food on her plate, "you seduced the little witch, eh?" She seemed unsure of herself, which was unlike Maelleen.

"How did you hear about that?" He wasn't sure he wanted to know the answer to that question, but he needed to ask anyway.

Her eyes widened and she grimaced. "I had to listen to the old woman detail any number of rather inventive ways of killing you. Most of them involved cutting up, or cutting off, various body parts,"—she leaned back and glanced down at his crotch— "usually beginning with that one. And they had one common thread: all of them involved keeping you alive for a very long time so you can watch your own little bits blacken, wither and rot away. She went into a lot of detail about the blackening, withering and rotting-away part."

Jax's heart climbed up into his throat.

Maelleen wouldn't meet his eyes, and she spoke tentatively. "What did you do to that girl?"

Jax had specifically promised Venessta he would not reveal their secret to either the Witch or Maelleen. Other than his thieving, he'd never kept any secrets from Maelleen, and doing so now made him uncomfortable. "I just . . . well . . . you know."

"Oh dear," Maelleen said. "You look rather pale." She reached out and touched his cheek, their eyes met for a moment, and she looked away from him immediately, as if he might see some hidden secret in her face. "Don't worry, I think I talked her into keeping you alive for another day or two. It helps that she really wants that figurine, and she's convinced you're the only one who can get it for her. And she's torn between wanting to cut those little bits off of you, and needing you to use some of those little bits to keep the little witch human. You did use those little bits to keep the little witch human, didn't you?"

Jax leaned back and looked at her carefully. She toyed with her food, still refusing to look him in the eyes. "What are you not telling me?"

"I . . ." she said. "I . . . uh . . ."

"Out with it," Jax demanded. To emphasize his point, he drummed his fingers on the table, while he sat silently staring daggers at her and waiting for her to speak.

"Venessta . . . and I . . ." She swallowed, as if gulping down something unpleasant. "Venessta and I were . . . alone, in her chambers. She wanted to know what I did to seduce a man, how I went about it. It was girl talk, nothing more. We laughed and giggled a lot, and then . . . she kissed me."

She looked to Jax for some encouragement, but he refused to soften the hard stare he aimed at her.

"She kissed me, not a peck on the cheek, but on the lips, a passionate kiss with heat and desire . . . and . . . well . . ."

She finally looked him in the eyes, a grimace on her face. "One thing led to another, and . . ."

Jax couldn't hold back a laugh. "You seduced her."

She shook her head and wrinkled her nose. "Well . . . we sort of seduced each other."

For once, Jax got to enjoy Maelleen's discomfort. "Did you enjoy yourself?"

She continued to toy with her food. "I did. I mean, there was pleasure, but I'm not that way. I much prefer a man, with man parts. But yes, I did enjoy myself. She is a lovely little creature."

Jax laughed again, and couldn't stop laughing until he had tears in his eyes.

Maelleen's eyes narrowed with anger. "It's not funny."

Jax got control of himself and wiped a tear out of his eye. He leaned close to Maelleen, planted a kiss on her cheek, then whispered in her ear. "It's hilarious, because I *didn't* seduce her."

She pulled away from him, her eyes widened, and her anger blossomed ten-fold. "You didn't."

Jax told her the details of his night with the little witch, and her anger slowly diminished as he related the story.

"So all you did was lay there with a naked young woman in your arms and you did nothing?"

He shrugged. "We talked, quite a bit, in fact."

"Interesting," she said. "You're her friend, and I'm her lover."

Jax asked, "Did she cry out in the throes of ecstasy?"

"Yes, she did do that."

"Did you cry out in the throes of ecstasy?"

Jax was really enjoying Maelleen's discomfort. "Not as loud as her, but . . . I did make a little noise."

"Did she tell you all her secrets?"

She shook her head. "No, not really. I learned nothing of value. Did you?"

He grinned. "I believe I did. She's never felt passion before. When it was time for her to lose her virginity—by the way, she referred to it as *giving herself to a man*—the Witch arranged for it. It all sounded rather cold-blooded."

"You're joking," Maelleen said as the corners of her mouth curled downward in an incredulous frown. "Just arranged for it, no groping and experimenting with some handsome young boy and foolishly losing her head? And how did they decide it was time for her to . . . give herself to a man?"

Jax held his hands out to his sides and shook his head. "Don't ask me. They probably discussed it very dispassionately. She described her prior relationships as mechanical."

Maelleen curled her nose up in distaste. "I can understand that. I guess I would use the word *mechanical* to describe what happens with the men who hire me. And men like Carkoska aren't much better, though he did give me pleasure when he seduced me. But I'll wager that after a few more times he'll get lazy and I'll have to start pretending."

She reached out and traced a finger along the line of his jaw. "I don't ever have to pretend with you, darling. That's why I like you: you *like* women. Do you like Venessta?"

He didn't have to think about that. "I do, when she's not being a childish imp."

"Good," she said. "That young woman needs someone who likes her."

"She's not so young," he said. "She's almost forty years old. I learned that too. And the old witch is probably four or five hundred years old, though that's just a guess."

Maelleen's eyebrows shot up. "I don't understand."

Jax told her how he'd learned Venessta's true age. "And yet, she doesn't act like someone that old. She's as emotionally vulnerable as any young woman."

Maelleen's eyes grew distant, she lifted her empty fork to her mouth and tapped it on her lower lip. "Perhaps, if the body doesn't age, the mind doesn't age as well. And living here in this palace all these years, under the thumb of that old woman, I can't imagine she'd accumulate much experience of life. It must have been a rather sad way to grow up."

Knowing the Witch, Jax had to agree with that. "And then there's all the magical witch stuff they do—at least I assume they do magical witch stuff. That must affect her in some way. The Witch told me they're forced to interact with creatures that have no emotions."

"Hmmm," Maelleen said. "I suppose they shut their own emotions down when dealing with them."

Jax leaned toward her and whispered, "And don't forget the forked tongue thing. Makes me wonder how much humanity the old woman can still claim."

He straightened and spoke in a normal tone. "She was absolutely furious with me. Not so much for seducing the little witch, but for making her happy. But apparently, it's you who made her happy."

Maelleen gave him a look, nodded and said, "I think we both make her happy. As I said, I'm her lover, and you're her friend. Someday Venessta is going to inherit the old woman's throne, darling. It will be a good thing if we can keep the little witch human, and I would think keeping her happy does that. You and I will keep her happy, and I'll work with the old woman to keep all your little bits in one piece and still connected to you."

"Thank you," he said. "I do appreciate that."

She leaned over and kissed him on the cheek. "My motives are somewhat self-serving, because I intend to continue making use of those little bits as well. And I can't very well do that if they're missing or damaged, can I?"

They were playing a dangerous game, and a thought occurred to Jax. "I don't think we should tell Venessta that I know you seduced her, and you know I didn't."

Maelleen considered his words for a moment and nodded. "I have to agree with you on that, darling. And if the young girl ever tells you the truth about me, or me the truth about you, we should pretend we didn't know about it until she told us."

In that, they were in agreement. They finished dinner talking about trivialities.

Venessta didn't come to Jax's room that night. He had mixed feelings about that. On the one hand he hoped she would, but on the other, he feared the Witch's wrath if she did. The next morning Venessta didn't show up at dance practice either, and the Witch was surly throughout the entire session. And while the old woman joined Jax and Maelleen for dinner that evening, without the little witch, the table conversation consisted of long swaths of silence, punctuated by a series of terse remarks and unpleasant looks from the Witch.

28

Buried Memories

THE WITCH HAD decided to resume the daily dance practice, so Jax dressed appropriately and the knights escorted him down to the sitting room. Only Maelleen and the musicians were present when he stepped through the door. Jax immediately pulled her aside and lowered his voice. "What's going on?"

Maelleen shook her head fearfully. "The old woman has kept Venessta locked in her room, and there's been a little war going on between them. So I had a talk with the Witch, then, with her permission, I had a long talk with Venessta. Apparently, I've managed to broker a truce, though hostilities could resume at any moment. Be very careful today."

Jax had watched Maelleen's relationship with the Witch grow, and it appeared that in many ways she had become one of the old woman's closest advisers.

Maelleen added, "The old woman needs her to remain human, but she also needs her to become a powerful witch. I think it's a delicate balancing act."

A few minutes later the two witches arrived, and when they entered the room the temperature seemed to drop considerably. As the young witch helped the old woman sit in her usual place on the couch, neither of them said anything, nor did they show any expression on their faces. The musicians struck up a tune on their instruments, Jax took Venessta in his arms—at an appropriate distance for polite company—and they danced.

Venessta wouldn't meet his eyes. They danced for a few minutes in silence, then she looked up and said, "She's kept me locked in my room."

He nodded. "I know."

"Have you missed me?"

"Of course."

She stopped dancing and he stopped with her. Looking in her eyes, his instinct told him she was about to do something defiant, but it didn't prepare him for exactly what she had in mind. She wrapped her arms around his neck and kissed him in a passionate way. She backed him across the room until he came up against the wall. The music died in a stutter of missed notes as she reached down, grabbed his hand and lifted it up to her breast. She pressed his hand heavily against it, and he was reminded of her comment in the vestibule outside Carkoska's office, and how he'd been ". . . kneading her flesh like a glob of lumpy dough."

He felt no pleasure or desire, and from the tension in her body he sensed that she felt none as well. Over her shoulder he saw the Witch staring at him, and he wondered if now he'd learn how to live the life of a toad, or sit alone in the dungeon and watch parts of him blacken and rot away.

Into the silence, the Witch said, "My dear, why don't you just drop his trousers, lift your dress, and have him pleasure you against the wall."

Venessta leaned away from Jax and looked at him, tears welling in her eyes.

The Witch said, "The musicians, Maelleen and I can watch. Perhaps I'll learn something new. Maelleen tells me he's quite talented."

Venessta buried her face in her hands, turned, and ran from the room.

••••

After two tense days of the Witch and Venessta snarling at each other, an uneasy truce settled over the Witch Palace. The old woman, Venessta, Jax, and Maelleen slowly returned to a state of normalcy. *That is*, Jax thought, *if anything about the four of us could be considered normal.*

Venessta didn't always come to his bed, but he noticed that when she did, she sought comfort or solace in some way. Sometimes the old woman had done something to upset her, and she complained about the Witch's stubborn and unyielding nature. One time, after listening to Venessta voice her complaints with considerable vehemence, Jax decided that the little witch herself had been a nasty, little snot. He used all his powers of persuasion to carefully point out to her that, possibly, it was she who had been unreasonable. When he finished he tensed, waiting for her to explode in an eruption of monumental proportions. But instead, she grimaced, and whined like a child, "You're right. I know. I should probably apologize to her."

The next morning the Witch intercepted Jax as the Witch Knights escorted him down to breakfast. "Thank you, little thief."

"For what? What did I do?"

She smiled, one of the few times she did so with a pleasant look. "I never realized you might be good for us both."

She would say no more, and he let it drop.

One time Venessta came to his bed in the wee hours of the morning, and her demeanor was cold and distant. As she climbed beneath the sheets next to him, she lay on her side facing away from him and said nothing.

He asked, "Did I do something to upset you?"

She shivered. "No. It's not you. We've just spent several hours dealing with some-thing . . . inexplicable and . . . very strange. It was . . . frightening. I've never experi-enced anything like that . . . and . . ."

She shivered again, and wiggled her rear until she slid it up against him. "Just hold me. Please."

He wrapped an arm around her and hugged her tightly. She felt cold to the touch, and beneath his arm her heart beat with a rapidity that had to be unhealthy. Little by little, as the minutes passed, her pulse slowed and he felt the tension in her back and shoulders recede.

Her breathing had slowed to that soft, comfortable rhythm where he thought she must be asleep. She surprised him when she spoke. "I love you."

He almost started, but controlled his reaction.

She laughed. "You don't have to say you love me too. Just hold me."

He had never in his entire life said those words. He might have said them to his mother, had he known her. He might have said them to his sister or his brother, had there ever been any love between them. He'd never said them to his father, because neither of them needed to voice those feelings. And though he had wanted to many times, he'd never said them to Maelleen, because she would just laugh in his face.

"I've never in my entire life said those words to another human being."

She sounded groggy and only half awake. "Really?"

"Truly."

"That's sad."

"Not as sad as you might think."

She shook her butt back and forth and snuggled more tightly into his embrace. "Maybe someday I'll let you touch me in that way you're not supposed to."

"And maybe someday I'll decline."

"You're just teasing me."

"Perhaps. Perhaps not. I don't really know."

They fell asleep that way.

••••

They had wasted a couple of days with the little war between the two witches. Jax was getting nervous because they still had a lot to do before Maelleen took up temporary residence in High House Carkoska. Maelleen told him she had found another oppor-tunity to make love to Venessta. Apparently, Venessta began paying attention to her lessons again, had left behind the stage of *walking around all mooney-eyed and gaga*, and that pleased the Witch greatly. Jax thought that perhaps he wouldn't have to learn how to live the life of a toad, at least not for the time being.

With Lady Carkoska about to leave for the coast, and Maelleen about to take up residence in High House Carkoska, the four of them met in the Witch's sitting room to do some planning. Maelleen and Venessta sat on one couch, the Witch on another, while Jax paced back and forth in front of them, relating what he'd observed during his nocturnal reconnaissance of the Carkoska property.

The Witch snapped, "Would you kindly stop pacing, young man? It's irritating."

Jax stopped and faced her.

"And what's bothering you so?" she demanded.

He held his hands up in a helpless gesture. "From the outside I can't tell which window to go into."

She frowned. "Explain."

"There are six windows on the back of the original structure on the second floor, all identical in size and appearance. That hallway clearly runs the length of the second floor, so if I assume one window per door, then the fourth door on the left would indicate it's the fourth window from the southeast corner."

Maelleen said, "One window per door is a dangerous assumption."

Jax smiled unpleasantly. "Exactly."

The Witch said, "I can understand that you don't want to climb up there and find that you're at the wrong window."

Jax shook his head. "But I'm not going to climb up there from below, I'm going to climb *down* there from above."

Earlier, he'd sketched the layout of the Carkoska property. Maelleen had confirmed that Carkoska had bedded her in an elegantly furnished guestroom in the far southeast corner of the newer addition, and it had a balcony facing east. Jax crossed the room, lifted a small table and carried it to the Witch, placed it in front of her and spread the sketch out on top of it. Venessta and Maelleen stood and stepped behind him to look over his shoulder.

He pointed a finger at the approximate location of the office window. "If I climb up from below, I'm going to have to cross a hundred feet of property that's heavily patrolled by guards." He stabbed a finger at the southeast corner near the wing that had been added. "But if he houses Maelleen here, I only have to cross about thirty feet from the east wall to the addition. And it'll be easier because Maelleen will throw a rope down to me. That southeast corner is not as heavily patrolled. I'll climb up to Maelleen, and at that point I can use the interior halls to get to the office, then pick the lock on the office door and enter as I did during the ball. Alternatively, the roof is flat, and I saw no guards making rounds on it, so I can climb up to the roof from her room, cross it to the office, then climb down and jimmy the window. We'll know which way I should go once Maelleen has spent more than a night or two there."

He glanced over his shoulder at Maelleen. "When you're on the inside, see if you can figure out a way of determining which window I need to go into when viewed from the outside. If you can't, I'll have no choice but to use the interior halls to get there. And I'll need the same kind of information to locate your room from the outside, though I'll be counting balconies."

She smiled. "Trust me, darling."

He returned her smile. "I always do."

From across the table, the Witch looked at him thoughtfully. "You said you'd cross to the addition from the east wall. So you're first going onto the property adjacent to High House Carkoska? Isn't that dangerous?"

He shook his head. "That depends. Can you get information on that particular property? Anything you can learn will be helpful, but I'd like as much detail as possible."

She lifted an eyebrow and frowned. "It depends on what kind of information you want."

"There is a small property adjacent to the southeast corner of Carkoska," he said. "I detected no guards there at night. Is the family taking a holiday on the coast, or are they just too poor to afford guards?"

Venessta said, "I can't imagine anyone who owns property in that neighborhood being too poor to hire night guards."

"That's a good point," the Witch said. "I'll see what I can learn."

Jax got the impression she was not unhappy with the peace they'd settled between them, and the truce Maelleen had negotiated with Venessta. He decided to be very careful to avoid anything that might upset the delicate balance Maelleen had established.

He smiled at the old witch. "Thank you, Mother. But please move quickly. We're running out of time." He didn't mention the fact that it was her war with the little witch that had compressed their schedule.

"My goodness," Venessta said. "This is really exciting."

The two younger women returned to their seats and sat down. Jax folded up his sketch of the Carkoska property and returned the small table to its original position at the far edge of the room.

As he walked back toward them the Witch said, "Oh, one more thing. Lord and Lady Naesmyth invited us to dine with them tomorrow. I believe you have yet to meet them."

Jax's gut tightened. He'd finally succeeded in removing Stephanna Naesmyth from his thoughts, and now he recalled their nights together long ago. Seeing her again at the ball had been a shock.

The Witch continued. "They've been on the coast and feel remiss that they haven't been properly introduced to Venessta's cousins. And their niece is visiting them from Palvestra. They'd like her to meet other young people her age, so they've invited House Carkoska as well."

"Is she really their niece?" Venessta asked. "Or is she their niece like Jax and Maelleen are my cousins?"

The old woman shook her head. "No, she really is their niece, the daughter of Lady Naesmyth's brother. Nathaniel had no difficulty confirming that."

Maelleen looked at Jax oddly. "Jax, you look white as a sheet. What's wrong?"

Venessta stood, crossed the short distance separating them, and touched his cheek lightly with a finger. "You do look rather ill."

Jax couldn't ignore the issue. "Someone there could recognize me."

The old witch gave him a calculating look. "And who might that be?"

He hurriedly made up a plausible lie. "Their man—I don't know his name, but he's the fellow with half his ear chopped away."

The Witch's eyes narrowed with distrust. "Lakorsa, a very dangerous man. And why would he recognize you?"

Jax continued to improvise. "I tried to pick his pocket when I was new at thieving, and botched it. He cornered me, got a good look at me in broad daylight, and I barely escaped with my life."

The distrust remained in the Witch's face as she said, "Don't forget that I'm a witch, my little thief. No one there will recognize you."

"The glamour?" Jax asked.

"That," she said, "and it has been a few years."

"Well," Maelleen said. "I hope I don't have to seduce Lord Naesmyth as well."

"You can't," Jax said, and the instant the words left his mouth he realized he shouldn't have spoken.

The Witch's distrust appeared to blossom like a flower opening its petals. "And why would you say that, my little thief?"

Venessta unknowingly rescued him. "He must have heard those old rumors about Lord Naesmyth."

Venessta's words didn't deflect the Witch's attention or her distrust, and she sat silently staring at Jax.

Maelleen asked, "What rumors?"

Venessta wrinkled her nose with distaste. "That he prefers young men."

"Really," Maelleen said. "How did such rumors come about? And is it true?"

The Witch had not taken her eyes off Jax through the entire exchange, and she continued to stare at him as she said, "Lord and Lady Naesmyth were married seventeen years ago. The wedding was the most talked of event in the city for months: he one of the most handsome, eligible bachelors, and she the most beautiful of all the properly-available young women. But after six years with no children, ugly rumors surfaced that she was barren. Then there followed unpleasant speculation that he couldn't father a child with a woman because he felt no attraction to the fairer sex. The same rumors said he could perform the necessary coupling only with young boys. Poor Lady Naesmyth lived in shame for several years, then miraculously he got her with child, and a little over eight years ago she bore a lovely, healthy, little girl."

Jax recalled Lady Naesmyth's words from their last night together, something about *a little bonus* that he'd given her. He'd been much too young and foolish to understand any hidden meaning in her words.

The Witch smiled, and her eyes still remained locked on Jax's face. "Amazing how the birth of one child quelled all the rumors. Never again did anyone whisper behind Lord and Lady Naesmyth's backs that she was barren, or that he might have certain disagreeable proclivities. And they've since had two more children."

Jax recalled the young boy who'd stepped into that carriage, and he wondered if Lady Naesmyth might be with child again. Or perhaps she had borne all the children she needed, and death was merely the price young men paid so she and her husband could sate their needs without complications.

The Witch leaned back, steepled her fingers in front of her and asked, "How long ago was it that you tried to pick Lakorsa's pocket?"

The old woman knew Jax's history and could do the math. "Nine years," he said.

"Yes," she said, nodding and appraising him carefully. She smiled, as if happy with his answer. "Nine years."

29

The Past Returns

THE NEXT DAY, in the carriage on the way to High House Naesmyth, Jax couldn't stop from reliving every moment of the time he'd spent with his murderous lover— he had long ago stopped thinking of her as Stephanna, and refused to think of her as Lady Naesmyth. He tried to recall the broken conversation he'd heard that night between her and Lakorsa when they had planned to dump him in the river. There could be no doubt of her guilt in his intended murder, the successful murder of the young boy, and the murders of any number of other young boys he didn't know about. But her final words to Lakorsa haunted him, and he wondered again if her husband had been complicit as well, or merely subject to the needs of his body, and ignorant of the young lives his wife had ended to keep their secret.

"My little thief," the Witch said, interrupting his thoughts. "You seem preoccupied."

Seated next to him, Venessta said, "Yes, you've been distant all day."

On the seat across from him and next to the Witch, Maelleen said, "Is something troubling you, darling?"

The Witch said, "You've been quietly thoughtful since I told you we'd visit High House Naesmyth. And as I recall, at the ball, you seemed quite taken with our dear Stephanna. What is it, my little thief? What bothers you so?"

He wasn't about the give up the sordid story of his prior relationship with Lady Naesmyth, so he quickly improvised. "I'm a bit preoccupied with how I'm going to get to that figurine."

The Witch smiled like a patient mother instructing a child. "I'm glad that you have your professional mind focused on the task at hand. But didn't *you* tell us not to overthink the problem?"

"Yes," Venessta said. "You should take your own advice."

"By the way," the Witch said. "As you requested, I made some inquiries about that unguarded house adjacent to the Carkoska property."

She had a habit of pausing and forcing her audience to ask her to continue. Jax gave her what she wanted. "And?"

She seemed smugly satisfied as she said, "And it's vacant. For sale. Has been so for a couple of years now. No furniture or property worth stealing, so that's why it's unguarded."

A stroke of luck like that could prove to be advantageous. "Can we get inside, see the place in broad daylight?"

Her smug satisfaction remained undiminished. "I've already taken care of that, little thief. Nathaniel is contacting the property agent as we speak. He'll repeat the lie you told Lord Tray'enall, that because of your financial interests here, you're thinking of relocating to Val d'Ossa to manage them properly. Nathaniel should be able to arrange a tour of the place. And as a potential buyer, you'll get to poke about in every room in the house, and walk the grounds freely. I'll see to it you're allowed to take all the time you need."

At that moment the carriage pulled onto the grounds of High House Naesmyth, and when it stopped Jax stepped out onto a gravel driveway in front of the house. As one of the Witch Knights helped the three ladies out, Jax examined the two-story building that towered over them. The house had been built in the same style as House Carkoska; no second-floor balconies in front, but they probably lined the sides and back of the place. He recalled the old castle to which Lakorsa had taken him nine years before, and in which he'd had his month-long assignation with the lady. It did not surprise him that this was not that place. He didn't remember the castle's exact location, but it had not been located in the District of Noble Houses.

In the vestibule a servant took Jax's greatcoat and top hat, and other servants relieved the ladies of their bonnets and cloaks. They were shown into a sitting room that already contained the Carkoskas and Naesmyths. The two High Lords stood near a hearth, while their ladies were seated on couches. The Carkoskas had brought their two young sons Martin and Samuel, who were focused on a young woman with curly, reddish-blond hair. She appeared to be about Martin's age, which would put her a few years younger than Jax. Sitting next to her, and ignored by the two young men, a young girl seemed ill at ease. She looked to be about eight years old, and Jax had to force himself to avoid staring at her.

Lord Carkoska perked up immediately when Maelleen entered the room. Jax noted that Maelleen had turned off the sex appeal, and yet Carkoska couldn't take his eyes off her. Jax saw Lady Carkoska look at her husband, then follow his gaze to Maelleen. Her eyes narrowed and her brow furrowed.

When Venessta introduced Jax to Lord and Lady Naesmyth as Roland, her cousin from Lieudess, Lady Naesmyth extended her hand, a fairly common gesture from a woman of higher rank. Jax reached out, gently gripped her fingers, bowed and touched his lips lightly to the back of her hand. The contact was brief and fleeting, but it brought back memories of the taste of her skin, and as he straightened it took all his willpower to look into the woman's striking, blue eyes without flinching.

"Master Roland," she said, frowning. "Have we met before?"

His heart raced, but he managed to smile and say, "No, Your Ladyship, I don't believe we have."

Her frown deepened. "Are you certain? You seem familiar, in some way."

"This is my first time in Val d'Ossa," he said. "Have you ever been to Lieudess?"

"Yes," she said. "Three years ago. Perhaps we met then. It may have been just a brief encounter, and if so I apologize for my forgetfulness."

"Perhaps," he said, "but I still think not. Had we met before, no matter how briefly, there is no doubt in my mind I would remember you."

That was actually the truth, but not in the way she took it. The flattery worked, the frown disappeared and her smile turned warm and inviting.

Jax stepped aside as Venessta introduced Maelleen, but he noticed the Witch eyeing him suspiciously. Her eyes darted momentarily to Lady Naesmyth, then back to him, and he wondered how much grief that little encounter would bring.

Lady Naesmyth introduced the young woman with reddish-blond hair as her niece, Celeste. The girl had an oval face, a pale complexion, and while her hair had been carefully pinned up in an elaborate structure atop her head, little, curly wisps of it had broken loose and fluttered against her cheeks. Jax's instinct warned him to be cautious, but it didn't give him the same kind of demanding and insistent danger signal he got from Lady Carkoska.

"Master Roland," Celeste said, "I've heard so much about you. I've never been to Lieudess myself, but I'd love to see the city some time."

He decided to lie. "And I'd love to be your guide."

At his comment, Lady Naesmyth frowned, and he wasn't sure how to interpret that.

Lady Naesmyth introduced the young girl as her oldest child, Tessa. Like her mother, she had dark brown hair and striking, blue eyes, but there was a shyness about the girl unlike the predatory nature of her mother. She had inherited the woman's beauty, but Jax saw none of Lord Naesmyth in the girl's features.

Lady Naesmyth leaned close to him and whispered, "This is her first time dining with the adults." Her lips actually brushed against his ear, which was inappropriately intimate, though no one else appeared to notice. Jax braced himself so he didn't instinctively lurch away from her. "She begged incessantly," she said, "and has been practicing her table manners ever since we told her she could."

The young girl reddened with embarrassment, so Jax said, "Well she seems like a perfectly elegant young woman to me, and pretty." He smiled at her. "I can see you got your looks from your mother, which means you're going to be quite a beauty someday."

Tessa lowered her eyes, while her mother smiled happily.

With the Carkoskas present, there were twelve of them. They sat down to dinner at a long, thin table, with Lord Naesmyth seated at one end, and his wife at the other.

The arrangement put Venessta at their hostess's left-hand side, with Jax seated on Venessta's left, and he was thankful he had the little witch between him and the lady of the house. Maelleen sat across from them with Celeste seated next to her.

Young Tessa sat on Jax's left, which made him exceedingly uncomfortable. "You're from Lieudess?" she asked excitedly. "I've never been outside of Val d'Ossa. What's it like?"

He tried not to let his discomfort show. "If you visit Lieudess you might be disappointed. I'm afraid it's a bit backward, compared to Val d'Ossa."

As the footmen served the first course, Lady Naesmyth said, "So, Master Roland, I'm told you're considering relocating to Val d'Ossa."

The look in her eyes made Jax think of a predator eyeing a tasty meal. He managed not to stutter as he repeated his earlier lie. "I have some financial interests here I'd like to manage more closely."

The smile she gave him reminded him of the demanding and unrelenting hunger he'd sensed in her the first night they made love, though he had to remind himself they hadn't really *made love*; he'd simply been her whore.

"Well if you do relocate," she said, "I'm sure we'll get a chance to see a lot more of you. And if you don't, I do hope we get the opportunity to see you again before you leave."

Venessta's eyes narrowed with jealousy, but she managed to smile and speak politely. "Anytime you wish to see him, Mother and I will be happy to make the arrangements."

Celeste struggled to suppress a smile as she raised her napkin and pretended to pat at her lips. Maelleen's lips turned upward in a slight smirk, though she kept her eyes on the dinner plate in front of her.

The rest of the evening progressed in much that way, almost as if Lady Naesmyth took pleasure in baiting Venessta with innuendo, though the younger woman handled it well. Jax noticed the Witch repeatedly glancing back and forth between him and their hostess, her face dark with suspicion. He was glad when the evening ended.

••••

In the carriage on the way back to the Witch Palace, Maelleen said to Venessta, "She was clearly baiting you, and you handled yourself nicely."

Venessta let out a long, slow sigh. "But she was also serious. I could see the hunger in her eyes every time she glanced at Jax."

Venessta looked at him pointedly. "You were certainly the hit with Lady Naesmyth."

Jax ignored her.

Maelleen nodded and smiled. "I don't think he'd have to try very hard to seduce the lady of the house. I saw that hungry look too."

The Witch gave Jax a knowing look. "Rumor has it that she does take the occasional lover, though she's not as prolific as Lady Carkoska in that respect. Perhaps you should seduce her."

"No," Jax snapped. It came out more harshly than he had intended, and Venessta and Maelleen gave him an odd look. The look on the Witch's face was more that of appraisal. Jax realized that she had intended to test him with her remark, and he had failed.

The Witch continued, "And how is it that Lady Naesmyth seemed to recognize you?"

Jax shook his head. "I don't know. I thought your glamour was supposed to work better than that."

"It does," the old woman said. She nodded and held her silence after that, but the cloud of suspicion that darkened her features remained unchanged all the way back to the Witch Palace. When they arrived, after the servants took their cloaks and coats and hats and bonnets, she said, "Come, let's retire for drinks in the sitting room."

Jax wanted to get away from the old woman and her suspicions. "I'd rather not."

She looked at him unkindly and smiled. "It's not a request, young man."

Maelleen arched a single eyebrow at the angry tone in her voice.

In the sitting room, Jax served them drinks, the ladies sat down, and he stood by the hearth. The Witch wasted no time. "I ask again, how is it that Lady Naesmyth seemed to recognize you?"

Jax held his ground. "And my answer is unchanged. I don't know."

The cloud of suspicion in the Witch's face darkened even further. "And I think you do."

"What about the glamour?" Jax asked. "Venessta told me it would prevent anyone from recognizing me."

"Exactly," the Witch said. "It's only necessary to keep someone from recognizing you if they've seen you before. So when did Lady Naesmyth see you before?"

Now, all three women frowned at him suspiciously.

Jax locked eyes with the Witch and they stared at each other for a long moment, like two stray cats facing each other in an alley. Even he was surprised that he didn't flinch or look away from those coal-black irises. Then all the anger he sensed in her dissipated and fluttered away like snowflakes in a stiff breeze.

She broke the silence. "The glamour is subtle. It doesn't actually alter your features, but instead alters any perception of familiarity for anyone who has ever seen you before. And combined with the natural changes in you after all these years, no one from your previous life should recognize you. It would not fail like that."

She stood, and did so without effort, as if her infirmities had all been cured. She crossed the room slowly and stopped a pace away from Jax. "There is one exception. The glamour is less effective if you were close to someone. And if you were truly intimate with them, I'd need to know so I could make adjustments. Otherwise, it might fail just as it did this evening."

Maelleen's face saddened as she looked at him. "Jax, my darling, tell us the truth."

He had no choice, but he wasn't going to give them the lurid details. He spoke in a monotone. "The rumors about Lord Naesmyth are true. He does prefer young boys, and cannot couple with a woman, not in any way that would produce a child."

Venessta's eyes widened and her jaw dropped, her mouth forming a large round O. In Maelleen's face he saw only concern.

The Witch looked at him with a blank, neutral expression. "Then how did he get her with child?"

Jax shrugged and didn't try to hide his discomfort. "Lakorsa procures young boys from the streets, destitute young men who will jump at the promise of a hot meal and a warm bed. They don't really know what they're getting into."

From the look on Maelleen's face, she immediately made the connection, but Venessta and the Witch didn't. The old woman asked, "And how does that help Lord Naesmyth couple with his wife?"

Jax tried to keep his expression neutral. "It's not her husband who fathers the children."

The round O of Venessta's mouth widened even further. The Witch merely smiled, nodded, and said, "How clever of our dear Stephanna."

Jax had managed to escape from Lakorsa with only a scar on his arm where a musket ball had grazed the flesh. And with the exception of the poor young boy they'd fished from the river, he didn't know exactly how it ended with the other boys, but he could guess. He added, "After she finishes with a young boy, her husband takes his turn."

"Interesting," the Witch said. She turned and walked carefully back to the couch, her hobbling limp once again present. She sat down, a thoughtful look on her face.

No lurid details, but Jax wanted her to know the whole truth. "Then, after her husband is done, she has Lakorsa drown the boy in the river to ensure he can't spread unsavory rumors."

This time, even the old woman's eyes widened. "So, Lord and Lady Naesmyth are cold-blooded murderers as well as rapists."

"No," Jax said. "Her husband won't take a young boy against his will. And I think he is unaware of how she and Lakorsa dispose of them afterwards. His wife considers him weak-willed."

The look on the Witch's face turned from thoughtful to calculating. "How interesting! Though I must admit I am not surprised at Stephanna's ruthlessness."

She sat silently for a moment, obviously thinking. Then she turned to Maelleen. "Lord Carkoska couldn't take his eyes off you this evening. And Lady Carkoska noticed. She certainly knows that he's bedding you, but you'll have to control him better than that or she might be a problem."

Maelleen lowered her eyes. "Yes, Mother."

To Jax, the old woman said, "And be careful of Celeste, my little thief. She's a witch, and I must assume that's why she's here."

Celeste, a witch! Jax realized he might learn a little about witches without directly inquiring about the two sitting in the room with him. "Does that mean she saw through the glamour?"

The Witch shook her head. "The glamour would affect her only if the two of you had met before . . ."

She let the sentence hang, an obvious question. In answer, he shook his head, she nodded and continued, ". . . but since you haven't, it would have no effect. For her, there would be no glamour to see through. On the other hand she might have detected it, and from that she could surmise that we're trying to conceal your identity for some reason. And that might spur them to look more closely at you. We'll have to be careful."

Venessta leaned toward the old woman. "How powerful is she, Mother?"

The Witch smiled and patted her on the wrist in a very motherly gesture. "Not as powerful as you, my dear, but still dangerous. The big question in my mind is: Did they bring her here because she's a witch, or because she's their niece and she just happens to be a witch? If the former, then they're planning to use her against us in some way."

Jax said, "And that raises the question: Are Lord and Lady Naesmyth aware of the figurine, and possibly hoping to acquire it for themselves?"

The old witch grinned. "It heartens me to know that you're not a fool."

Maelleen leaned toward her and patted her on the wrist in the same motherly gesture the old woman had used on Venessta. "Mother, Jax has never been a fool."

All three women looked his way, and the Witch said, "I'm beginning to realize that."

Jax thought that if they knew all the lurid details of his long-ago liaison with Lady Naesmyth, they might change their minds.

30

In High House Carkoska

TWO DAYS LATER Lady Carkoska left Val d'Ossa to join her lover at her villa on the coast. And the day after that, Maelleen temporarily moved into the suite Lord Carkoska had prepared for her in his mansion.

Nathaniel had arranged for Jax to view the vacant property adjacent to High House Carkoska. Jax tried to get the Witch to remain at the Witch Palace so he could inspect the place unhindered, but she wouldn't hear of it. The next morning, with the old woman leaning on his arm and Venessta following, as they crossed the courtyard to the waiting carriage, Jax gave it one last try. "I really think I can do this better alone."

"Absolutely not," the Witch said. "With me present, the agent will fall all over himself to do anything you ask of him. And in any case, I'm curious myself."

Nathaniel climbed up into the coach box and sat down next to the coachman. Apparently, he'd be coming along as well. And of course, a dozen Witch Knights stood by their mounts near the carriage, waiting to escort the Witch of Val d'Ossa properly. Any hope Jax had of being inconspicuous had long ago disappeared.

They met the property agent just inside the main gate of the vacant estate, a short, bald fellow with sunken cheeks and hunched shoulders. The presence of the Witch who ruled the city had exactly the effect on the fellow that Jax had hoped to avoid. "Mother," the little man said as he bowed, took a step back, bowed again, took another step back, then bowed a third time. He held the final bow and said, "I am deeply honored to serve you."

She waved an imperious hand at him, her words clipped with impatience. "Let's get on with this."

He bowed again. "Yes, Mother."

As he straightened, she said, "And stop bowing."

He bowed one more time. "Yes, Mother."

"Ah!" she cried, then marched past him, leaving him standing there bent over. With Venessta on Jax's arm, and Nathaniel behind them, they followed her, while the Witch Knights waited in the small courtyard. The house was certainly much smaller than Carkoska, though larger than his father's had been.

Just within the main entrance, a double stairway arced both left and right up to a landing on the second floor, with a chandelier hanging down from above. The agent paused in the vestibule between the stairs and said, "As you can see, the entry is quite dramatic. Such elegant, little touches can nicely reinforce one's place in Val d'Ossan society."

The vacant house had been stripped of furniture, and after two years a fine layer of dust had settled on everything. The agent proved to be an insufferable snob. He insisted on pausing in each room and extolling its virtues, noting how they would help Master Roland solidify his relations with Val d'Ossans of appropriate rank. The place even had a small ballroom, though nothing compared to that in Carkoska. Jax tried to hide his impatience, because his main interest lay in the rooms on the west side of the second floor. Near the back of the house he took note of a narrow staircase meant to allow servants access to the upper level. And while the agent was occupied answering a question Venessta had asked, Jax looked carefully at the lock on a servant's entrance next to the kitchen in the back of the house.

They spent almost an hour on the main floor before proceeding up the stairway to the rooms above. Jax really wanted to break away from the group and snoop around on his own, but he couldn't figure out how to do that without being obvious. Then Nathaniel took the agent by the arm, saying, "I have a question about the security of these back rooms." He marched the fellow away toward the back of the second floor and the Witch followed.

Venessta leaned close to Jax's ear and said, "We'll keep him occupied so you can look about on your own."

Jax didn't try to hide his surprise. "Tell Mother I realize now that I should have had more faith in her."

"Exactly," she said, then walked away to join the others.

Jax turned immediately and headed for the west side of the house. A single bedroom occupied the front corner of the building. Since it was not part of a suite, it had probably been meant as a child's room or nursery. The back corner contained a large suite of rooms: a bedroom, boudoir, small sitting room and private privy. The sitting room had large double doors in the west wall. He opened one door and stepped out onto a balcony that ran almost the entire length of the building. Bright sunlight slanting down from overhead illuminated the balustrade and a thin strip of masonry next to it, but the balcony had been roofed over, leaving the rest of it in deep shadow.

Below him, the small vacant property ended at the wall separating it from Carkoska. The wall was a little taller than him, but it hadn't been constructed with security in mind. Some of the stones in it jutted out slightly in a decorative pattern, which should make it reasonably easy to climb. Beyond that, about ten paces of manicured grounds separated the wall from the new wing of High House Carkoska, with second floor balconies directly opposite him. Jax made a mental note that they'd have to ask Maelleen if the Carkoska side of the wall also included such decorative little outcrops.

As he stood there surveying the ground he'd have to cross, and the wall he'd have to scale, movement on one of the Carkoska balconies drew his attention. He stepped back from the balustrade and huddled deeper in the shadows there. Across from him Maelleen emerged into the sunlight. She wore one of the dresses the Witch's seamstress had sewn for her, and she looked incredible. She rested her hands on the balustrade and didn't look his way, so he wasn't sure if she had spotted him.

High Lord Carkoska stepped out of the shadows behind her and joined her, stopping beside her. Their lips moved as they spoke briefly, though Jax couldn't hear their words. Then they turned to each other, Carkoska took her in his arms and kissed her. Jax felt a moment of jealousy, as he always did when Maelleen gave herself to another man. He wondered if she had felt any jealousy during the brief time she thought he had bedded Venessta.

Carkoska and Maelleen turned away from the balustrade and disappeared into the shadow's there. That certainly settled the issue of which balcony Jax would need to climb up to.

Jax waited a few minutes, then opened the door behind him and stepped back into the sitting room. He heard voices out in the hallway, and a moment later the property agent, Nathaniel, and the two women stepped into the room.

"Ah," the agent said. "There you are Master Roland." He swept his arms out dramatically. "This master suite is magnificent, isn't it?"

"Yes," Jax said, "it certainly is."

Jax coasted through the rest of the tour and didn't see anything that needed his specific attention. They finished back in the vestibule at the front entrance. As the agent prattled on, Jax quickly examined the lock on the front door, and decided he'd make his entry through the small servant's entrance at the back.

The agent noticed him inspecting the door lock and said, "Let me assure you, Master Roland, that security is not an issue in this district. Even with a vacant property such as this, the constabulary checks regularly to ensure that no vagrants take up residence here. Lord Carkoska has made it known that he would be greatly displeased if that were to happen."

Jax said, "That's reassuring. Do the constables enter and check the rooms?"

"No," the fellow said. "They just check the doors and windows to make sure everything is locked up tight, and that no one has broken in. After all, there's nothing of any value inside the place."

A good piece of information to know, Jax thought.

••••

Sneaking about like a thief was certainly not Maelleen's forte, but she had no choice. She had only taken up residence in the Carkoska mansion two days earlier, and with

Carkoska and his sons dining at their club that evening, the place was all but deserted. Her chance had come to get Jax the information he needed.

She put on a fairly conservative dress, then added a shawl for the night air. Stepping out of her room, she made her way to the stairs and down to the first floor, where she encountered a young cleaning girl on her hands and knees scrubbing the floor.

At her appearance the young woman started and stood. "Mistress, is there something you need?"

Maelleen smiled and shook her head. "No. I desire a little fresh air, and it's a pleasantly warm night, so I thought I'd take a stroll through the gardens."

Maelleen realized she could turn the situation to her advantage. "I don't yet know my way around. Could you point me in the right direction?"

"I'll show you the way."

The girl led Maelleen down a hallway to the back of the house, opened a large door and held it for her. "I'll warn the night guards not to lock this door until you've returned."

Maelleen again smiled. "Thank you."

She stepped out into the night and made her way through the gardens to the gazeebo where Carkoska had first kissed her. She sat down to kill some time.

She had planned to use a stroll through the gardens as an excuse to leave her room, but the encounter with the cleaning girl had been fortuitous, allowing her to establish that she didn't know her way through the interior of the estate and might get lost. She spent a short while sitting in the gazeebo, then strolled through the gardens for a time, making sure some of the night guards saw her doing so. After about an hour in the gardens, she returned to the main building.

Jax had sketched out what he knew of the layout of the property, which wasn't much, but enough for Maelleen to navigate her way through the halls of the ground floor. She paused at the bottom of the stairs that led up to the office that contained the figurine, and tried to still her racing heart. As she climbed the steps, she marveled that Jax could remain calm when the danger of discovery seemed so imminent.

The hallway at the top of the stairs was empty and dark, lit only by a single gas sconce. She didn't waste any time and immediately opened the first door on the left, a storage room with a single window easily visible because the grounds outside were well lit. She closed the door and moved on. The second door opened into a large bedroom with two windows, thankfully unoccupied. The third had only one window, and the fourth opened into the vestibule Jax and Venessta had described.

She closed the door and heard someone grunting as they climbed the stairs. She looked back, panicked and froze just as the cleaning girl cleared the top of the stairway. Carrying a heavy bucket, mop and other cleaning gear, the young women stopped and frowned. "Mistress, what ye be doin' here?"

All Maelleen could think to say was, "I . . . uh . . ." and then she remembered their earlier encounter. "I was returning from the gardens and I must've turned the wrong way. I'm terribly lost, completely turned around."

The girl's frown disappeared. "Sure, 'tis a big place," she said, speaking with an accent not unlike that Jax had helped Maelleen eradicate. The young woman put the bucket and mop down, and said, "Follow me. I'll show you the way."

As Maelleen followed the girl back to her rooms, she thought it might be wise to draw Jax a map of the upper floors of Carkoska.

••••

The Witch grew exceedingly impatient and wanted Jax to go after the figurine at the first opportunity. "But we need more information," he told her. "Let's wait until Venessta has had lunch with Maelleen again. I still have questions I need answered."

Jax had a hidden agenda. If he broke in and succeeded at stealing the figurine, every day Maelleen remained in High House Carkoska after that, the possibility grew that the theft would be discovered with her still there. Hopefully, Carkoska didn't check on the figurine daily. Jax tried to stall; ideally, he'd do the job the last time the High Lord and his sons dined at their club before Maelleen's departure. If all went well, she'd be out of there before anyone learned the little statue had been taken.

A little over a week into Maelleen's stay at High House Carkoska, Venessta met her for lunch, followed by an afternoon of shopping. When the little witch returned, she and Jax joined the Witch in her sitting room.

"What did you learn?" the Witch asked.

Flushed with excitement, Venessta said, "All of the other rooms in that hallway are unlocked, so Maelleen was able to enter and check each one. The second door on the left opens into a large bedroom with two windows, so his office is the fifth window from the southeast corner, not the fourth."

Jax asked, "And the servants?"

"Lady Carkoska has a lady's maid who sleeps upstairs in a room not far from the master suite, but she's on the coast with her mistress. The rest of the servants retire in early evening, and their quarters are all down below, so the upper floor is deserted. And as you requested, I asked Maelleen about any servant activity when Lord Carkoska and his sons return from their club. There's a footman who waits up for them, but he's an old fellow who usually sleeps sitting in a chair near the front entrance, and he only wakes up when they come through the door."

Jax asked. "And is she still in that same room with the balcony I saw her on? They haven't moved her, have they?"

"No," Venessta said. "She hasn't been moved. And she confirmed that the wall between the two properties has little protrusions on the Carkoska side as well, so you should have no trouble scaling it on either side."

It occurred to Jax that it wouldn't hurt to have a little backup muscle in place, though he had no idea how they might help if the job went wrong. "When the time comes," he asked the Witch, "can you hide a couple of your knights in the small day park across the street from High House Carkoska? Be sure they're dressed incognito."

She raised a single eyebrow. "And how will that help?"

"I don't know," he said. "But it might in some way I can't anticipate. Could you do so . . . when the time comes?"

She smiled unpleasantly and said, "I do believe the time *has* come. Tomorrow evening Carkoska and his sons will dine at his club,"—she turned her black-eyed gaze on Jax—"and tomorrow evening I'll make sure those knights are in place, and you'll get that figurine for me. Won't you, my little thief?"

Jax knew he could no longer stall, so he simply nodded.

••••

Late the next day, Jax donned his lurking-in-the-shadows outfit and cloak, threw the strap of the canvas valise over his shoulder, and slipped out of the Witch Palace into the oncoming darkness of early evening. Nearly two weeks had passed since his last nocturnal visit to Carkoska, and the moon had waned to a thin crescent that wouldn't rise until the wee hours of the morning, so he'd be working under a moonless sky. He'd need to employ a different set of reflexes from those he used when a full moon lit the night, though with gas lamps lighting the streets of the District of Noble Houses, there'd be plenty of shadows to aid him.

Jax had chosen his timing so he arrived at the end of the street behind Carkoska under the cloak of full darkness. He squatted in the shadow of a shrub and watched the lit street for a few minutes. When his instinct told him to move, he stayed close to the wall and darted quickly to the first main entrance. Jax waited for the next nudge from his instinct, then raced past the wrought iron gate. He had plenty of time so there was no need to hurry.

The walls around most noble houses had been built for privacy, with little concern for security. He retrieved the rope from the canvas valise, tied a loop in the end of it, then tossed it up and around a decorative crenellation on the wall. With the valise secured over his shoulder, he scaled the wall in seconds, lay flat on top of it while he disengaged the loop from the crenellation, then dropped down to the ground on the other side. No lamps lit the grounds of the vacant property, so he crouched in the shadow of the wall and surveyed his surroundings. He listened and waited.

Nothing seemed out of place or untoward, so he sprinted in a crouch to the front of the house. Staying close to it, he worked his way carefully around the east side to the servant's entrance at the back. He didn't dare light a lamp, so he knelt down and retrieved his pick set. During his inspection of the property under the eyes of the agent, knowing that he'd have to pick the lock in the dark, he'd carefully noted the type of lock in the door of the servant's entrance. Back at the Witch Palace he'd found one like it and practiced on it for several hours. Working purely by feel it took some time, but the lock eventually clicked as it disengaged. He opened the door, stepped inside, then closed it softly. He carefully relocked it, just in case the constabulary came by to check.

He climbed up to the second floor, then made his way to the master suite on the west side. From a window in the bedroom he looked across the intervening distance to the balcony where he'd seen Carkoska embrace Maelleen. Through the glass panes of her balcony doors he saw the dim light of a single, flickering candle flame somewhere in her bedroom. When Carkoska and his sons left for their club, and the servants retired, she'd block the light of the candle three times in rapid succession to tell him it was time for him to move.

He stood there for some time and watched the guards on the Carkoska grounds make their rounds. One difficulty with securing a well-guarded property was that nothing ever happened, night after night, week after week, month after month. Eventually, boredom set in, and even the best of guards slipped unconsciously into routine. Jax watched a single watchman walk beneath Maelleen's balcony twice an hour, and he did so with such regularity that Jax could have set a clock by the fellow's schedule.

Jax backed away from the window, crossed the bedroom, then stepped into the private privy where there were no windows through which a Carkoska guard might see the flare of a match. He retrieved a small, shuttered lamp from his valise and lit it.

He opened his pick set and carefully selected a medium sized pick and tension tool that he wouldn't need that evening. Like most residents of the slums he had learned to use a needle and thread for the occasional repair job on his clothing. After the night in his flat when the knights had thwarted his plans to squirrel away a few of his tools, in his room in the palace he had carefully sewn two tiny pockets beneath the collar of his *lurking* shirt. If someone knew to look, his modifications wouldn't withstand any close inspection. But the additions were quite small, and hidden beneath his cravat or the collar of his coat, no one would notice. He carefully inserted the pick beneath his left collar, and the tension tool beneath his right. Both were long, thin pieces of stainless steel, and didn't produce any wrinkle or bulge in the material. Without doubt the knights had inventoried the tools in his pick set. If he successfully escaped from Carkoska with the figurine, he would hide the discrepancy by discarding the entire pick set, and claim he lost it in a hasty retreat from the Carkoska property.

Jax tucked the pick set into the special pocket he'd had sewn into the lining of his coat. He turned the lamp's flame down and closed the shutter, then returned to the estate's master suite to wait. The flickering candle flame in Maelleen's bedroom still showed brightly through the balcony doors.

Another hour passed, during which he confirmed the timing of the guard's rounds. Drowsiness set in and he yawned several times, but that ended in an instant when the candle flame in Maelleen's bedroom went dark. He watched closely and it immediately flared, went dark again, flared once more, then went dark a third time. He waited for the Carkoska watchman to pass beneath him one more time, then backed five paces from his window so the light of the lamp couldn't be seen from below. He turned the lamp flame up, aimed the lamp toward the window, and opened the lamp's shutter three times in rapid succession. A few seconds later the candle flame reappeared in Maelleen's bedroom, which was his signal to move. Everything had gone according to plan—at least so far.

Jax extinguished the lamp, and from the valise he retrieved a small backpack constructed of heavy canvas. It contained the few items he'd need for the job that night, and once he slipped his arms into it, it left his hands free. He wouldn't need anything else from the valise, so he left it in the master bedroom and raced down to the bottom floor. He unlocked the servant's entrance, opened the door just a crack, and listened for several seconds. When Jax heard nothing unusual, he stepped out into the night, closed the door and locked it.

He edged his way along the back of the house toward the western side of the property, but his instinct warned him to beware, and when he reached the corner of the building he heard voices. He squatted down low and leaned forward to peek with one eye past the edge of the house. He saw two constables stop near a window. He heard them speaking casually to each other, but he couldn't make out their words. One of them tapped on the window, and when satisfied that it was secure, they moved on to the next, slowly coming his way.

Jax backed away from the corner and looked around carefully. The grounds hadn't been kept up and were in poor repair, with shrubs and gardens thin from lack of water. But he had no choice, so he raced in a crouch toward the back of the property, dropped down behind a small bush, and waited in the dark, his heart pounding in his chest.

He and Maelleen had agreed that they would use the watchman's passage beneath her balcony to control their timing. When she first gave her signal, he'd waited until the guard passed by beneath them to respond with three flashes. That gave Jax the maximum amount of time to make his way down to the wall and be in place. He'd wait there until the guard's next pass, and as soon as the fellow was out of sight, Jax would have one full circuit of his rounds to scale the wall, climb the rope Maelleen tossed down from above, then retrieve the rope so it wasn't dangling there at the guard's next pass. Jax needed to get in place, and he was running out of time.

The two constabulary guards came around to the back of the house strolling casually and in no hurry. They tapped lightly on each window as they circled the place, then stopped briefly and jiggled the handle of the door in the servant's entrance. They stood there and talked about something for several seconds, then moved on. They never looked over their shoulders, never looked away from the house. Jax could have probably stood out in the open and they wouldn't have noticed him.

When they rounded the corner on the east side of the house, Jax waited a couple of seconds then sprinted toward the west wall. He slowed down as he approached it, conscious that if the watchman was beneath Maelleen's balcony, the sound of running feet might carry to him. Jax moved carefully the last few paces. His caution turned out to be justified, for just as he crouched at the base of the wall he heard the guard walking past on the other side of it.

He knew the guard's timing well enough to predict how long it would take him to reach the front of the house and round the corner. He waited, counting the seconds, and when the time was right he scaled the wall. The decorative pattern of stones that protruded from it helped immeasurably.

He reached the top with ease, peered over it and looked left and right. No watchman. He scrambled up onto the wall, then lowered himself down onto the Carkoska side and sprinted to the base of the building. Just as he got there, a rope dropped down from above and hit him on the head. He gripped it, tugged on it once to test it, then climbed upward.

He was good at such climbing, had had quite a bit of practice, but it still seemed to take an eternity. When he reached Maelleen's balcony, she stood there waiting for him. She leaned out, hooked a hand under his armpit and helped him over the balcony's stone rail. He heard her breathing heavily, probably more from nerves than anything else.

He turned around to retrieve the dangling rope, but she hissed, "Wait."

The watchman had just rounded the corner at the back of the house, so they both crouched down behind the balusters of the railing. They could do nothing about the rope but wait and hope. For a moment Jax wondered what had happened to change the fellow's timing, but he noticed this guard wore some sort of hat, whereas the fellow who had last made the rounds had been bare headed. They'd changed guards.

Jax held his breath as the fellow approached. The rope rested snugly against the side of the building, and if the man looked to one side they were done for. Maelleen gripped his arm almost painfully as they listened to the fellow's footsteps approach, walk beneath them, then continue on. When the watchman rounded the corner at the front of the house, Jax retrieved the rope, coiled it up and left it on the balcony, still attached to the baluster. Maelleen quietly opened the balcony door and they stepped into her bedroom.

31

Trapped

"THAT WAS CLOSE," Maelleen whispered, breathing rapidly.

Jax sat down in a chair next to a small table that contained the lit candle. He paused to catch his breath, and Maelleen stood over him doing the same. He looked at her, and by the light of the candle he realized she wore a translucent night gown, through which he could see the dark shadow of her nipples as her chest rose and fell. He rather liked the way that gown fit her, and if he hadn't been pressed for time would have been happy to sit there and watch her chest all night long.

She noticed the look on his face, looked down at her chest and her eyes widened. She curled her fingers into fists, planted them on her hips and hissed, "Your eyeballs have that erection again. Keep your mind on the job."

Jax said, "It's rather difficult with you wearing that."

"This is what Carkoska wants me to wear. It excites the old lecher."

Jax nodded and said, "I can certainly understand why. Can't you throw on a robe or something?"

She looked toward the heavens and said, "You men are impossible."

Jax didn't waste any more time arguing. He stood, crossed the room to the door and put his ear against it. As he listened, Maelleen approached him and stopped beside him. He didn't hear anything in the hallway beyond, but he couldn't count on that. Maelleen leaned toward him and kissed him lightly on the cheek.

"Be careful," she whispered. "I don't want to lose you."

It occurred to him that if he failed, he might never see her again, so he put his arm around her waist, pulled her tightly against him and kissed her passionately. She responded warmly, and when their lips parted she had started breathing heavily again. "You shouldn't distract me that way," she said. "And if we weren't here in this place right now, I'd let you do something about it. But you really should keep your mind on the job."

"It occurs to me," he said, "that if I'm caught, they won't fail to connect us. You should probably get dressed, and be ready to sneak out of here if you hear an uproar.

If you can get to the day park across the street, you'll find a couple of Witch Knights there who can help you."

Her eyes saddened. "I can't leave you behind."

"Then they'll have us both, and your capture won't do me any good. Better that one of us escapes."

Her eyes glistened in the light of the candle with an unshed tear and she stepped away from him. He carefully turned the latch on the door and opened it a crack.

Gas sconces lined the walls of the hallway, though only one in three had been lit. With his eyes reasonably adjusted to the darkness Jax had no trouble seeing. He slipped out into the hall and closed the door.

Maelleen had sketched a map of the upper floor of High House Carkoska. She had passed it on to Venessta at one of their lunches, and Jax had committed it to memory.

When they'd added the new wing the builders had punched a hole through the outer wall of the old structure to connect the hallways of both upper floors. Jax wouldn't have to descend to the ground floor, cross over to the old house, then climb back up. But he still had to cross almost the entire breadth of the two structures, which increased the chance that he might stumble upon a servant on some legitimate business they hadn't anticipated.

When he and Venessta had first scouted out the location of Carkoska's office, he'd told her, "Walk like you own the place." But that advice didn't apply in the dark in the middle of the night. No one who came across him would think for a second that he belonged in the house, so he moved on tiptoe down the hall. If a legitimate resident was up and about, they wouldn't go out of their way to be silent, so by moving quietly, Jax hoped he would hear them before they saw him. He wasn't sure what he would do if that happened, but it gave him some little advantage.

Through Venessta, Maelleen had warned him that the architects had miscalculated slightly when adding the new wing. The elevation of the second floor in the older structure was a bit lower than that of the newer. So when he came across a stretch of hall that had a slight slope to it, he knew he'd left the addition behind and entered the original structure. From there he worked his way slowly to the back of the house, and found the long hallway that led to Carkoska's office.

He gripped the latch on the fourth door on the left and was thankful it had not been locked. It opened easily, he stepped into the vestibule, and closed it. From the inside the lock could be engaged with the simple turn of a lever, so as a precaution he gave it a quick twist and heard the bolt click into place.

The small lamp he'd used before still rested on the little writing table. He retrieved it and lit it, then glanced around the room. The cushioned chair, writing table, two unlit sconces on the wall, and shelves of books remained unchanged from his last visit. Kneeling down in front of the door to the inner office, he made quick work of the lock with his pick-set, turned down the wick on the lamp and eased the door open. He stepped in and closed the door. Unlike the outer door, this one required a key on both sides so he used his pick-set to lock it.

The inner office remained unchanged as well, with the small statue still displayed openly on a pedestal, the desk in the middle of the room, and the window behind it. Other than a quill pen, bottle of ink, and a letter opener, the top of the desk remained bare.

Curtains covered the window, but they weren't completely opaque. Jax shrugged out of the backpack, opened it and retrieved a piece of thick, folded black cloth and several pins. He unfolded the cloth and pinned it over the curtains, careful to be sure it covered the window completely. Confident now that none of the guards on the grounds below would see shadows moving about, or flashes of light against the walls in a room that should be empty, Jax turned up the wick on the lamp.

His instinct hadn't warned him off, but since he would attempt to open the hidden strongbox now, he had resolved to be extra cautious. Before doing anything further he got down on his hands and knees and aimed the lamp's beam under the desk. He looked carefully for any wires or connection to the floor that might provide the linkage for a mechanical alarm. Moving slowly, he swept his hand across the floor in an effort to detect any filament too thin for him to see in the dim light and shadows. He moved the hand back and forth slowly until he'd covered every inch of space beneath the desk.

He straightened and retrieved a small piece of paper from the backpack. He knelt down at a corner of the desk and lifted that one leg a fraction of an inch off the floor. It was heavy, but lifting one corner at a time was doable. He slid the piece of paper underneath the bottom of the table leg and it moved freely without any hindrance. He repeated that process at the other three corners to ensure that no elaborate mechanism of wires had been hidden by running a thin cable through the center of a leg and into the floor.

Satisfied that no mechanical alarm had been rigged to the desk, Jax pulled the chair up to it, sat down, and opened the bottom drawer that contained the hidden compartment. The contents of the drawer appeared unchanged: just a few books stacked on top of one another. He took note of their position, lifted them out and placed them on the desk, then removed the wooden slat that hid the compartment below. The strongbox also appeared unchanged, and nothing about his instinct warned him away from it. With the help of the lamp and his pick-set, he went to work on the lock.

It wasn't a terribly complex lock, and in a matter of minutes he heard a soft click as he disengaged it. Again, his instinct didn't warn him off, so he slowly raised the box's lid, rotating it upward on its hinges. Inside, a small figurine lay in crumpled, black-velvet cloth. He lowered himself to his knees beside the open drawer, pointed the lamp at the statue and examined it closely without touching it. It appeared to be identical to the other figurine openly displayed on the pedestal: the figure of a woman wearing a cloak, and holding a small box. To confirm that, he rose and crossed the room to examine the statue on the pedestal, and he saw no difference whatsoever. Perhaps an expert in such artwork might distinguish an old antique from a recently fabricated forgery, but Jax did not have those skills.

He knelt down again beside the figurine nestled in the strongbox, and examined it once more to confirm that the two were identical in every way. His instinct remained silent, so he reached out and lightly touched the little statue with the tip of his finger.

Jax had never had a vision before, and didn't consider himself the type for that kind of thing. But at that moment he saw dunes of yellow sand under a hot sun stretching for as far as the eye could see. He felt the strain of trudging up the side of a hill of sand; for every two steps he took he slipped back one, but eventually reached the top. Then he struggled not to lose his footing as he slipped and stumbled down the other side, only to be faced with another dune. Inside him, an overwhelming urge pushed him to leave Val d'Ossa, so he stood and faced the direction it wanted him to go: south.

The vision ended abruptly, but he still felt that urge. He closed his eyes and the pull tugged at him most strongly. He turned a little to his left, then a little to his right to be certain of the direction of the pull. He opened his eyes and stood facing due south.

A muffled shout broke the stillness of the night. He turned about, trying to determine from which direction it had come. Another shout, and he realized it had come from the other side of the office door, probably in the office's vestibule, or perhaps the hallway beyond. He raced around the desk and put his ear against the door in time to hear another shout so heavily muffled he concluded it had come from beyond the outer door. Locking the hallway door had bought him a few precious seconds of time.

Jax had left his pick-set in the drawer next to the strongbox. He quickly stepped around the desk, retrieved it and returned to the door. The uproar might not be because of him, so he pressed his ear against the door again and waited. A few seconds later he heard the door to the hallway slam open, accompanied by another shout. The guards had gained entry to the vestibule.

He selected one steel pick at random, jammed it into the office door's lock and snapped it off. Hopefully, that would buy him more than just a few seconds.

With no time to formulate some elaborate plan of escape he moved purely by reflex, grabbed the fake statue on the pedestal and lifted it. No vision came to him when he touched it. When he lifted the real figurine out of the strongbox, the vision of unending sand tried to cloud his thoughts again and he struggled to suppress it. Apparently, he could somehow tell the real from the fake.

A scrabbling sound at the office door drew his attention, someone attempting to use a key to unlock it, probably Carkoska, or the captain of his guard. This time he heard the words clearly, "Damn, it's jammed. Get an ax and break it down."

Jax placed the fake statue in the strongbox, nestling it carefully in the black, velvet cloth. He closed the lid and used his pick-set to engage the lock. Then he reset the slat of wood that hid it, and replaced the books on top of it, taking care to ensure they were positioned as they'd been when he'd first opened the drawer. As he closed the drawer something thudded heavily against the office door and splinters of wood scattered across the room. Buried in the door, he saw the sharp edge of an ax blade protruding from it. Someone on the other side of the door grunted and yanked the blade out of the door.

He shoved the original figurine into his small backpack, tossed the pick-set in with it, and quickly tied the straps that sealed the pack. Then he stuck his arms through its straps and shrugged it into place. Another thud of the ax and more splinters flew across the room. The ax had torn a jagged hole in the middle of the door, and one of the men on the other side tried to push his hand through it, but the opening would only accommodate a few fingers.

Jax ripped the black cloth and curtains off the window and threw them aside. He popped the window's latch and shoved it open, then climbed up onto the sill and squatted there. Just beneath the window, a narrow ledge about as wide as his shoe offered his only chance. Holding tightly onto the inner edge of the window, he stepped out onto it, wondering why his instinct had failed him that night.

••••

As Maelleen dressed, her thoughts fluttered back and forth, carrying on an internal argument with herself. If Jax were discovered she should stay and find some way to help him. But she'd be going into a completely unknown situation, and any sway she might have over Carkoska would end the moment he connected her with the thief. Oddly enough, that didn't frighten her, and she realized in that moment she would gladly risk her life for Jax. She'd never had to think of it in those terms before, and for the first time she understood he would do the same for her. In the end, she decided that she could best help Jax by leveraging her influence with Venessta and the Witch. If Jax were captured it would be just like the old woman to throw him to the wolves, and Maelleen could remind the Witch of her promise to do what she could to help them. If nothing else, she'd be a thorn in the old woman's side, and Venessta might even help her a bit with that.

She had just pulled on a hooded cloak when she heard the first cry of alarm. She hesitated at the door to her room and listened carefully. And then the sharp crack of a musket told her she must act.

She opened the door and stepped out into the hallway, then marched down its length as if she were the lady of the house. Shouts and musket reports, muffled by the building's walls, told her the entire estate had come alive, but she didn't encounter anyone until she reached the front of the house and stepped out into the night. There she encountered the old retainer who always waited for Carkoska. He stood talking to a lone guard. The guard eyed her narrowly.

"Milady," the retainer said, "why are you up and about?"

"The shouts," she said, a carefully controlled tremble in her voice. "The musket shots. I'm frightened. I thought I saw an intruder inside, so I fled."

"Inside?" the retainer asked. "I must warn them." He turned to the guard. "Watch her closely. Lord Carkoska will be extremely displeased if any harm comes to her."

The retainer turned and rushed into the building.

Maelleen couldn't simply march to the front gate, then across the street to the small park, not with the guard standing there watching her. And even if she had a weapon, she wouldn't know how to use it. But then she realized she did have her own type of weapon.

After Jax had entered her life she had slowly come to realize she could turn on and off her sexuality like the flame in a lamp. She lit that flame now, and let it blaze as she turned to the guard. It had an immediate effect on him and he gasped as she said, "I'm frightened, and when I'm frightened I need the protection of a strong man."

The fellow's eyes blinked rapidly. She touched her hand to her throat like a terrified maiden, but used the gesture to release the clasp on her cloak. As it billowed open, the man saw the low-cut gown she wore, and the ample flesh it exposed. She closed the short distance between them. "At this moment I desperately need the comforting touch of a strong, virulent protector, someone I can count on to shield me from harm."

He gulped and swallowed.

She leaned close to him. "I'm so frightened I can no longer control myself, and won't be able to restrain my actions if I can find such a man. I find myself willing to do anything to be protected. Please protect me."

His eyes widened and he nodded. "I . . . milady . . . uh"

She whispered into his ear. "There's a small park across the street. It's very private."

"Yes," he grumbled. "Yes. Private."

He led the way, and only when they approached the main gate to the estate were they challenged by another guard. But he snarled, "I got orders to protect her. I'm taking her where it's safe."

In the small park he spun toward her and desperately grasped one of her breasts. Behind him a Witch Knight stepped out of the shadows and clubbed him in the head.

••••

The narrow ledge barely supported Jax. He would have fallen without the edge of the window to hold onto. The dormer wasn't deep, but it was short enough that he managed to hoist his body upward and climb onto the roof slates on top of it. Balancing precariously, he prayed that none of the slates came loose.

The pop-crack of a flintlock echoed through the night, and a musket ball zinged off the side of the house, spattering him with sharp chips of stone. Another pop-crack, and another musket ball thudded into the dormer beneath him. He heard someone shout, "Don't shoot him. Take him alive. Lord Carkoska will want to question him."

Jax rose slowly to his full height, balancing precariously on the roofing slates of the dormer. He reached up and his fingertips just barely touched the bottom of the balustrade that lined the edge of the roof. He took a chance, crouched a little, then leapt up, thoughts of the ground far below sucking at his confidence. He managed to get his fingers securely around the base of a baluster.

He grunted and swore as he heaved and struggled to pull his weight upward. Thankfully, the baluster was tapered, its base thicker than its top. Had it been the other way around, he could never have lifted his weight off the dormer's slate tiles. He tried to ignore the shouts on the ground below and hoped that all the guardsmen had heard the orders to cease firing musket balls at him. He got one hand over the top of the balustrade, then the other. Adrenaline coursing through his veins helped him inch upward until he could swing his hips to one side. He got an ankle over the top, then the entire leg, balanced there for a moment, then pulled his chest up onto the balustrade so he straddled it. He pushed off and landed on the roof, hit hard, rolled, scrambled to his feet, bent into a crouch and ran east.

As he crossed over to the roof of the new wing, he heard shouts behind him, and realized there must be some sort of hatch for roof access. Keeping his head down and staying low, he glanced over his shoulder, and saw Carkoska guardsmen spilling onto the roof and fanning out. They didn't know he'd come from Maelleen's room, so they didn't know to head in that direction and concentrate their search there. He kept moving, but since this was his first time on the roof, he had to guess at the location of Maelleen's balcony. He skidded to a stop near the balustrade at a spot he hoped placed him just above it.

Staying low, he climbed over the balustrade and lowered himself behind it, his feet dangling beneath him. At least that put him out of sight of the guards on the roof. They'd have to search the entire length of the edge to find him, which might buy him a few more seconds. He eased down further until his feet touched the roof tiles of a balcony, hopefully the right one. He dropped into a crouch on top of it, hugging the wall and praying the balcony roof didn't collapse under his weight.

He had a short climbing rope in the backpack, but he didn't have time to retrieve it. Luckily, the balcony roof had a sharp lip of small stone crenellations. Again, he thanked whatever architect had chosen to decorate the place with such attractive little touches. He griped two of the protrusions, yanked on them to ensure that they wouldn't break loose, then eased his legs over the edge, followed by his hips. At that point he slid all the way, but managed to hold on and hung there for a moment. He swung his legs forward and back, forward and back, then dropped onto the balcony.

He had chosen correctly. The rope Maelleen had dropped down to him earlier remained tied to the stone rail and coiled up next to it. He opened the door to her room, stuck his head inside and snarled, "Maelleen, are you there?"

He didn't know what he'd do if she hadn't heeded his advice to dress and try to sneak away, but he had to make sure. Thankfully, there came no answer, so he assumed she'd made the attempt. There was nothing he could do to help her now, so he'd have to hope she succeeded without him.

Jax closed the door, retrieved the coiled rope, tossed it down so it once again dangled all the way to the ground, then swung his legs over the rail and began his descent. Above him he heard the guards searching the edge of the roof, trying to determine where he'd made his escape. Descending went much faster than climbing and his boots touched the ground in a matter of seconds.

Someone hit him hard and slammed him against the wall of the house. A rifle butt crashed into his side, sending a shock of pain through his ribs. He cried out and doubled over.

While two guards held his arms twisted painfully behind his back they removed his backpack, then pulled a black, cloth sack over his head. It had a drawstring, and one of them tightened it painfully around his neck.

"You're choking me," he said, coughing uncontrollably.

One of the guards said. "Loosen it a little."

"Why bother?" another asked.

"Because Lord Carkoska won't be happy if we kill him before he gets to question him."

They loosened the drawstring, but only a little.

One of them said, "Bring him and follow me."

32

Captured

THE CARKOSKA GUARDS gripped Jax by his armpits and elbows and hustled him away. He tried to keep up with them, but with the black sack over his head he tripped over something and fell to his knees. The guards didn't stop to give him a chance to recover, but continued on, dragging him with them. He managed to get his feet beneath him again, but his guards forced him into a bent-over shuffle. Without warning they reached some stone steps. He stumbled and fell painfully to his knees. They hoisted him up by his elbows and ascended the steps with his feet dragging behind them.

They halted, and the two guards hoisted him up, which allowed him to get to his feet. He assumed they didn't do that out of any kindness for him, but rather because they grew tired of supporting him. A guardsman with command in his voice said, "Not in the main house. Take him to the stables. We'll interrogate him there."

They reversed course, descended the steps, and Jax didn't stay upright for long. Every time he got his feet beneath him, something tripped him and he wound up carried by his elbows, with his feet dragging on the ground behind them. It proved to be a painful way of getting from one place to the next.

When they stopped again, the guards forced him to sit down on a hard surface. They tied his hands individually to the sides of his seat, and from that he concluded they had put him in a simple wooden chair. They tied his feet to the legs of the chair as well, binding them uncomfortably tight. Then all the frantic activity came to a stop.

Even with the black sack over his head, he smelled horse manure and straw. A horse neighed, and another spluttered. Somewhere nearby two guards spoke quietly in hushed tones, but he couldn't make out their words. Jax sat there listening to the sounds of the stables for what seemed like an hour, though under the circumstances, he knew his sense of time was anything but accurate. His hands and feet grew numb from the ropes that bound them.

He sensed the guards perk up, then he heard the soft clump of boots on the ground.

"Captain Vorkees," one of the guards said, and Jax heard them snap to attention.

The guard captain didn't respond, but Jax heard him breathing and knew the man stood a few paces in front of his chair. Jax smelled a faint scent of perfume, heard the rustle of what sounded like skirts and petticoats, and assumed there must be a woman present as well.

A strong male voice said, "You were right, there was an intruder." That had to be Vorkees.

A young female voice responded, "Of course I was right. Have you sent for my aunt and uncle?"

Jax heard something familiar in the young woman's voice, but he couldn't place it. And he wondered how she had known an intruder was present in Carkoska's office before Jax had touched the figurine on the pedestal.

"No, we've sent word to Lord Carkoska and we're waiting for him to return from his club."

The young woman said, "Please send for them now. They'll want to be involved in questioning this thief. And I have no doubt your lord will want them present. They're not far away, so if you send a man to fetch them, they can be here quickly, probably before Lord Carkoska returns."

"As you wish," the man said. The sound of his boot steps dwindled into the distance as he walked out of the stables.

Jax heard the woman approach and walk slowly around him, the soft pad of her slippers on the dirt floor of the stable far different from the thud of the captain's boots. She made a full circuit of his chair, then stopped in front of him. The smell of her perfume wafted over him and he heard her soft inhale and exhale of breath, telling him she'd leaned close to him. "We're going to have your secrets, thief," she said, speaking softly, "all of them. And we'll learn your identity too. And if you're working for someone, which undoubtedly you are, you'll tell us who that is. Believe me, you're going to tell us everything, and if you cooperate nicely, then we'll give you the benefit of a quick, easy death. If you don't . . . well, I'm sure you can imagine how unpleasant that will be for you."

He heard the rustle of her dress and petticoats, then the diminishing sound of her soft footsteps as she walked away.

If he and this young woman were acquainted in some way, which was a distinct possibility, she hadn't recognized him because of the cloth sack over his head. He tried to remember all the young ladies he'd met at soirees and other events during his captivity in the Witch Palace. He strained to recall their voices, but so many of their conversations had been no more than a brief introduction, with a few polite sentences of meaningless chatter and idle talk, and maybe a dance or two.

It occurred to him that the moment they removed the sack, Carkoska would recognize him, and all of the young woman's questions would be answered in an instant. It also occurred to him that if removing the sack answered all their questions, they might have no further need of him and execute him out of hand. He dearly hoped

Maelleen had managed to escape while the guards chased him across the roof. Though, even if she had attempted to do so, he doubted the guardsmen on the grounds would have allowed her to simply leave the property late at night. But he could hope she had figured something out.

Some minutes later he heard the footsteps of a small group entering the stables. From the sounds they made, which included both the clomp of boots and the pad of soft slippers, he thought it might be a mixed group of men and women.

A woman said, "Remove the hood so I can see his face when I question him."

Jax's heart pounded up into his throat. He would never forget that voice: Lady Naesmyth, his Stephanna.

"I'm sorry, Your Ladyship," Captain Vorkees said. "I know my master well, and Lord Carkoska will want to be here during any questioning. You'll have to wait until he's present."

"I insist," she demanded.

"Again," Vorkees said, "I do apologize, but I will not deviate from what I know my lord would want. You'll have to be patient."

"If I must," she said coldly.

The young woman said, "Don't worry, dear aunt. We'll learn all his secrets in short order."

Now that he knew Lady Naesmyth stood in front of him, he realized the young woman must be her niece, Celeste, a witch, and he easily recognized her voice. Jax guessed that Lord Naesmyth probably stood there with them as well, though the man did not speak. He heard them walk out of the stables as a group. He tried to hear every word they said, but their voices quickly diminished with distance and he heard nothing of benefit.

The Witch, Venessta, Maelleen and Jax had never considered the possibility that two High Houses might collaborate. The Witch had told them that Celeste had witch powers, though apparently Venessta was stronger. True witches weren't that common. Jax had met women who claimed certain mystical powers, but when he observed them practicing their arts, everything they did could easily be accounted for by misdirection or slight-of-hand, skills that a thief knew well. And if only a true witch could tap into the figurine's powers or magics or whatever it contained, then cooperation between the two High Lords seemed obvious: Carkoska had the figurine, and Naesmyth had a witch. Not for the first time Jax wondered what strange benefit they hoped to gain from the tiny statue, and he resolved to never reveal that something odd happened to him when he touched it.

It occurred to him that his instinct had failed him in Carkoska's office that night because of some witchery Celeste had conjured. Perhaps she'd cast some spell on the strongbox to alert her to a thief's presence even before he'd touched the alarmed figurine, something that didn't trigger his special talent. It would be good to confirm if his instinct could be circumvented by a sorceress's influences, but he had no idea how to determine that. And given his present circumstances, he probably wouldn't live long enough to make use of that knowledge.

He heard the clump of boots on the dirt of the stable, a lone man approaching. "Lord Carkoska has returned," Captain Vorkees said. "Untie the thief and bring him, but keep the hood on."

Jax didn't resist as they unbound him and the prickly sensation of returning circulation set his hands and feet on fire.

"Stand up," one of them said.

"I can't," he pleaded. "My feet are numb."

He felt four pairs of hands haul him to his feet. They twisted his arms painfully behind his back and dragged him out of the stables. Once more, they ascended the stone steps. He heard a door open, then he heard the boots of the guards dragging him as they clomped down a hallway of what he guessed was the main house. He heard another door open, they apparently passed through it, came to a stop, and held him there dangling between them.

The numbness had left his feet, so he finally managed to stand, though with two guardsmen holding his elbows in vice-like grips, he was not free to move.

"Let's see what we have here," he heard Lord Carkoska say. "Remove the hood."

One of the guards tugged at the cloth sack, but the drawstring was too tight to clear Jax's chin. It took them a moment to loosen it, then they yanked it off his head.

Jax stood in a large study in front of an enormous desk made of dark wood, a room quite unlike the small office on the second floor where he'd found the figurine. Carkoska sat behind the desk making no attempt to mask the smoldering anger in the look he gave Jax. Lady Naesmyth and Celeste sat to one side on a couch, with Lord Naesmyth seated in a large comfortable chair nearby. The small statue had been carefully placed upright in the middle of the desk, facing Jax, with the rest of the contents of his small backpack strewn about it. The empty backpack lay on the floor to one side.

Celeste recognized him before anyone else. Her eyes widened and she touched her fingertips to her lips. Carkoska recognized him next; his mouth opened and he stood, leaning forward with his hands on the desktop. Then Lady Naesmyth grinned, while her husband frowned.

"Master Roland," Carkoska shouted. With his face a mask of fury he stormed around the desk, drew his fist back, and buried it in Jax's solar plexus.

Jax's abdominal muscles seized up. He grunted and doubled over as his diaphragm spasmed. The guards didn't let Jax fall and he hung between them supported again by his elbows. He gasped and choked as he struggled to get air into his lungs.

Lady Naesmyth said, "Don't hurt him yet. Damaging him at this time might be somewhat premature. We need information, then you can do to him whatever you want."

Jax slowly recovered, got his feet beneath him and stood upright again, still breathing heavily.

Carkoska returned to the other side of the desk and sat down. His jaw muscles clenched as he gritted his teeth. Then his eyes widened and he said, "The woman, get her."

"The woman?" Captain Vorkees asked.

"Yes," Carkoska shouted. "Lady Katrina, she's his sister."

To his credit, Captain Vorkees immediately recognized the implications, and didn't need Carkoska to spell it out for him. He spun on his heel and shot out of the study.

As the door closed, Carkoska said to Jax, "I'll hang the both of you from one of the trees outside the front gate, though I'll probably give the woman to my guardsmen first. We'll let them enjoy her for a few nights."

Lady Naesmyth stood and approached Jax. She reached out and ran a finger delicately along his jaw line, and he managed to not react to her touch. "Once again," she said, "it occurs to me you look familiar in some way. Why is that?"

Jax said, "I wouldn't know."

She smiled, and he saw that hungry look in her eyes he remembered from long ago. "I do find you rather handsome. Perhaps I can . . . put you to some use before he hangs you."

She glanced over her shoulder at Carkoska. "If your guardsmen get to have the woman before you hang her, let me have him for a while before you hang him."

Her husband frowned and spoke softly. "Stephanna, stop acting like a tramp."

Celeste's eyes widened at the interplay between her aunt and uncle.

Captain Vorkees returned, breathing heavily. "The woman's gone."

Carkoska erupted out of his chair. "What do you mean gone?"

Vorkees stood facing his master stiffly, clearly fearful of the news he must impart. "Just to be certain, we're searching the property and the house now, but we have a few witnesses who saw her leave."

Jax quietly breathed a sigh of relief.

"Witnesses," Carkoska demanded. "Your men allowed her to leave the property."

Vorkees's voice trembled as he spoke. "One of my men was foolish enough to believe her when she offered him sexual favors. She led him to the day park across the street where he thought they'd have some privacy. All he got for his efforts was a bump on the head. After we're done whipping him, he'll be dismissed."

Maelleen had turned on her special charms, and having been the recipient of them any number of times, Jax knew no man was immune to her. He couldn't really blame the poor guard.

Carkoska screamed at Vorkees, "I should have you whipped and dismissed as well."

••••

It took some time for Lord and Lady Naesmyth to get Carkoska calmed down. He didn't have Vorkees whipped, and the man got to keep his job, though it was a close thing. And it pleased Jax that they ignored him for a while, but once Carkoska's temper dissipated, that ended.

Lady Naesmyth returned to her seat and asked Carkoska, "Did you confirm that the original remains untouched?"

Carkoska gave her a displeased look. "Before we discuss this further we need a smaller group."

He opened a drawer in the desk, reached in and retrieved a large flintlock pistol, then placed it on top of the desk next to the figurine. Looking at Vorkees, he said, "Captain, please take up this weapon, then stand behind Master Roland."

Vorkees stepped forward, lifted the heavy weapon, turned and walked around Jax and the two guards holding him.

Carkoska said, "Now raise the weapon, cock it, and aim it at the back of Master Roland's head."

Behind him, Jax heard the hammer click back on the pistol, then he felt the barrel of the gun press against the back of his head.

Carkoska leaned forward on the desk and said to Jax. "I'm going to instruct the two guards holding you to release you and leave. During and after that, if you so much as look like you might try something, I'll have Captain Vorkees splatter your brains all over the room."

Lady Naesmyth wrinkled her nose and said, "That's a disgusting thought." To Vorkees she said, "Captain, be sure to angle the gun to one side. Celeste and I don't want our dresses spoiled by nasty spatters of blood and brains."

Carkoska continued to look at Jax and raised an eyebrow in question.

Jax shrugged. "Don't worry. I'll be a good little prisoner."

Carkoska spoke to the two guards, "Release the prisoner and leave."

The two men released Jax's arms and stepped back. He heard the door behind him open, heard footsteps, then the door closed again.

Carkoska looked at Lady Naesmyth. "Now, in answer to your question, yes, I checked, and the original statue hasn't been touched." He reached out and lifted the small figurine from the desktop, then wagged it at her. "The fool took the forgery."

During the stress of the moment, up in the small office when he'd been about to be discovered and possibly killed, Jax had not had time to think his actions through carefully. He realized now that his instinct must have guided him when he'd replaced the figurine in the strongbox with that from the display pedestal. And since he'd carefully relocked it, and returned everything to its original position as if the strongbox had never been touched, Carkoska's ruse of employing the fake figurine as a decoy had appeared to work exactly as he had intended. Carkoska had seen what he wanted to see and hadn't looked that closely at the figurine in the strongbox, or perhaps they did need an expert to tell the statues apart.

Jax could think of any number of ways to use that to his advantage, under other circumstances. Unfortunately, at the moment, he couldn't think of any way to use it to stay alive.

"Tell me, Master Roland," Carkoska said, waving the little figurine at Jax, "how did the Witch learn I have this statue?"

Jax shook his head. "I honestly don't know."

Carkoska's lips tightened into an angry pucker. "Why does the Witch want it? What will it do for her?"

Jax found it interesting that he would ask that. That question clearly meant they didn't understand the nature of the statue and its use. Conscious of the gun barrel pressed to the back of his head, he said, "I don't know that either. The Witch did not choose to enlighten me on anything more than what I needed to know to break in and take the statue."

Carkoska slammed a hand down on the surface of the desk and stood. "Nonsense. If you won't cooperate, I'll make this very unpleasant for you."

Jax had nothing to gain by concealing anything. "I have no vested interest in the statue, or in what it can do. I came here to steal it because I was forced to, not because I want to."

"Forced to," Lady Naesmyth asked, "how so?"

Jax shrugged. "The Witch Knights abducted me off the street, and the Witch told me she'd execute me if I didn't steal it."

Celeste said, "I think he's lying." She stood and walked toward him, stopping a short step away from him, her nose only inches from his. "We need to make him tell us what he knows."

Behind her, Lady Naesmyth said, "Only because you failed so miserably."

The young woman spun to face her. "I did not. If there were anything arcane in that statue, I would know it. Its true value must be some mundane aspect of which we're unaware. Perhaps there's some key hidden within it, or an old formula of powerful magic, or a map or something."

Jax got the impression they'd already had this argument a number of times.

Lady Naesmyth gave Celeste a knowing smile, clearly meant to irritate her. "You say that only because you failed and you're trying to cover up your ignorance. Or is it simply inexperience?"

Celeste said, "I—"

Lord Naesmyth cut her off. "Be silent, both of you."

Celeste looked like she wanted to argue, but kept her mouth shut.

Lord Naesmyth said, "I think he's telling the truth. We all know the Witch well. She keeps her secrets to herself, and only reveals something if she must."

He stood, walked forward, stopped in front of Celeste and said, "Return to your seat, young woman."

She pouted like a chastened child as she crossed the room and sat down.

Naesmyth turned to Jax and looked in his eyes. "You're just a thief, aren't you, hired to steal the figurine?"

Jax corrected him. "Hired isn't exactly the word I would use."

Naesmyth nodded. "Hired, coerced, or cooperating willingly, does it make any difference?"

They'd allowed Jax to hear too much, so he had no doubt they intended to kill him. His only chance lay in stalling for time and praying he could figure out some means of escape. "If I hadn't been hired or coerced, then I might know the answers to your questions, and I'd gladly give them up to save my life."

"Perhaps," Naesmyth said.

"It doesn't matter," Carkoska said. "My lady wife will want to be present for any thorough questioning. So for now, we need a place to lock him away and hide him from the Witch." He glanced at the walls around them. "Unfortunately, they stopped making dungeons before they built this place, and we can't very well lock him in a city constabulary cell."

"I have a solution to that," Lady Naesmyth said. She stood and crossed the room, walked past her husband and stopped at an intimately close distance from Jax. "Our property on the edge of the city, in the Charbourg suburb, is part of an old castle. We don't use it much, just upon occasion, so we don't even maintain a permanent staff there. It's small, but it has turrets and everything, including a dungeon with a couple of old cells." She smiled at Jax. "I think the dungeon has only been used for storage for some years now, but that can be remedied in short order."

"Excellent idea," Carkoska said, "and it's not far from here, so that'll be a lot more convenient than my villa on the coast. And I'd have to kick my wife's lover out, which would upset her."

Throughout the conversation, Carkoska had continued to hold the small statue in his hand. He looked at it for a moment, then looked at Jax and smiled. "And you might as well have this. You certainly earned the worthless piece of trash."

Without warning he tossed the figurine into the air. It arced across the room toward Jax and he caught it by pure reflex. The images of sand and hot sun flooded through his mind again and he staggered as he struggled to suppress them. Celeste started and her eyes narrowed as if she sensed something, but she merely looked at Jax oddly and said nothing.

They called the guards back in to restrain Jax. One of them took the statue from him and stuffed it into Jax's coat. Celeste watched him with a piercing look as they tied his hands behind his back, and the last thing he saw was the calculation in her eyes as they pulled the black, cloth sack over his head again.

Vorkees said, "We'll tie him to a horse."

"Absolutely not," Carkoska said. "I don't want him paraded through the city. Put him in a carriage."

"If you're worried about the Witch," Lady Naesmyth said. "She's got her spies everywhere. She'll know by noon tomorrow exactly where he is."

"I don't care," Carkoska said. "Just put him in a damn carriage and draw as little attention as possible."

The ride to the old castle in the Charbourg suburb proved uneventful. Because of the cloth sack over his head Jax didn't see the walls and battlements that enclosed the courtyard, but he imagined that they hadn't changed much from the first night he'd met Lady Naesmyth there so long ago.

33

Betrayal Within Betrayal

WITH THE CLOTH sack still over his head, Jax gave up trying to stay on his feet as the guards dragged him out of the carriage, into the old castle, and down a flight of stone steps.

Vorkees shouted, "Clear out one of those cells."

They sat Jax down in a chair, and he listened to the guards grunting and straining as they moved some sort of stored goods around. He heard the scrape of heavy crates sliding across the floor accompanied by more grunting and groaning. At one point they had a discussion about the old locks on the cell doors. Vorkees sent a man to ask Lady Naesmyth for the keys, but the fellow returned empty handed. The lady did not have the keys, and had no idea where they might be, or even if they still existed.

Vorkees said, "Damn locks look rusted out anyway."

Jax heard Vorkees give another man orders to find a padlock and a length of chain. When he returned, two guards hoisted Jax out of the chair and dragged him across the floor. They pinned him face-on against a stone wall and removed the cloth sack. He glanced around and saw that they held him in a cell. Celeste walked into the cell and approached him on one side, carrying a wicked little knife. At the look he gave her, she said, "Don't worry. I'm not going to harm you. I just need a couple strands of your hair."

"Why?" he asked.

She smiled and said, "If you survive, perhaps I'll tell you." She reached up, pinched a small lock of his hair, and used the knife to cut it loose. She examined it for a moment and nodded.

"Oh," she said. "A little blood will be helpful as well."

To the guard closest to her she said, "Hold his hand out."

Jax didn't resist as the man forced him to extend his hand palm up. Celeste pinched the tip of his thumb between the fingers of her left hand, and with her right made a small puncture using the point of the knife. A drop of blood welled up, and with a white handkerchief she dabbed it away. She looked at the red stain on the handkerchief and said, "That'll do."

Celeste raised her face to Jax and their eyes met. The look she gave him made him wonder if she really needed the hairs and blood for some arcane rite, or if this little gambit was some sort of act for the benefit of Carkoska and the Naesmyths. She smiled at him unpleasantly, then turned and walked out of the cell to join the others.

The guards untied Jax's hands and released him. He stood there for a moment facing the wall and wondering what came next, but no one restrained him and he remained free to move.

He slowly turned around. Two guards stood facing him, watching him warily, both holding cudgels about the length of a man's forearm. The three of them stood in a cubical cell little more than a stone box about three paces across. It had a door that consisted of crossed, riveted, heavy, iron straps spaced about a hand's width apart. Vorkees and another five guards stood outside the cell. Behind them, in a group, Lord and Lady Naesmyth, Lord Carkoska and Celeste looked on.

Vorkees walked into the cell carrying a blanket and a wooden bucket. He put the bucket in a corner and handed Jax the blanket. Then he and the two guards backed out of the cell.

When Vorkees closed the cell door, its hinges screeched like a demon from one of the hell-pits. The captain secured it with a short piece of chain and a padlock, then turned and handed the key to Lord Carkoska.

The High Lord asked, "Did you send out a rider?"

"Yes, Your Lordship," Vorkees said, "before we left High House Carkoska."

"Good," Carkoska said. "We'll question him as soon as my wife returns from the coast."

Lord Naesmyth stepped forward and gripped the bars of the cell door. He looked at Jax for a long moment, like someone trying to recall an old memory. That frightened Jax, because he suspected he wouldn't live long if Lady Naesmyth connected him to this old castle, and their nights in her bed long ago.

They left a single Naesmyth guard seated at a table near the crates of stored goods they'd moved out of the cell. A torch in a bracket on one wall provided the only light in the dungeon.

Jax reached into his coat and removed the figurine. He'd become reasonably good at suppressing the visions that came to him when he touched it. He placed it carefully on the floor in a corner, then sat down in the shadow against one wall to watch the guard and wait. It didn't take long for the fellow to grow drowsy and nod off.

Jax rose to his feet, careful not to make any sound. Without touching anything he examined the padlock and length of chain securing the cell door. With the pick and tension tool hidden beneath his collars he could easily open that lock, but the thing hung on the chain outside the cell. Getting the padlock into a position where he could work on it might make enough racket to wake the guard, but even if it didn't, the screech of the door's hinges certainly would. He would have to bide his time.

Jax backed quietly away from the door, wrapped the blanket around his shoulders, and lay down on the stone floor to sleep.

••••

"Please leave us. I want to speak with the prisoner alone."

At the sound of a man's voice issuing orders, Jax opened his eyes. He hadn't slept well because the stone floor proved to be . . . as hard as stone.

He rolled over and sat up. Lord Naesmyth stood outside the cell, again looking at Jax as if trying to recall an old memory. Behind him the guard trudged up the stone steps and out of sight.

Jax put his back to the wall, crossed his legs in front of him and remained seated.

"I remember you," Naesmyth said, his voice soft and melancholy. "My wife doesn't, but I do, even though I only saw you briefly. Strange how fate brought us together again."

Jax wondered what motivated the man to come down here and admit that. "It wasn't fate that brought us together back then. It was Lakorsa and your wife."

"Yes," he said. "She certainly has her appetites,"—he shrugged and his eyes clouded with sadness—"as do I."

Jax sympathized with the man. "I do thank you for not . . . making me do . . . what I couldn't do . . . that night long ago."

Naesmyth's back stiffened. "You were clearly terrified and unwilling that night. I don't rape anyone."

Jax said, "And I thank you for that."

Naesmyth frowned and relaxed a little. "I suppose you think me reprehensible . . . for my . . . appetites."

Jax had broken his share of laws and rules, so he couldn't fault the man. And Jax's lawless acts may have been committed out of desperation, but they were still done by choice, whereas he suspected the man who stood before him merely succumbed to the needs of his body. "If you had taken me against my will, then I probably would judge you harshly. But since you did not, I don't judge you at all."

Naesmyth closed his eyes momentarily and nodded his head. "Then I thank you for that."

Jax added, "And I am certainly not one to judge anyone."

"Why do you say that?"

"I'm a thief."

Naesmyth grimaced. "Well, there is that. Unfortunately, that will probably get you hung."

Jax thought a little shock value might take the conversation in an interesting direction, and perhaps he'd learn something. "Am I the father of your first child? Tessa is her name, is it not?"

Naesmyth sucked air into his lungs in a sharp hiss. "Don't let my wife know you've come to that conclusion. I'm not sure what she'll do, but I know she can be ruthless."

Jax looked pointedly into the man's eyes and said, "She'll have me murdered."

Naesmyth sighed. "It's not murder to execute a thief."

"She'll have me murdered because I know your secret, not because I'm a thief."

Naesmyth shook his head. "You're being unfair."

"She has them all murdered, you know."

Naesmyth squinted as if trying to judge the truth of Jax's words. "Them . . . all . . ."

"Yes, all the young men Lakorsa picks up off the streets."

He shook his head angrily. "I don't believe you. She's not that heartless."

"That last night I was there, I overheard her and Lakorsa agree that he'd dump me in the river. As I recall, he said something like, 'I'll take care of him like the others and dump him in the river.' But since I overheard them, I had some warning, certainly more than the others. As the carriage came to a stop near the river bank, I broke for it and ran. The coachman—I think Carlos was his name—and Lakorsa chased me. They tried to shoot me with pistols, but missed. Then they searched for me all night long but I eluded them."

"No," the man said, still shaking his head. "That doesn't prove that they intended to kill you, only that they overreacted to you running like a thief. In fact, that's probably why they shot at you. They assumed you ran because you had stolen something."

"I did," Jax said.

"There you have it."

Jax knew he must be relentless if he wanted Naesmyth to face the truth. "A few months ago I saw a young boy get into an unmarked carriage on the street, identical to the one I got into all those years ago."

Naesmyth shook his head slowly. "That proves nothing."

Jax remembered the young boy's face as if he'd last seen him only the other day, and he described him easily, providing every bit of detail he could. As Jax spoke, the look on Naesmyth's face slowly darkened, his brows furrowed, and the skin around his eyes tightened noticeably. Jax finished with, "He was an inch or two shorter than me, mid-teens, and he had unruly, curly, blond hair that hung down into his eyes and covered the upper half of his ears, leaving just the earlobes exposed."

Jax gave Naesmyth a moment to absorb the description, then said, "A few days later he washed up on the bank of the river, nothing more than a bloated corpse, though some creatures in the river had dined on him a bit. The constabulary carried his body away and disposed of it. But you wouldn't have heard about that, because he was nothing more than a nameless boy from the slums."

Naesmyth turned away from Jax's cell and he spoke in a whisper. "No."

Looking at the man's back, Jax spoke just as softly. "Yes."

Naesmyth stood with his back to Jax for the longest time and didn't move, his head bowed, his shoulders hunched. The silence of the room was broken only by the man's breathing, which sounded strained. Then he raised his head and straightened his back. He didn't turn to look at Jax as he said, "If you're executed, it will be because you are a thief, or because you're foolish enough to reveal to my wife that you know her secrets. I'll not be the one to tell her."

He walked across the floor, then up the stone stairway and out of sight. A few seconds later the guard returned to his seat at the table.

••••

The dungeon apparently had a single window open to the outside. Jax couldn't see it from his cell, but as morning arrived, sunlight passing through it cast a bright square of illumination on the opposite wall just beyond the iron bars. That lit up the entire room reasonably well.

Jax recalled his fear of wasting away in some hellish dungeon, spending the last of his days eating gruel and suffering unimaginable torment while they chopped off little bits of him and fed them to the rats scurrying around his cell. Thankfully, they hadn't yet chopped off anything—he didn't count the hair and blood Celeste had taken— and there didn't appear to be any rats present to eat his bits if they had chopped them off. And breakfast turned out to be bread and cheese, probably because they didn't have any gruel on hand. Jax didn't think there was much of a market in Val d'Ossa for gruel. They gave him a pitcher of water to wash down the bread and cheese, and to his surprise, the water didn't taste like it had been retrieved from a piss pot or a mud puddle in the street. He had more than enough left over to wash up a bit.

He had a nasty bruise where one of the guards had slammed a rifle butt into his ribs when they'd first taken him captive. And he had a few minor bruises from being dragged around. But other than that, he remained relatively unscathed, though he feared that would change as soon as Lady Carkoska returned from the coast.

After breakfast he sat on the floor of his cell with his back to the wall, in much the same position he'd sat the previous night during his conversation with Lord Naesmyth. The furnishings in his cell—a bucket and a blanket—pretty much limited him to sitting that way. The only alternative was to stand and pace back and forth, or lean against the bars of the cell door.

Carkoska had said they'd begin questioning him after his wife returned from the coast. If they had immediately dispatched a messenger the night before, and upon his arrival she dropped everything to return, she couldn't be back until late that evening. Fashionable ladies of unquestionable repute didn't torture and interrogate prisoners late in the day, so he assumed they'd begin the questioning the following morning. Jax quickly grew bored, though he was absolutely certain that when his boredom ended, it would involve a sweaty torturer with knives and unpleasant things of that nature, so he decided to enjoy the boredom.

About an hour after dawn they changed guards. The new fellow had corporal's stripes and sat at the table playing with a deck of cards, clearly bored. Jax continued to sit on the floor with his legs crossed, his back against the wall, and dozed fitfully.

"Hey, prisoner."

Jax snapped awake. The guard with corporal's stripes stood at the bars of the cell. "You look as bored as me." He shuffled the deck of cards. "Know how to play *Kiss the Witch's Tit?*"

"Yah," Jax said. He didn't want to play cards, but he thought it best to keep the guard happy. "But I have no coin on me."

"That's okay," the guard said. "You can owe me."

Jax grimaced.

"Don't worry about it. After they hang you, you'll be free of the debt."

Jax and the guard sat on the floor, their legs crossed, facing each other, the bars of the cell door between them. They found it awkward, passing cards between the bars, but it did alleviate the boredom, and it took Jax's mind off his low expectations for his continued survival. He learned that the guard's name was Danoka, and the fellow had a wife and two young sons somewhere in the city. Jax and Danoka were evenly matched at cards, so Jax only lost a bit of money to the fellow. After an hour of play, they both grew tired of the game so the guard returned to his table, and Jax returned to sitting against the back wall of the cell.

He dozed on and off through the day, which turned out to be a mistake because that meant he slept poorly that night. He was awake and sitting with his back to the wall when he heard a door open up above at ground level, then clank shut. A few seconds later Celeste walked down the stone stairs to the dungeon floor. It was certainly not an appropriate hour for a young woman of respectable circumstance to be about, nor was the dungeon a proper place for her to visit without an escort, so Jax wondered at her presence.

She approached the guard and said exactly the same words Lord Naesmyth had said the night before. "Please leave us. I want to speak with the prisoner alone."

The guard stood, walked around the table and trudged up the stairs. Celeste approached Jax's cell, but stopped a couple paces away, as if she feared he'd reach out and throttle her.

It would gain him nothing to be rude, so he stood, and gave her a friendly smile. In return, the look she gave him was one of unbridled distrust. He thought back on his few interactions with her, and recalled that suspicion had always clouded her features. After the argument he'd heard between her and Lady Naesmyth about her failure to unlock the figurine's magic, he supposed she had good cause to be distrustful.

"You've now had a night and a day in that cell," she said. "Have you thought about your present circumstances?"

He assumed that the Carkoskas and Naesmyths were not aware she had come to question him alone, and would be unhappy if they learned of it. He wondered if he could use that to his advantage in some way.

He shrugged. "My present circumstances are not something I really want to think about right now."

She smiled unhappily, almost a sneer. "But your present circumstances are so dire, I would imagine you could think of nothing else."

"That is true," he said.

"And?" she asked.

She wanted something, but he couldn't think what. The argument she'd had with Lady Naesmyth the previous night had been enlightening. Clearly, she was under pressure from the Carkoskas and the Naesmyths. "One doesn't have to think terribly hard to understand that my future doesn't look too bright. Yet you're down here, most likely without the knowledge of your aunt and uncle, or the Carkoskas, so perhaps my future might include some circumstance under which my prospects will improve."

Her brow furrowed. Good. He'd touched a nerve.

She looked askance at him. "What makes you think I'm down here without the knowledge of my aunt and uncle?"

He thought it interesting that she didn't include Carkoska in that. "Instinct," he said, though she had no idea what that really meant for him.

"You're a glib one."

His patience had come to an end. "Mistress Celeste, I must assume you've come down here for a reason. Especially since you risk the ire of your aunt and uncle and Lord and Lady Carkoska by questioning me without them present. So why are we wasting our time with guessing games? What is on your mind?"

She hesitated for a long moment, eyeing him warily. Then she seemed to come to a decision and pointed at the little statue in the corner of the cell behind him. "That's the original isn't it?"

He thought he did a good job of keeping his expression neutral and not letting her know that *she'd* now touched a nerve. "Lord Carkoska said it's a worthless fake. Didn't he call it a piece of trash?"

She smiled and took a small step forward. "How did you accomplish it? You must have switched the two. How did you do that?"

He shook his head. "I don't know what you're talking about."

Her smile broadened, and he thought that if she ever controlled the power of a High Noble House, she would be as ruthless as Lady Naesmyth, though he wasn't sure she'd be as good at it, or as dangerous.

"Go pick up the statue," she said.

He turned around, crossed the cell and looked at the small figurine standing upright in the corner. He turned back to her and said, "I think not."

She took the last few steps to the cell and gripped the bars. "What is it you feel when you pick it up?"

He wasn't about to tell her. "And why do you think I feel anything?"

"I don't think," she said, "I know."

"And how do you know?"

"When Lord Carkoska tossed it to you, you flinched."

"Of course, I flinched," he said, putting as much scorn in his voice as he could. He recalled the calculating way she'd looked at him in Carkoska's study when visions had flooded through his mind just as he'd caught the little statue. "That blasted statue is going to be the death of me, and at the time I had a loaded and cocked gun pressed to the back of my head. Had I moved too much to catch it, I would have ended up with my brains splattered all over your pretty dress."

The calculating look returned to her eyes. "You know what I am?"

"I'm told you're a witch."

"And who told you that?"

"The Witch."

She raised her chin and lowered it in a single, careful, satisfied nod. "When you touch that statue, I sense a flow of magic. You heard my argument with Lady Naesmyth, so you know I'm not revealing anything when I tell you that I, with my abilities, have been completely unable to discern anything about that little figurine. But when you touch it, you do, don't you?"

He stepped toward the bars, and as he did so she stepped back and stopped only when out of reach. He gripped the bars and said, "I don't know what you're talking about."

"Be careful, thief," she said. "If that's true, then you're of no value to us, and your life is forfeit."

She turned and walked to the bottom of the stairway, but she stopped there and looked back at him. "Because of my talents, I can help you . . . in ways my aunt and uncle and the Carkoskas cannot. But you'll have to help me in return."

She turned her back on him, walked up the stairs and disappeared from view. A few seconds later the guard trudged down the stairs and returned to his seat at the table.

Jax wasn't sure if she hoped to double-cross her aunt and uncle as well as the Carkoskas, or if she and the Naesmyths were working together to betray the Carkoskas; possibly both, or more likely, some scheme beyond his limited ability to concoct diabolical machinations. For the first time in his life, Jax actually felt glad he'd been disinherited. The more he got to know the morals of the High Noble Houses, the more it felt like wading through a cesspool of intrigue and betrayal.

34

Deception

JAX AWOKE NEAR dawn, stood and paced back and forth in the small cell to loosen up the stiffness in his limbs and spine. His butt told him it didn't want to sit on the stone floor anymore, so he leaned against the bars and watched the square of light from the unseen window crawl down the wall and start its march across the dungeon floor.

They probably wouldn't start cutting little bits off of him until close to noon. Since the women would be involved in any interrogation, their schedule would most likely determine the timing. The dictates of Val d'Ossan society would not allow fashionable ladies of leisure to begin torturing someone before sitting down to a casual breakfast. And that wouldn't happen until a few hours before noon.

An hour after dawn Corporal Danoka arrived to relieve the night guard. A servant brought Jax a simple breakfast of bread, jam and water. Danoka made the servant pass it to him in pieces through the bars of the cell door. Jax used some of the water to wash his face and clean up a bit. He'd grown accustomed to the luxury of hot baths in the Witch Palace, and guessed that a request for something of that nature under his present circumstances would fall on deaf ears.

Four guards came for him about an hour before noon, two with the crest of Carkoska sewn onto the breast of their tunics, and two with that of Naesmyth. To Jax's utter surprise, when he looked at one of the Naesmyth guards, his instinct told him the man should be wearing the red, black and silver of a Knight of the Witchguard.

One of the Carkoska guards with sergeant's stripes on his uniform said, "You're coming with us, thief."

As the man unlocked the padlock to open the cell, Jax turned to retrieve the little figurine standing upright in the corner. But when he reached for it the sergeant said, "No, leave that. You won't need it, and it's not going to get up and leave on its own while you're gone."

Jax didn't like the idea of letting the thing out of his sight, but objecting now might bring unwanted attention to a supposedly worthless copy.

Thankfully, they didn't tie his hands or make use of the black sack, which made it easier on all of them. They didn't have to half-carry Jax most of the way, and he didn't have to bang his shins on every unseen object that got in the way. Two of the guards simply gripped his elbows with a firmness that bordered on unpleasant and walked beside him, while the third walked in front of him and the fourth behind.

They marched him up the dungeon steps then through the main building of the old castle. During his time there nine years before, he'd been confined almost exclusively to Lady Naesmyth's suite of rooms, so little of what he saw now triggered any memories. The guards escorted him into a sitting room on the ground floor where the Carkoskas and Naesmyths were waiting with Captain Vorkees. Jax didn't see any sign of Celeste, and he thought that odd.

Lords Carkoska and Naesmyth sat in identical, large, wingback chairs. Close to hand, each had a small side table that contained a snifter of some amber liquid, and a heavy flintlock pistol. The two ladies sat on a nearby couch, both looking elegant and quite beautiful. Interestingly enough, while Jax knew without question that Lady Naesmyth was a heartless murderess, his instinct reacted most strongly to Lady Carkoska, telling him she was far more dangerous than the other woman or the two lords. Jax realized his instinct was pointing to Lady Carkoska as the dominant predator in the room.

She smiled at him invitingly, then licked her lips as if about to devour a delicious meal. He was reminded of the first time they'd met. She had invited him to call upon her for "... afternoon tea," though there had been the clear implication that there wouldn't be any *tea* involved, and she'd find something else to do with their time together.

While the guards held Jax standing in the middle of the room in front of them, Lord Carkoska reached over to the side table, picked up his pistol, cocked the hammer back, and placed it in his lap. "Captain Vorkees," he said. "We have this situation well in hand. You and your men may leave."

Vorkees bowed, and he and the four guardsmen walked out of the room.

Lady Carkoska turned to Lady Naesmyth and asked, "Where is Celeste? I'm most interested to hear the results of her little experiment yesterday."

"She was delayed," Lady Naesmyth said. "She sent her apologies, but she'll be here shortly."

Lady Carkoska frowned thoughtfully. "Well we don't have time to wait for her." She looked Jax over carefully, her eyes starting at his toes and slowly working their way up to his face. Then she stood and approached him, stopping only a pace from him.

Lord Carkoska said, "Be careful, Darthea."

She ignored him, looked Jax up and down again, then slowly walked a full circle around him. Jax felt like a mouse fully exposed in the presence of a large cat. All he could do was stand there in frozen stillness and hope the predator didn't strike.

She finished circling Jax and stopped in front of him at an intimately close distance. He caught a hint of her perfume as the tip of her tongue emerged from her mouth and slowly made the circuit of her lips, wetting them so they glistened brightly. She had cold, gray eyes that looked upon him hungrily, and while in every sense she was a truly beautiful woman, she held no attraction for him. It occurred to him that if she ever learned he found her beautiful but not desirable, she'd be insulted and displeased. He thought that making this lady unhappy in any way might be detrimental to his health, so he smiled pleasantly and tried to pretend he found her appealing.

"So," she said, and Jax almost jumped, but managed to control his reactions and remained still, "this is the thief I've heard so much about."

Jax thought he now understood the difference between the two women and why his instinct reacted so strongly to one and not the other. Lady Naesmyth had a specific motive for bedding young men: she and her husband needed heirs, and she needed to diffuse those scandalous rumors about her lord. She used young boys to get with child so they could pretend her husband had fathered the infants, then she eliminated the loose ends. The woman was cold-blooded and calculating, to say the least, but she did have a purpose. On the other hand, Jax suspected that Lady Carkoska's motives were simply self-fulfilling and predatory.

She reached out and ran a finger along the line of his jaw. "I'm making you nervous." She leaned close to him and whispered, "Don't worry, sweetheart, I don't bite. You needn't fear me." She frowned thoughtfully for a moment, then said, "Actually, that's not true. I do bite."

She started to turn away from him, but hesitated and whispered. "I think I might have to take a big bite out of you. But don't worry." She leaned away from him and grinned. "I'll certainly enjoy it, and perhaps you will as well."

She spun about, walked back to the couch and sat down next to Lady Naesmyth. She gave Jax a hungry smile.

The door opened and Celeste walked in. She greeted each of them and apologized for being late, then crossed the room and sat on the couch with the two older women. Lady Naesmyth patted her on the wrist and said, "I've ordered tea, dear. It should be here shortly."

Lord Carkoska lifted the pistol out of his lap and held it aimed toward the ceiling. "Now that we're all here, I want answers, and I have yet to hear any, so my patience is growing thin. Start talking, young man."

"Dear," Lady Carkoska said. "Be careful with that pistol. Killing him is so final, and it'll badly limit our options."

"I don't have to kill him," Carkoska said. "I can shoot him in the knee, shoot one part here, another part there. We can keep him alive a long time that way."

Apparently, Lady Carkoska considered that an acceptable solution, because she nodded her acquiescence. Jax thought he'd rather have Lord Carkoska shoot him to pieces bit by bit, than let Lady Carkoska take a big bite out of him.

"So, thief," Carkoska said. "Perhaps I should start by shooting you in the foot. Give me a reason not to."

Jax didn't have a good reason, but he had to try. "I . . . uh . . . I'm just an innocent third party here."

"Innocent, bah," Carkoska said. "I have no doubt you were a thief long before this. I should shoot you just to save the constabulary the trouble of hanging you."

"Calm down, dear," Lady Carkoska said. She looked Jax over again, appraising him from head to foot. "I'm told the Witch coerced you into working for her."

At that moment the door opened and a servant entered carrying a tea service on a tray. To Jax's astonishment his instinct told him the fellow should be wearing the red, black and silver of the Witchguard, and he was pleased he let nothing show on his face. The servant placed the tray on a low table in front of Lady Naesmyth and mumbled, "Will there be anything else, Your Ladyship?"

"No," she said. "You may go."

While Lady Naesmyth poured tea for the three women, Lady Carkoska said, "So, she coerced you. How did she do that?"

Jax knew his life could end in the blink of an eye in that room. "She threatened to torture me." He wasn't going to tell them the Witch had used Maelleen as a hostage, because if these people knew he cared for her that much, they'd probably try to use her against him as well.

Lady Carkoska nodded thoughtfully. "Very well, we'll accept that you were forced into helping her and are not an enemy of either of our houses. And my husband told me you claim no knowledge of the figurine. Is that true?"

Here, Jax had no choice but to lie. "It's just a piece of fired clay to me. The Witch told me it's very old, and that it's described in some texts, but that's all I know."

Lady Carkoska lifted her teacup to her lips and sipped, eyeing him over the rim of the cup. She lowered the teacup and said, "So, since you're of no use to us, you do need to give my husband a reason why he shouldn't shoot you in the foot, or just turn you over to the constabulary to be hung."

Jax's thoughts raced as he desperately tried to think of something, but failed miserably. Celeste leaned forward and said, "I can give you a reason, Your Ladyship."

Lady Carkoska's head pivoted slowly toward the younger woman, and the look she gave her could have chilled the tea in their cups in an instant. "It appears our witch has something to contribute. Did you learn anything yesterday with your little experiment?"

Celeste lowered her eyes, yielding to the more dominant woman. "I did, Your Ladyship."

"Why now?" Lady Carkoska asked. "After nothing but failure, you suddenly succeed. What was different yesterday?"

Celeste kept her eyes lowered. "I took some of the thief's hair and blood. He has been close to the Witch and her apprentice for some time now, which influences all arcane aspects regarding him."

Celeste had succeeded in getting their attention. Both Lords leaned forward intently and Lady Naesmyth perked up.

Lady Carkoska sat motionless and expressionless as she said, "Explain."

Celeste raised her eyes and spoke softly. "I had a hunch, a woman's intuition, you might say. With physical samples of him, like hair and blood, I can perform certain incantations directly related to him and not possible otherwise. And since your husband graciously granted me access to the original figurine yesterday,"—Celeste and Lord Carkoska traded looks that made Jax wonder if the man had bedded her as well—"I was able to establish that there is some sort of arcane connection between the statue and him. I think it came about because he's been in close proximity to the Witch for some weeks now, but that's only a guess."

The original figurine! The only figurine Carkoska could have given her access to would have been the fake Jax had placed in the strongbox. And Celeste damn well knew that. What kind of game was she playing?

Lady Carkoska raised an eyebrow and said, "Really! What kind of connection?"

Jax tensed as Celeste said, "Some sort of sympathetic connection. Perhaps, with a bit more time, I can determine more. But it would be best if he remained unharmed."

"Very well," Lady Carkoska said. She hadn't consulted her husband, which confirmed that she was dominant, and not he. "For the time being we'll let him live undamaged, but I want results."

Celeste gave Jax a look that seemed to say, *See, I helped you, now you must help me.*

They called the guards back in, and they and Vorkees escorted Jax back to the dungeon where he discovered that the figurine no longer stood upright in the corner of his cell. He glanced around quickly, but it was nowhere to be found. He recalled the guard and the servant who should have been wearing the Witch's livery, and wondered if one of them had taken it. If the Witch now possessed the statue she so coveted, would she feel the need, or even care, to rescue the thief who had failed to deliver it to her?

He waited until Vorkees and his men had departed, leaving him alone with Danoka, who sat at the table shuffling his deck of cards. Jax leaned on the bars of the cell and tried to sound casual and uncaring as he said, "Corporal Danoka."

The fellow paused mid-shuffle and looked Jax's way.

"The figurine?" Jax asked casually. "The little statue that was in the corner of my cell here, do you know where it is?"

"Yah," Danoka said. "That pretty young girl came down and took it right after they took you upstairs."

That would have been during the time Celeste had been absent earlier that morning. Jax asked, "Do you mean Mistress Celeste?"

"Yes," the man said. "That's her." He returned to shuffling his cards.

Celeste had planned this carefully, and had chosen to play a deadly game against Lady Carkoska. Jax didn't want anything to do with dancing so close to the jaws of such a predator. But he feared Celeste was too foolish to see the danger inherent in a contest with that woman, and she was unlikely to give him a choice in the matter.

35

The Dominant Predator

WRAPPED IN HIS blanket and curled up on his side on the stone floor, Jax's instinct woke him sometime after midnight, warning him to be fearful. His special talent didn't usually wake him that way, and he wondered why it did so now. It must have sensed some danger. He sat up and put his back against the wall.

The night guard sat at the table with his head resting on his arms snoring softly. A lone sconce on one wall cast dim illumination and indistinct shadows across the dungeon floor. Jax peered carefully into all the shadows in the room, but saw nothing out of the ordinary.

It didn't surprise him when, up above, the door of the dungeon clanked open, then shut with a loud thump. The guard at the table snapped awake and sat up straight.

As a dark silhouette descended the stone steps to the dungeon floor, Jax listened carefully for the thump of a man's boots, but could hear only the faint rustle of moving cloth. A man might wear soft, comfortable shoes that made no more sound than a woman's slippers, so he drew no conclusion from that. From the shape of the silhouette he could tell only that his visitor wore a floor-length cloak, with a hood thrown over his or her head.

The guard jumped to his feet, his chair scraping across the stone floor as the back of his legs pushed it away from him. The visitor approached the guard, and only when she spoke did Jax recognize Lady Carkoska. "Please leave us. I want to speak with the prisoner alone." She had spoken exactly the same words Celeste and Lord Naesmyth had used.

When Celeste had come for a chat the previous night, the same guard had barely acknowledged the young woman and trudged wearily up the stairs. But now he bowed deeply, fearfully, and said, "Yes, Your Ladyship." He stepped around her quickly, and marched rapidly up the steps. The woman stood without moving, facing the empty table and chair until the door above opened and thudded shut, then she turned to face Jax's cell.

Jax rose to his feet as she approached. Unlike Celeste, she stopped less than a single pace from the bars, almost within reach had he been foolish enough to attempt murder. But while Celeste might need to fear something of that nature from a prisoner about whom she knew almost nothing, Lady Carkoska simply stood within easy reach and stared at him. He crossed the cell and stopped one pace from the barred door.

He bowed, and as he straightened he said, "Lady Carkoska, to what do I owe this honor?"

He stepped forward to stand with his nose only inches from the bars of the cell, and within easy reach of her, but she didn't flinch.

She reached up and eased the hood of the cloak back so it draped around her shoulders. Even in the dim light of the single sconce on the wall to one side, her beauty struck him with a diamond hard coldness. He could not deny that any man would find her desirable, and yet again, within him nothing stirred and he felt no attraction for her.

She stood inhumanly still for a long moment, appraising him with the look of a hungry predator. "You made it much farther than any other thief so far. No one has ever gained access to the inner office before."

From her words he surmised that others had tried, a valuable piece of data. Unlike Celeste and Venessta, she was not one to inadvertently give up such information with an unguarded statement, so she clearly wanted him to know that he had not been alone in seeking the figurine. On the other hand, during the ball her husband had discovered him and Venessta kissing in the outer vestibule. If he had told his wife of that incident, she surely would make the connection. Had her husband failed to recognize the link? Or had he intentionally not informed her of it? Jax's head spun with all the possibilities of treachery and betrayal.

Jax cocked his head slightly to one side. "So I take it there have been others?"

She smiled, though there was nothing pleasant in the look she gave him. "Of course, there have been others. Some of the best, and hired at considerable expense, no doubt. So how did you get farther than all the rest?"

Jax shrugged. "I had the Witch's help."

"No," she said, shaking her head from side to side so slowly she appeared to be carefully evaluating him. "No, you had no more help than they. They knew the layout of the property and the inside of the building. They knew the location of the office, and any whore could have seduced my husband, as many have, so I don't credit your sister with providing any significant advantage."

She turned her head and gave him a side-long look. "No, thief, there is more to you than meets the eye."

Jax did not want this woman's attention focused on him. "I'm just a thief; and after all, I did fail, so apparently, I'm not a very good thief."

She stood silently for a long moment. "But still, better than all the rest."

She stepped forward so that she too stood within inches of the bars, and Jax flinched. His instinct warned him that he was in danger, but looking into her eyes he didn't step back, couldn't step back. She reached out, extended her hand through the bars and touched her finger to his lips. Again, Jax felt like a mouse under the hungry gaze of a cat.

"If you survive this," she said, tracing her finger across his lips, "I may have use for the best thief in Val d'Ossa."

Her finger traced the full circuit of his lips then slid down his chin to the collar of his shirt. She opened her hand and pressed it against his throat, an intimate gesture that might be either a lover's caress, or the prelude to strangling him there in his cell. And even though he stood taller than her and easily out-massed her, had she chosen to take his life at that moment, his instinct told him he could not have stopped her. Dominant predator, indeed!

She withdrew her hand and took one step back. Jax felt a bead of sweat trickle down his back, and he released a breath he hadn't realized he'd been holding.

She turned and took two steps toward the dungeon stairs, but paused and looked over her shoulder. "If you do survive this, I think I'll take you as a lover."

There was no question of Jax's desires in the matter; she would take him with or without his consent, and he'd be powerless to stop her. Somehow she knew he found her beautiful but not desirable, and she wanted him to understand that.

She turned back to the stairs, lifted the front of the cloak and her skirts to avoid stepping on them, and walked carefully up the steps.

••••

Jax didn't recognize the guardsman who relieved the night guard an hour after dawn, and he wondered what had happened to Danoka. He'd gotten to know the corporal a little and had come to like him. The fellow just wanted to keep his head low, draw his pay, raise his family, and stay out of trouble. Jax could sympathize with such simple needs.

The new guard simply wanted to sit at his table and roll dice, so Jax spent a boring morning in his cell. But about mid-afternoon the door to the dungeon burst open with a loud crash. Vorkees, with his sergeant and three guardsmen in tow, rushed down the stairs to the dungeon floor. Jax stood and backed away from the cell door as the captain fumbled at the padlock with a key, his face livid with anger. The man threw the barred door open and the four guardsmen rushed Jax.

Jax didn't struggle as two of them grabbed him by the elbows. They held him as their sergeant curled his fingers into a fist, drew it back and punched him in the stomach.

Jax cried out and doubled over as his gut clenched up.

"Hold," Vorkees shouted. "Don't hurt him. Not yet. I doubt he's going to live much longer, but that's not up to us."

While two of them held Jax, the sergeant lifted his blanket and shook it out. One of his men looked in the wooden bucket, shook his head and said, "It's not here."

The sergeant thoroughly patted Jax down, then said, "It's not on him either."

They tied Jax's wrists behind his back, then put a loop through his elbows and cinched it painfully tight. They tied his ankles together, stuffed a dirty rag in his mouth, bound it in place with a length of rope, put the black sack over his head and dragged him away. His bound feet banged painfully on the dungeon stairs, but once they reached the main floor he had no idea where they took him, only the sensation of his feet dragging across stone floors, then across something smooth like polished wood. He heard shouts and screaming that rose in volume as they approached a group of people arguing: men's and women's voices raised in anger, all interrupting each other. Then a door slammed open and they hauled him in among the angry voices, which abruptly went still. They dragged his feet across plush carpet, then dumped him. With his hands tied behind his back, his cheek smashed into the carpet and a shock of pain shot along the side of his face.

Vorkees said, "It wasn't in his cell, and it's not on him."

He heard Lord Carkoska say, "Remove the hood."

The guards lifted Jax by his elbows and propped him up on his knees, two of them on either side of him supporting him. Then one of them ripped the cloth sack off his head.

He knelt facing Carkoska. The High Lord stood over him holding a figurine in one hand, and Jax had no idea if it was the original or the fake. Lady Carkoska, the Naesmyths, and Celeste stood behind Carkoska looking on. They were in the same parlor where they'd interrogated him the day before.

The High Lord's face turned a vivid red as he extended the small statue and held it just beneath Jax's nose. "Where's the real one?" he shouted. "What did you do with it?"

Somehow they'd discovered he'd switched the statues. Jax tried to say, "I don't know where it is," but with the gag in his mouth his words came out as a series of unintelligible grunts.

Carkoska raised the statue, drew it back, swung out and slapped Jax in the face with it. The small figurine wasn't heavy and didn't make a good club, but it rocked his head to one side and opened a painful cut on his cheek. A small stream of blood trickled down to his chin.

Carkoska raised the statue again, but his wife stepped between them and said, "Now, dear, let's hear what he has to say before you damage him."

Carkoska backed up a step, lowered the statue and gave Jax an angry look filled with malice. Celeste stood behind them all and to one side. She appeared uncertain and fearful, and Jax wondered if she knew he'd learned from Danoka that it was she who had taken the statue from his cell.

Lady Carkoska said to Vorkees, "Dismiss your men, then remove the gag so he can talk."

Vorkees turned and barked, "Leave the room, but don't go far."

The sergeant and his three men hurriedly left and closed the door behind them.

The knot in the rope that held the gag in place had tangled in Jax's hair, and the captain was not kind removing it. Jax did not cry out as a small clump of hair came away with the rope. Vorkees then yanked the gag out of his mouth, almost taking a few of his teeth with it.

Lady Carkoska stood over Jax and planted her fists on her hips. "Well now, thief," she said, "you switched them, didn't you. Put the one from the pedestal into the strongbox, and took the original with you."

There was no use denying it, so Jax shrugged and nodded.

"Why did you do that?" she demanded. "What did you hope to gain?"

Again he shrugged. "I had heard the uproar and was moving quickly, didn't really have time to think anything through, was operating strictly on instinct."

"Instinct, eh?" she said. She smiled and nodded. "Very clever of you. And then my husband actually tossed the original to you. That must have been a surprise."

Jax got the impression she actually approved of his little trick.

"So," she continued, "what have you done with the original? Where is it now?"

Celeste stiffened as if she feared he might give her away. Her eyes narrowed into diamond hard points as she looked at Jax uncertainly. He felt no loyalty toward her and he had nothing to lose by revealing her duplicity. But it occurred to him that if they suspected someone among them had taken it, and didn't know who, that could work in his favor.

Jax said, "I don't know."

Celeste's shoulders relaxed and the look on her face softened.

Carkoska stepped forward to stand beside his wife. He shouted, "You had it in your cell. Where did you hide it?"

Jax tried to keep his voice calm. "The only time I've been outside that cell was under the watchful eyes of your guardsmen, and always with my hands tied or restrained in some way."

Lady Carkoska looked past Jax at Vorkees. "Is that true?"

"Yes, Your Ladyship," the guard captain said.

She returned her gaze to Jax and her eyes narrowed. "Then where is it now, thief?"

Again, Jax shrugged. "The last time I saw it was yesterday morning when your men brought me up here for questioning. Your sergeant told me to leave it in my cell, which I did, and it was gone when we returned."

Lady Carkoska looked past Jax and asked, "Captain?"

Behind him he heard Vorkees say, "One moment, Your Ladyship."

Jax heard the door open and Vorkees shouted, "Sergeant, get in here."

Jax heard a mumbled reply then boots thudding on the floor and the door closed again.

Lady Carkoska said, "Yesterday, did you tell him to leave the statue in the cell?"

Jax couldn't turn to look at the man, but he recognized the sergeant's voice. "Yes, Your Ladyship. We thought it was worthless junk." Jax heard the tremble of fear in the man's voice.

Lady Carkoska continued, "And was it gone when you returned him to his cell?"

"I don't recall, Your Ladyship."

Vorkees said, "I do, Your Ladyship. There was no statue, though I didn't think anything about that at the time."

Lady Carkoska asked, "And who was the guard on duty in the dungeon while the thief was up here with us?"

"That would be Danoka," the sergeant said.

Vorkees demanded. "Bring him up here, now."

"I can't, Captain," the sergeant said, the tremble in his voice now quite pronounced. "He got sick late last night. We think he ate some bad meat."

Carkoska waved the figurine at the sergeant. "I don't care if he's shitting his guts out. He can still talk, can't he?"

"No, Your Lordship," the sergeant said, lowering his eyes. "He ain't doing so well. He ain't conscious no more, and we ain't sure he's going to make it."

Celeste relaxed even further, and her air of confidence returned. Jax concluded she didn't know he'd learned from Danoka of her treachery, so she thought she now had nothing to fear. If Danoka died, and she believed he was the only one who knew she had taken it, she could be confident there'd be no one to expose her.

Carkoska turned on Vorkees. "Have my personal physician see to him. We need to learn from him who took that statue."

Celeste didn't react to that. *Bad meat*, Jax thought, *or perhaps poisoned meat*. If she had been the architect of Danoka's illness, she would know if a physician could help the poor corporal. That her air of confidence remained, did not bode well for the unfortunate man. Again, Jax thought Celeste didn't truly understand the danger she faced in betraying Lady Carkoska.

They dismissed the sergeant again.

Lady Carkoska turned away from Jax to face the rest of them. "So," she said. "One of us has the statue."

Lord Naesmyth frowned and asked, "Why do you say that?"

Lady Carkoska turned back to Jax and gave him the predatory smile. "Since our thief here doesn't have it, and obviously didn't hide it, who else would know its worth?"

Behind them all, Celeste frowned thoughtfully, and it took Jax a moment to understand what had pierced her confidence. Lady Carkoska was anything but stupid, and it wouldn't take her long to reconstruct the events of the previous morning. She would quickly conclude that only one of them had had the opportunity to steal the statue from his cell, and Celeste would find herself at the mercy of the predator. Jax watched the young woman's confidence slowly crumble and disappear completely.

"And you, thief," Lady Carkoska said. "You're no longer of use to us, so we might as well dispose of you."

"But wait," Lord Naesmyth said. He turned to Celeste. "Didn't you say he is connected to the statue in some way?"

Celeste's voice came out in a barely audible whisper. "Yes, he is."

Naesmyth turned back to Lady Carkoska. "Then let's not act in haste. We may need him in some way we don't yet understand."

Lady Naesmyth said, "It occurs to me that it wouldn't hurt to interrogate him . . . more forcefully."

Lady Carkoska had not taken her eyes off Jax, and at Lady Naesmyth's words she smiled. "That's an excellent idea, Stephanna. In fact, I'll handle the interrogation myself."

At those words a large lump formed in Jax's throat.

Lord Carkoska frowned and stepped forward. "Be careful, dear. We probably do need him alive, and you have been known to . . . get carried away."

Lady Carkoska looked at Jax with such ravenous need he thought she might see right into his soul. "Don't worry, my dear. I won't harm him . . . at least not too much. And please don't begrudge me a little pleasure. After all, you had your pleasure with his whore of a sister, so let me have mine with him."

She leaned forward and bent down, her face on a level with Jax's. In her eyes he saw lust and desire. He marveled at the way her gray pupils appeared almost colorless, and in them he saw the predator stir. It had been quiescent until that moment, but now it wanted to feed, and he couldn't look away.

She leaned forward a little more and brushed her lips lightly across his. Her touch sent a shock through his heart, and her need wrapped its tendrils around his soul. Her desire and lust became his, her needs his, and he craved to fulfil her wants. He fantasized about kissing her, caressing her breasts and licking her nipples, biting them until he drew blood, and tasting every inch of her body.

As quickly as it had come upon him, the moment ended and he snapped out of it. A wave of nausea almost brought his meager breakfast boiling forth. When he'd looked into her eyes, somehow she'd taken control of him, and he quietly vowed never to look into those cold, heartless eyes again.

She brushed her lips across his one more time, but now it had no effect. She sniffed at him, the predator taking the scent of its prey, and her lips brushed lightly across his cheek. Her breath tickled his ear as she whispered, "You intrigue me, thief. Something about you fascinates me in a way I haven't felt in a long time."

Her tongue darted out and licked at the trickle of blood on his cheek. When she tasted it she shivered and a soft grumble escaped her throat. "Who knows, when I strip you of all your secrets you might find it quite pleasurable, or you might find it unbearably painful. Though, in fact, I think you'll probably find it both. I always do."

36

Corrupted Magics

JAX'S INSTINCT TOLD him that two of the four guards who dragged him back down to his cell were of the Witchguard. And he recognized the guard who sat down at the crude table to take the dungeon-watch night shift. He was one of the knights who had arrested Jax on the street the day the Witch had abducted him. Something was going to happen, and soon.

Locked safely in his cell again, Jax wrapped the blanket around his shoulders and curled up on the stone floor. He dozed fitfully, but came fully awake at the sound of the dungeon door opening and closing with a thud. He had no idea of the time, but it was clearly well into the night.

Four guards marched down the dungeon stairs, and this time they didn't rush him or assault him. They opened the door to his cell and their sergeant said, "Come with us."

They didn't tie him or bind him, but held him securely between them as they marched him up to the ground floor of the castle, then up another flight of stairs to the second floor. Long ago Lady Naesmyth's boudoir had been located on that floor, and when they hustled him into a lady's sitting room, he wondered for a moment if he'd now be confronted by her—and her appetites. Though it occurred to him her appetites might be more palatable than Lady Carkoska's

The guards held him securely and waited standing in the middle of the room. At the far end of the room an open doorway filled with shadows led into a dark and unlit room, probably a lady's bedroom. From within it he heard a soft moan in a voice that sounded familiar, though he could not tell if it had been a sigh of pleasure or a whimper of pain.

Lady Carkoska emerged from the dark doorway into the light of the room. She wore a rich, velvet brocade robe secured snugly around her neck. It covered her completely down to her ankles. Jax was pleased to see that she had not let her hair down and still wore makeup. Hopefully, all she intended to do was question him.

She crossed the room, walking the way a lioness might stalk a young deer, stopped in front of him at an intimately close distance and looked him over carefully.

In her face he saw the hungry look of the predator again, so he lowered his eyes and refused to meet her gaze, but that left him looking at the swell of her breasts beneath the brocade robe, so he looked aside. She reached out and caressed his cheek, then lightly gripped his chin between two fingers and turned his face from side to side. "You'll do nicely."

She waved a hand at the guards in a gesture of casual dismissal. "Leave us."

The sergeant said, "But Your Ladyship, he's—"

"I said leave us." She gave him a stern look. "I don't need you to protect me."

The guards released Jax, but still hesitated.

Lady Carkoska didn't move in the slightest, but the sergeant cringed. She looked again at Jax and he kept his eyes diverted.

"Our thief here," she said, "would not have survived as long as he has if he were a foolish man. I doubt he'll try anything. But even if he does,"—she turned her head slowly and settled her gaze on the sergeant—"for me he'll prove to be nothing more than a pleasant challenge."

The sergeant averted his eyes and said, "Yes, Your Ladyship."

The four men scuttled out of the room like fearful rodents.

Jax and the lady had not moved, and she still stood with her chin only a few inches from his. With his gaze diverted and trying not to look into her eyes, he saw the figurine standing on the mantle above an unlit hearth, and its presence startled him. "The statue," he said, and made the mistake of looking into her face.

Their eyes met.

Once more, the tendrils of her hunger and desire wrapped around his heart, imprisoning his soul in a cascade of want and need. She smiled, opened the front of her robe, and he saw that she wore nothing beneath it. He struggled to resist as she took his hands in hers and pressed them against her bare breasts. But her desire became his need and he could not have denied her in the slightest, no matter how hard he tried. A piece of him screamed and cried and begged to be released, but she would allow him no retreat.

Her skin beneath his fingers was soft and smooth, like that of a young woman half her age. He traced the circle of her areolas with his thumbs, then lightly pinched one nipple. She groaned and writhed against him. He tried to turn away from her, but her grip on his soul remained unrelenting. And instead of denying her, he could only give her what she wanted as he ran his hands down her sides to her hips and wrapped his arms around her waist, pulling her tightly against him. As he kissed her she thrust her tongue into his mouth, and he had a demanding erection that he pressed against her stomach through the cloth of his trousers. She rubbed her belly against it, and a growl escaped her lips.

"Yes," she said. "You're everything I knew you would be."

He kissed her neck and nibbled at her ear. She bit his earlobe, and his entire world centered on one single need: to touch and kiss every inch of her body. He had no desire to make love to her, but he desperately longed to rut with her, to feel her skin pressed against his, their sweat mingling as he stabbed his erection into her. Something within him needed to hurt her while he spilled his seed within her. And as she groaned and cried out in his arms, he knew without a doubt that she would gain pleasure from the pain.

In an effort to end this, he tried to bite her neck viciously, but his body ignored his own desires and he planted kisses on her cheek, then slowly worked his way down her throat. He covered her upper chest with kisses, then licked and sucked on her nipples. He planted more kisses down her belly as he lowered himself to his knees, and she cried out as his lips explored her navel.

She leaned down and whispered in his ear, "You are a tempting treat, young man, but not tonight."

She stepped away from him and said, "Enough."

Whatever had entrapped him ended as abruptly as it had begun. All desire left him and his erection quickly withered. He retched, gagged and swallowed bile to keep his supper down, but he failed, turned to one side, fell to his hands and knees and vomited. What had she done to him? She had controlled him like a puppet on strings, and he would have done anything she demanded, no matter how corrupt or degrading. He gagged and retched until nothing remained in his stomach, but still his abdomen spasmed and convulsed. When the seizures finally ended he lay on his side, gulping for air.

She stood over him. "You're stronger than most, and your attempts at resistance excite me even more, though in every way that counts, you are now mine."

He rose up onto his knees. She looked down at him and smiled triumphantly. She leaned close to him and ran her tongue along his cheek. "I'm saving you for another time, darling. And you're welcome to resist as much as you can, because that only excites me all the more. But when I want you, I'll have you. That, you can believe in the deepest part of your soul."

She straightened, turned, and walked to the hearth. She retrieved the statue from the mantle and carried it toward the dark, open doorway from which she had emerged earlier. "Come," she said without looking his way, "I have something I want you to see."

Jax struggled to his feet and had to lean for a moment on the back of a chair to keep from falling over. As he stood there panting like a frightened animal, trying to suck air into his lungs, he considered making a run for it, but the guards outside the door would stop him easily.

From within the darkened room, she called out, "You mustn't keep a lady waiting, darling."

Jax walked slowly on unsteady legs. As he stepped into the darkened room, with his eyes still adjusted to the light of the parlor, he saw nothing. He heard another soft moan, and again he couldn't have said if he heard pleasure or pain in that sound.

To one side a match flared. Lady Carkoska lifted the glass off a lamp and lit its wick. As she replaced the glass and turned up the wick, light filled the room. She stood there, no sign of the figurine, the front of her robe open, her breasts and belly glistening with his saliva, but still she stirred no desire in him.

Another soft moan drew Jax's attention and he turned away from her. They were standing in a lady's bedchamber, and on the far side of the room he saw movement in the shadows against one wall. He squinted, and thought he could make out the shape of a person standing there, arms outstretched to either side.

Lady Carkoska crossed the room carrying the lamp. As she approached the person against the wall and the globe of light from the lamp enveloped the figure there, Jax could make out pale, white skin; small, bare breasts with dark brown nipples; curly red hair both on top of her head and where her legs met.

Celeste dangled from ropes tied to the wall in some way, naked, her arms outstretched, her legs spread. She hung limply by her arms, her head lolling down and to one side. Small, red welts covered her body, each nothing more than a thin red line no longer than an inch or two.

The figurine stood on a small table nearby. Lady Carkoska placed the lamp next to it, then reached out and put a finger delicately beneath Celeste's chin. She nudged the chin upward and said, "Look who has come to join us, darling. He thinks he can resist me, just as you thought you could deceive me only a few hours ago. You still have a secret or two to tell me, but I'm going to enjoy wresting them from you."

Celeste raised her head, and when Jax saw her face he gasped. Grayish bags darkened the skin beneath her eyes, and she appeared to have aged several decades in a single night. A soft moan escaped her lips, and this time there was no question she uttered it in pain, not pleasure.

Lady Carkoska turned her head to look at Jax. "Our young witch has been a very naughty little girl." She looked down at the figurine. "But all is forgiven, now that she's returned that to me."

She looked at Celeste. "You like my forgiveness, don't you? You crave it, you need it, you want it more than anything you could imagine."

Celeste moaned again and said, "Please, no more . . . more . . . more."

"Ah, my poor dear," Lady Carkoska said. "You're in pain, and pain without pleasure is so unfair."

Again, she looked at Jax. "Pain should always be rewarded with pleasure, don't you think? And pleasure with pain. The two together make for a delicious, never-ending circle of sensation and need."

She retrieved something from the table. It was about the width of a man's finger, and a little longer. With both hands she carefully unfolded it, and Jax saw that she held a straight razor. She raised the blade toward Celeste's chest, and when Jax realized what she intended to do he took an involuntary step forward. Lady Carkoska glanced his way and said, "No, thief, don't even think about it, or you'll take her place."

Jax backed up a step and glanced frantically about the room for some sort of weapon, but saw nothing he might use to overcome the monster he faced.

Lady Carkoska pressed the edge of the razor carefully against the pale, white flesh high on one of Celeste's breasts. A trickle of blood traced a line down her soft skin and dripped off the girl's nipple. Jax now understood how all the thin, red welts had been created, though a piece of him noted that, while none of them could be more than a few hours old, most appeared to have already healed.

Lady Carkoska leaned forward, licked at the blood and sucked at the small wound with smacking, slurping sounds. When she lifted her head away from Celeste's breast, she looked at Jax and smiled, her lips and teeth stained red with the younger woman's blood. Then she gripped the hair on the back of Celeste's head, and pressed her blood-soaked mouth to the young woman's lips.

Celeste's eyes widened and she responded with desperate need. She moaned with pleasure as Lady Carkoska pressed their naked bodies together, while Celeste thrust her pelvis frantically against the older woman's hip. When the kiss ended Celeste pulled one of her arms out of the ropes holding her suspended against the wall, and only then did Jax realize she hung there willingly. But then, if the woman controlled her the way she had controlled Jax earlier, there was nothing voluntary about it, and bile rose in his throat.

Celeste reached down and put her hand between Lady Carkoska's legs. The woman responded with an animal-like growl, then raised the straight razor and cut Celeste again.

This time the cut was deeper and bled more freely. Lady Carkoska reached out and pressed the palms of her hands into the trail of blood. She turned to Jax and he avoided looking into her eyes as she smeared it on her own breasts and stomach, then down between her legs. She smiled at him and turned back to Celeste. The younger woman licked the blood away hungrily as Lady Carkoska grumbled with pleasure.

Jax turned and staggered out of the room, gulping hard and fighting down nausea. Had he not emptied his stomach earlier, he would have vomited then and there. In the parlor he leaned against the back of a couch and struggled to breathe. Lady Carkoska had orchestrated that entire scene as a little demonstration for his benefit. She wanted him to know the fate that awaited him. She wanted him to know he would be helpless in her clutches.

"Well, thief, what do you think?"

Jax turned around to find her standing behind him, the front of her robe open, her lips, breasts and belly smeared with Celeste's blood. Again he resisted the urge to look into her eyes as she reached out and clamped a hand around his throat with crushing force, then lifted him off his feet as if he weighed nothing. As he dangled from her hand, choking and gasping for air, she said, "Pleasure and pain; when properly applied, the boundary between one and the other is gray and indistinct, and that makes both so much more enjoyable, don't you think?"

With his toes dangling inches off the floor, Jax was too busy struggling for air to attempt an answer.

She set him down on his feet, then closed the robe and cinched it carefully. She raised a small handkerchief to her mouth and wiped away the blood and saliva there, leaving no outward sign of what had just transpired. If Jax had not seen it with his own eyes, he would doubt his sanity.

She crossed the room to a bell pull near the hearth and yanked on it. The door opened and in walked the sergeant and three of his men, their eyes fearfully downcast.

She looked Jax's way and gave him a predatory smile. "Take him back to his cell."

The guards surrounded Jax, two of them secured his arms tightly, and they marched him to the door. As the sergeant opened it, Lady Carkoska halted them by saying, "Just one more thing."

The guards turned Jax about so he could look her way, and even though the robe now hid any last traces of Celeste's blood, Jax could not look at Lady Carkoska without seeing her blood-smeared breasts and belly. He realized in that moment that she now appeared even younger than when he'd first seen her that evening. He recalled that her breasts had stood up like those on a young woman, and the belly he'd licked had been flat and hard. He wondered at that.

"Our witch has one more secret to reveal," she said. "She still must tell me how you are connected to the figurine, and once I know that, you'll take her place. You might even enjoy yourself, at least for a time. But like her, I doubt you'll survive either the pleasure or the pain."

37

Old Loose Ends

OF THE THREE guards escorting Jax and the sergeant, the two holding his arms clamped to his sides and the fellow following behind them were Knights of the Witchguard. Jax's instinct told him that the sergeant leading them was appropriately attired in Naesmyth livery, so he couldn't count on any help from him. Jax wondered what the three knights had in mind, and he hoped there'd be an opportunity to speak with them where no one else could hear.

They hustled him down to the main floor, but Lady Naesmyth intercepted them there. It had to be well past midnight, and yet she wore a day-gown with her hair still pinned up. If Jax hadn't been so consciously aware of her murderous past—and present—he would have marveled at her striking blue eyes. And the slight swell of her breasts, carefully exposed above the top of her gown, might have stirred some desire in him. But he could never forget his own past with her, nor could he forget the face of the young boy who had washed up on the banks of the river.

"I want to speak with the prisoner," she said. "Follow me."

The sergeant said, "Yes, milady."

She led them into the sitting room where earlier that day she and Lady Carkoska had interrogated him. Her husband stood by the hearth waiting. A heavy pistol lay on the mantle near his hand.

"Leave the room," he said to the sergeant. "But stay close."

The four guards scurried out of the room and closed the door.

Lady Naesmyth stood a few paces from Jax and looked him over carefully. She opened her mouth to say something, but a distant, muffled cry broke the stillness of the night. She hesitated, smiled, and looked upward. Her husband cringed and also looked upward.

Lady Naesmyth turned the smile on Jax and said, "It sounds as if Darthea is instructing our wicked little Celeste in the error of her ways."

The way she said it, Jax got the impression she would like to join the two women upstairs. She clearly longed to share the pleasure and pain of their activities.

Lady Naesmyth asked, "Did Darthea show you her method of instruction?"

Jax swallowed bile and refused to answer.

"Ah," she said. "I can see by the look on your face she did."

Lord Naesmyth said, "Her proclivities are disgusting."

She approached Jax and stopped a short pace from him, looking into his eyes. "I find her proclivities fascinating. They produce the most interesting results."

Her husband looked at her with undisguised distaste. "You envy her."

She turned her head slowly and looked at him. "I do envy the power and strength she controls. Perhaps someday she'll show me how she twists the minds of men so easily. And many would say your proclivities are disgusting as well, my dear."

He shook his head. "And many would say yours are."

She returned her attention to Jax. She reached up and put a finger beneath his chin. She turned his face to the left, then to the right, examining him carefully, much the way Lady Carkoska had done only a few minutes earlier. "Ever since I first met you, there has been something familiar about you. And now I think I remember you."

"What do you mean?" her husband demanded, and Jax heard the fear in his voice.

Without warning she stepped forward, wrapped her arms around Jax's neck and kissed him, thrusting her tongue into his mouth. She ended the kiss after only a few seconds and stepped away from him. "I certainly remember the taste of you. Do you remember the taste of me? It was a long time ago, but we did enjoy each other, didn't we?"

She cocked an eyebrow thoughtfully. "Perhaps I should have the guards leave you with me for the night, just for old time's sake. You did prove your worth, all those years ago."

She looked at her husband. "And this time don't be so squeamish. Take your pleasure in him and enjoy it."

His eyes hardened. "So you can have him murdered in the morning?"

"Ah," she said, her eyes widening. She looked from her husband to Jax, then back to her husband. "He's been telling you little stories, hasn't he? You know, I can't allow him to spread such nasty rumors."

Lord Naesmyth clearly had trouble containing his anger. "And I have no doubt they're true. They are true, aren't they?"

She gave him a flirtatious smile. "You don't know what you missed, my dear. At first he was tentative and a bit hurried, but he learned his lessons well and proved to be quite the willing student."

Her words humiliated Jax, and cold fury boiled up in his gut. "Perhaps I was willing then, but not now."

She turned toward him in a swirl of petticoats. "He finally speaks." She stepped forward, forcing him to step back a pace. She leaned close to him. "I still have needs, and I know from experience I'll enjoy going through the motions with you. I did thoroughly enjoy your touch all those years ago."

She turned and walked to her husband. "For a brief time, we needed him. But he knows too much, and Darthea will soon know all of Celeste's little secrets, so he's no longer necessary. I think we'd be wise to clean up this loose end. After all, it is nine years overdue, isn't it?"

Another distant, muffled cry sounded through the walls. Jax decided it was time for the Witch Knights to get him out of that building.

Lady Naesmyth called out, "Lakorsa, please join us."

The man with half an ear stepped out through the darkened doorway of an adjoining room. "Milady," he said.

She nodded toward Jax. "This young man has proven to be . . . a dangerous liability."

Lakorsa nodded. "He's the one who escaped, isn't he?"

"Yes," she said. "An error you need to correct right now."

Lakorsa reached into his coat and pulled out a double-edged dagger with a wicked point. "Easily done," he said, and started across the room toward Jax.

"Hold. Not another step."

At the sound of Lord Naesmyth's voice, Lakorsa froze in mid-stride. He, Jax, and Lady Naesmyth looked to her husband, who held the pistol aimed at Lakorsa. He cocked the hammer back and said, "I'll not let you harm another innocent."

The lady rolled her eyes. "He's a thief, dear. How innocent is that?"

He snarled, "I don't care."

She shrugged. "Be that as it may, you can't stop us, darling. I had Lakorsa foul the charge in the pistol."

Lakorsa grinned and resumed his march toward Jax, the dagger held in front of him. Lord Naesmyth pulled the pistol's trigger, the hammer clacked, a flash of sparks flared upward from the flintlock's pan, but no loud report thundered in the room, and no musket ball felled Lakorsa.

Jax backed away from the man and shouted at the top of his lungs, "Guards!"

The four guardsmen burst into the room, their sergeant in the lead. Lakorsa froze again.

"Sergeant," Lady Naesmyth said, "do not hinder Master Lakorsa. He has an unpleasant task to perform, so stand aside."

The sergeant wore Naesmyth livery, so he had no choice but to obey. "Yes, milady," he said, lowering his eyes.

Her husband intervened, "And *I'm* ordering you to take that dagger away from Lakorsa. I'll not allow murder in this house."

Lady Naesmyth snarled, "Don't be a weak-willed idiot."

The sergeant looked back and forth between husband and wife several times. "But . . . I . . ."

At that moment one of the Witch Knights swung out with his fist and clubbed the sergeant in the side of the head. Lakorsa lunged at Jax, crossing the last few steps between them and leading with the dagger.

Jax had had nine years on the streets to learn how to defend against a short blade, and how to fight with one as well. He'd also grown in that time, now stood as tall as Lakorsa, with shoulders just as broad. And perhaps Lakorsa still expected him to be a naive, clumsy, sixteen-year-old boy.

Jax side-stepped the dagger thrust, grabbed Lakorsa's wrist with his left hand, spun and slammed his right elbow into the side of the man's head. Lakorsa slashed out as he staggered away, slicing a fiery red line across Jax's forearm.

Lakorsa lunged again with the point of the dagger aimed at Jax's heart. Jax blocked the thrust to one side, spun and kicked Lakorsa in the knee. The man cried out and stumbled back two steps limping badly, but retained the dagger and thrust out again. Jax back stepped just out of reach of the dagger's point.

One of the knights stepped between them and placed the point of a sword at Lakorsa's throat. Another cornered Lord Naesmyth and held him at bay with a flint-lock pistol aimed at his chest. The third held a blade against the lady's throat and shouted, "Hold, or the woman dies."

Lakorsa looked at the blade at his throat, dropped the dagger and raised his hands. He staggered and clearly had trouble standing on the knee Jax had kicked. The knight backed him up two limping steps with the point of his sword, then without taking his eyes off Lakorsa reached down and picked up the dagger.

Lying on the floor, the Naesmyth sergeant groaned and rolled over, but didn't rise.

The Witch Knight holding the knife at Lady Naesmyth's throat said, "We're leaving, and the thief is coming with us."

"You'll answer for this," she hissed. "You'll answer dearly."

He grinned. "You'll have to speak with Mother about that, because I answer only to her."

••••

The adjoining room from which Lakorsa had emerged had a solid wooden door. While one knight bandaged Jax's arm with a strip of cloth torn from his shirt, another dragged the Naesmyth sergeant into the room. They quickly forced Lakorsa, and Lord and Lady Naesmyth, in there as well. One of the knights closed the door, and another jammed the point of Lakorsa's dagger into the door jamb, then snapped it off. He said, "That won't hold long, but long enough for us to get out of the building if we move quickly."

Out in the hallway beyond the sitting room the castle remained eerily silent. "Wait," Jax said and paused for a moment to listen. No more screams or cries from Celeste, nothing.

One of the knights asked, "Where's the figurine?"

Jax lied. "I don't know, and we don't have time to search for it." He wasn't about to attempt to face Lady Carkoska, even with three Knights of the Witchguard to lead the way. And recalling the way she'd easily lifted him off his feet with a single hand, he didn't have time to explain to them why four men couldn't handle one woman. He also couldn't take the chance that one or more of them might look into her eyes, and be trapped within her sordid control.

One of the knights handed Jax a short blade. "Do you know how to use this?"

He nodded. "I do."

They moved carefully down the hallway toward the main entrance. The absolute silence that had descended on the place bothered Jax no end. He wouldn't want anyone to suffer at the hands of Lady Carkoska, but he would have felt better if Celeste had let out a scream or two, just so he knew the predator was occupied sating her desires. And Celeste had no one to blame but herself for her predicament.

When they reached the base of the stairs that rose to the second floor, they huddled in a small group and Jax cautioned them to move carefully. Three of them waited while one of the knights ran in a crouch past the stairs—nothing. Another knight followed him, moving quickly to join the first, and still nothing. It was Jax's turn, so he stayed low and ran, but just as he reached the base of the stairs, an ear-splitting shriek above him broke the silence.

He looked up the stairway and saw a naked and bloodied Celeste screaming at the top of her lungs and charging down the steps toward him, taking them two at a time. Smears of blood covered her from face to ankles, and she waved her arms wildly, her breasts bouncing with each step. She plowed into him and they both tumbled to the floor in a tangle of arms and legs. He tried to shove her away, but she grabbed at his wounded arm, tore the makeshift bandage away and clamped her mouth over the wound. He expected to feel the pain of her teeth sinking into his flesh, but all she did was suck and slurp at the blood. He grabbed the hair on the back of her head and tried to pull her loose, but she growled like an animal and ignored him, the tendons of her neck straining to keep her mouth clamped on his arm. She looked at him with eyes that had long ago lost any semblance of sanity.

One of the knights leaned over them and clubbed her in the side of the head with the hilt of a dagger. Her body went limp, her mouth slack, a runnel of blood and saliva dripping down her chin. She sat up, her eyes crossed and rolling wildly. She tried to stand, but her arms and legs wouldn't cooperate and she fell back to the floor. The knight extended a hand to Jax. "Let's get the hell out of here, thief."

Jax took the hand and the fellow pulled him to his feet.

"Thief," Lady Carkoska screamed, and Jax and the knight both looked upward. She stood at the top of the stairs, her robe again open at the front, exposing her breasts, belly and the dark shadow between her legs, all covered in smears of Celeste's blood.

"You cannot escape me, thief," she cried, her lips, face and teeth stained with more of the girl's blood. "Our dear Celeste has revealed the last of your secrets, so I now know all, and you will be mine. You are the key we've sought."

Jax averted his eyes and shouted, "Don't look in her eyes," but the knight beside him had already done so. He stood stiff and frozen, looking up at the insane vision of the woman standing above them.

She spoke softly. "Come to me, darling."

The knight's hand opened and his blade clattered to the floor, the look on his face slack and distant, his eyes focused on the woman above them. He continued to look at her as he lifted a foot and placed it on the first step. "Yes," he said, his voice dreamy and distant, "come to you." He took another step.

"No," Jax screamed, careful to keep his eyes averted. As the knight took another step Jax reached out, grabbed the man's wrist and tugged. The fellow hesitated, but still refused to look away from Lady Carkoska.

Jax hit him in the side of the head with the hilt of his blade and the man staggered. The knight stumbled into him and they both fell on top of the semi-conscious Celeste. She stirred, wailed like an infant crying out in the night and tried to grasp Jax's wounded arm.

One of the other knights appeared beside them and aimed a pistol up the stairway. When he pulled the trigger it erupted with a thunderous blast of flame and smoke. The musket ball tore a chunk of masonry out of the wall at the top of the stairs, and Lady Carkoska ducked out of sight, screaming like a demon from the grave.

As the knight with the pistol helped his stunned comrade to his feet, Celeste clamped her hands around Jax's wrist and craned her neck to get her mouth on the wound in his arm, her lips and teeth already stained with his blood. The third knight leaned over them, gripped her shoulders and lifted her off him as if she weighed nothing. She kicked and screamed maniacally, so he struck her in the side of the head with his fist and she went limp in his arms. He dropped her to the floor and helped Jax to his feet.

The knight Jax had clubbed in the head could stand, though he was stunned and unsteady on his feet. Jax tried to support him and help him walk as the other two knights led the way, short swords held in front of them. Shouts and cries sounded from the interior of the building as they moved cautiously but quickly down a long hallway to the front of the house. They encountered a Carkoska guard armed with only a cudgel. Everyone froze for just an instant, but a lone guard with a club against two knights with short swords stood no chance. Seeing the odds stacked against him, the guard backed away and didn't hinder them.

By the time they reached the front of the house, the knight Jax had clubbed could stand on his own and move without aid. One of the knights eased the door open and peered out. "The courtyard's clear," he said. "Let's make a run for it."

The four of them spilled out into the front courtyard and ran. Halfway to the wall that surrounded the place a musket roared and a ball whizzed past their heads. Another musket blast sounded just as they reached the main gate, and one of the knights went down. As musket balls hissed past them, zinging off the cobblestones around them, Jax and another knight lifted the wounded knight by his armpits and dragged him out into the street. Then the hand of some unknown god slapped Jax down in the middle of the street. His head slammed into the cobblestones and he lost consciousness.

38

Allies

"MY POOR LITTLE thief!"

Jax recognized Venessta's voice.

"No, little witch," Maelleen said. "*Our* poor little thief. He's mine as well, you know."

Jax wondered if they might cut him up into pieces and share him between them. He wanted to tell them not to do that, that he didn't mind being shared, but he had trouble making his lips work. He drifted in and out of consciousness for some unknown time.

"Mother got the musket ball out of you, and she says you'll be fine. We're treating the wound to ensure it doesn't fester."

Jax wasn't sure which one of them had said that.

"Yes," the other one said. "All you need is a little rest."

Jax dreamed about staggering naked down a deserted street in Val d'Ossa, a horrible wound in his shoulder. A cold, blustery rain pounded down on him and he huddled beneath a stone bench to shield his body from the weather, but the wind blew the raindrops sideways, and nothing protected him for long. He ended up lying in the mud, shivering, his teeth chattering like the sound of a horse's hooves clomping down the street.

"Mother says we should keep you warm," one of them said.

The other added, "And this is the best way."

Jax became conscious of a lithe body huddled against him beneath the sheets on his left side, and a round curvaceous one on his right, both completely naked. He decided it was a good way to keep warm.

"Oh my goodness," Maelleen said. "You're certainly feeling better. Dear, look at that."

"Oh yes," Venessta said. "He must be feeling better. Do you think we should . . . do something about that?"

"What did you have in mind?"

"Oh . . . I don't know. Something rather conventional, I suppose. But you'll have to take care of that."

"I . . ." Maelleen said, and she hesitated for a moment. "No . . . no . . . let's let him rest. We should let him rest. I'm sure that's the right thing to do."

"You don't sound terribly convinced."

"I'm not."

And neither was Jax, but they did let him rest.

●●●●

The musket ball hadn't done too much damage to Jax's shoulder, and apparently the Witch had all sorts of magical tricks to ensure that the wound didn't fester, and to help him heal rather quickly. Jax never sensed any magic or sorcery, but then he didn't expect he would. In a week he was up and about with his left arm in a sling, and in another week he felt well enough to remove the sling completely, though the shoulder remained stiff and sore.

The Witch thought the slash on his arm most unusual. It healed almost instantly, almost miraculously. Jax recalled that one of the wounds Lady Carkoska had made in Celeste's skin had been rather deep, and it seemed unlikely she would have cut her that badly only once. The young woman's injuries couldn't have been more than a few hours old when he'd first seen them, and yet only the most recent were anything more than unpleasant welts, as if they had healed unusually fast. Celeste had sucked hungrily on the slash in his arm. He didn't want to believe that had anything to do with the way it had healed so rapidly, so he put that thought out of his mind.

Venessta slept in his bed and refused to leave his side, though as always nothing happened between them. Maelleen welcomed him back to health most passionately one night, and had no trouble with their unusual relationship, but he wondered about Venessta. She had shown some signs of serious jealousy, and he hoped that wouldn't become a problem. Maybe they'd have to put a little more effort into getting Maelleen her rich husband. But at that thought, Jax felt a pang of jealousy, so he decided not to mess with the status quo. He'd just hope for the best.

Jax didn't want to talk about the unpleasant few days he'd spent as a captive guest of the Carkoskas and Naesmyths, and he managed to put it off until one morning about two weeks after his rescue. During breakfast the Witch announced, "The Lords and Ladies Carkoska and Naesmyth wish to meet with us on neutral ground outside the city. And I believe Mistress Celeste will accompany them."

Jax wasn't sure if he was pleased or disappointed that Celeste had somehow survived Lady Carkoska.

The Witch turned her attention on him. "So it's time you tell us what happened in that old castle, my little thief."

"Why are they coming?" Jax asked her. "Aren't we sworn enemies, or something?"

The old woman's apparent age dropped by about two decades as she said, "You've put it off long enough, so don't try to delay this further with a lot of questions."

Venessta intervened. "Mother, I think he sincerely doesn't understand. The politics are rather complicated."

Maelleen said, "I think I sincerely don't understand as well. I would think that, at this point, we'd have open war, or something."

The Witch gave her a furious look, but thankfully she didn't turn any younger. "Open war is out of the question."

Maelleen gave her a questioning look. "But why?"

"Because I would crush them."

"Then why not just crush them and be done with it?"

"Because I need them. And I need them powerful, but not too powerful. The balance of power between the High Noble Houses and the Witch Palace allows us to hold sway over the other city-states: Lieudess, Palvestra, and Del Fransika. A shift in that balance might be seen as an opportunity for one or more of them to break away, and then we'd be vulnerable to the barbarian hordes."

Jax had never seen a barbarian, though like every child he'd heard stories of their atrocities. "Is that what this is about, a grab for power?"

"Yes."

"And the figurine has this power?"

Apparently, the Witch had realized their confusion was honest and sincere, because she returned to her proper age. "No, it doesn't contain the power. But it's probably a key of some sort, though to exactly what, we're not sure. I'm certain I could discern more if I could get my hands on the blasted thing."

She gave Jax an angry look. "That's what you were supposed to accomplish, little thief."

Clearly, the Witch thought that being a witch would help her gain some greater understanding of the nature of the statue. But Jax recalled that Celeste's qualifications as a witch hadn't done much for her in that regard. In fact, everything would be so much simpler if all the witches would just go away. Well, he didn't want Venessta to go away, but he wouldn't consider it any great loss if she stopped being a witch.

"Now, thief," the Witch said, "your story. All of it. Leave nothing out."

From Maelleen they already knew what had occurred up to the point where Jax left her in her room in House Carkoska. He took up the story from there and described the events in detail until his rescue. He told them nothing of the sensation he got when he touched the original figurine, nor that Celeste had sensed something when he did so. And to keep that piece of information a secret, he adjusted certain aspects of the story. He did tell them about Lady Carkoska and her appetites, though he didn't go into any great detail on the almost hypnotic control she induced when she looked into his eyes.

"Interesting," the Witch said. "She's practicing blood rites. I wonder where she got such knowledge and power, and where she learned the proper techniques."

"What are blood rites?" Jax asked.

Jax had never seen the Witch look uncomfortable before. "It's a kind of magic, though you don't have to be a witch to practice it. It's dangerous, and if she keeps feeding on Celeste that way, it'll certainly destroy the young woman, but it could backfire on Lady Carkoska as well."

Venessta asked, "How so?"

"I don't know much about blood rites," the old woman said, "because I don't practice them. But I've heard a thing or two, and they can be dangerous to the practitioner."

Maelleen spoke tentatively. "You used the word . . . feeding. You said Lady Carkoska was feeding on Celeste."

The old woman's wispy-gray eyebrows shot up in surprise. "I did, didn't I? I think that was completely subconscious. I suppose Jax's description left me with the impression of a dangerous predator feeding on a kill."

She tapped a spoon on the side of a teacup for several seconds, her eyes focused elsewhere. Then she looked pointedly at Jax and asked, "My knights tell me you told them not to look into Lady Carkoska's eyes, though one of them did and he immediately went into some sort of trance. He said she controlled him completely, that a series of disgusting sexual images flooded through his mind and that he would have done anything she asked. I must assume you knew not to look into her eyes because you had done so yourself. Did she control you that way?"

Jax couldn't meet her eyes as he said, "Yes."

"Was her control something like the way Maelleen controls men with her charms?"

Jax shook his head. "Maelleen doesn't really control men. Not in that way, and not so absolutely. She just makes men intensely want to do to her what they naturally would want to do to her."

Maelleen reached out and touched his cheek with a smug look on her face. "That's very sweet, darling."

The Witch looked at him for a long moment, and her eyes narrowed. "I need to know about this, little thief. It may be important."

Jax tried to explain the wanton need that had overcome him when he'd looked into the woman's eyes. "I would have done anything she commanded, even while it turned my stomach. It wasn't that I wanted to please her, but more that I had to obey her. And I wanted to hurt her. Hurting her would have . . . given me pleasure, though I don't understand why I felt that way."

"My goodness," Maelleen said. "I suppose I should be envious of her, that she can control men so completely."

"No," Jax said. "You make a man desire you. She makes a man desperately need to . . . to simply couple with her, to rut like animals. With her, the line between pleasure and pain blurs. They become one and the same, and her victim wants to give both, as well as receive both. And when the trance is broken, you're left feeling degraded and used."

Jax looked into Maelleen's eyes. "With you, the desire is genuine and never goes away."

Maelleen smiled, while Venessta frowned in a jealous pout.

"Hmmm!" the Witch said. "I find it interesting that you used the word *victim*. There are certain demons who elicit a similar response from humans. I'll have to think on that."

"These blood rites," Jax asked. "Would they give her super human strength?" He described the way Lady Carkoska had gripped his throat with crushing force and lifted him off the floor with one hand. Venessta's and Maelleen's eyes widened as he spoke, while the Witch remained expressionless.

"I don't know," the Witch said. "We witches can't practice blood rites. To do so would open gateways that would allow some extremely powerful beings access to our souls. Believe me, a horrible, painful death would be preferable to the fate we'd suffer. So I know very little about that kind of magic."

That implied that Lady Carkoska's lack of arcane powers protected her in some way, whereas a witch's infernal abilities made her vulnerable in a way mundane mortals need not fear. That thought only confused Jax.

Venessta sounded subdued as she asked, "Did the Carkoskas and Naesmyths tell you why they want to meet?"

"Indirectly," the Witch said. "They want to cut a deal, to cooperate,"—she looked at Jax pointedly—"and they specifically asked that you be present."

All three women looked at Jax. He felt like a felon in a magistrate's court as the evidence stacked up against him. He hadn't told anyone about the visions that came to him when he touched the statue, not even Maelleen, and had privately vowed that he never would. She, like the two witches, now gave him an odd, suspicious look.

The Witch continued, "They want to pool resources, little thief. They said they have the figurine . . . and we have you. They'll bring their resource to this meeting on neutral ground, and we're supposed to bring ours."

The Witch leaned back, steepled her fingers in front of her, and looked at Jax over the top of them. "What are you not telling me, little thief?"

••••

Jax continued to deny all knowledge of the figurine and swear vehemently that he had held nothing back. As breakfast broke up, when the Witch and her apprentice left the room, he had Maelleen alone for a moment. She leaned close to him and whispered, "I know you're holding something back, but if it keeps us from wading deeper into the cesspit of politics these witches are digging, I'm with you. And if I can do any-thing to help, just let me know."

The Witch scheduled the meeting with the Carkoska's and Naesmyths for two days hence. It would take place at an inn at the intersection of two main roads east of the city. Each side would be allowed to bring twenty armed men, plus a carriage, one coachman, and a footman.

The night before the meeting Jax slept alone, and poorly. He lay awake wondering what Celeste had actually sensed when he'd touched the figurine. Was it some vague sensation of witchcraft, or did she see his visions as he saw them, and if so how clear-ly? If she could relate to Lady Carkoska nothing more than ambiguous and ill-defined impressions, if all she could say was that some sort of arcane connection existed be-tween the statue and him, he had some hope he could discredit her. Somehow he had to avoid further involvement with these witches, and he never again wanted to en-counter the monster he'd seen in Lady Carkoska's eyes.

With autumn approaching, the morning of the meeting broke with gray clouds hanging low in the sky. The Witch had given Jax strict instructions on how to dress that day, with clear orders that he should be prepared to ride on horseback. He donned one of the day suits the Witch had had tailored for him, with riding pants and knee-high boots. With pewter skies outside threatening rain, he pulled on a greatcoat and selected a broad-brimmed hat. When the four of them assembled in the court-yard, Jax assisted the two witches and Maelleen into the carriage, then climbed in to join them. Darganna and his twenty knights mounted their horses, the coachman cracked his whip, and the carriage lurched out of the palace's courtyard.

Sitting next to Jax, Venessta asked, "Does the shoulder still bother you?"

"Only a little," Jax said, "and it gets better every day."

She smiled. "You have Mother to thank for that."

An unpleasant thought occurred to Jax, but he decided to keep it to himself, though when the Witch spoke, it was as if she had read his mind. "Why should he thank me, dear, when I'm the one who put him in front of that musket ball in the first place? If it weren't for me, he and Maelleen would probably be back at her father's tavern making love right now."

The old woman gave Jax a warm smile, not the knowing grin she often threw his way. "It is I who should apologize for doing so. But I won't, because, for some reason I don't yet fathom, I need you, my little thief, and in all likelihood I'm going to put you in danger again. Know that I won't hesitate to do so, if that's what I have to do to protect this city."

She said it without rancor, and they rode in silence after that.

About half an hour east of the city the coach lurched to a stop. Jax glanced out the window, but saw no inn, only open countryside. The Witch must have noticed the curious look on his face. "Come," she said. "We need to stretch our legs a bit before we arrive."

Jax stepped out of the coach and saw immediately that they had stopped on a small rise in a wide road that snaked off into the distance both east and west. As Captain Darganna helped the ladies out of the coach, Jax surveyed the terrain around them. The landscape consisted of tilled fields interspersed with open grassland, all separated and blocked off by mile after mile of waist high, mortarless stone walls. An occasional tree or bush dotted the uncultivated acreage. Three hundred paces east of them, a three story building sat amidst a cluster of trees at the intersection of another road that ran north and south, streams of lazy smoke drifting into the sky from four chimneys. Across the road from the inn, a single-story building appeared to be a stable.

Another carriage had stopped in the middle of the intersecting road three hundred paces north of the inn, with twenty armed men standing by their horses. At that distance Jax couldn't make out the crest on the side of the other carriage, but it would be either Naesmyth or Carkoska.

Darganna and the three women walked up and stopped beside Jax. Looking at the other carriage in the distance, the captain said, "Good. They're already here."

"Last to arrive," the Witch said, "first to leave."

She looked at Jax. "The Carkoskas and Naesmyths may be our enemies in this, but there's no reason we can't still be civil about it, is there?"

Darganna and three of his men mounted up. The coachman stood up in the coachbox and waved a standard containing the Witch's crest. In the far distance, two coachmen stood up in the coachbox of the other carriage and waved the standards of Carkoska and Naesmyth.

Darganna and his three men rode east at a trot. Simultaneously, four mounted riders broke away from the group in the distance and rode south toward the inn at the intersection of the two roads.

The Witch said, "That would be Vorkees and three of his men. Their men and our men will pair off and carefully examine every room in the inn and the stables, and the surrounding grounds. I've paid good money to see to it that no one but the owner and his wife are present. When both sides are certain we'll encounter no traps or dangers, only the carriages will ride forward for the meeting. We'll leave the soldiers behind."

Jax now understood the arrangements for the meeting. Both sides were evenly matched, and with a nearly flat, open countryside around them, if either side tried to bring up reinforcements, there would be plenty of warning.

"We're supposed to come unarmed," the Witch said. "But I don't have an honest bone in my body, and it never hurts to be prepared."

She handed Jax a bundle wrapped in silken cloth. He unfolded the material carefully. To his surprise it contained one of the daggers he'd worn the day her knights had arrested him. He'd carefully designed the sheath so it fit snugly against his inner forearm. It wouldn't show any sort of suspicious bulge, but could be reached in an instant if needed.

She gave him a knowing grin. "The knights who rescued you from the Naesmyth castle told me you handled yourself well, even though you were unarmed against

Lakorsa with a dagger. That you bested yourself against such a dangerous man impressed them no end."

"Won't they search me?"

"No." she said. "As I said, we're all being very civil about this. No one will be able to conceal something as large as a flintlock pistol, so we have nothing to fear there, but I doubt you'll be the only one with a blade. You and Captain Darganna are our insurance."

Jax pulled off his greatcoat, then the tail coat. He secured the dagger in place, then shrugged back into the two coats. Down near the inn the guardsmen accompanying Darganna and Vorkees mounted their horses. Three of them rode north toward the other carriage, while three headed west toward the Witch, her apprentice, the thief and the harlot.

As the four of them stood there watching the men approach, the Witch said, "One more thing: None of you need fear looking into Lady Carkoska's eyes. Not today. Not with me present."

The three knights reined their horses to a stop ten paces in front of them and dismounted. One of them, a sergeant, stepped forward, dropped to one knee in front of the Witch, and said, "Mother, Captain Darganna says it is safe for you to proceed."

The knights brought forward the sleek mare Jax had ridden before. Jax helped the ladies into the carriage, then climbed into the mare's saddle. He spurred the animal forward, and as he rode out ahead of the carriage, a light drizzle of rain pattered down from the gray skies. In the distance he saw two men, probably Carkoska and Naesmyth, on horses leading the other carriage toward the inn. He carefully paced the mare so both carriages arrived outside the inn at the same moment.

As Jax approached the two High Lords he touched the brim of his hat and greeted them. "Your Lordships."

Lord Carkoska refused to acknowledge him. The High Lord swung his leg over his horse's rump, then stepped down onto the dirt road. The rain was not yet heavy enough to form puddles, so the road remained reasonably dry. Carkoska tied the reins of his horse to their coach, turned and walked into the inn without saying a word. Lord Naesmyth politely touched the brim of his hat and said, "It's really Master Jaxon, is it not?"

Apparently, they'd done their homework while Jax had recuperated from the musket ball. No doubt, they also now knew Maelleen's true identity.

Jax nodded, though he said nothing.

Naesmyth said, "I do apologize that you were wounded."

"Of course you do," the Witch said, startling Jax.

He glanced over his shoulder. She stood near Jax's stirrup holding an umbrella while Darganna helped the two younger women out of the carriage. Vorkees had already helped the Ladies Naesmyth and Carkoska from their coach.

"Of course you regret his injury," the Witch said to Naesmyth, "because you need him."

He touched the brim of his hat and said, "As do you, Mother."

She shrugged. "That remains to be seen." She turned and walked into the inn.

While Jax dismounted and tied the mare's reins to the Witch's carriage, Darganna and Vorkees hustled the ladies into the inn like two chaperones hovering over a group of maidens. As Jax stepped out of the rain at the front door of the inn, he found himself alone with Naesmyth for a moment. On impulse, he asked, "Why did you try to stop her and Lakorsa from killing me?"

Naesmyth shrugged and said, "I promised I wouldn't let her murder you just for knowing our secrets." He hesitated for a moment, then asked, "Does that make me weak-willed?"

Jax grimaced and said, "I don't know, but I think maybe it means just the opposite."

Naesmyth frowned and looked at Jax carefully, as if not sure how to take his remark. "Just remember that I won't stop anyone from executing you for being a thief."

Jax ignored the remark and turned toward the inn's door, but Naesmyth caught his arm and forced him to turn back. Jax saw only pain in the man's eyes.

Naesmyth lowered his voice. "My wife is not yet aware of your conclusions regarding the parentage of our children. Be careful, because if she ever realizes you've made that connection, I doubt even that old witch can stop her from having you murdered."

39

The Statue and the Thief

JAX FOLLOWED LORD Naesmyth through the front door of the inn and into the common room. He and the High Lord both removed their greatcoats and hats and hung them on pegs near the door. But as Naesmyth crossed the room to join the others near a large hearth, Jax hesitated and held back.

The ladies had all taken seats in large comfortable chairs. Celeste and Ladies Naesmyth and Carkoska sat to one side of the hearth, and on the other side, the Witch, Venessta, and Maelleen sat facing them. The two High Lords stood near their seated ladies. Sconces on the walls lit the room poorly, while a blazing fire in the hearth cast flickering shadows across the floor and ceiling in front of it. Vorkees stood in the shadows a few paces behind Lady Carkoska, and Darganna stood a few paces behind the Witch.

The innkeeper and his wife hovered among them, serving what appeared to be cups of tea for the ladies, and some sort of amber liquid in glass snifters for the men. When everyone had been served, the fellow and his wife stepped to one side and stood nervously awaiting further instructions. Jax was content to remain across the room and watch the tableau develop from afar. Unlike the two guard captains, he suspected that if the two predators decided to draw blood, he couldn't avoid being caught in the middle, though he hoped Maelleen would survive unscathed.

A small strongbox rested in Lady Carkoska's lap. She raised its lid and retrieved the statue, then closed the box. Lord Carkoska took the strongbox from her lap and placed it on a nearby table. The lady stared at the statue for a long silent moment, then said, "So, we are at an impasse." She raised her eyes and looked at the Witch.

The old woman lifted her cup to her lips and sipped at its contents. She turned her attention to the innkeeper and his wife. "You make an excellent cup of tea, good sir and mistress. But we're now content, so you may go. We'll let you know if we need anything more."

The couple scurried away, clearly eager to be gone. They exited through a door near the back of the room.

The Witch turned her gaze on Lady Carkoska. "I'm under the impression you have a proposal that will solve this impasse."

Lady Carkoska nodded in Jax's direction. "What is his connection to the statue?"

Jax had no doubt that, under Lady Carkoska's bloody hand, Celeste had revealed everything she knew, and that question meant she didn't know much. It also implied that Lady Carkoska assumed the Witch knew more than she did. Jax breathed a little easier.

The Witch turned her head slowly to look his way. "Little thief," she said. "How like you to stand across the room lurking in the shadows. Come, join us."

Regardless of what the Witch had said, Jax was not about to tempt fate by looking into Lady Carkoska's eyes. He kept his eyes locked on the figurine in her lap as he slowly walked forward and stopped next to the Witch's chair.

The Witch said, "Tell them about your connection to the figurine."

Jax tried to keep the look on his face neutral as he shook his head. "There is no connection. It's just a lump of clay to me."

Celeste jerked upward out of her chair and stood. "That's a lie. He is connected. I can sense it."

Until that moment Jax had not gotten a good look at Celeste. But standing only three paces from him, her face illuminated by the flickering light from the hearth, he forced himself not to visibly cringe. Only a few weeks ago she had been a pretty young girl with curly, red hair, but in that brief span of time she had aged decades. The gray bags that darkened the skin beneath her eyes that night in Lady Carkoska's boudoir had grown even more pronounced. Crow's feet creased the skin beside her eyes, the skin around her mouth had wrinkled visibly, and her face glistened with a sickly sheen.

She pointed a shaking finger at Jax. "He's lying. I tell you he's lying."

Lady Carkoska's voice snapped with impatience. "Sit down, and be silent."

Celeste turned to the older woman, rubbing her hands together fearfully. "I'm sorry. Please forgive me."

Lady Carkoska said nothing, but stared at her, making her displeasure clear. Jax saw the predator emerge, and so did Celeste, for without another word, the young woman returned to her seat, placed her hands carefully in her lap, and lowered her eyes.

Without speaking to anyone in particular, the Witch demanded, "So which one of them is lying?"

Maelleen leaned forward and addressed Lady Carkoska. "Did not Mistress Celeste try to betray you?"

Lady Carkoska's face remained expressionless as she nodded. "Yes, whore, she did."

Maelleen smiled. "So how can you trust anything she says?"

Lady Carkoska's lips curled upward in a predatory grin. "Trust me, at this point I know all her secrets and she cannot tell me anything but the truth."

The Witch asked, "And what does she say, exactly?"

Lady Carkoska turned her head slowly to look at Jax. He refused to flinch and look away, but met her eyes with an equally cold stare. As promised, the Witch had apparently neutralized the compulsive effect of the woman's gaze, and Jax felt none of the sadistic desire she induced in her victims. She looked at Jax as she spoke. "She tells me that when he touches the statue, she senses the flow of magics, some sort of arcane forces that she doesn't understand, but can detect."

The Witch leaned back and considered Celeste for a long moment. "Then let him touch the statue now."

Still looking at Jax, Lady Carkoska asked, "Why?"

The Witch raised a single eyebrow. "With me present, to observe."

"Ah," Lady Carkoska said, her eyes widening with anticipation. To Jax she said, "Come forward, thief."

Jax took a step back. "No."

The Witch lost a couple decades of age as she said, "Do so now, or I'll have you executed on the spot."

Jax shook his head. "No."

The old woman's age returned and she smiled triumphantly. "The fact that you refuse tells me a great deal."

She glanced over her shoulder at Darganna. "Captain Darganna, please restrain Master Jaxon."

Darganna responded without hesitation and lunged. Jax turned and back stepped, pulling the dagger from the sheath strapped to his forearm. Carkoska shouted something as Darganna halted, facing Jax and wary of the dagger he held between them. Someone hit Jax from behind, and in seconds Vorkees and Darganna had relieved Jax of the dagger and pinned his arms behind his back. Venessta and Maelleen had risen from their chairs, and Jax noticed Maelleen held a small dagger close to her side. He met her eyes, shook his head slightly, and the dagger disappeared in the folds of her dress. Darganna and Vorkees held Jax upright and he couldn't move.

"Now," the Witch said. "Let us all calm down."

She looked pointedly at Venessta and Maelleen. Both hesitated for a moment before sitting down.

The Witch said, "Lady Carkoska, would you be so kind as to touch the figurine to our thief. Be sure to make contact with his skin. It can be his hand or his cheek, but I believe direct contact may be necessary."

Lady Carkoska smiled and nodded. "Certainly, Mother."

She stood, and holding the statue she approached Jax. He didn't waste any effort trying to cringe away from her as she raised the small figurine and touched it to the side of his neck. The visions pushed at his thoughts, but he'd now had enough practice that suppressing them proved easy.

Lady Carkoska lowered the statue and looked at the Witch.

The old woman said, "Interesting." She stood without any signs of frailty and approached them. She lifted her right hand and peeled her glove half way down to her fingers, exposing her wrist. She extended the hand to Lady Carkoska, palm down. "Please touch the figurine to the back of my wrist. Again, direct contact with my skin is necessary."

Lady Carkoska's eyes narrowed suspiciously, but she slowly extended the statue and pressed it against the old woman's skin.

Again, the Witch said, "Interesting."

The old woman completely removed the glove, then reached up, gently gripped Jax's chin and turned his face toward her. He didn't want to meet her eyes, but something compelled him to do so. Still holding onto his chin with her bare fingers, she said, "Now please touch the figurine one more time to the thief."

When the figurine touched Jax's neck he felt a shock arc through his body and into the Witch's hand where it touched his chin. He fell into the old woman's eyes, and once again he saw the dunes of yellow sand under a hot sun stretching for as far as the eye could see. He struggled to climb one, then fought to keep his footing as he slid down the far side, only to face another dune and an eternity of sand. He looked over his shoulder and saw an army of strange beings following him, something he hadn't seen before. Some were just wisps of gray shadow, while others appeared to be reptilian, horned nightmares, and many were deformed shapes beyond description.

In an instant it all disappeared, and he stood unrestrained in the middle of the inn's common room, facing a little to one side of the main door. Recalling its orientation, he knew he stood looking due south. The blasted thing wanted him to go south.

"Did you feel it as well?"

That had been the Witch behind him. He turned to find that everyone had returned to their original positions, the ladies all seated, the men standing, Vorkees behind his master, and Darganna behind his mistress.

Apparently, the Witch had addressed the question to Venessta. The little witch said, "Oh, most definitely, Mother, a very strong flow of magic. Did you see anything?"

The Witch shook her head, her features clouded with anger and disappointment. "No, nothing."

Turning her head to look at Jax, the old woman said, "And what did you see, my little thief?"

Jax couldn't simply deny it. "Strange . . . strange beings." He wasn't about to tell them about the sand and dunes, or the compulsion to go south.

The Witch looked at him for the longest moment, nodding slowly.

Lady Carkoska's eyes narrowed with distrust. "What kind of strange beings?"

Before Jax could answer, the Witch abruptly stood and announced, "This meeting is done."

Lord Carkoska said, "Not so fast, Mother. What did you learn?"

The Witch's apparent age dropped a couple of decades. She took a step toward Jax and it dropped further, and by the time she had crossed the distance between them, he faced the beautiful young woman with coal-black irises. He couldn't see her forked tongue, but he didn't need to.

She said, "I learned that he is the key. He can help us, but I don't yet know how."

She turned away from Jax to face the Carkoskas and Naesmyths. "But I will know . . . and soon. And when I do, we'll act in unison."

They argued for a bit, but the meeting broke up, and Jax and the three women rode in silence back to Val d'Ossa.

••••

When they pulled into the courtyard of the Witch Palace, any small sense of freedom Jax had felt in the presence of the Witch Knights abruptly disappeared. The Witch ordered Darganna to have four of his men escort Jax and Maelleen to her sitting room. Maelleen sat, while Jax stood with two knights hovering on either side of him, and Darganna behind him. The Witch and Venessta joined them a few moments later, and Venessta sat next to Maelleen on the couch.

The Witch did not sit in her usual place, but approached Jax, pointed a finger at him and said, "When I touched that figurine I felt nothing. It was just a cold lump of fired clay. But when you touch it, I sense hellfire coursing through your soul, not merely magic. What is it you're not telling me?"

"Strange beings," he said. "That's all I saw."

She cocked her head slightly to one side, appraising him. "What kind of strange beings?"

Some of the things he had seen had been little more than wispy tendrils of vapor or smoke. He had to give her something, so he described them in a few terse words, and didn't mention anything about reptilian, deformed, horned monsters.

"And why did you turn to face south?"

"I don't know."

The old woman spoke to Captain Darganna. "Throw the little thief in the dungeon."

The knights standing on either side of Jax grabbed his arms and pinned them to his sides.

"Don't treat him badly, but I want him to compare the wonderful life he's lived for the last few months, with his future where he gets to live in his own shit."

Venessta stood. "Mother, wait a minute."

"What, little witch. Don't tell me not to throw him in the dungeon. He's going in the dungeon until he decides to cooperate."

"I'm not going to tell you that." She squirmed uncomfortably from side to side. "Just . . . clean him up and bring him up to me every now and then so he can . . . be nice . . . to me."

Jax and Venessta had continued to maintain the pretense that he made passionate love to her each time she came to his bed, when in fact all they did is talk and laugh, and sleep in each other's arms.

"Be nice to you?" the old woman asked, raising an eyebrow.

"Yes," Venessta said, still squirming, dancing back and forth from one foot to the other like a young child who's been caught stealing sweets from the kitchen. "I need him to . . . be nice . . . to me sometimes."

Maelleen stood to confront them. "If you get to have him come up and . . . be nice . . . to you, then I get to have him come up and . . . be nice . . . to me."

"Wait," the Witch shouted. "This is getting out of hand. How often do I have to clean him up so you can bed him?"

Still squirming, Venessta said, "Just once or twice . . . a week. Maybe three or four—"

"Now wait a minute," Maelleen shouted. "You get him four times a week, and I only get him three? I had him first."

Venessta put her fists on her hips. "I don't care."

The Witch shouted, "Will the two of you shut up."

Both women went silent.

The Witch's brow furrowed in thought.

Jax saw the corners of Maelleen's mouth quivering as she tried to suppress a giggle. Clearly, she had purposefully goaded Venessta and the Witch. She said, "Don't forget, Mother, he's good for the little witch."

The old woman gave her an unhappy look and said, "I'll tell you what, I'll bring him up once a week, and the two of you can share him."

Jax watched Maelleen cover her mouth with her hand to suppress a laugh. He began to think she was definitely due for a spanking, though he knew that wouldn't do any good.

Venessta asked, "You mean . . . the three of us . . . together?"

The Witch said, "Exactly."

"I could never do that," Venessta said, lifting her chin.

Maelleen shrugged. "Wouldn't be the first time for me."

Venessta asked, "You mean you and he and another woman?"

"No, not him," Maelleen said. "He's too poor. He could never afford two of us at once. It was another customer, and another woman."

Maelleen got a look in her eyes, reached out and brushed a lock of hair out of Venessta's face. "You may be kind of skinny, and your breasts are nonexistent, but you are quite pretty. I could enjoy myself with you and him." Jax didn't miss the hidden meaning in her words. He'd never told Venessta that he had revealed to Maelleen the true nature of the relationship between the little witch and little thief, and Maelleen certainly hadn't.

Venessta's eyes widened, she frowned, looked thoughtful for a moment, then reached out and delicately caressed a handful of Maelleen's curls. "You are so . . . exotically beautiful."

Jax shouted, "I'm standing right here, you know."

The Witch snarled. "I've changed my mind. I'm not bringing him up at all."

She turned angrily to Darganna. "Captain, do you think you can find some gruel. I want him to learn the taste of gruel, as well."

He frowned with confusion. "Gruel? That's just tasteless, watery porridge, right? I'll have to think on it, but I can probably come up with something."

"Mother," Maelleen said, and the quiet tone of her voice calmed them all. "I think I can help."

The Witch looked at her with clear distrust, but nodded her permission.

Maelleen crossed the room to Jax, took him by the elbow, looked at the knights hovering near him and said, "He and I are going to speak quietly in the corner for a moment."

The knights backed away as she and Jax crossed the room.

She turned to face him and lowered her voice to a whisper. "Darling, we have no choice."

"You know," he said, "she can hear everything we say, regardless of how quietly we say it."

She acknowledged that fact with a pained smile. "We have no choice. You have to cooperate with her, tell her everything. She has good reason to treat us better than the Carkoska's will."

Jax grimaced, because she was right. Maelleen hadn't said it aloud, but they both knew that as long as the Witch needed them to feed Venessta's humanity, they had a small chance of surviving this.

Maelleen turned her head and looked at the Witch. "Mother, will you protect us from what I saw in Lady Carkoska?"

The Witch nodded. "As much as I can."

Maelleen looked into Jax's eyes again. "At least she's being honest with us. That's better than nothing. That's all we have."

Jax closed his eyes for a moment and couldn't deny the truth of her words. "The figurine wants me to go south."

The Witch demanded, "It tells you to go south?"

Jax opened his eyes and looked at the old woman. "No. It tells me nothing. I get visions of strange beings, and I feel a compulsion to go in a particular direction. And when I look that way, it turns out to be south"

"How far south?"

Jax shook his head. "That I don't know. It just wants me to go in a particular direction. It tells me nothing of what awaits me there, or of how far I must travel."

The Witch turned away from them and paced back and forth across the room, clearly lost in thought. She stopped abruptly, looked at Darganna and said, "Captain, send a message to Lords Carkoska and Naesmyth. Tell them to prepare for a short journey. I would estimate no more than five or six days. Tell them we're going south, and our little thief is going to lead the way."

Venessta asked, "What lies south, Mother?"

The Witch looked at Jax. "Del Fransika hugs the coast due south of here. It's about a day's journey on horseback, perhaps two in a carriage."

The old woman crossed the room to stand a pace in front of Jax and looked up into his eyes. "Due south, is it?"

Still wondering about the dunes of sand, Jax felt a sense of relief at the Witch's words. He'd never been to Del Fransika, but he knew for a certainty its streets weren't buried in dunes of sand. Jax nodded carefully. "Yes, due south."

She grinned, but the look in her eyes told him she didn't believe him. "Good, because east of Del Fransika is the Valley of Bones, and I'm glad it's not pointing us there."

Maelleen's lips flattened into a straight line of distaste. "That sounds ominous."

The old woman's eyes lost focus as if contemplating a distant memory. "Yes, east of Del Fransika the land changes abruptly and descends into a waste of sand and dunes. It's a scorched wilderness of desecration ruled by chaos, and wherein the hell-pits of Senigoth tempt even the most vigilant souls to their eternal doom."

If you enjoyed this story, more on Jim
and other books he's written can be found at
www.jldoty.com

Acknowledgements

I'D LIKE TO thank my betas Jaime, Dan, Clyde, Tory and Dave for fixing all my dotted t's and crossed i's, and for their invaluable insight, criticism and advice—in my world you're all alphas. I'd also like to thank Karen for both supporting my dream and being my most valuable critic.

I want to add a special thanks to Jennifer L. Carson for her invaluable advice on the cover design. This one was quite difficult, and went through several iterations, but with her input the final cover is far superior to what I started with.

Books by J. L. Doty

Series: The Treasons Cycle
Of Treasons Born
A Choice of Treasons

Stand Alone Novel
The Thirteenth Man

Series: The Gods Within
Child of the Sword
The SteelMaster of Indwallin
The Heart of the Sands
The Name of the Sword

Series: The Dead Among Us
When Dead Ain't Dead Enough
Still Not Dead Enough
Never Dead Enough

Series: The Blacksword Regiment
A Hymn for the Dying
A Dirge for the Damned
A Prayer for the Fallen
A Requiem for the Forsaken

Series: Commonwealth Re-contact Novellas
Tranquility Lost

Series: The Deck of Chaos
The Thief of Chaos
Chaos Unbound (working title)

About the Author

JIM IS A full-time SF&F writer, scientist and laser geek (Ph.D. Electrical Engineering, specialty laser physics), and former running-dog-lackey for the bourgeois capitalist establishment. He's been writing for over 30 years, with over 16 published books. His first success came through self-publishing when his books went word-of-mouth viral, and sold enough that he was able to quit his day-job, start working for himself and write full time—his new boss is a real jerk. That led to contracts with traditional publishers like Open Road Media and Harper Collins Voyager, and his books are now a mix of traditional and self-published.

The four novels in his new hard science fiction series, *The Blacksword Regiment*, were released in July 2020, and *The Thief of Chaos*, the first book in *The Deck of Chaos*, was released in July 2021. Right now he's fleshing out ideas for the next book in *The Dead Among Us*, he's writing another episode in *The Treasons Cycle*, and he's working on the second book in *The Deck of Chaos*, a Regency fantasy of seduction, betrayal, and dark magic.

Jim was born in Seattle, but he's lived most of his life in California, though he did live on the east coast and in Europe for a while. He now resides in Arizona with his wife Karen and two little beings who claim to be cats: Julia and Natasha. But Jim is certain they're really extra-terrestrial aliens in disguise.

Visit the author's website at http://www.jldoty.com
Contact the author at jld@jldoty.com